PORTLAND
PUBLIC LIBRARY

ENRICHING OUR COMMUNITY,
EXPANDING OUR WORLD.

CITY OF READERS TEAM

Creating a City of Readers

Please return when finished

or *pass it on*

to another reader.

SURPRISING MYSELF

MYSELF

A NOVEL BY

CHRISTOPHER BRAM

An Owl Book

HENRY HOLT AND COMPANY
New York

Henry Holt and Company, Inc.
Publishers since 1866
115 West 18th Street
New York, New York 10011

Henry Holt ® is a registered trademark
of Henry Holt and Company, Inc.

Published in Canada by Fitzhenry & Whiteside Ltd.,
195 Allstate Parkway, Markham, Ontario L3R 4T8.

Library of Congress Cataloging-in-Publication Data
Bram, Christopher.
Surprising myself.
"An Owl book."
I. Title.
[PS3552.R2817S8   1988]   813'.*54*   *88-3244*

ISBN 0-8050-0669-9 (An Owl Book: pbk.)

Henry Holt books are available for special
promotions and premiums. For details
contact: Director, Special Markets.

First published in hardcover by Donald I. Fine, Inc., in 1987

First Owl Book Edition—1988

Printed in the United States of America
10 9 8 7 6

Because of Draper
and Mary

For my families

"ONLY THE SHALLOW KNOW
THEMSELVES."

Oscar Wilde

1

MOTHS THUMPED THE screens of the dining hall. More moths batted around the bare light bulb overhead, shedding scales and bits of wing on the page of *Atlas Shrugged* I tried to read. The fat book had plumped up like a sponge in two weeks of damp Virginia heat. The long table where I was sitting shook each time the card players at the other end threw down their cards and grabbed their spoons. These guys turned even a friendly game of "Pig" into a riot.

"You blocked me, asswipe."

"Chuck you, farley."

"Queerbait, cut the cards."

Damn parent, I thought, and brushed a dying moth off Ayn Rand.

Not that I hated my father. I was in awe of the man, even now. But Jake was halfway around the world and I could at least be angry with him for his carelessness. This was the summer job he had found for me in the States. After four years abroad in an American school in Switzerland, after four years of living with civilized Swiss relatives, I'd been sent home to work in a Boy Scout camp.

"And it's close to your mother's little farm," Dad had announced, sounding so pleased with himself for what he'd done. "So you can see the Three Graces on weekends. You're supposed to be a registered scout, but Major Hawkins can fake something for you there."

"Oh Jo-el," Aunt Bertie sang in her singsong English.

"You will wear the uniform and be outdoors all day long. Just like a real boy."

I didn't want to be a real boy. I was seventeen years old and wanted to work in a brokerage firm, or somewhere similarly adult, as a warm-up for Harvard or wherever I went before I made my mark in the corporate world. My father could've arranged anything for me; he had a government job so important that Swiss cousins were always asking him, "But what exactly do you do, Jacob?" Before he left Zurich to return to Zaire, having arranged everything with two overseas calls, he'd convinced me that this would be better, more interesting.

"Pig-fuck, pig-fuck, pig-fuck," the card players chanted, pounding the table with their fists. These were my peers, the counselors my age or younger.

What had my father been thinking of? I sometimes wondered if Jake were testing me, challenging my ability to adapt. If so, I wasn't doing very well. There was the work, but I enjoyed that. They had me in the commissary, doing inventory, signing invoices, doling out the food the campers took back to their campsites to cook themselves. I enjoyed being with goods. My problem was people.

The staff toilets and showers were right off the dining hall, the door was wide open and I could hear Wyler Reese in there, singing the words and doing the guitar noises to "Jumpin' Jack Flash." Reese was a bony kid with thick, pouty lips that he claimed made him look like Mick Jagger. He was probably singing into one of the mirrors over the sinks after his shower. I needed to take a shower but didn't want to go in there until Reese was finished. Reese mocked and abused anyone who was smaller than he was. I was short for my age. Insult was the universal language here, but Reese's insults were different, personal and creepy.

Corey Cobbett strolled out of the office, carrying his *Time* magazine, good liberal that he was. I was a Goldwater Republican. I had nothing but contempt for the liberals and radicals who couldn't understand why we were in Vietnam, but I could've made an exception for Cobbett. He was nineteen, more mature than the others, quieter. He was tall and hairy but there was a shyness in his adult face and black-framed glasses that made him seem approachable.

"Hiya, Cobbett," I said as he sauntered past the table.

"Hi, uh, Shirtsy." He barely remembered who I was. *Scherzenlieb* was too much to bother with, so they had reduced me to Shirtsy. It could've been worse. They'd tried Shitsy and, briefly, Heidi.

Cobbett walked toward the washroom and frowned when he recognized Reese's singing. He turned around and sat at the bench at the other table, facing me. He gave the noisy card players a quick, bored look, then read his magazine.

The only counselors I wanted to be friends with were the ones who were older than me. But they thought I was just another twerp; they had no idea who I really was.

I thought about hiking out to the highway to try my mother, sister and grandmother again. The nearest outside line was two miles away at the entrance to the camp, a lone telephone booth beneath a lone street light beside a dark country road in the woods. It was too late for me to call them tonight. This was another of my father's ideas that had come to nothing. Surely they knew I was here, but I'd already called them twice and nobody was home. This new farm of theirs was on the other side of the James River, two hours away when the ferry was running. I began to suspect I'd finish my summer and return to Switzerland without ever seeing them. We hadn't seen each other in four years; I wondered what I could say to them, anyway.

Reese came out of the washroom in white underwear and flip-flops, tossing his bangs and strutting to the music he still mumbled to himself. He spotted me, narrowed his

11

eyes maliciously and slapped his flip-flops in my direction. "What'cha reading?"

I said nothing; I didn't want to encourage him.

"You still reading *that?* Shit, my dog can read faster than you." He stood on the other side of the table, propped a foot on the bench there and leaned on the raised knee, threatening me with a long stay. His undershirt was tucked into his underpants and his head was too big for his body; for all his swagger, Reese looked like a kid up past his bedtime.

I noticed Cobbett at the other table look up from his magazine to watch us.

"Please, I'm trying to concentrate."

"Hey, you can't fool me. You're not really reading that book. You just want people to think you're hot snot. I don't even think you're from Switzerland. You just made that up so people wouldn't know what you *really* are."

He was determined to get a rise out of me; I refused to give it to him.

"Shit," he finally said, took his foot off the bench and strutted down to the Pig players. He glanced at me one last time across his knobby shoulder and sneered, as if he knew something I didn't, before he told Bryant to give him a spoon and deal him in.

When I looked back at Cobbett, he was bent over his magazine again.

A car rumbled into the dirt parking lot out front. We heard laughs and shouts as people tumbled out and car doors slammed. Heads turned toward the screen door, knowing what was coming.

The screen door flew open and the moths scattered. In charged Bob Kearney, alias Kahuna, the waterfront director. "Honor bright! Be square!" He waved the scout sign in front of him. He wore a sharky grin tonight, and civvies. Kearney was smoothly muscled and tan—in swim trunks he looked like solid milk chocolate with a blond crewcut.

Yo-yo and Flash stumbled in behind their leader. Nights when there was nothing scheduled for the campers after dinner, Kearney took his waterfront staff into Claremont for beers. I was never sure how drunk they really were after these trips. I wanted to believe most of it was play-acting, Kearney's in particular. Because I wanted Kearney to be better than this. At the end of the summer, he was going into Officers Candidate School. He planned a career in the army. I wanted to be able to admire him for that, but he made it awfully difficult.

"Play the game!" he howled. "While you people all sat on your thumbs tonight and played the game, I've been laying the groundwork for a summer of nooky."

"Girls?" Reese cried. "Where, Kahuna? I'm so horny, man, I could fuck a frog."

"How many? How old? How did you meet them?" the other card players pleaded. Their fever was all play-acting, these fifteen- and sixteen-year-olds pretending two weeks without women could make them crazy. I never pretended.

"Shut up, dumbasses. There's only one and she's all mine."

The card players groaned.

"She got any sisters? I'll do anything if you'll introduce me to her sister, Kahuna." Reese positively fawned over Kearney.

Yo-yo announced, "He's promised her the stars but he'll give her the moon," and he and Flash went cryptically hysterical.

Kearney solemnly laid his hand on his heart. "She's a waitress for the summer at the Claremont Bar and Grill."

"Hey, Kahuna," said Flash. "You gonna give her a tip?"

"Tip, hell. I'll give her the whole thing."

I hated seeing Kearney play the ass. He was an adult; he was twenty-two. He could debate circles around Cobbett when they argued about Vietnam. Yet here he was, acting out the fantasies of this adolescent audience. I assumed

13

Kearney was the experienced stud he said he was. I just thought adults would keep such experiences to themselves.

Cobbett suddenly stood, rolling up his magazine. He moved toward the screen door with his head lowered.

"Uh oh," said Kearney. "I think we've offended old Corny's ears."

Cobbett looked up and saw Kearney and the others watching him. "Huh?" He produced a bashful smile. "No. Not offended, Bob. I have to get some things from my tent, that's all."

"Kahuna not fooled!" Kearney went into his pidgin English, an old joke between him and Cobbett. "Kahuna know Corn-on-Cobbett disapprove!"

Cobbett hesitated at the door. "Yes, well... what can I say?" he went in his sluggish Southern voice. Until, embarrassed to say it, he said, "I think you're misrepresenting yourself. And setting a bad example for the others."

Kearney stared at Cobbett, then turned and shared his shark grin with the rest of us. He burst out laughing. "You old preacher, you. Don't give me that. You don't shit roses either, Cobbett."

Cobbett didn't take offense, only shook his head and said, "I don't like being the prig, but you asked, so I told you. Good night." He went out the door.

"Jealous!" Kearney shouted after him. "You're just wishing it was your wick that was getting dipped, Cobbett!"

Kearney and Cobbett confused me. This was 1970 and a person's politics should mean everything to me. But the man whose manner I liked was politically wrong and the man with the right politics was a barbarian. Not that it really mattered, since neither of them knew I existed. I hoped Kearney would see what I was reading—he had to approve—but Kearney stayed at the other end of the room, waxing joyfully on the pleasures of sex without love. Without Cobbett there to shock, he quickly grew bored with us, told Flash and Yo-yo good night and lurched off towards the woods and his tent.

Reese and the others began to moan about how much they needed a woman and exactly what they would do with one. My tentmate, Alvin Bryant, fifteen years old, stretched out on a bench on his stomach and said that was his favorite position.

"Dumbass," said Reese. "This is the best way." He stretched out on the other bench on his back, hands supporting an imaginary shape above him. "That way you make *them* do all the work."

Such talk had been bad enough from Kearney. From peers who were as virgin as me, it was grotesque. I snapped my book shut. I groaned and got up.

"What's the matter, Shirtsy? We turning you on?" Reese sneered. Prone on the bench, he leered at me across the lump in his underpants. He opened and crossed his knees at me.

"Shirtsy doesn't know what we're talking about," said Flash, the rowing instructor. He was squat and overweight, his crewcut head shaped like a bullet.

"He knows. Don't you, Shirtsy." Reese made his voice very small and insinuating.

I had no idea what he was insinuating, but I couldn't walk away from that voice without saying something.

"All I know is——You're nothing but a pack of pathologically insecure . . . retards!"

My outburst stunned them. It stunned me. I'd never spoken out to them and they blankly stared at me, for an instant. I used that instant to make my exit. I was at the front door before Reese forced up a loud, derisive laugh.

I marched furiously into the darkness, away from the lights of the staff building, across the parking lot to the threadbare grass of the parade ground. I began to feel stupid. I'd finally given them a piece of my mind, and the piece had been hopelessly inarticulate. Retards? When I crossed the chalky dirt road that divided the parade ground, I remembered that I hadn't intended to leave, that I had wanted to take a shower. It was as warm and muggy outside as it had been indoors. I wasn't going to let them shame me out of a shower. I could hardly slink back through the dining hall after my little outburst, but the staff building had a back door, a separate entrance for the latrine and washroom. I circled around to the rear of the building, the clatter of cicadas in the weeds there louder than the voices inside. I quietly opened the baggy screen door and slipped back in.

The door into the dining hall was still wide open, but a row of lockers blocked the view. Not that I was hiding from anyone. They'd hear me when I turned on the water. I heard them groaning about how late it was and how tired they'd be in the morning and how much they hated working here. They'd already forgotten my flubbed tirade, which was fine by me. The front screen door began squealing open and shut: They were leaving. I sat on the upended wooden milk crate to take off my shoes and knee socks.

The washroom was its usual mess. There were wet towels everywhere and a smell of soap and mildew. At one end were two exposed toilets, which I hated using; at the other end, a cement-floored gang shower with only two shower heads. I saw myself in the water-spotted mirror over the middle sink. I looked ridiculous in a Boy Scout uniform: sunburned knees, pink little hands, a blandly childish face. No wonder nobody took me seriously.

I had turned away from the mirror to unbutton my shirt when I heard voices on the other side of the lockers. I wasn't alone after all. I recognized Reese's nasal whine —all American voices sounded nasal to me, but Reese's more than the others—and the muddy, garbled voice of Flash, who talked as though he had a golf ball in his mouth.

"Makes me want to puke, man. Having to work all

summer with a homo. I don't want to be alone with him, afraid he'll go grabbing for my meat."

I relaxed. Reese wasn't talking about me. I listened anyway, curious to know who he was slandering this time. I knew there were no homosexuals at Camp Wolf.

"You should've been here last year," Flash said eagerly. "Then it was the waterfront director. The guy before Kahuna. Everyone kind of suspected something, and I *know* he was doing things with one of the trainees. But one night he and a camper were missing. The whole staff went out looking for them. We had walkie-talkies and the motorboat and Fisher going up and down the trails in his jeep—"

The front screen door squealed again.

Flash paused, then continued. "We called it the Great Queer Hunt. You were there, Cobbett. Remember?"

Cobbett must've returned, because I heard a reluctant, "Yeah. It happened."

"We found 'em on the beach," said Flash. "Doing it."

"Gross." said Reese.

"They fired the waterfront director that night. And sent the kid to a psychiatrist."

"Well, I'll bet you money," Reese said, "that we'll be having our own queer hunt before this summer's over. Did you see the way he was looking at my squirrel-shot tonight? I was testing him, and you could tell. He was watering at the mouth, man. Even if he is Swiss, I hear they're all homos over there."

I jumped to my feet, to keep from falling off the crate.

Wicked cackling from Flash. "'Let's go tell Bryant. I want to see the look on his face when he hears his tentmate's hot for weinies."

A homosexual? Me? I was too surprised to move. I stood there with my shirt undone, staring back at myself in the mirror. I'd never imagined anyone calling me queer.

"You think Bryant doesn't know? Shit. The two of

17

them are making out with each other every night in their tent, I bet."

With Bryant? Bryant was a timid, acne-faced imitator of Reese. The idea of kissing Bryant was disgusting. Then why was I still standing here? I should go out there and call Reese a liar. But, ridiculous as the accusation was, it left me feeling helpless. I was terrified of letting them know I'd even heard it.

"What is this bullshit!"

That was Cory Cobbett's voice.

"Not bullshit," sniffed Reese. "It's true."

"It's bullshit!" snapped Cobbett. "You keep your paranoid little fantasies to yourself, Reese! Bad enough that you stab your own friend, Bryant, in the back. But you have no business spreading trash about Joel Scherzenlieb. You hear me?"

Cobbett knew who I was. He even knew my full name. I was overjoyed, then ashamed, because he was fighting the battle I should be fighting for myself.

"Come on, Cobbett," said Flash. "You're too goody-goody to see *anything.*"

"Oh no? Well, I see two cases of homosexual panic that are projecting like crazy."

"And what the hell's that supposed to mean?" asked Flash.

"It means..." He paused to catch his breath, or maybe he paused to regain control. I'd never imagined Cobbett had so much passionate righteousness inside him. "It means the two of you must be wanting to do it, too. Or you wouldn't be so quick to smear other people."

"What!" screeched Reese.

"You're full of shit," said Flash.

"Maybe I am. But I do know this. I hear either of you talking trash about Joel or anybody else, I'll knock you on your rears."

"You and whose army?" Reese's voice cracked.

"You want to try me, Reese? You don't believe me? I don't hear you saying anything, Flash. Jesus. You morons look at me like I've been talking in tongues. Y'all make me sick."

I heard Cobbett head for the washroom. I stepped around and pressed my back against the lockers. But as soon as Cobbett turned the corner, he caught sight of me in one of the mirrors.

"Oh, God." He covered his red face with one hand, turned around and almost went back into the dining hall. He kept turning until he faced me, grimacing. His eyes locked with my eyes for a second. Then he groaned and sat heavily on the crate.

We heard Reese and Flash grumbling and spitting at each other, the front door again, and silence.

Cobbett didn't look at me, only at my empty shoes on the floor beside him. He picked at the label on the towel he had with him. "Did you hear much of that?"

"Pretty much," I said, sounding as embarrassed as he did.

"Nonsense. All of it. Don't let it bother you. Typical American teenage behavior."

It embarrassed me that Cobbett knew I'd heard Reese and done nothing. I wondered what Cobbett was embarrassed about. I'd heard him come to my defense, but that was nothing for *him* to be ashamed of. I was ashamed as well as grateful, but making shame easier to bear was learning that Cobbett actually knew who I was.

Cobbett suddenly gave his head a shake. "Jesus, I made an ass of myself out there."

"Don't say that. You handled yourself quite well." I could thank him that way, without having to mention my helplessness.

"No. I was wrong to lose my temper with those idiots. Just talking to hear myself talk out there."

"Do you really think Reese and Flash are latent homosexuals?" I asked matter-of-factly.

Cobbett turned to look at me. He stared at me. He had a big face and his look of surprise made him look faintly stupid. "No. Not really. I was just giving them a dose of

19

their own medicine. But I shouldn't have called them names. Uh, homosexual panic is as common as rain around here." He looked at me a moment longer, blinked and stood up. "I came back to take a shower," he explained, turned his back to me and began to undress. "But you seem remarkably cool for someone who's just been called a homosexual."

"Of course. Because it's not true." And it wasn't, although the accusation lingered, like a memory of something I might've done wrong.

"Good. I'm glad. That's a very mature attitude." He kept his back to me as he yanked his shirt tail out. "Because it's the sort of thing that could upset anyone who's not sure about themselves. Here especially." He shook his shirt off his broad shoulders and freckled back. My eyes were level with the shoulder blades shifting under his skin.

"I'm a very mature person," I told him.

The belt went slack and he lifted his legs out of the green shorts. Then he stepped out of his underpants and there was the long, bare length of him, a red line across the small of his back, a flat bottom lightly penciled with hair. I could look without feeling funny. I knew I wasn't queer. What bothered me was what it *meant* to be called queer. It meant that I was weak, helpless, that I wasn't the captain of my fate and all that. Which hurt, because it was true. I needed someone with whom I could be myself.

The sides of Cobbett's bottom dimpled with each step as he walked toward the shower. He didn't turn around or even speak to me again until he'd turned on the water and was covered with spray. "Be different if there were girls around," he called out. "Fantasies wouldn't be so free-floating."

The front of his torso looked thickly hairy from across the room. He had genitals, of course. But the most striking thing about Cobbett naked was that he'd taken his glasses off. The scrupulous black frames now sat cross-legged on the milk crate with his underpants.

"I don't have any fantasies," I called back to him.

"Well, good then. Good. You're lucky."

He kept glancing out at me, as if wanting me to join him, squinting when he glanced, as if worried I'd be shy after the accusation. I preferred taking showers alone. But I wanted to be naked with Cobbett. Not because of anything sexual, but because being naked with a guy I liked suggested intimacy, trust. When I resumed undressing, Cobbett smiled and began to wash.

I lightly stepped past him to the other shower head, turned it on and arched my front against the cool cone of water. "Oh, that feels good," I sighed.

"Feels great." Cobbett stood three feet away, smiling at me while water drilled the back of his head. Without glasses his face looked half-finished, not boyish really, but not yet adult either. He had a short round nose like half a strawberry. His brown eyes were looking me over. We knew who we were and could look at each other's body without fear of being misunderstood. It felt very comfortable.

"Can I ask you a personal question?" said Cobbett.

I laughed. We couldn't get any more personal. "Of course." Although I hoped it had nothing to do with being called queer.

"Why . . . are you reading Ayn Rand?"

But he didn't sound scornful, only curious.

So I told him a little about the virtue of selfishness, the beauties of free enterprise and the individual's duty to seize whatever he wanted with both hands. Cobbett would have none of that, but he had a respectful way of disagreeing, treating his distrust of Rand as a personal whim of his, not a condemnation of me.

"I'm just a little surprised," he admitted when we were out of the shower and drying off. "That a gentle, well-mannered person like yourself would believe in such a dog-eat-dog philosophy."

I laughed at him. "But I'm not gentle. Wait until you get to know me a little better. You'll see."

"Yes?"' But he didn't laugh at me. "I want to know you better. You seem like someone worth knowing."

A bubble of gratitude rose in my chest. "Thanks," I said. "That's very flattering. Coming from you."

Color rose into Cobbett's throat and face as he turned away; he was blushing. For some reason, that made me blush, as if we'd gone too far with each other, said too much. But it was nothing to be ashamed of, two men admitting they wanted to be friends. It was good to find a friend here, even one with whom I shared nothing but this wish to be friendly.

Cobbett began to chuckle and moan. "Yes, well. What can I say?" He stepped back into his underpants and shorts, although his bottom was still wet. "But I have my dark side, too. My . . . hypocrisies."

"Me too," I said, wanting to be agreeable, wondering what he was talking about. But I put some of my clothes back on, to keep us equal.

We became cheerfully friendly, asking about each other's schools, families, futures. We combed our hair and brushed our teeth, but stayed in the washroom, reluctant to go our separate ways to humid tents and sour cots. Cobbett was quietly humorous about himself, his three summers as a counselor, his rinky-dink college in Norfolk. Only when I mentioned my parents' divorce did he turn solemn again, until I assured him that, like so much else in my life, it had worked out for the best.

Over the next few days, summer camp began to seem more promising. It was still the same silly children and woodland squalor, but I could look forward to each evening when Corey Cobbett and I searched each other out and talked. Or sometimes we didn't talk. Sometimes knowing I had a friend sitting in the same room with me was enough to make life interesting. Things really do work out, if you give them time. The following Monday, I even saw my mother and sister.

I saw them only for an hour and a half. They were on

their way to Wakefield in a pickup truck for free manure and stopped at Camp Wolf long enough to embarrass me with their kisses and bib overalls. I took them down to the river so we could escape the looks everyone was giving us, only there we ran into Kearney.

Face to face, I wasn't sure what to make of my mother and sister, my mother in particular. I hadn't seen them since Dad went overseas and left me in Switzerland, but I'd heard about all the classes and jobs Mom tried before she decided she could achieve true independence only as a farmer. She and Dad divorced when I was twelve, which had been a surprise, although they seemed to think it perfectly reasonable. Mom had said Dad didn't take her seriously and fourteen years of genial condescension had reduced her to a neurotic pet. Dad genially went along with her request for a divorce. He liked to joke with me that they decided custody by flipping a coin. Dad was full of jokes about Mom.

Last winter she had borrowed money from Gramma Bolt and bought herself a failed farm in Charles City County. Mom was so proud of it, she could talk of nothing else while we walked to the river and back. She seemed absolutely nutty about it. My big sister, Liza, kept biting one side of her smile. After I finished here, I was to spend a week with them and Gramma before I flew back to Switzerland.

I was relieved when they drove off, then ashamed of feeling relieved. A family such as ours made for such mixed responses and confused loyalties.

Late one night, a month later, Jacob Scherzenlieb, my father, came to Camp Wolf. While everyone was sleeping, he loaded me and my things into his rented car. We drove all night while Jake explained. There'd been a change of plans.

2

THE GARDEN WAS all green confusion: my mother's garden. Vines ran everywhere, some loose, some snared by stakes, others twining along strings that drooped like clotheslines. A house stood a hundred yards from the road, backed up against the woods to escape its own garden. It was nothing but a tall box, shingled in grey and topped with a pocked tin roof. The garden frothed around the house as crows croaked and the sun peeked over the trees.

"Dis do look like dah place," teased Jake. He swallowed before he put the car into gear again. We swung down a rutted dirt drive that ran through the garden's center, barbed wire fences on either side and, at the end, a low barn built of corrugated metal.

Jake parked between the house and barn and immediately stepped out to stretch. His knit shirt rode up, exposing his thin belly. Jake didn't look like a father to me unless he wore a suit and tie, but I no longer trusted him as a father, not now. I sat in the car longer than I should've, staring out at the land flat as a table and the high, empty sky. I was being left at the end of the world.

Jake had been transferred to the Far East. There was no point in my returning to Switzerland, he said. I was to live with my mother, here. I tried arguing with him about school in Kilchberg and even my final week at camp, but he genially stuck to his decision. He had a

24

plane to catch to Bangkok the next night and this was his one chance to tie things up. Catherine was expecting us. And it was only for a year, he said, before I went to college. He made it sound perfectly reasonable. Yet he didn't convince me, not this time. It was too strange, too sudden. I couldn't believe it: Was it really possible that I wasn't going back to Switzerland? But beneath that shock was the sinking realization that my father was throwing me away, handing me over to women he had mocked and laughed at for the past five years. Why? What had I done?

"Hey, lad. Come out of there and look at this place. Wonderful place," said Jake, thin face creased in a dry smile, salt-and-pepper moustache pinched under his nose. He stood there with both hands fidgeting in his pockets, amusedly rocking on his heels while he surveyed everything. "Is that an *outhouse* back there?"

I saw it through the windshield. "Yes, sir."

"Wonderful. Simply wonderful. Old Black Catherine has really outdone herself." He swallowed again, then walked briskly up to the front of the house, climbed the concrete steps and tried the door. He pushed lightly, but it didn't open. I stepped out of the car. When I came up behind him, he was running his fingers along the jamb.

"Locked from the inside," he whispered. His eyebrows went down for the joke: "*Bolt*-ed."

"Can't we just knock?"

"No. Oh no. They're probably all asleep. I want to surprise them. Let's try the back."

He hopped down the steps and I followed him around the house. He seemed weirdly excited, even manic. I couldn't remember ever seeing him giddy like this. The grin he shared with me over his shoulder lacked its usual control. He danced gently up the wooden steps at the side and bent down to examine the door knob.

"Did you see the goat?" he whispered.

"What goat?"

"The goat under the stairs."

I looked under the stairs and there, on a pallet of hay, was a young goat, forelegs folded beneath its chest, a skittish look in its eye.

"Must be their watch-goat," said Jake.

He was a ratty goat, with none of the confidence or beauty of Swiss goats.

I heard the door open, looked up and found Jake caught in his crouch at door knob level. He straightened up and I followed his eyes to the face of my mother. The two looked at each other and froze.

There was an extra ring of wrinkles under my mother's eyes, but she was awake and fully dressed. Her dull brown hair was tied up in a red bandanna. There was a shotgun in her right hand, muzzle against the floor. A ribbon of smoke rose from her cigarette.

"Catherine. Why *hello.*"

"Hello, Jake." Each syllable was deliberately hushed, giving her words a tone of careful fondness. "You idiot. I had no idea who was picking at my door." She ducked around the corner to put the gun away.

Jake looked at the gun. Then, as if remembering a trick, he let his face go soft and sheepish. "It's good to see you, Cat."

She looked over his shoulder so she could avoid that face. "Hello, Joel. How are you, dear?" Her voice was stuck in the tone of businesslike fondness, but she gave me a watery smile that was genuinely sympathetic.

"Fine, Mom. And you?"

"Just fine. You look tired, dear. Here. Come in. Both of you come in. I have a pot of coffee on."

Jake led the way into the kitchen. At the door, Catherine gathered me under one arm and took me with her to the stove. "What were you doing out there, Jake? If you knocked, I just *might* have let you in." She gave my shoulder a squeeze to let me know that this was a joke.

"I didn't know anyone was up. I just thought we'd sit in the kitchen and fix some coffee while we waited for you."

"Oh, but the day starts early here. We're up with the birds, or at least I am. The work never ends." She kissed my forehead with the side of her mouth and released me. She remained by the stove although there was nothing for her to do there but watch the coffee perk. "You're lucky I didn't shoot you."

"You wouldn't shoot me," Jake said confidently.

He had seated himself at a table by a window that looked out on the garden's bright confusion. Inside, everything was dark and shaded; the woods kept the kitchen in shadow. It was an old kitchen, with a dank, marshy smell that seeped through the aroma of coffee. There was a new sink beside the stove and an aluminum shower stall with a plastic curtain. The new refrigerator looked too heavy for the floor and had settled at a tilt against the wall. I walked cautiously to the table, afraid the floor wouldn't hold me either. I saw a box of tampons on the kitchen counter.

"That's quite a garden you have out there. Quite a piece of land." Jake winked at me when I sat down. "Reminds me of parts of Africa."

"*We* like it."

"You should. Africa can be lovely." He cleared his throat behind his hand. "Where's Mom and Liza? They still sawing wood?"

"I'll shake Liza shortly. Mom gets up whenever the spirit moves her. Did you see our goat?"

"Yes, saw him under the stairs. Scrawny little fellow. What do you call him?"

"Jacob." She brought the coffee and cups to the table, her mouth pinched at the corners so she could hold back her grin. Catherine had a wide rubber mouth.

"Jacob the goat," said my father, nodding agreeably. "Do you have any other animals?"

"Just chickens." She stood behind me and squeezed my shoulder again. "The goat's a gift from a neighbor. We're going to use him to trim the grass around the house."

"Very practical."

"I'm a very practical person, Jake. Something I never suspected. But I can plant gardens, repair barns, shoot a gun, understand mortgages, lease land, handle goats—"

"I'm impressed." He nudged my foot under the table. "I hope you pull it off, Cat."

"I will. It's a challenge, Jake, but I'm happier than I've ever been before." She looked straight at him, daring my father to contradict her.

But Jake only nodded. "Good, Cat. I always had the highest respect for your potential."

My mother's eyes narrowed. The cords of her neck slowly tightened beneath her skin. "Drink your coffee," she said. "I'll go wake Liza."

Jake sighed as soon as she was gone. "That woman." He didn't elaborate, but only shook his head and smirked, assuming I understood and supported him. He was so busy reacting to his ex-wife he had forgotten his real purpose in being here: to get his son off his hands. If he'd remembered, he would've tried to make my mother's life seem attractive, not ridiculous. It didn't matter. I couldn't believe in my mother's life, but I no longer believed in Jake's. There was no milk or sugar for the coffee.

"Liza'll be right down," said Catherine when she returned. "Can I interest either of you in some breakfast? There's some nice eggs. *Tons* of nice eggs."

"Here, Cat. Have a seat." Jake stood up. "I'll fix breakfast."

"No! It's *my* kitchen. Sit down!" She bit her lip, yanked open the refrigerator and hid her head behind the door. "You're only a guest, Jake. I won't have you make me feel incompetent in my own kitchen."

Jake hesitated, then shrugged and smiled. "Only trying to be helpful. I thought I could fix everyone omelets."

"And I was going to fix plain old scrambled eggs. Sit down and be a guest." She took out a bowl of brown eggs. Not wanting to seem harsh, she flashed a smile at us.

Liza swaggered into the kitchen, hands tucked into the bib of her overalls. "Daddy!" she sang, but kept her hands where they were. "Hello there."

"Hello, Kitten. You have a kiss for your old man?"

She gave his cheek a cautious peck. "Hey. Your white hair looks good with a tan."

"Like the moustache?" he asked.

"Naw." She hurriedly turned to me. "Hello, Shrimp. How *you* doing?"

"Fine, thank you. Yourself?"

Her hands came out of the bib and she gave me a hug and a kiss. She bent over me a moment, hanging on my neck while she looked sadly into my eyes. Finally, she sat in the chair beside mine.

"You make me feel old, Kitten. How long has it been? Two years since my last visit? My God. You're growing into quite a beautiful woman."

"Yeah. That's what people tell me." Liza turned sideways in her chair so she wouldn't have to look at Jake. At nineteen, she was beautiful: long, darkish blonde hair, strong, sharp profile. She was my sister and I might not have noticed how good-looking she was if not for all the gawks she drew when she and Catherine visited Camp Wolf. Kearney had managed to talk to her and, afterwards, pretended to be my friend, the jerk, hoping he could see my sister again. There was no chance of that now. I wished that it'd been Corey Cobbett who'd been interested in Liza, but Corey said she wasn't his type.

"Hey, baby brother? You plan to wear that Boy Scout uniform the rest of your life?"

I looked down and saw the green shorts and ridiculous knee socks. It embarrassed me now that Boy Scout camp was as far away and long ago as Switzerland. "No. I just haven't had time to change," I muttered.

"Gramma's going to be so happy to see you. She talked about your visit all last month. And when she heard you were going to *stay* . . . oh, she was excited."

"Do you still play the guitar, Kitten?" asked Jake.

"Huh? Ooooh. Yeah. A little."

"I'd love to hear you play. And Joel's never heard you. Why don't you go get your guitar and give us a little concert."

Liza thought about it without looking at him. "Uh uh. Too early for me to sing."

"Aw, come on. Don't be modest. How often do you get to see your old man anyway?"

"No. I don't like to sing this early. Mom? Shouldn't I go wake Gram? I know she wants to see Joel." Liza was dying to escape the room.

"Yes, dear. Why don't you do that."

"Back in a jiffy," said Liza and swaggered out.

My mother broke eggs and pretended to be at ease. There was a brief, accusing stare from my father. He then sipped his coffee and pretended that he didn't notice the discomfort he caused.

I could only sit and watch. I understood everything, but couldn't react to it. I too wanted to escape. "Where do I sleep?" I asked.

"What's the matter, dear? Are you sleepy? Why don't you go lie down for a bit after you eat." Catherine winked with her entire face, scrunching her cheeks up and squeezing both eyes shut. It was a gesture both she and her mother used to express concern when they were busy thinking about something else. "For the time being, we'll stick you on the sofa. But Liza goes back to school next month and you can have her room."

"Thank you," I said and stood up.

"Where you going?" demanded Jake. "You don't need to go to sleep now. Wait until after breakfast."

I had Catherine's attention too. "Stay, dear. Please? Just for breakfast," she pleaded.

I lowered myself into my chair.

"Liza's *away* at school?" said Jake. "I didn't know that."

"She wanted to study painting, so she transferred to

Virginia Commonwealth in Richmond. They're supposed to be good for studio art."

"Nice, practical field of study," said Jake, shaking his head. "I would think she would've learned from your mother's example." Gramma Bolt was an artist who had never been able to support herself by her art. She too had been divorced, twice, and had worked most of her life as a bookkeeper.

"I think she has learned," said Catherine proudly. "She's going into it with no illusions. It's what she wants to do."

"Well, good. And maybe after a year's study, she can paint the house. Ho ho ho. I'm only teasing, Cat. Don't look so stern."

"Joel? Are scrambled eggs okay with you?"

"Yes, ma'am."

"They're easiest." She was beating the eggs in a bowl. "I took a psychology course last year and the professor said adolescent boys prefer scrambled eggs to fried. It has something to do with guilt over masturbating. Is that true?"

"I don't know. *I* like fried eggs." Did she really say that?

"Hmmmmm. Maybe that's a sign that you're well-adjusted."

Jake covered his eyes and began to chuckle.

"What's wrong?" my mother asked scornfully. "You find it funny?" She turned to pour the eggs into the pan. "You're such a prude, Jacob. Always were."

My father dropped his hand and winked at me, but I couldn't accept his conspiratorial advances any longer. I had to strike back. "It's not that I don't masturbate. But it's never affected the way I like my eggs."

Jake glared at me.

"Anyway, they'll be scrambled this morning," said Catherine. "But it's going to be a real education for me, Joel, having you live here. I know almost nothing about

31

adolescent males. You'll have to bear with me at first."

"Me too. I know almost nothing about middle-aged women."

Jake rallied and turned everything to his advantage. "I knew you'd be happy together."

Stairs creaked—the staircase was on the other side of the kitchen wall—and there was a clatter of toenails on wood. A tiny dog bounced into the kitchen, a toy dachshund with short brown fur. The dog stopped at the sight of strangers and began yipping furiously, confident that he could drive us from the kitchen.

"Hush, Max, hush," said Gramma Bolt from the stairs.

Liza called down. "They're relatives, Max."

The top of my grandmother's head appeared, then the rest of her: back and shoulders slouched forward, tiny feet racing to keep up with a chubby body. She raised her head to look at us with eyes that shined. "Hello, everybody. Hello, Joel. Hi, Jake. Now hush, Max. Don't be rude."

Max clicked across the floor to hide behind the advancing hem of her housecoat.

"Oh, it's so nice to see you, Joel. My God. You look so big now."

I had stood up and had to bend down to kiss her on a quilted cheek. The pressure of my hands on her waist squeezed a sweet, dusty odor up through the collar of her housecoat. I hadn't grown that much; it was she who had changed. She seemed shorter and rounder. And she wore a wig now. An auburn hat of strange hair covered the white wisps that had once made her look like an elderly statesman—noble and androgynous. The wig made her look more like a woman, but it also made her seem older, less eternal.

"No. Don't be silly. I can sit down on my own power. Here, Max. Hop up." She lifted the little dog off the floor and let him nest in her lap. "Ah, it's good to see you." She swatted me on the knee. "I was so envious when I heard that your mother and Liza got to see you. I was positively green. But now you're here." The twinkle in her eyes was even brighter than Aunt Bertie's. She was silent for a moment, so she could affectionately twinkle at me.

Jake reached across the table to touch her hand. "Hello, Mom. You're looking chipper."

"What?" The twinkle vanished. "Did you say . . . " She angrily thrust her head at him. "How can I . . . "

Jake withdrew his hand. He looked confused. He was expecting cordial courtesy from his mother-in-law, relief from all the buried tension.

"Jake? What was . . . Oh!" She made a face. She reached down the front of her housecoat to tinker with something. "Aaaaah. I was wondering why you were all so quiet." She chuckled and faced her daughter. "I was so excited, Cathy, I forgot to turn my hearing aid on." She smiled, happy to hear the breathing and the sighs. "Now what was that you said, Jake?"

"Nothing. Just hello."

"Well hello." She petted his hand. "I don't like you with a moustache. You don't have the lip for it. But it's good to see you anyway, even if you did bring a moustache."

"But he brought Joel too, Gram," said Liza. She stayed in the doorway, preferring to watch us from a distance.

"Yes. He did do that." Gramma Bolt turned to twinkle at me again. "I hope you and your father had a chance for a good long chat on your way over here. Cars are good for that."

Catherine served breakfast and Liza was coaxed from her doorway into a chair. Bits of egg were burnt, but I was too sleepy to taste the food. I ate simply to keep my mouth occupied. I didn't want to talk.

"Do you play chess, Joel?" my grandmother asked. "Could you teach me? That's something I've always wanted to learn."

"Have you been doing any painting, Mom?" Jake asked. "I would think this country would be excellent for that."

"Have you shown your father any of your pen and ink?" Gramma Bolt asked Liza.

Only Jake and Gramma Bolt really wanted to talk, wanted it only to keep everything covered with a skin of civility. You could feel muscles tense beneath that skin even when something as simple as the economics of the farm were discussed. A smug look crept into Jake's face when it was admitted that two-thirds of the property was leased out to a farm co-op.

"But that's only until we can afford our own tractor," said Catherine defensively. "Until then, we have enough work with the patch around the house."

"Of course," said Jake. "Very practical."

"Jake," said Gramma Bolt, determined to stitch the skin together again. "I've been meaning to ask you— you're the one to know. But what we're doing in Asia now—do you think it's good?" She thought she had found a safe, impersonal topic.

"I'm an Africa man, Mom. I don't know much more about it than anyone else does."

I saw Liza staring at the floor.

"But as a man on the street, what do you think?"

Jake took on a dark tone of faked uncertainty and went through a standard line on our position in Vietnam: It was a mistake to be there, but now that we were, we were committed, for the sake of our allies. "But it is a mess. There's no denying that."

"It's not just a mess," said Liza, not looking up. "It's wrong."

Jake remained utterly smooth. "Yes. Some people think that, Kitten."

"We should get out and leave those poor people alone."

Jake only nodded. "It *is* a mess. But we're in no position to simply mind our own garden." He looked out the window, then smiled at Liza. "Although it does look like the garden needs quite a bit of minding."

My mother's eyes kindled.

"What is it you're growing out there anyway?" Jake asked Liza.

"Beans... tomatoes... squash." Liza was confused by the shift of subject.

"Any cannabis? I'd think that would be a profitable crop."

"Cannabis?"

"Don't be square, Kitten. Marijuana. *Pot.*"

Catherine put down her fork. "You're the last person on earth, Jake, to criticize the way *other* people mind their gardens."

"Criticize? Who's said a word of criticism?"

Catherine clenched her jaw and looked at the ceiling. "I must be an idiot," she said. "I *wanted*—I *hoped* you would show some respect for what we'd done here. But you treat the whole thing like a joke. I feel like an idiot for *wanting* you to respect us. Your respect should mean nothing to me."

"I do respect you!" He gestured with the blade of his hand, ready to argue, but then dropped both hand and voice. "If I don't seem appreciative of what you've done, Cat, maybe it's only because I didn't see the condition the farm was in when you bought it."

"No, Jake. It's not that at all. You know what I'm talking about. You treat the whole thing as a joke. You mock your daughter, you mock... everything. You treat *us* as a joke. You always have."

"I only tease you. I've never understood why you have to be so thin-skinned about teasing. I don't really think you're growing pot out there."

"Momma," Liza pleaded. "He was just making a dumb joke. Let's talk about something else."

"Jake is in an uncomfortable position," said Gramma bolt benignly. "He should be allowed a few jokes."

Catherine considered this. "Is that it, Jake? Are you uncomfortable? Do we threaten you? I'm curious. I want to know."

"Just because I make a few bad quips doesn't mean I feel threatened. I make jokes to be social."

"It's not the jokes," Catherine insisted. "It's the lack of respect. Why can't you respect us?"

The contained anger, the questions and defenses: It was all part of the past. I was twelve years old again. The exhausted buzz in my head thickened into sleepiness. My eyelids rolled over my eyes. I snapped them open again only to find my mother still waiting for an answer.

"What is it about us that threatens you? Is it our independence, Jake? Because if it is, then I should be flattered by your disrespect, shouldn't I?"

Jake leaned back and conceded everything with both hands.

"But Jake, I'd rather have your respect. Independence should make us admirable. We don't need you, Jake, but you shouldn't feel guilty about that. You should like us for it."

He raised both hands again, but his gaze wandered off. "Oh, before I forget," he said and reached into a pants pocket. He extracted a checkbook and opened it on the table. "Should I write out Joel's costs for one month or two? Or, if it's easier for your bookkeeping, I can make out an amount covering him through the end of the year."

There was a missed beat in my mother's expression. She shot a frightened look at me, then snapped her head forward to face Jake again. "Suit yourself. Whatever's convenient for you."

The rest of us watched as Jake coldly cut figures in his checkbook. I knew I would be paid for, just as I had been paid for in Switzerland.

"Jake," said Gramma Bolt calmly. "That's dirty pool."

"What's dirty? Just being practical." He tore the check

out and passed it to her. "I assume you keep the books, Mom. That is the correct amount, isn't it?"

My grandmother accepted the check, smiled nervously as she showed it to me. "We're not making a profit off you, dear."

Three hundred dollars for September through December, 1970. Jake had paid that much a month when I had been in Switzerland and, although the payments had not been a secret, they had been kept polite and private. The financial facts stayed at the back of the mind, unexamined, like faith. I looked at the check as it was folded and slipped into a pocket in my grandmother's housecoat.

"I *can* pay more," said Jake. "But that was the amount you stipulated."

"Yes," said Catherine. "And you can make even that seem like a slap in the face. It doesn't compromise my position. Don't think it does."

I didn't put a price tag on my father's affection, and yet... Money now seemed to be my only link with Jake. And this money that should've been fatherly love was used to show contempt for my mother. I tried to untangle what it meant, and the harder I tried, the more I wanted to sleep. I felt sleep setting in, breaking circuits, ending thoughts protecting me.

"If you like, I can take it back," said Jake.

"Jake. Please, don't mock me," Catherine said sadly.

"I'm dead serious."

"You know full well I have to take it. We can't afford the luxury of being *that* indignant."

Jake smirked triumphantly. He couldn't share his triumph with anyone else at the table so he thoughtlessly smirked at me.

"I've finished eating," I said. "I want to go to sleep."

Jake became annoyed. "Have another cup of coffee, lad."

The women watched me, hoping I'd change my mind.

37

They all wanted me to stay, although it was clear by now that my presence stopped nothing.

"No thank you. Mom? Is there someplace where I could lie down?"

Catherine reluctantly nodded. "Certainly, dear. I'll fetch a pillow and you can stretch out on the sofa. You *do* look tired. Maybe an hour nap and you can rejoin us?"

"I'll get the pillow," said Liza.

"No. I'll get it. You keep your father company."

"Sweet dreams, sleepyhead," said Jake. "Sorry to have kept you up past your bedtime." The sarcasm was meant to hurt, but didn't.

I followed my mother into the living room. I recognized some of the furniture: the walnut coffee table, matching table lamps with sleek brass bases, squarish armchair and sofa covered with tweed. It was furniture from my childhood and none of it looked right here. I sat on the sofa and undid my shoes.

"Joel?" said my mother. "Are you angry?"

"No. Sleepy."

"You have a right to be angry, you know. Or hurt. Not over the money. That's all me. But... you know. Men can feel hurt, too. There's nothing wrong with it."

"Yes, ma'am. But I'm just sleepy right now. That's all." I refused to surrender to her so easily, at least not before I had time to sort things out for myself. "Honest."

I turned away to avoid her benign, understanding look. I saw one of my grandmother's paintings on the wall, a portrait of my mother at twenty. With red-rouged lips and jet-black eyelashes, she looked like a magazine cover from the forties. She posed beside a plaster bust that was all slabs and cubes.

Catherine followed my eyes. "Me in my mannequin days," she said. She stood with her weight on one leg, her hands in the back pockets of her overalls. "You remember it from Gramma's old studio, don't you? 'Two Blockheads.' That's what your father called it. He had no idea how right he was. You sleep," she whispered. "Join us when you're ready. Oh! I forgot. I promised you a pillow." She turned and ran up the stairs, work boots chasing each other into the ceiling.

I lay down on the sofa while I waited for my pillow, intending to make a start in deciding what I should feel. Money, love, betrayal; out of the kitchen, I no longer felt sleepy. But as soon as my head touched the rough tweed of the cushion, I was asleep. And I was dreaming of the Bahnhofstrasse in Zurich.

It was an autumn evening when the sky was still light. I sat at an outdoor cafe with Uncle Arthur, who consoled me by buying coffees with whipped cream, one after another. He took me through the cafe to a meadow out back, where it was late afternoon, as though the day were running backwards. The meadow was full of knowing cows and each cow wore an alarm clock around its neck.

I woke with a pillow beneath my head. "*Was uhr?*" I mumbled, then remembered where I was and wanted only to go back to sleep, back to Zurich.

"He's not twelve anymore." It was my mother's voice somewhere in the house. "You can't shunt him around like a sack of potatoes, never talking things over with him."

"I told him enough. Anyway, Joel's in a world of his own."

"Hmmph. Like somebody else I know." A pause, then, "You and your holy reticence, Jake. If you had any sense, you would've talked to him and gotten his sympathy. You should've spent some time with him, instead of coming straight here. He's not going to like it here at first, but you've been so cavalier about this that he's going to be resenting you on top of that."

"He's seventeen. I'm not going to hold his hand."

"That's what you said when he was thirteen and you packed him off to Switzerland."

"And it worked out fine. He was very happy there."

"Then why couldn't you leave him there? You keep

contradicting yourself. A minute ago you said Switzerland wasn't good for him."

"I did not contradict myself. If you'd listen . . . I said he was happy. And I said it wasn't good for him. Two very different concepts. Life isn't a bed of roses and it's high time Joel learned that. Being unhappy for a little while isn't going to hurt him. And if that means he's going to hate me, it's a sacrifice I'm willing to make."

"You *martyr*. I don't believe for a minute you believe one word of what you're saying, Jake. You might be a fool, but you're not the son of a bitch who could really feel that."

"Believe what you like."

I wanted sleep. Sleep and dreams. When I was eleven and twelve, I'd been able to tune myself out, lose myself in sleep and television and schoolwork. I wanted to be able to do that again. I dragged the pillow around my head and shut the angry voices out. I fell back into sleep, without the voices or my visions of Switzerland.

3

I WOKE UP drenched with sweat in a foreign house. The sun had moved and the light burned on the screens of the windows. I lay on the sofa and looked up at a ceiling that was as cracked and scabby as a desert. I did not want to be here. I wanted to be on the Bahnhofstrasse or in the garden in Kilchberg or even my tent back at camp.

The house was silent. The voices were gone. Had I only dreamed them? No, I had heard the words too clearly, the stifled whispers and hisses. Everyone else gone from the kitchen, my parents had been finally faced with each other. But now they too were gone and the fighting was finished.

I felt like crying, not for my parents, but for myself. With *my* life at stake, all my father and mother could do was criticize each other, score points off each other. What about me? Couldn't they forget their own disaster long enough to deal with mine? Because it was a disaster to be left at the end of the world. My setting, my schooling, all the worldly influences that had promised to produce a successful man—thrown away by two people too preoccupied with themselves to understand what they were doing. I blamed both of them. If my father hadn't offered me, if my mother hadn't accepted, things would've stayed the way they were. But together they had closed the great door of my future.

The flood of self-pity was disquietingly deep and satisfying. All sharp feelings of anger and resistance melted away in an emotion as clean and simple as feeling sorry for myself.

Catherine and Gramma were sitting alone at the kitchen table, their faces turned toward the door when I walked in.

"Hello. Guess I slept longer than I should've."

The two pairs of grey eyes shifted nervously.

"You must've needed it, dear," said Gramma.

"Here. Sit down and have some lunch," said Catherine. "All we have is egg salad, but there's plenty of it."

"Not hungry. Where is everyone?"

"Uh, out," said Catherine. "Your sister's doing her chores. I should be getting back to mine shortly."

"And Dad?" But I already knew the answer. I looked out the window and saw the hard, empty clay yard.

"Jake... your father... left." She cocked her head and guiltily lifted one eyebrow. "I'm afraid I scared him off."

"Now don't say that," said Gramma. "Jake had no intention of staying here any longer than he had to, and we both know it. He was only using your squabble as his excuse."

Catherine noded. "He wanted to say good-bye to you, dear, but didn't want to wake you. And, as you know, your father doesn't like scenes. He said to give you his love."

"Ah." I quietly accepted the news, fitting it into everything else. My self-pity was so deep I was impervious to any new pain.

"Be angry with him, dear. But give him his due. You might not believe this, but he *means* well."

I stared at her in disbelief.

Gramma Bolt skeptically cleared her throat.

"Okay," Catherine admitted. "I know I'm the last person on earth to defend him. But somebody has to. He certainly does a lousy job of it himself." She looked ashamed for a moment, then continued. "Joel, your father . . . your father felt that you were too isolated in Switzerland. That you didn't have enough contact with real life. He said he was afraid—I'm only quoting, dear—that it wasn't preparing you for real life."

And a year stagnating on a farm in the middle of nowhere was going to prepare me for the life I'd chosen? She was a fool if she actually believed him.

"I wish he'd talked to you a little more about it. But you know how highhanded your father can be. I don't really know if he's right or not, Joel. You seem fine to me. A little too polite, perhaps, but not unfit for real life. But there you have it. That's what he feels. So don't be too hard on him. He *is* thinking of what's best for you."

"Yeah. Sure," I muttered.

She sighed and nodded at that. "Okay. Only natural for you to be angry with him right now. But give yourself time and try to understand him. Okay?"

"Give yourself plenty of time," Gramma added kindly.

"And give us time, too. I hope you'll be happy here, Joel. You might find our way of life a little peculiar at first, until you get used to it. But, until you do, we must promise to be patient with one another."

Patient? With people who were so far from understanding me that they thought defending my father might make me feel better? I lied and mumbled, "No problem."

Catherine smiled, petted my hand, then rested her elbows on the table and looked at me warmly. "Joel?" she said. "What do you know about goats?"

"Goats?"

She innocently shrugged and said, "I was hoping that, being in Switzerland, you might've had some goat experience."

"The people in nice neighborhoods don't keep goats," I said stiffly.

"No? Oh. I'd been thinking that maybe you could take charge of Tango out there."

"Tango? I thought it was Jacob."

Catherine laughed. "Noooo. I was only needling your

43

father with that. No, just plain old Tango. Wouldn't want to have to think about Jake every time I had to drag that fool goat out of our garden. But we'll think of something for you. I want there to be something special you can do around here. So you can feel you belong."

"But I don't want to belong! I had nothing to do with my coming here! I don't even want to be here!"

Catherine frowned; she glanced at her mother.

I was too proud to apologize for letting my emotions get the better of me.

"Yes," said Catherine, looking down. "Yes, I understand. Okay. We'll talk later, dear. These things take time and I know my talking isn't going to persuade you before you're ready. So, if you'll excuse me, I should get back to the chicken coop I'm building. Why don't you just take it easy this afternoon, Joel. After all, this is your first day. Make yourself at home. You okay, Mom? Okay, I better be getting back to work." She took a carpenter's apron down from a hook beside the door and smiled at me while she put it on, so I would know she wasn't running away. "See you two later."

Gramma watched her go, then turned to me. "She's right, you know, even if she does sound a little daffy at times. We'll give you a few days to be snappish with us, dear. But after that, I sincerely hope you get your act together." She scrunched her eyes and twinkled at me while she lifted herself out of the chair. "And now, if you'll excuse me, it's time for my nap. See you later, dear. When your fur's back in place." And she went around the corner and up the stairs, Max clicking his toenails behind her.

I felt guilty for driving them off like that, but I knew they'd be back, fingering and picking at my emotions with their gingerly understanding. Men were so much easier to deal with, but I was surrounded by women. I heard my mother hammering outside. It was hard for me to sit there doing nothing when I could hear her working.

I did not want to be one of them, but my self-pity felt shameful to me now. I had to get outside, where solitude wouldn't feel so criminal or arrogant.

A hand saw snarled behind the barn. I deliberated over walking towards the snarl, when I saw Liza in the field on the right, jabbing with a hoe in a bog of green leaves. My mother was too articulate. If I were to join anyone, I should join my sister. Another hoe leaned against the house and I took it with me, wanting to appear useful.

Liza was bent down, her face hidden by a straw hat that had a green visor in its brim. She straightened up when she heard me rustling down the furrow.

"Hi," I said. "Need a hand?"

"Sure," she said. "Could use a little company." She studied me sadly, as if she knew everything that had happened, then pulled back from all that and said only, "Hoeing out the weeds. Here, you take that row and we can work side by side."

We worked side by side, separated only by a row of leaves like saucers that came up past our ankles. My knee socks were down and the fuzzy leaves made my legs itch. There was the gritty clop and chit of our hoes, an occasional ring when a blade hit a shard of baked clay.

"What ever happened to that guy who gave Mom and me a tour of the waterfront at your silly old camp?" Liza asked.

"Kearney? He's still there. Although he's going into the army at the end of the summer. Career army."

"Army?" Liza groaned. "Figures. What a dork."

That was about all we said to each other. I needed to forget my emotional aggravation in work that was perfectly mindless. Our hoes broke the earth into chalky plates. It was summer squash we were hoeing, recently planted where the tomatoes had been. The blossoms on the stalks looked like shriveled trumpets. The sun was low enough to flash on the pie plate that hung on a pole in the middle of the field: something to scare the crows away, I decided. I was bent down so long that my back began to cramp, and I had to straighten up and stretch. "Tedious," I said.

"Amen," said Liza without looking up. "Thank God I only have four more weeks. Then it's back to school for me. Back to normal life."

And self-pity suddenly flowed again. Liza could return to normal life while I was left here at the end of the world. I swung my hoe harder, fighting the pleasurable sadness that threatened to make me into a child again. And that was what shamed me most, that here, among women, my identity as a man would dissolve in self-pity, like sugar in warm water. I couldn't give in to it.

Two hours later the sun dropped below the trees and we went inside. Gramma Bolt and I began a game of chess in the living room while Liza and Catherine took their showers in the kitchen. When they were done, they moved to the living room and left the kitchen to me. It was lonely in the cylindrical stall, with no Corey to talk to while I washed off at the end of the day. I fought back by telling myself it was good to have privacy again.

Dinner consisted of salad, crackers and coffee. Catherine was cocky after her carpentry and talked about a score of subjects—tools, the farmers' market in Williamsburg, the distance to the nearest public school—but never mentioned Jake's visit or my anger.

After dinner, we went out on the back porch to catch the coolness of the evening. A chair was brought out for Gramma and she mixed herself a highball. Catherine cajoled Liza into bringing out her guitar so I could hear her sing. She sat on the bottom step and sang softly towards the woods, singing with the sweet, thin voice of someone who preferred to sing only to herself. She seemed embarrassed that we knew she bothered to sing without being great at it. The songs were accompanied by the deep-throated thunk of a bullfrog who mistook Liza's bass string for the call of a rival. It was all traditional folk songs, and then "White Rabbit."

At ten sharp we went inside to bed. Catherine threw some sheets over the sofa and everyone kissed me good night, repeating how happy they were that I was here. One by one they made their trips to the outhouse, then trooped up the stairs to their rooms. Lights were turned off and I was alone.

I thought I wanted sleep, thought that sleep would come quickly, but I only lay there in the darkness. I leaped from the sheets and turned on the light.

I would not surrender to my feelings. I had to keep myself occupied. I would read. I was finished with Ayn Rand, but I saw the bookcase by the stairs, a heavy oak bookcase full of books that had once been my father's. They were all history books from his graduate school days: *The Education of Henry Adams, The Decline of the West, The Decline and Fall of the Roman Empire.* There were no books about business. He had left behind nothing useful.

But why should usefulness matter to me now? I had no future now. I shouldn't care anymore. To care only fed my hopes, and hopes here would only mean continued pain and self-pity. If I were going to read, I should read to kill all hope of hoping. Only then would life become bearable.

The Decline and Fall of the Roman Empire sounded suitably depressing. It came in six volumes. I opened the first, bent on starving my hopes, and read about the extent of the empire under the Antonines. By the end of the first chapter, tears were running down my cheeks, as if in sympathy for the doomed future of a sovereignty that had once comprehended the fairest part of the earth.

4

THEN CAME THE longest year of my life. I rotted all winter, read my father's set of Gibbon and taught Gramma Bolt how to play chess. The whites in Charles City went to private schools and the black public schools didn't want me, so they declared me graduated. But when it was time for college, Dad pleaded poverty. He did it in a letter from halfway around the world and sent me a check so small I spent it on a secondhand motorcyle. That was all I could do for myself, now that the bastard had stranded me in the middle of nowhere. That's what he'd been doing all along: washing his hands of a son, slyly, in stages, without even his ex-wife understanding what he was up to. Catherine was infuriated. Somehow, I'd known all along. I was hurt, but I wasn't surprised. I took a job at a motel in Williamsburg, the nearest town, just to escape the farm for a few hours every week. Liza was away at college, but I saw no point in college now that I couldn't afford to go to the best.

One day that spring, I was out in our woods with the chainsaw that had been Catherine's idea of a Christmas present. I was cutting firewood that we could sell in the fall, when a car pulled into our yard. It was Bob Kearney, or rather, Second Lieutenant Kearney, now stationed at Fort Eustis on the other side of Williamsburg. I was embarrassed that he saw me like this: A little redneck hick whose overalls were blond with sawdust. But he wasn't looking for me. It was Shirtsy's sister he wanted, and since he happened to be joyriding in the neighborhood— "Not too many Scherzen-whatevers in the Charles City County telephone directory." I told Kearney where Liza was, just to get rid of him. He had only been with her briefly at camp, but she had obviously made an impression. He was still a jerk, but Liza would see that and give him the treatment he deserved. He was so bent on seeing Liza he didn't even stay long enough to meet Catherine, but shot off down the road again, like a setter scenting a quail. Still, his mindless pursuit of women didn't seem like such a vulgar waste of time to me, now that I, for one, wasn't doing anything better with my life.

That fall, when I was almost nineteen, I took a part in a play. A William and Mary drama student who waitressed at the motel was directing a college-community production: *The Persecution and Assassination of Jean-Paul Marat as Performed by the Inmates of the Asylum of Charenton Under the Direction of the Marquis de Sade.* I seemed to be in love with her. I'd never been in love, nothing else was happening in my life, and Jan Terwiliger was even shorter than I was. I tried out for her play, but I saw little of her once I was in it. She rehearsed the leads while an assistant handled me and the other lunatics. The odd energy of the play began to affect me. Images of efficient, faceless secretaries, accessories of a future I'd never have, no longer appeared to me whenever I had sex with myself. My imagination turned inventive: Jan, of course, naked and flat-chested; Karen, the assistant director, who joshed about wanting to have two men at once; and, out of sadism, Wyler Reese's mouth—forcing an enemy to take you in his mouth seemed like a beautiful way to humiliate them. I was surprised and pleased with how original my imaginings had become.

I sat on a bench in Williamsburg one afternoon, killing the hours between my bellman's job and rehearsal that

49

night. If only I could impress Jan with how good I was, even in a minor role. Real images, she had told us. I was basing my lunatic on Odie, the big retarded dishwasher at the motel. A red sun sank into the October trees of the college at the end of the street while I sat on the bench and tried to be Odie. There were more students than tourists now, but nobody knew me here. I continued to be Odie, slowing my thoughts, going slack in the face. Odie's hands always seemed very heavy and useless, so I had to do something with the motorcyle helmet I was holding. I put it on my head, which immediately seemed like something Odie would do.

I'd been sitting there for fifteen minutes when a blonde, big-boned girl sat at the other end of my bench. She had a fistful of mail in her lap that she eagerly tore open and read. We were under a mock-Colonial streetlamp and the envelopes were decorated with rainbows and yellow smiley faces. She glanced at me once or twice and went on with her letters.

I was irritated by the way she ignored me. College students lived in their own pampered world. I wanted to annoy her, then realized Odie could do it just by being friendly. And I could test Odie's believability. I squirmed on the bench, getting deeper into Odie, then said, "Hel-Low."

"Hello," she said and went back to her letter. She paused over it and abruptly looked up again. "Yes, hello there. My name's Patty. What's yours?"

She chirped at me, as if I were a toddler. She thought I was retarded. Eastern State Hospital was nearby and there were always patients wandering around town. I wondered how long I could keep her thinking I was one of them.

I told her my name. "Oh-deee."

"What a pretty name."

I congratulated myself. I wasn't even an actor. "Pretty letters. Boyfriends?"

"Oh no. Friends. I belong to a great big club of friends, all over the world. We write to each other all the time, sharing."

"What d'ya share?"

"Love," she cooed. "And our belief in the Lord Jesus Christ."

Gibbon came to mind, and the theater people's jokes about "Jesus freaks," and I had to push it all back to stay in character. But I was so intent on my performance there was no temptation to smile.

"Do you know who Jesus is?"

"Uh huh." What would Odie know? "Jesus loves the little children."

"That's right! Jesus loves you, me, everybody. He died to save us from our sins."

I had Odie change the subject. "Can I be your boyfriend?"

She laughed and petted my knee and said yes. She dropped religion and talked about other things: circuses, balloons, playing in leaf piles and our favorite colors. I invented a life for Odie and he told Patty all about it. His routine at Eastern State was so bleak I began to feel sorry for him myself.

"Odie? Would you like some ice cream? Or maybe a nice piece of cake?"

"Yeaaaah!"

She was meeting some friends for dinner and wanted to take me with her. I couldn't resist the challenge. I had to see if I could convince other people as easily as I had Patty. Patty took my hand and proudly led me to the college. I took a couple of steps before I remembered Odie's lead-footed walk.

We went behind the Campus Center, where I'd parked my motorcycle, to the college dining hall. Patty convinced a woman in white to let me in as a guest, then took me up a narrow flight of stairs to a balcony that looked out on the clattering, cavernous room. There were four or five tables up there and two males at one of them greeted us with "Praise the Lord." Their smiles froze when Patty explained that I was from Eastern State.

"He hasn't run away?" asked the one with the thick, murky glasses.

The other one, Randy, had the same scrubbed sweetness as Patty: blue eyes, dimples and a sheaf of blond hair. Normally I couldn't have paid much attention to how cute a guy was, but Odie was free to stare.

The ugly one continued to grumble that it was late and I was probably missing the bus back to the hospital. Randy shared his chocolate milk with me.

"Pay Walter no mind," said Patty. "He likes to worry. It's his way of showing his love. I'm going down to get my dinner now, but I'll be back in two shakes of a lamb's tail. And I'll bring you *ice cream.*" She went down the stairs with the proud bounce of a Good Samaritan.

I was nervous for a moment. These two couldn't be as gullibly kindhearted as Patty.

"Odie? It's considered rude to wear a hat indoors," said Walter. "Or a helmet."

Odie shook his head. I was afraid I'd look too normal without the helmet.

Patty returned with a tray of food, and a Fudgesicle for Odie. We all bowed heads while Patty thanked the Lord for cafeteria food, this beautiful day and me.

They tried talking to Odie, but he was more interested in his Fudgesicle, so they talked to each other, now and then remembering me with a smile or bite of their dessert.

"I'm not studying for the chemistry test," said Randy. "If the Lord feels I should pass it, He'll give me all the help I need."

Walter cautioned him against using faith as a disguise for sloth.

Patty suddenly asked Randy if that was his friend, Middlemarch, down below, putting up his tray.

Randy looked over the railing and said that it was.

"Hey! Marchy!" he shouted and waved to someone below. "He waved back. I guess that means he's coming up."

"I think Middlemarch has been avoiding us," said Walter.

"Marchy! Long time, no see," cried Randy, making room at the table.

Odie turned around with his whole body to see who it was. Up the steps, with a forlorn slouch and wary smile, came Corey Cobbett.

I jerked my head around, so the side of my helmet hid my face. But it couldn't be Corey. He went to college near his home in Norfolk. I looked up from under my eyebrows and watched him go around the table to the chair beside Randy. Middlemarch had sideburns and his hair was shaggier than Cobbett's had been, covering his ears and the collar of his army jacket. He wore glasses, but little wire-rims, not the black-framed glasses Cobbett had worn. He looked bulkier too, but then, I'd known Cobbett only in the summer and never seen him in a coat. Books stuck out of the coat pockets on either side, like the stumps of wings. But Corey Cobbett had been a liberal and an atheist: He wouldn't be with these Jesus freaks. And "Middlemarch": It didn't sound like a nickname.

"Hi Marchy." "Where you been, Middlemarch?" "The Lord finally returns you to us."

He shrugged apologetically and lowered himself into the chair. "What can I say?" said Corey. "I guess I've just been busy."

It was definitely Corey. It was the same drawled voice and the same open face that couldn't hide a thing: He clearly didn't want to be with these people. He briefly greeted Patty and Walter and glanced at the person in the helmet. Then glanced again. Then glanced a third time and stared.

I lowered my head, hoping that when I looked up, it would only be a stranger who reminded me of someone from Boy Scout camp. But, inconvenient as it was, I wanted it to be Corey Cobbett.

"Oh, and this is Patty's friend," said Randy. "His name is Odie. He lives out at . . . Eastern State?"

"You shouldn't stare. He's very shy," Patty whispered.

"Sorry. I just—" He squinted at me, then quickly turned away. "Patty's friend? Oh. And Eastern State? Oh. I see. Nice to meet you, Odie," he told me over his shoulder.

"Odie's in the second grade," Patty boasted.

"Oh? Okay." He leaned towards Randy. "So where were you in history this morning? Strong was asking for you."

Now that I had a name and a situation, I couldn't be who he thought I was. He ignored me and talked to the others, only his eyes kept coming back to me.

It was maddening. I itched to shake his hand, slap his back and cry, "Yes! It's me!" The more he glanced at me, the happier I was to see him. But I felt trapped inside Odie. I was afraid to break out of Odie in the presence of the others. I tried using a smile to let Corey know we knew each other, but it was only Odie's smile—blissful and meaningless.

"We think we know who painted 666 on Randy's door," Walter was telling Corey.

Corey only nodded and turned to me. "Odie? Do you have any brothers? Or cousins maybe? What's your last name?"

"Looooong name," I said and counted out three names on my fingers. "Joel Odell Scherzenlieb."

His eyes went blank and his lips parted.

"Sounds Jewish," said Walter.

"Or Mennonite," Patty insisted.

Corey looked horrified. His eyes locked on me.

It wasn't the reaction I wanted. I meant for him to know it was me, Joel Scherzenlieb, buried in this impersonation of a damaged child. Instead, he thought the damaged child was me. His sympathy made me feel ashamed.

I regained control of my face, closed my mouth and winked at Corey.

He cocked his head at me.

I winked again, then nodded at the stairs.

The signals startled him. He glanced at the others to see if they'd noticed.

"Have to go," Odie announced and stood up.

"You mean you have to...*wash your hands?*" said Patty.

"Uh uh. Have to go back to the bus. Time." I tried signaling Corey out of his chair by scratching my chin with a finger that pointed at the stairs. "Bye."

"I'll walk you to the bus," said Patty. "You might not know the way."

"*I know.* Not stupid." I looked pleadingly at Corey.

And he finally stood up. "Maybe I should walk him over. I'm leaving anyway and you just started eating, Patty." He still didn't know what was going on and couldn't look at either Patty or me.

"Thanks, Middlemarch. But he's my responsibility."

"No, no," Corey insisted. "You're always doing good turns for people. Why not let me do one?"

"He's right," said Walter. "You shouldn't be selfish with your good works."

Patty looked ashamed and irritably thanked Corey. She made me promise to meet her at the same bench next Wednesday. "You're still my boyfriend, Odie. I want you to remember that. And Middlemarch? Promise me you'll hold his hand when you cross the street. I worry about him in traffic."

But before Corey could promise, Odie grabbed hold of his hand.

His fingers stayed limp, then nervously closed around mine. His hand was surprisingly small for someone his size. Or maybe it was only because my hand was so hard from farmwork and luggage. He looked off into space and said, "Let's go, Odie. See you, people. You too, Randy."

"Bye. Bye," I said and waved my free hand at them as Corey pulled me down the stairs. The woman in white stared as Corey hauled me out the door. He looked straight ahead, lost in worry, but I was grinning, not like Odie, but like myself.

I waited until we were safely outside. I pulled loose and cried, "Cobbett! *Damn!*" And I threw my arms around him.

There was the clunk of his chin hitting my helmet.

I jumped back and pulled off the helmet. "Damn but it's good to see you. I thought we were never going to get out of there!"

He stood in the light from the door, looking at me as if I were a ghost. "Joel? You...? But what're you doing in...?"

"*Me?* What about you? You're supposed to be in Norfolk or somewhere, studying to be a lawyer or something. Oh but it's so damn good to run into you, Corey!" I seized his hand again, but only to shake it. "Yes! It's me!" I laughed at his unconvinced face. "Joel! From summer camp!"

"And... you're at Eastern State now?"

"No! Are you crazy. Why would I be...? That was only a put-on up there. Couldn't you tell? That girl met me on the street and thought I was retarded and I played along and it snowballed and... and *you* walked into it!" I laughed and shook my head.

"Then you're okay?"

"I'm wonderful! And I can't tell you how glad I am to see you again!"

He began to smile, then closed his eyes and lifted his eyebrows. Then he looked down at me and rubbed his chin where my helmet had banged him. "Uh, we shouldn't stay here. They might come out this way and, well... They have their foolish side, but it'd be mean to let them see it was just a joke."

We walked down the brick sidewalk toward the Campus Center, the use of our legs bringing both of us back to earth.

"You again?" he said, sounding less stunned and more pleased. "I still can't believe it."

"And I can't believe I'm talking to you. What're you doing here anyway?"

"Oh. I won a scholarship. Through my mother's church group. No big deal. But it gave me enough money to transfer to a real school. So here I am."

"You're not one of them, are you?"

"One of...? Oh, them." He quickly laughed. "No, I haven't been born again. At least not as a—" he kept glancing at me and his sentences seemed to snag on his glances—"But no. I met Randy in a class and... no, it's not an association I think I'll continue. But what about you?" He looked straight at me. "You're not at Eastern State?"

"No!" I laughed at his refusal to let go of that.

"But shouldn't you be in Switzerland or Harvard or somewhere important? Hey, and what happened to you back at summer camp? Why did you disappear so suddenly?" He laughed, remembering something else. "It wasn't because of any of us, I hope."

"Not at all." And I told him my story, or a doctored version of it, one that left out my father's betrayal of me and reduced it all to circumstances. I didn't want to sound as if I were asking for his sympathy. It was easier talking about the last few months, when I'd actually started doing things.

We ended up under the windows of the Campus Center, standing on either side of my motorcycle, which Corey petted while he said, "Huh. And I've been picturing you in a Ferrari all this time. But a farm, huh? A motel and *Marat/Sade?* You've certainly changed, Joel.

57

And your little stunt back there with Randy and them? I never would've imagined it a year and a half ago."

"You've changed too." But had he? "New glasses. William and Mary. Longer hair. No wonder I couldn't decide if it was you. And they were calling you 'Middlemarch'?"

"That's Walter's idea of humor. It was the book I always had with me, when I saw them for lunch every day. Good book. Not as long as *Atlas Shrugged*. But long."

We nodded and smiled about *Atlas Shrugged*.

But remembering that made me wonder why we should be so happy to see each other. We had been friends at summer camp, searching each other out whenever we wanted somebody to talk to, but what we talked about had been nothing special. We argued about Ayn Rand, who Corey hated, and graduated income tax, which I thought unfair. He treated me as someone intelligent, which showed that he was intelligent too, but that was back at a time when I assumed my intelligence would come to something, not waste away in the flatlands of Virginia.

"So. How was camp this summer?" I was afraid we had nothing in common now but that.

"I wasn't there. I spent the summer in, uh, New York."

"New York? *You?*"

Corey became sheepish—I had said it accusingly. "Yeah, well. I knew I had this scholarship, so I didn't have to worry about saving money. Worked in a bookstore and it took all my salary just to live there. But—Big city. I was curious. I needed to see what it was like."

"And what was it like?"

"Interesting. Very interesting." He gazed at me, as if he expected me to agree or disagree, then broke off his gaze, as if afraid I wouldn't know. "But it spoiled me for this place. I'd been so excited about getting away from home, but after New York—" He looked at the dark lawn and lit windows around us. "Hey. Um. I can't help feeling that Randy and company will come around the corner any minute. Want to go get a beer somewhere? Or we could go to my place. It's not far from here."

I wanted to continue this, just to assure myself that there was no reason for me to feel glad to see Corey. He had gone up in the world and I had gone down. "Sure. I've got another hour to kill."

He asked where my rehearsal was and I told him.

"Oh! I'm just around the corner from there. What about there then?"

"Sounds good," I said and shrugged.

"Good. You can see where I live. Not much really, just a basement in somebody's house, but it has a kitchen and I can fix us some coffee, if you don't mind instant. Or there's some bourbon left, only you're going to rehearsal and you probably won't want that on your breath when you..." He was suddenly speaking in a quick, careless manner that I'd never heard him use at summer camp. He caught himself, grinned and suggested we walk.

But I didn't want to leave my motorcycle here. "I'll ride us over. I've got an extra helmet." I always took two helmets to rehearsal, in hopes that I might get Jan to take another ride with me.

Corey squeezed his head into the helmet: No wonder nobody'd had trouble believing I was retarded.

"And there's no safety bar in the back, so you'll have to hold on to me."

But Corey held on to the seat. I kicked the engine on, took us down the sidewalk to the curb and swung onto the street. This was a side to me that Corey'd never seen: a free man on a motorcycle. I tapped the bike into a higher gear and threw us backwards. And Corey grabbed my waist. Then let go. Then he put his hands back, on my hips this time, only to let go again.

And I remembered something else from our summer at camp.

A ride back from Claremont in an open convertible, Corey and I squeezed into the backseat with Wyler Reese.

And Corey's hand on my leg. It was Saturday night and most of the staff had gone home for the weekend, and those of us left drove to Claremont for beers. I drank Coke and beat Corey at pinball. Reese used a fake I.D. and passed out on the drive back, sprawling in his corner of the backseat until my legs were forced against Corey's. Corey must've misunderstood; he'd had a few beers. But when he laid his hand on my knee, I was amazed, and flattered by his interest in me. He couldn't look at me; his hand stayed perfectly still. I wanted to show that I liked him, too. His shoulder was level with my mouth; I leaned over and gently bit it. When I tasted shirt I wondered what we were doing. But I was intrigued. My confusion excited me. We sat there motionless, night air and darkness rushing around us. Only when we stepped out of the car at camp could Corey look at me. He didn't mention the hand or bite. I casually invited him to spend the night on my tentmate's empty cot, just so I might find out what was happening to us. He was so silent I thought I heard his teeth chatter before he accepted. We shut ourselves inside the dark, mildewed tent, sat on two cots, removed our shoes and... discussed Ayn Rand, graduated income tax and Bobby Kennedy. Until my confused excitement passed, and I remembered neither of us was female. There was nothing we could do together without looking ridiculous. Corey seemed relieved when it became clear we weren't going to do anything. Maybe he'd forgotten he had defended me when I was called queer, remembered again and realized how close we were to making liars out of each other.

But I was suddenly curious about what might've happened if memory had been a little slower that night. Being in a play about the Marquis de Sade made it easier for me to think about such things.

I got to rehearsal that night, but missed one a week later.

* * *

Fields flew past. A soybean field they'd been harvesting a day ago was shaved clean this morning. A white dog ran at a slant across the furrows toward a distant row of trees that raced with me against brown fields and blue sky.

The motorcycle strained to race out from under me on my way home. The roar of the engine and the pressure of wind woke me up, continued to wake me, wider and wider, until I realized I wasn't just waking up, I was happy. I seemed ventilated with happiness.

I knew why. Sex, of course. But more than sex, less itchy than sex, more future tense, while the sex had been already seven or eight hours ago. I knew exactly why I was so happy, but could only nod at the reason, pretend I didn't know it yet, delay the moment when I finally looked it in the eye. Because it frightened me. And because I wanted to protect it. I was in love with Corey.

It frightened me because Corey was a guy. I wanted to protect it because such a love was so ridiculous and frag-ile. Love was for marriage, and I couldn't marry Corey. There were no practical uses for falling in love with him. And yet, it was such a wonderful feeling. I kept postpon-ing the moment when I would have to admit it was ab-surd and throw it away. I couldn't distinguish the excitement of my fear from the excitement of love. And I wasn't alone with this; Corey was in love with me.

When we had parted that morning, I had been glad to get away. I wasn't sure what else we could say to each other and I needed to change my clothes. But, ten miles out, I still felt him near me, as if he still rode the back of my motorcycle, and I was pleased to have him near me. Then I started waking up to how happy I was, and took my happiness with me the thirty miles out to my mother's farm.

Here was our house, pressed up against the woods by our dead garden. But the grey-shingled carton didn't look so dismal to me this morning. Even our squat shed of a barn looked good, the red rust and blue steel of the corrugated metal glowing purple in the low angled sunlight. I walked my bike toward the barn, past a new car I'd never seen before. It was too nice a car for a Bible salesman. I decided it was another man from the co-op, here to renegotiate their lease on two-thirds of Catherine's land. I parked my bike inside the barn and stopped. I could still feel Corey's weight pressing on the inside of my legs, like a memory in the muscles. I covered my bike with its tarp to protect it from Catherine's chickens. I protected my love by deciding it didn't have to mean I was gay.

Corey said he was gay, but that wasn't why I was in love with him. I was in love with Corey because he was Corey, if I really were in love with him. It was just bad luck that he was a guy, but at least he was a gay one. And people fall in and out of love all the time. Love isn't one of those unrepeatable choices, like college, that can make or break you. I wanted so badly to be in love. I should enjoy it while it lasted. There would always be a next time, when I could be more practical and fall in love with a girl.

I went out into the yard and saw the car again. My mood was too fine for me to deal with some condescending businessman posing as a farmer. I knew Catherine would be talking to him in the kitchen, so I went around front and fished out my keys. We never used the front door, but I could go through the living room and avoid the stranger. I jiggled my key in the rusted lock. The door was swollen and needed painting.

One of our roosters was crowing.

Then I heard someone on the other side, fumbling with the bolt. The door was pried open for me. On the other side, in stocking feet, stood my father.

"Lad! So you finally made it home. Yes, it's me. Don't just stand there like you've seen a spook. Come on in. Not heating the outdoors, as your mother succinctly puts it."

I stepped past him and he bolted the door behind me.

He looked different, as always. He wore a beard this time, almost as white as his hair. Beard and hair needed trimming. His face was thinner and darkly tanned, except around his eyes where his sunglasses must've been. There were circles around his eyes and a deep pair of crow's-feet. He wore an old sweatshirt of Catherine's and, over that, a buttoned-up cardigan sweater.

"Well. Aren't you going to greet your father in a kinly manner?"

"Hi, Dad," I said and numbly shook his hand.

He didn't behave like a man who'd done anything wrong. I remembered him as my father before I remembered him as a son of a bitch.

"Does Mom know you're here?"

"Ho ho!" His usual mirthless laugh. "Give me a little credit, lad. Graces One and Two are out at the moment, but, in answer to your question, yes. Your mother knows I'm here. Didn't exactly receive me with open arms, but she seems willing to let me stay here for a few days. They gave me three months R. & R. while they decide where to send me next. Last time I had so much time on my hands, I married your mother. So, rather than do something like that again, I thought I'd swing out here and see how everyone was getting on without me. And get a better look at Dogpatch Two."

And he winked at me: Jake's old knowing wink, the wink of complicity. As if he never dreamed that I hated him now. I followed him into the kitchen, where he was fixing coffee.

"I heard about this little gal and the play you're in. Glad to see you're making up for lost time. Point of fact, one of the reasons why I thought Switzerland wasn't doing you any good. But now that you're too busy tomcatting to get home at night..."

He was so smugly paternal and chummy, it made my skin crawl. I wanted to kick in his fatherly intimacy by saying, "No, not a girl. A guy, Dad. Your son's been queering off with queers, Jake. How do you like that?"

"No," I said and lowered my eyes. "Nothing like that. I had too much to drink last night and slept on a friend's sofa. That's all."

Because I couldn't say it aloud, not even out of hatred. And feeling that with Jake, I was shocked at how blithely I'd been saying it to myself all morning.

Liza came home for a visit three weeks later, and Jake was still with us.

Catherine went to pick her up at the drugstore in Charles City Courthouse. We waited for them in the kitchen—Gram, Jake and me. I was cooking dinner. Gramma Bolt was playing chess with Jake.

She sat at the table with Max nestled in her lap. She rested her four chins on the twisted claw of her hand. Gram used to paint, had even taught art classes, before her arthritis forced her to quit. Now she spent her days reading murder mysteries and, when she found an opponent, playing chess. As long as she could get a game out of Jake, she didn't seem too worried about what he was doing here, or why Mom let him stay. Both of Gram's marriages had ended in divorce and she was never squeamish around my father, but she knew an unnecessary complication when she saw one. She kept her own life uncomplicated by staying out of our squabbles, keeping her words of advice to a minimum and, when necessary, turning off her hearing aid.

"You're quite the wise man. At chess," she said when he beat her again. She let Jake know what she thought of him, in a friendly way. "Much too good for an elderly duffer like me."

"Nothing but habit, Mother Bolt," Jake said cheerfully, winked at her and set up the board for another game. "I've spent so much time holed up in places where there was nothing to do but play chess. You develop the habit of thinking ten moves ahead. And checkmate in seven is nothing to be ashamed of." But he barely followed their

64

games, concentrating instead on my copy of *Marat/Sade*. I wished he were reading something else. He looked more respectable now, even fatherly, with his beard trimmed and the haircut Catherine had given him. "Leave it to the Germans," he chuckled at me over the book. "But interesting. In its cockamamie way."

"I look forward to seeing it," said Gram. "But only for you, dear. After all, I know already that Charlotte Corday dunit." She scrunched up her face and twinkled her eyes at me.

I suddenly wondered if reading my play were Jake's way of showing affection. I hoped not. I was sick of the play. I wanted to quit it, only that would've spoiled any chances I had with Jan, and it did give me somewhere to go in the evenings while Jake was here. One of the leads had dropped out only last week and Jan was already in a fever over that. And I didn't want any affection from Jake. I could be perfectly cool and aloof with the man, never mentioning what the bastard had done to me. He never mentioned it, either, and I refused to be the one who brought it up. His presence might've unnerved me for a day or so, but that had actually been something else and I'd settled that. I wished he'd go away, but I wasn't going to let him have the satisfaction of getting under my skin. That, I'd decided, was why he'd come here and not, as Catherine claimed, because he was lonely, confused or changed. He only wanted to make us uncomfortable, and prove to himself that he still mattered to his family. Well, he didn't matter and I was going on with my life as if he weren't even here.

I had pounded the meat loaf into its pan and was washing my hands when our pickup truck rattled out in the yard.

"Ah. She's here," said Jake and suddenly concentrated on the chessboard.

Gram looked excited, straightened her wig and tapped her hearing aid. "Oh good. I just hope she's brought her portfolio with her." She had more affection for her artistic grandchild, which was only natural. It was Gram's money that sent Liza to college.

A suitcase thumped the porch railing and there was a moment of whispering. Max spilled to the floor, yipping and clattering his toenails in front of the door. The door flew open and in came Liza, peering over the top of a large cardboard box.

"We're here!" sang Catherine, following with suitcase and guitar case. She wore a huge grin that displayed her gums and smoke-stained teeth and made her look like she'd tied her bun too tight.

Jake jumped up. "Need a hand, Kitten?"

"No." Liza dropped the box. It hit the floor and bounced, as if empty.

"She refuses to tell me what's in there," said Catherine, setting the other things in the corner and taking off her red mackinaw. Her mouth remained stuck in that grin. "I think it's a surprise."

"No surprise. Just junk," muttered Liza. She sniffed at the room without looking at any of us. She was thinner than I'd ever seen her. Liza's weight changed from visit to visit, but there was a caved-in look to her cheeks today and her mouth was as straight and thin as her hair. There was a peace sign and a dove embroidered on the seat of her jeans.

"Kitten! You look great!" said Jake, stepping around the box. "Remember me? The prodigal father?"

Liza watched him with her hips cocked against her smirk. "I remember," she said flatly. "Guess a kiss won't poison me." She quickly kissed him. "What's this thing? You turning into a freak or something?" She gave his beard a yank.

Jake winced but kept his smile.

"Gram? Shrimp?" She went around the room, giving kisses, then sat at the table, groaned and picked Max up from the floor, as if already bored with the humans.

Gram leaned over and smiled. "In the box? Is that something you did for a class?"

Liza made a face and guiltily nodded.

Jake sat down across from her. "So you made it home in time to see the old man."

Liza only narrowed her eyes at Catherine.

Catherine repeated what she must've been saying to Liza ever since she picked her up. "We didn't tell you on the phone, dear, because we didn't want to scare you off. Such a blue moon when we get to see you anyway." She lost some of her grin while she felt her pockets for a pack of cigarettes.

"No. I would've come home anyway. It just bothers me that you were keeping it a secret, that's all."

"Not a secret. I was just afraid you might get the wrong idea. If you didn't see the situation with your own eyes."

"And what idea's that?" said Liza nastily.

Catherine frowned at her, eyes half-closed against the cigarette she was lighting.

"Ho ho," went Jake, grabbing for his pipe.

Liza nastily studied him. "So Jake? What brings you back here?"

He calmly shrugged and continued to fill his pipe. "Ohh...just wanted to see how everyone was doing."

"And we've been letting your father know we're doing splendid, Catherine announced."

"So why did you want to know? You couldn't have missed us all that much. I know none of us have missed you."

"Elizabeth," said Catherine.

"But it's true, isn't it?"

"Yes, but...you shouldn't rub your father's nose in it."

Jake tried to seem indifferent, tried to light his pipe, but he'd packed it too tight.

"Why not be honest? I'm sick of being polite with all these...male egos."

"Oh," went Catherine.

"Oh, what?"

"Oh, that's it. Something went wrong with some boy you're seeing and that's why you wanted to come home. And why you're taking it out on your father."

Liza glanced at me, but I hadn't told Mom her secret. "Mu-*ther*," she moaned. "I'm just up to here with males in general. Male egos, male reticence, the whole male trip. I'm sick of males, sick of all the space they take up."

"We can't all be as thin as you, Kitten," said Jake.

"Dad doesn't faze me in the least," said Liza. "But I won't behave differently just because he's here. I came home to get a breather from men. Just a house full of women, no male egos, and Joel." She faced Jake again. "I don't *like* being thin. Men just think you're prettier when you take up less space."

She didn't make a friend of me by classing me with the women. I was annoyed with her anyway, because she was doing what I felt I should be doing, and because I knew there'd be nothing gained from it but frayed nerves.

"Now Kitten," Jake said good-humoredly. "I'm not out to affect anyone. In fact, we've been pretending"—he drew a breath through gritted teeth—"I'm no bigger than a mouse."

Gram nodded her head in full agreement.

"I'll bet," sneered Liza. "If there's one thing worse than an egotistical male, it's an egotistically humble male."

Everyone's patience was strained; someone had to snap.

Catherine snapped. "For crying out loud! Who put you on such a damn high horse! Nobody's asked you to give up a damn thing. Nobody's so much as said boo to you. But here you are, already swinging, as if all of us were guilty!" Her jaw was out, the cords of her neck taut. She stopped to adjust the temper in her voice, so it would sound like firmness. "No need for you to be so testy. Your father came a long way. I don't understand why you're making it so hard for us to be civil with him. Be yourself. Nobody's asking you not to. Only . . . can't you be yourself without snapping at us?"

Liza's stare was as hard as Catherine's, only Liza was grinning. "Be myself?"

"Well. Within reason."

"Okay. I will." Liza stood up and went for her cardboard box.

"Uh, what're you doing, dear?" asked Catherine.

"You were right, Gram," said Liza, hoisting the box. "This is something I did for class. Didn't go over very well. Hasn't gone over with anyone. I brought it home just to get it out of the way. And maybe show Joel. But! Since everyone is so hot about me being myself..." She beamed wickedly at me as she went out the door. "Right back," she said.

We listened to Liza go up the stairs. Whatever it was, I felt it was only going to make the situation worse. I assumed it had something to do with men, a vicious caricature or a vivisected male, even though her pictures were generally of children and old people.

Catherine drew on her cigarette and listened to Liza in her room overhead. "I don't care what she says, she isn't being herself today. I had no business losing my temper."

"Quite the little spitfire," said Jake.

Catherine frowned. "You don't help matters any. Everything she said, you had coming."

Jake raised both hands in a genial surrender.

"Still, she worries me. Keeps meeting boys and breaking off with them. That's all it is today, nothing more. But it's not healthy. I can't help wondering if it's something *I've* done wrong." But she looked at Gram, not Jake.

She was right to worry, but not about the many boyfriends. Because the many boyfriends were all one boyfriend, Bob Kearney. Kearney had found Liza and my sister had recognized immediately he was a jerk, but that didn't stop her from getting involved with him. Catherine had never met Kearney, and Liza wanted to keep it that way. She had invented a string of boys that she dated only once or twice and never saw again, never had a chance to bring home. When she had been home over the summer and working with me at the motel, I had helped her keep track of these fictional males, but only out of loyalty to Liza.

With Liza out of the kitchen, we hypocrites felt very close and safe with each other. "Been ages since Liza's shown us her work," said Gram. "I'm dying to see how she's developed."

There was a rap on the door jamb.

Everyone turned.

Catherine let out a squeak.

Liza stood just outside the door. She was stark naked, pink as paint and monstrously fat.

"Liza?" said Gramma Bolt.

She stepped forward, so fat she had to turn sideways to squeeze through the door. Bulbous breasts rasped against the door frame, flicking two red pom-poms where her nipples should've been.

"I see said the blind man!" and Jake burst out laughing. He applauded and looked at the rest of us to see if he were responding correctly. "Bravo, Kitten. Bravo."

Gram looked confused. Catherine and I were stunned, even when we understood.

It was a suit. A fat woman suit. There was a seam at the waist. It would've been no more disturbing than a giant doll, except that Liza's hands and hard, lean face stuck out of it She had embroidered the crotch with bright red string.

Liza slapped the pink mound behind her. "Foam rubber. You won't believe what a bitch it is to mold this stuff around a pair of longjohns. And it drinks up paint like there's no tomorrow. Well? What do you think?" She held out her arms, knowing perfectly well we didn't approve. "Is it me?"

Gram said plaintively, "Doesn't anyone do watercolors anymore?"

"You did this for a class?" said Catherine. "For a grade?"

"Advanced Form and Space. We had to come up with something that used everything we'd learned. This was mine. I wanted to see what it felt like to be humongous. To take up lots of space. Everyone was disgusted. I can't understand why." She strode over to Catherine and shook her pom-poms at her. "Want a touch?"

"No!" Catherine folded her arms over her own breasts. "I don't understand. Now, I don't claim to know the first thing about modern art, Liza. But I see an unhealthy amount of self-contempt here."

"She just wants to be a lard bucket," laughed Jake. "So those dreaded males won't waste their time with her."

She contemptuously shook her breasts at Jake, then turned to me. "Go ahead, Joel. I know *you* want to touch it."

"Uh uh," I said and slid out of my chair, trying to keep away from her. The idea of touching it disgusted me.

But she was too far into her teasing to recognize I was dead serious. "Touch. Please. Touch me, Shrimp. I know you want it," she teased and pursued me into the corner.

And with Liza's face still a foot from mine, I was pressed against the wall by foam rubber crusted with paint. The texture alone was repulsive and the idea that it was supposed to be a body, a naked body, horrified me. I tried pushing her away, but my hands only sank into her.

"Flessssh!" she hissed. "Warm, meaty flessssh."

"Dammit to hell! Get that shit away from me!"

Her grin broke.

"Come on. It gives me the creeps. It's *not* funny."

Liza stepped away, the suit popping back where I'd left my dent. She raised her chin and glared at me down the gunsight of her nose.

I tried rubbing the gooseflesh off my arms. "I find it in very bad taste, and repulsive. I can't help it. Things are weird enough already. Why do you want to make them weirder? You're acting like a brat."

"Joel," said Catherine. "There's nothing to be gained

by talking to your sister that way," even though she'd spoken the same way ten minutes ago. "And Liza. There's no point in being obnoxious. You've made your point. Your point eludes me, but you've certainly made it."

Liza paid no attention to her. She continued to glare at me with her lips curled.

A shrug of her shoulders caused the suit to shudder. "Fickle," she muttered. "I should know better than to count on *anyone.*" She shambled out of the kitchen, the pink butt bumping behind her.

She was down again a few minutes later, her stringy, moody self. "Stuffy in here." She cut her eyes at me. "I'm going for a walk. Joel?"

There would be accusations and defenses, but I knew we had to do it. "Mom? The meat loaf's in the oven, but could you start the beans?"

Without looking at each other, without explaining to the others, we put on coats and knit hats and went outside.

Jake called after us, "No bloodshed, children."

"Hush," said Catherine. "They don't need your sarcasm."

I intended to strike first, but we were going down the steps when Liza growled, "What's eating you? You got a pine cone up your ass?"

"Me? What about you?"

"Looking so damn smug and self-righteous in there. Everyone else weird as hell, but I thought you'd be on my side. And were you? No way. Acting like an old maid in there. With a pine cone up the ass."

We walked into the woods, fists in our pockets.

"You were the one making an ass of yourself. All that women's lib anti-male crap. That grotesque costume—"

"I was being honest. Which is more than the rest of you are doing."

"We have to live with it. You're just visiting. You don't

72

know what it's been like around here, Liza. I was finally learning how to live with it when you—"

"If I don't know what it's been like, whose fault is that? Everybody keeps me in the dark and then—Pow! There's Jake in our kitchen, being his old creepy ho-ho know-it-all self. You and Mom playing right along. Gram staying out of it. What's he doing here anyway? And why's Mom letting him stay? They're not making up, I hope."

"I don't think so. Mom's enjoying the chance to lord it over him, that's all." Which was what Catherine told me, only it didn't explain why Jake submitted.

"Family," Liza grumbled and looked back to see how far we were from the house. She reached into her coat and brought out her own cigarettes. This was another habit that Catherine didn't want her daughter picking up from her.

I cupped my hands around her cigarette while she bent down and lit it. "You had another fight with Kearney, didn't you?"

She blew out some smoke and grimaced. "What if I did?"

"And that's why you're so pissed with everybody."

"Bull. You've been living with Mom too long." She walked on, proudly smoking her cigarette, stepping over the stumps of all the trees I'd cut down. "Anyway, Bob means even less to me now than that old fart back there. We broke up. For good this time."

"So that *is* what's wrong."

"No way. That's what's right. It's over. About time too. I can stop compromising myself and go back to being me. Which is a big relief."

But she'd broken off with Kearney so many times, I needed to know what made this break different from the others. "What happened?"

"Classic Bob. It was Brunhilde."

"Another woman. I was wondering when that would happen. Good."

"No way. Not Bob. No, Brunhilde's what I call my fat lady. Brunhilde von Scherzenlieb. You should've heard that jerk when I put it on. He was outraged. The asshole."

"But... it is kind of outrageous."

"Why is that? What's this thing everybody's got against fat people? I mean, wouldn't you like to see what it's like to be *big*? To have some weight to throw around? Don't you get bored with being smaller than everyone else? Shrimp?"

"Jake seemed amused."

"Yeah, Jake," Liza muttered, admitting my point. "He probably thought I was making a mockery of myself. But it's not debasing. It's not."

"Kearney thought you were debasing yourself?"

"Not me. He thought it debased him. Can you believe that? He said he worshipped me, loved me, all that crap. And for me to wear that thing was like painting 'Fuck' on the American flag. And he gave me this fat ultimatum. But I went ahead and wore it to class. Went over like a lead balloon, but I wore it. I called him up afterwards and told him I'd worn it. And he said I'd *profaned* his love, polluted it forever, debasing myself in public. And how it hurt him more than it hurt me, but good-bye, good-bye forever. Can you believe that? The jackass. So I say good riddance. Eight months of royal bullshit and I could never bring myself to end it once and for all. But he could. God bless him for finally doing something right."

I didn't know what to say. It certainly sounded like Kearney. Liza's voice was so gloriously vindictive I didn't think sympathy was in order. We walked in silence through the open, dusky woods.

"But—" She sniffed up the moisture collecting in her nose. "You know what's really sick?"

"Oh Liza," I groaned.

"You want to hear the sickest thing about the whole sick mess!" she spat.

"You don't already miss him?"

"Sicker than that." She felt her hips and thighs through her coat, as if missing her extra layer of Brunhilde. "I feel like I've done something wrong. And I don't know why."

"You feel guilty?"

"I guess."

"But Liza! He was a jackass. He made you miserable. You're better off without him. You've been saying that for eight stupid months now."

"I know. It's dumb. But it's tough to cut somebody out of your life. Without feeling bad about it."

"When they cause you nothing but grief, you have to do it."

"That's easy to tell someone. It's not so easy when you have to do it yourself."

"I've done it myself."

Liza looked at me; she couldn't help smiling. "Oh, you broke up with that spacey theater girl? But that was never anything serious. Was it?"

"No. This was somebody else. A ... another person." The example embarrassed me. And it didn't seem quite appropriate. But I wanted to tell somebody what I'd succeeded in doing. And I could use Liza's need to justify sharing the secret. I winced to show her I was still disgusted by it. "A guy," I said.

Liza's face lit up. "A guy? You mean a friendship or a ...?"

The quickness of her interest startled me. "The latter. Yes."

"A guy, huh? With a guy?" She kept turning the idea over in her head. "Wow."

"But I ended it, Liza. Without feeling guilty. Which is what you should be able to do."

"I often wondered about you, Joel. Always wanted to ask but never knew how to bring it up. I couldn't tell if you were the way you were because of Switzerland, or if you might be queer. But you've been involved with a guy?"

"But I'm not queer. That's why I had to end it."

It didn't dampen her interest. "How involved?"

"Enough for it to get messy. When I broke off with him, I mean."

"Were you in love with him?"

"Of course not. I'm straight."

"Was he in love with you?"

"I guess. He said he was." I didn't like her interest. She seemed overjoyed that she could forget her problems for a moment in order to frolic in mine.

"Did you have sex with him?"

"Let's walk back this way." We'd reached the field of stubble on the other side of the woods and I pointed at the path that ran back into the trees. I didn't want to go out into the open.

"Did you?" she asked, walking ahead of me so she could see my face.

"Yes," I said. "Twice."

"What was it like?"

"What do you mean, what was it like?"

"Oh. Just, I've been to bed with men, too," she said with a pleased shift of her shoulders. "Be fun to compare notes."

"Nothing to compare. You're designed to enjoy sex with men. I'm not."

"You didn't enjoy it?"

"No. Which was why I ended it."

"But you did it twice, you said."

I'd outrun my conscience, that's all. It wasn't until the second time, shortly after Jake showed up, that my conscience caught up with my body and I felt sick over what we'd been doing. But that was too complicated to get into, so I told Liza, "I was drunk twice."

She seemed to weigh that claim.

I wondered if I should cover myself with another lie, tell her this was somebody of no importance whom I'd never see again. I wanted to see Corey again, but couldn't yet. I'd run into him on the street only a week ago, had

76

tried to be civil with him, but I could smell his body right there on the street, something so subtle not even his own mother would notice it. But I did. I kept my greeting brief and hurried off. "I had to break off with him so it wouldn't happen again. It ruined a good friendship."

But that wasn't what Liza was weighing. "Did either of you ever . . . well, I guess you had to. What else can guys do to each other? But . . . " She rolled her eyes sheepishly. "What did you think of fellatio?"

"Liza!"

"You did do it, didn't you?"

"I don't know. I was drunk." I had done it, and didn't want to be reminded.

"I do it to Bob. Or did it, past tense. Took me a long time to get used to it. Your mouth never seems big enough, right? And there's something childish about it. Associations with popsicles, I guess. But I got to like it. Sometimes more than intercourse, because I could do it to him and not get anything out of it myself. It made me feel superior to Bob. He went down on me, too, but Bob looked so damn pleased with himself when he was down there. Like he'd discovered America or something."

It was sex she wanted to talk about, not me, but I didn't like her assumption that I was someone who could appreciate the finer details of cocksucking. I didn't want to talk about sex either. I hadn't even masturbated while my father was here and I didn't like having those feelings aroused again.

"Sounds to me like you're *still* horny for Bob," I sneered.

Liza looked as annoyed with me as I was with her. "To be sure. But I can talk about it, can't I? That proves it has no hold on me. Good to talk about it," she insisted. "Helps me know that Bob was nothing to me but a good fuck."

"Talking about it only makes it worse."

Liza answered with a lip fart. "That would be your attitude. Yours and Mom's."

That topic, but I preferred it to sex. "If you can be of

two minds about Kearney, why can't we be of two minds about Dad?"

"But I'm not of two minds. I've made up my mind and got what I wanted."

"So why do you feel guilty about it?"

"Habit," she said, laughed, then groaned.

The path had taken us out into the open again, behind the barn and Catherine's chicken coop, where the chickens percolated. Liza and I stopped and looked at the high, bare house that was as grey as the overcast sky. Irritated as we were with each other, neither of us were in any hurry to go back inside.

Liza laid her hand on my shoulder and smiled. "Oh Lord," she moaned. "Why did we have to come from such a bourgeois family?"

"Bourgeois? Us?" I burst out laughing. "Oh God, I wish."

Liza laughed too. "Or something less uptight. So I could dump guys without feeling guilty. You could sleep with guys without feeling—"

"But Liza," I said, still laughing. "I don't want to sleep with guys."

"Whatever. We could do what we pleased, invent the messiest life we wanted. Right now, we've got all the hang-ups of the middle class, and none of the money."

"No," I told her. "When I get to invent my life, it's going to be neat. Neat and orderly, because that's the way I am. I don't have anything to repress."

But across the flat fields, against the grey sky, I noticed the Yoders' silo: a thick shaft crowned with a helmet. I pinched my mouth shut—I'd been forming an O with it—and shook the associations from my head. Liza's sordid talk had muddled my thinking.

J. Scherzenlieb,

A letter is melodramatic but it's my only resort when you won't talk to me. I'm not certain I want to talk to you, either. Better a letter than a silent, convenient forgetting.

First, I blame myself. You didn't ask me to fall for you. I fell in love with an idea, a memory, a possibility. It was your misfortune, and mine, that you stood in my field of fire. Who are you anyway? Only a mildly attractive, bright, erratic, young, self-absorbed guy who was my first infatuation back when I didn't know what to do with such feelings. Now when I know, you reappear and even go to bed with me. I trust in everything I ever imagined about my past and commit myself to a fantasy. You.

You say you're straight. I need to believe that (it makes your rejection less personal) although part of me can't help feeling that with enough dynamite I could convince you otherwise. It's unfair of me to deny you your free will like that, so I won't, even though I can't help feeling you're turning your back on the best thing that might've ever happened to you. The egotism of love, I admit. But it all seems like so much egotisical dreaming on my part that I begin to doubt you were the one who said, "Let's take off our clothes," or that you actually enjoyed what you enjoyed. You did, for a time. But you were only using my feelings as a chance to test your own fantasies, fears or temptations, your homosexual panic perhaps. So now you know. I should be glad to have made you wiser about yourself. I've spared some other gay oaf the trouble of teaching you. And I at least got some sex out of it. It was my Whimsburg celibacy that was causing my hair-trigger infatuations. I live too much inside my head. I need to commit myself to something larger than me, but love isn't it.

Of course, this letter is for my sake, not yours. All of this is only to say, if you catch me avoiding you, it's out of prudence, not hatred. When you snubbed me on the street last week I wanted to kill you. Even before you ran off I was torn between wanting to punch you in the face and wanting to throw up. But it's only anger with myself, not you. I don't even know you. Good luck with your life.

C. Cobbett

5

THE CURTAIN ROSE at last on *Marat/Sade*.

Every night, when the curtain lifted and we held our breaths while the audience applauded our costumes and lighting, I wondered if this were the night when Corey was out there. We were giving only three performances and there wasn't much theater in Williamsburg; Corey had to see the play, even if I were in it. But if he were out there in the great brown murk, I would never know. He couldn't come backstage and congratulate me on my performance. I didn't blame him.

I wanted to see him again, for many reasons, and the strongest was why I couldn't. I wanted to have sex again. It'd been over a month since our sex and my body harassed me with morbid thoughts and itches. Once I satisfied those itches I'd probably feel bleaker than ever and strike back more violently. I couldn't do that to myself, or to Corey either. His letter frightened, depressed and excited me. To have been so important to someone without ever knowing, or so importantly unimportant—the letter read differently each time I looked at the cramped handwriting with enormous spaces between each word. It was a terrible obligation. I had to settle it with him, clear it all up, but couldn't yet. Not until I was sexually involved with someone else would it be safe for me to see Corey.

The applause died out. There was a fanfare of organ

music and the play began. Coulmier rose from his chair downstage and addressed the audience.

As Director of the Clinic of Charenton
I'd like to welcome you to this salon.
To one of our residents a vote
of thanks is due, Monsieur de Sade who wrote
and has produced this play for your delectation
and for our patients' rehabilitation.

He was clean-shaven now, his hair cut short, his body lean as a knife in frock coat and knee-britches. But the voice trumpeting at the darkness had traces of the old, amused superiority. And it was printed in the program: Coulmier was played by Jacob Scherzenlieb, my father.

It wasn't until the last night of the play that our family came. With them were Kearney, who'd made up this time with Liza by getting engaged to her—which meant he finally met Mom—and Major Hawkins and Istvan Podnark, two of Jake's friends. He'd mailed them tickets and they'd driven down from Washington to see Jake make a fool of himself. They *all* came to see Jake, surprised and tickled by this unexpected eruption of exhibitionism. He'd been getting restless out at the farm—he continued to linger, as if hoping for something from us—and had come to rehearsal one rainy night to give me and my motorcycle a lift home in the truck. He stayed to watch, then stayed to compliment Jan, then, egged on by me, read for Jan, who desperately needed a new Coulmier. I'd only been mocking him for his sudden, insincere interest in theater; he could be so charming with strangers. I never dreamed he'd listen to me, or that Jan could be interested. The next thing I knew, Jake was coming with me to rehearsals every night. I didn't want him there, courting my favor by sharing my interests, stifling me with his subtle, judgmental presence. Only he didn't

81

court me, and his presence had none of the aloofness needed for judgments. He continued to be his cool, joshing, ironic self at home, but Jake at rehearsal had the eager awkwardness of a foreigner determined to fit in. He almost seemed like just another actor, like Fred who was Marat or Bambi who was Charlotte, people who were so serious about their roles it was hard to take them seriously as people.

We took our places on the bright stage. My make-up smelled like wet fertilizer. The curtain went up, I thought briefly about Corey, the play began and I gave myself to that. I wasn't anyone important—I didn't even have a name—but I enjoyed moving here, then there, shouting "Freedom!" a few times and occasionally having a seizure. The play ended, those who remained in the audience applauded, the curtain fell and my life in the theater was over.

"Did we wow them or did we wow them, lad?" Jake went straight for me the instant everyone broke character. All the others looked relieved or depressed, but Jake was still feverish, giddy, strange. "Did you see them out there? Ten rows back, Hawkins all lit up like Christmas with his brass buttons? Podnark's fat bald head? Who-hooooo! I can't wait to see the looks on their faces!" He abruptly snapped his mouth shut and pulled his head back in, which made him look like a child busting with a secret. He seemed totally unhinged. How had I ever worried about what this man might think of me?

Jan Terwiliger was in the wings, spinning her hands, howling and sighing as the cast went out. "You were so *wonderful* tonight! Each and every one of you! Oh err... geef... gaw... floof"—words often failed Jan—"God but I'm going to miss you!" She seized people and cried on their shoulders. She cried on mine and remembered my name, but pushed me aside to seize Jake and call him, *"A lifesaver!* I can't ever thank you enough. And you were *fabulous!"* But it didn't hurt me. I'd realized weeks ago I wasn't in love with Jan and never would be, which was somehow a relief.

The corridor was packed with aristocrats, lunatics and nuns, and the flood of civilians who'd come backstage to congratulate or be catty with their friends. There was to be a cast party in the greenroom and everyone was getting invited. I shouldered my way through the mob so I could get to the dressing room and change before I faced my family. They were here for Jake but I didn't want to be teased for my loose grey uniform or the hairspray that made my hair stand straight up. I wanted to blend back into the world again.

The crowded corridor ran past the doors to the women's dressing room, the greenroom and the men's dressing room before it ended in the glass double doors that opened outside. Standing by those doors was Corey.

He stood alone with his hands in his pockets. His glasses were fogged, his ears were pink and he wore his army jacket. He must've left the auditorium by the front door and come around by the side to avoid the crowd. Or left and changed his mind. Or maybe he hadn't even seen the play tonight. I considered all the possibilities as I continued to walk towards him.

He saw me come out of the crowd.

He stood up straight and looked straight at me, only his lenses were fogged and I couldn't tell how he saw me, or if he could see me at all. His hands shifted inside his pants pockets. Then he nodded at me.

I was frightened at how frightened I felt to see Corey again. I nodded back and wanted to walk straight into the dressing room. I decided to be brave. I wanted to seem casual. I walked up to him, stopped and said, "Hello."

"Hello." He was curt with it.

Here was his smell again, a cross between old upholstery and fresh pancake batter. But the emotion I breathed with the smell wasn't painful this time. What was painful was that neither of us spoke. His lenses were clearing.

He suddenly looked into the air just above my head. "I only wanted you to know I saw your play. That's all."

"Good. That you saw it, I mean. Hardly my play. But good. I thought you'd like it."

"I did. It was very... political."

"Very."

He looked so stern with his eyes staring past me. He hated me. Then why should I feel so pleased to see him again? Why did I feel, in my chest, that something wonderful was about to happen?

"Then you saw the play tonight?"

"Uh huh." His eyes drifted down towards me. "And last night. And the first night too. Interesting play. Confusing politics. I could never quite figure it out."

The way he looked at me: He was as frightened as I was. Corey was still in love. I didn't want him to hate me, would rather he only liked me, but love was better than hatred and I was glad. "I'm glad you liked the play so much."

His gaze suddenly sharpened and he withdrew it. "Okay. That's all I wanted to tell you. I better be going."

"Oh? Okay." But I didn't want him to go yet. "There's going to be a party. You're welcome to stay for that."

"No. I don't enjoy parties where I don't know anybody. I should be getting home."

We refused to mention what had passed between us, but it was the one thing that might keep Corey here a moment longer. "I got your letter," I said.

He cut his eyes at me before he stared into the air again. "Yeah. Well. What can I say? I'm sorry. But I meant every word of it."

His discomfort made me curious, and cocky. "So what do you feel now? Do you want to puke or punch me in the nose?"

"Neither. I better be going." But he didn't move.

I was surprised at how pleased I felt to be with someone who was in love with me. "You sure you won't stay? Just a little? Long enough to have a beer."

"A beer's the last thing I need right now, but... sure. Long enough to have a beer," he said resentfully.

He followed me into the greenroom, where the party was just starting up. Most of the cast were changing their clothes. I wanted to change, too, but knew that Corey wouldn't wait for me. I saw Jake in the corner, still in his costume, guffawing beside the stone-faced army major. The beer was in a plastic garbage can full of ice, but Corey went for the coffee urn on the table beside it. "My mind keeps blanking out; this is what I need," he said. The stuff had been cooking since before the play. It looked like hot black ink in Corey's cup.

"And that's your father over there?" said Corey accusingly.

"Uh huh." I directed Corey into a corner where I could stand with my back to Jake. But knowing Jake stood somewhere behind me only made me more self-conscious. "So. How have you been doing?"

"Busy. I've put my name in for a couple of social work programs. So I could have something to care about besides the things I talked about in my letter."

"Ah."

"I meant everything I said. I wasn't just making a play for your sympathy or something like that." Corey kept glancing over my shoulder in Jake's direction.

"I know. I never thought that." I heard how blithe and casual I sounded, but couldn't break out of it, not in this room full of people. "Maybe we shouldn't talk about this here."

"I thought you wanted to talk about it."

I didn't; I'd brought it up only to keep Corey here, and now that I had him.... "I do. But not now. Not here. And I feel funny, talking about it while I'm still wearing this."

Corey looked annoyed. "You want to talk about it? You really want to talk?"

"Of course."

"Okay then. Change your clothes and we'll go to my place." He said it like a challenge.

I pictured it. I noticed the dark fizz of hair in Corey's open collar. "Uh uh," I said. "But someplace else. Sure."

"What's the matter?" he whispered angrily. "You afraid I won't be able to keep my hands to myself?"

I didn't want him angry with me. I wanted to be honest. "No. It's my hands I'm worried about." It embarrassed me to say it. I didn't know how to explain.

He stared at me. He glanced around the room. I was afraid he misunderstood and would be overjoyed. But he thrust his head at me and hissed, "Why're you doing this to me? Does it give you a thrill? Make you feel important? Does it give you a feeling of power knowing you can wrap me around your finger?"

"All I meant was—"

"Dammit, Joel. I'm just beginning to get it under control and you . . ." He looked at his fist, his coffee, his foot. He looked like he wanted to hit me with something. I snatched the coffee cup out of his hand and emptied it on my head.

"I'm sorry, Corey. God but I'm sorry. I am, I really am sorry," I said, standing at the sink in the toilet across the hall.

"Don't apologize to me. You did it to yourself," said Corey, ripping paper towels out of the dispenser. He took a handful of them and pressed them around my head.

"You know what I mean. I've been a real shit to you. Will you forgive me? Can you ever forgive me?"

"Your ears look sunburned," he said, but his face in the mirror looked worried, timid, touched. "Why the hell did you do that? What were you trying to prove?"

"Don't know," I admitted. I took the towels from him and lightly rubbed my head. They kept sticking to my hair. "My way of saying I'm sorry?"

He pulled out more towels and mopped my neck and

shoulders. I was glad to have Corey touch me again, even with paper towels.

"There's safer ways to say it," he told me. "That coffee was hot, you know."

"I know." My ears burned; my head was freezing.

"I might've wanted to do it to you. But I would never have done it."

"I know. But I deserved it. I did."

"Here. I better let you do this," he said and let go of me.

I didn't want him to let go—

He still stood behind me—

The coffee hadn't said what I wanted it to say—

I spun around, threw my arms around his chest and buried my face in his shirt.

And suddenly, I didn't feel guilty anymore. I felt very round and full. It wasn't sexual. It was all in my arms and chest. I held on to him as tight as I could.

He stood very still. Then I felt a hand on my head trying to find a spot that wasn't gummed up with coffee and hairspray. The hand closed around the back of my neck. "You really know how to confuse me," he said.

"I confuse myself," I muttered against his shirt, but I didn't release him. I seemed to be in love with Corey. That was the only explanation. But it didn't frighten or confuse me this time. It ended confusion.

He gently pried me loose and looked down at my face.

I couldn't help smiling at him.

"Don't do this to me, Joel," he said nervously. "Unless you mean something by it."

"I think I do."

But that didn't end his confusion. He closed his eyes and sighed, "But you're straight, remember."

"Maybe I'm not." I diligently brushed at the shirt, where I'd left a little make-up washed with coffee.

"Maybe? Maybe's not good enough. Maybe you're bi —that's what you told me way back when. Then poof!

Your father shows up, you remember you're straight, sorry, good-bye. I'm not going to go through that again, Joel. I won't."

I couldn't understand why he made my sexuality the issue. Love was peculiar enough. "If I'm in love with you, I can be gay. I don't mind. And my father's out there right now. But I *still* think I'm in love with you." It was love that was the difficult thing to say, and I'd said it.

There was a knock on the door. "Hurry up in there! My teeth are floating!"

I was watching Corey, to see how he responded to my mention of love.

"We shouldn't hog the bathroom," he told me.

"You are in love with me, aren't you?"

He nodded. "Against my better judgment. Yes. But we better talk about this. Not here. Change your clothes and let's get out of here. But not my place. Not yet."

"Okay. Not yet," I agreed.

We opened the door and Tweed Humbolt came in. He looked at us funny, but then my hair did look like it had been badly shellacked.

Corey waited in the corridor. In the dressing room there was only de Sade, tying his sneakers, and Michael, the costume designer, who sulkily folded up costumes. He scolded me for not having changed and for spilling something on the front of my tunic. "Never mind. The lunatic outfits aren't important. But if Coulmier doesn't get his tail in here soon, I'm going out there and undress him myself. I'm saving that costume."

I sat at the counter and leaned into the bright mirror. I wiped away the smeared worry lines, the runny blush on my cheek, the coffee-colored bruises, everything but the fact that I was in love. Because the longer I thought about it, the more convinced I was. Even knowing we wouldn't have sex tonight convinced me I was in love, because sex didn't feel urgent. We'd have sex again, eventually. Love made me patient. I needed to be patient because I still had to convince Corey.

I gave Michael my costume and pulled on my street clothes. My undershirt had a brown stain around the neck. I was combing my hair with a plastic fork when Michael opened the doors to the greenroom—the party at full boil—and the corridor. Corey looked in, worried.

"I'm still here," I called out to him. "I haven't gone anywhere."

He stepped cautiously into the room. "I didn't think you had." He frowned at the noise in the greenroom. "You almost ready?"

"Almost," I said, looking for my coat.

"Here he is!"

I looked up; Liza stood in the greenroom.

"Found him!" she shouted behind her and breezed in, followed by Kearney. Each of them held a can of beer.

"Where have you been?" She kissed me on the forehead; she smelled a little drunk. "Everybody's asking for you. Join the party. Wonderful party. Wonderful play." She was very drunk. "You were good, Shrimp. Even Daddy was good, although we're sure the hell not going to tell him." She fell against Kearney and put an arm around his waist. "Bob and me have been keeping Gram company. You ought to come in and talk with her. I think she's bored."

"Corny Cobbett!" cried Kearney. "Many moons, no see!" He was nowhere near as drunk as Liza, but the sight of Corey sent him back to his pidgin English. "You good? Great Kahuna, he do no good. He no like pinko play."

Corey smiled and shook Kearney's hand. "Bob. Yeah. Joel's told me you're seeing his sister."

"No just see. Marry. Buy woman from mother. Two cows and one tractor. Good deal. Woman worth twenty cows, easy."

"Bob!" Liza groaned. "Behave." But she beamed and gave him a squeeze.

Corey glanced at me and shook Liza's hand. "Congratulations. We met once, but you probably don't remember me. When you and your mother visited Camp Wolf?"

"Yep. You all looked alike, I'm afraid. Except for a certain smartass hunk."

The hunk beamed, too. "So you and Shirtsy have been keeping in touch?"

"In touch? Yes. Sort of." His smile turned guilty.

"Which one were you tonight?" Liza asked.

"Which . . . ? Oh, in the play? I wasn't in the play. Just a friendly spectator."

"I thought you were because you have some of that brown gunk on your shirt."

Corey and I looked. The mark was barely visible on the red plaid. Where I'd pressed my face. I grabbed a paper napkin and passed it to Corey.

"Horny Corny Cobbett," Kearney clucked. "Neckin' with the chorus girls, I see."

Above her indiscriminate smile, a bit of light came into Liza's eyes. She glanced from me to Corey, and back to me again.

"The ol' fascist needs another brew." Kearney crushed his beer can to show it was empty. "Anybody else? You want another, babe?"

Liza shook her head, her eyes still fixed on me. When he was gone, she leaned in and whispered, "Is this the boy?"

I forced more napkins on Corey. "What boy?"

"You know. You can tell your sister. The boy you talked about when we talked about . . . things you can do with your mouth."

A hundred thoughts ran through my head. I was terrified. My first urge was for lies. But to renounce Corey in front of him was exactly what he feared from me. And, mixed with my terror, was a strange ticklishness, as if I were pleased by Liza's interest.

"Yes," I said.

"Then I was right!" she cried. "I *was* right, wasn't I?"

"Yes, yes," I began to chant, finding myself grinning with her, finding myself amazed at how good it felt to say this out loud. "Right about what?"

"That you were (gay)." She gleefully whispered the word. "The vibes you gave off. They weren't Goody-Two-Shoes, or European, they were (gay)."

"Uh, yes. Yes. I guess you were right." I turned to Corey, proud that I'd said it, wanting to see his look of approval.

He looked stunned.

Liza followed my eyes. "And you're (gay) too? I'm sorry, but I've already forgotten your name."

Corey slowly nodded and continued to nod until he said, "Corey. Corey Cobbett. Gay, yes. Uh, would anybody like a beer?" But he couldn't keep it up; he burst out laughing. "Nothing's wrong. I'm just..." He continued to laugh and shake his head. "I'm not running away. I just need a beer right now." And he walked off, breathing deeply, trying to catch his breath.

Liza watched him with me. "You are, aren't you? In love with him?"

"Uh huh." The second syllable stuck in my throat on a high, pleased note.

"You look it."

"It shows?" I was pleased to hear that. "I am in love, aren't I?" as if I needed Liza for verification. "I still have to convince him," I admitted.

"I think he's in love with you, too. I can tell."

"You can? Really?" I thought so too, but it was wonderful to hear it from a third person. "Uh, what do you think of him?"

Liza laughed. "I've hardly spoken to him, Shrimp."

"First impression," I insisted.

"Oh, only that he's large. And he doesn't *look* gay. Not just swish but something... absent? I went out with a few from art classes before I learned to tell the difference. If they seemed like a brother to me, that meant they were gay. Which is why I began to suspect my brother might be gay himself."

"Does it... repel you at all?"

"That you're gay? Not at all. I'm just happy to see you

91

happy, Shrimp. I was afraid you were going to turn into one of those cold, perfect yucks. It's a relief to know that you're human too."

"It's a relief for me too," I said, surprised by the idea. "What I'm feeling is like a wonderful sigh of relief."

Liza nodded, like a sage. "Yes. It can be like that." She winced at some new thought, then smiled and said, "Anyway, I'm in love with Bob. So I'm in no position to throw stones at what other people fall in love with."

"There they are, Mrs. S."

Kearney's voice startled Liza. Our mother came through the door as Kearney went back into the room.

"Hello, dear. Was wondering where you'd run off to," said Catherine, looking too tired to have overheard anything. She smiled at both of us, but she didn't look herself tonight. Her clothes were strange: women's knit slacks and a peach blouse with ruffles. It was the same lean face without lipstick and the same loose turkey's throat, but, as a concession to Jake's guests, Catherine wore earrings. Simple earrings, pearl buttons, but to see them on either side of that head was like seeing a crystal chandelier in a farmhouse.

"Hi Mom. Having a good time?"

"No, dear. Can't say that I am," she sighed. "Too many . . . people."

"You should've brought the chickens. They would've enjoyed it." Love made me witty.

"Too bushed for jokes, kiddoes. And you two look full of them. Full of something."

I saw Liza shining guiltily. I probably gave off the same guilty shine.

"I just want to go home," Catherine moaned, smiling at her exhaustion. "And I'm out of cigarettes. Your darn father."

"You don't have to wait on me, Mom. I've got my motorcycle. I might be a little late tonight anyway." I exchanged looks with Liza.

"No, it's your father I'm waiting on. With his cronies.

Your grandmother and I are stuck here until Jake and his pals finish swapping their secrets or magic decoder rings or whatever it is they're up to. Look at him out there. Still dressed as Napoleon."

"Did you like the play?"

She narrowed her eyes at me, as if I were asking for trouble.

"Would you like Bob to give you and Gram a ride home?" Liza offered.

Catherine looked sideways at Liza. "Why are you so hopped up on throwing us together? I have nothing to say to Bob. You're the one he's marrying. We'll see plenty of each other when the time comes." She folded her arms and pretended to concentrate on the party. "But thank you anyway. Just the same. I'll wait for your father."

Liza looked hurt and turned to me for support. All I could do was shrug and smile; it didn't seem important to me. But wheels began to turn behind her eyes.

She suddenly smiled. "Mom?" she announced. *"Joel's in love."*

"Liza!" The blood rushed into my face.

"I know you don't approve of Bob. But love is weird for everyone."

Catherine was busy watching Jake. "Not now, Liza. I'm too tired. And I've already met Joel's little friend."

"This one's not so little. Would you like me to point 'em out?"

I was all grimace and grin, waiting for Liza to back down. I wanted to tell everyone—telling made it more real—but this was not the right time to tell Catherine.

"There." Liza pointed into the room. "Talking to Bob." She gave me a guilty smile.

The panic subsided. It had been five minutes since I told anyone. I wanted to be able to say it again.

Catherine tried to be indifferent, but Liza's tone made her suspicious. "Where?" she said irritably. "All I see is Bob talking to a large, absent-minded looking boy."

"That's the one," said Liza.

Catherine stared at both of us. "You two have the weirdest sense of humor."

"Mom?" I began. I had to see if I could finish what my sister had started. "Not a joke. It's true. I'm in love with the large absent-minded boy."

You could see my words work their way into the corners of her mouth and eyes. Her face grew longer. "Oh, Joel," she said, but as if I'd only knocked something over.

"I *am* in love. With a guy. I don't want you to be shocked. But it is surprising, isn't it?"

She looked concerned, then annoyed. "Oh, I'm sure it's nothing to worry about," she said haphazardly. "What you're feeling is probably nothing but... friendship. In excess. And psychology says most boys go through a homosexual phase. No, nothing to worry about."

"But I'm not worried, Mom. I'm overjoyed. Funny as it is."

"And he's nineteen," said Liza. "Not a little boy anymore."

Catherine glared at her for ruining that explanation. She tried looking at me, but turned and faced the party instead.

I thought she was looking for Corey. "Wire-rims and needs a haircut," I said.

"He looks perfectly normal," said Liza. "Would you like to meet him?"

"No!"

"Oh Corey?" Liza sang out. She beckoned him over with a sly wave of her hand.

She was making it seem cruel, confronting my mother with Corey. I wanted to share him with my mother, generously. "Mom, I *want* you to meet him. You'll like him. I know he admires you and what you're doing with the farm."

Catherine looked skeptical, then flustered when Corey approached. But she held her ground, tensing the muscles in her neck.

94

Corey came through the door, glancing warily at each of us. He became bland for the sake of my mother. "Oh, Mrs. Scherzenlieb. Hello."

They fumbled their handshakes: Corey attempted to treat her as a lady, but Catherine shook hands like a man. Corey looked a little less real standing over my mother, but my mother was someone I saw everyday. Corey told her they'd met at summer camp.

Catherine was biting her lip.

Corey asked about the farm.

Then Catherine blurted it out. "Joel? What the hell do you expect me to say?"

"I don't know. That you're pleased to meet him?"

"She's been told," Liza told Corey.

Corey flinched, stared at me, then tried to look strong.

"My son tells me," Catherine began. She threw up her hands. "I don't want to talk about this. Not here. Too many damn people and I don't have a damn thing to say to you. Or to anybody!"

Corey was so intent on not being intimidated, he registered nothing else.

"This is something that should be talked about in private. At home." She turned on me. "Why in blazes did you have to tell me anyway?"

Because... because I love you. And I wanted you to know."

Catherine only groaned. "Well, maybe I didn't want to know. Not tonight anyway. If there's nothing wrong, I'd rather you hadn't told me, Joel. Keep it a secret. Sons are supposed to have secrets. Mothers aren't expected to worry about their sons." She rubbed her throat and gritted her teeth. "We can talk about it later. If you really want to talk about it. But right now, I'm going to see if I can tear your father away from those pompous asses. And find myself a cigarette." She marched off with her arms swinging at her sides.

"Well, kiddoes," chirped Liza. "Time to make sure Bob's behaving himself. Corey, congrats. Joel, good luck." She gave us pats on the arm. "And Joel, be sure to say hi to Gram before you go. She'll think you're avoiding her." And Liza traipsed off.

"Let's get out of here," said Corey. "Where's your coat?"

I pulled on my coat, feeling very good about myself. I'd passed through the dangers of telling my sister and mother, and I still felt in love with Corey. Surely, after that, he had to believe I loved him. "One more thing," I said. "Let me stop off and say hi to my gramma."

"Why? Do you have to tell her too?"

"Corey? Is something wrong?"

"No. Should something be wrong?" he said sarcastically. He leaned toward me and lowered his voice. "You pour coffee on your head and say you love me. And before I have time to understand *that,* you're telling everyone you love me? What the devil's going on with you?"

"I'm trying to prove I love you. Whether my family's here or not."

He could accept that, but.... "You're going about it the wrong way. It doesn't seem authentic, Joel. You're spooking me."

"I'm sorry. I'm new at this. How did you tell your family?"

The righteousness went out of his face. "My family? Well, they don't know yet."

I had to grin at him. I'd been a homosexual for less than an hour and already I'd outdone Corey.

"Can't we get away from here?" he pleaded. "Please."

We went out through the greenroom. I thought I might say hi to Gram if she were alone, but she stood in the corner with Catherine, Jake, Podnark and Hawkins. Gram hunched over her cane while Catherine held her by one jowly arm. Gram looked smaller and frailer than she'd ever looked at the farm, but this was the first time I'd seen her with strangers. Her wig looked a little too large for her tonight. Her smile looked like iron, as if the muscles in her face had cramped after hours of grinning at foolish people. Catherine apparently had brought her over to convince Jake that it really was time to go.

Jake paid no attention to them, but went on with whatever he was saying, laughing at the Jacobin hat he flipped in his hand. Podnark and Hawkins were staring at him in disbelief. Even Catherine stared at Jake, as if, after everything she'd seen and heard tonight, there was something that could still shock her.

I didn't want to deal with them. I left with Corey.

I left with Corey and as soon as we were outside, nobody else mattered. We walked away from the lights, across a dark, open playing field. The stars overhead seemed to quiver, I was so excited. Excitement, fear, relief: Each emotion I felt seemed bonded to the next, like something molecular, or the trembling constellations above us, so I didn't know where I ended and everything else began.

Corey walked beside me, stealing fewer glances at me the farther we went, growing more careless in letting his body knock against mine. Until his arm went across my shoulders and my arm wrapped around the small of his back, and we walked too close to look at each other.

"Where we going?" I asked.

"Oh, my place, I guess. Yes," he said, looking straight ahead. "My place. Let's get it over with. See what happens *this* time."

6

ONE DAY IN September, almost three years later, I returned to Switzerland.

Dim and echoing, half-empty at noon: the Bahnhof in Zurich. I stepped off the train, expecting to find myself in my past, only to find myself in nothing but a train station. And even that wasn't as I remembered it. There were no milky shafts of sunlight or spidery ironwork, only pale fluorescent lights and walls of blue lockers. I didn't know whether to blame memory or the fact that things can change in four years.

"Joel!"

I was still wiggling into my knapsack when a woman called out. I looked all around, across the tracks and platforms, even at the high glass roof overhead, because the voice seemed to come from everywhere. We weren't supposed to be met by anyone and my relatives would never shout in public.

"Over here, Shrimp!"

And I knew.

There she was, just beyond the end of the track, waving both arms over her head. When she saw that I saw her, Liza dropped her arms, put her hands on her hips and proudly smirked.

I smirked too. I walked toward her casually, my thumbs hooked under my shoulder straps. We were both elated at seeing each other, and were being ironical about our happiness.

"What the hell are *you* doing here?" I threw my arms around her and the weight of my pack threw me forward. Her breasts felt very large, the rest of her very thin and her hair smelled like crushed flowers. My sister's kiss was stickier than it used to be.

We released each other and smirked some more.

"You made it," I said. "I was going to give you a call tonight and see if maybe you could make it down for the weekend. But hey, you're already here."

"Brown-nosed the brass, Shirtsy, took some leave and got our butts out of Mainz."

There stood Kearney, an army captain in civvies, standing like an official at the entrance to my own past. I wanted my sister to be part of this past, but Kearney?

He'd aged badly. His face had kept its strong-jawed good looks, but Germany had given him a big beer belly.

"And we brought Joan," said Liza, patting Kearney's belly. A small blonde head grew out of Kearney's chest. It wasn't a beer belly; it was their baby.

"You woke her with your shouts," Kearney chided.

The little head rolled around and looked. She was strapped to Kearney's chest in a sack with holes for her stubby legs. I looked at my new niece, trying to feel something tender and uncle-like. This was the first time I'd ever seen her.

"Go ahead and gawk," said Liza. "That's all there is to see. She sleeps, cries, eats and stares off in space. She's one stoned baby."

"She's a beautiful baby," Kearney cooed and addressed her with clucks and snorts. I hadn't had much contact with babies, but Joan seemed slightly ugly to me: shriveled face, little scowl, big nose. Still, they had said Liza had been an ugly baby and she had turned out well.

"Where's your buddy?" Liza asked.

"Oh! He was right behind me when—" I swung around in a panic, but here was Corey coming towards us, stooped beneath his cock-eyed pack, unable to get his arm through the other strap because of the book in his hand and because he was too busy grinning at us.

"Dummy," I said, took his book and lifted his pack.

"Hey! You're already here!" he sang at them, hoisted the pack on his shoulders and straightened up. He stood taller than Kearney.

"Don't I get a kiss?" said Liza. "You been taking good care of my little brother?"

He gave her a hug and peck. "He's been taking care of me. Bob! Hey! How's the old Kahuna?"

"Hello, Cobbett," said Kearney, without looking up from his daughter.

"Ohhhhh. And that's the baby?" Corey lurched at her.

"No, it's a hamster," said Liza.

"This," said Kearney warily, "is Joan." He watched Corey ogle the baby, as if afraid Corey might stop looking and suddenly bite his daughter. After all, Corey Cobbett was someone he had once worked with, and had thought he'd known, but who'd turned out to be someone else altogether. Kearney hadn't seen Corey since the great change, only heard about him.

Corey noticed nothing but the baby. "What amazing little fingers she has."

"What? The fingers, yes." Still eyeing Corey, he held Joan's tiny hand and lightly stroked it with his thumb. "Remarkable fingers. See? Fingers, fingernails, knuckles. It's all there. And toes too." He suddenly showed Corey her foot, then her knees and ears and gossamer hair, smiling as he did it, growing more relaxed with Corey. "And look at this, Cobbett. The little white spots on her lips? They're calluses. From nursing."

"Amazing," said Corey, too engrossed in it all to notice Kearney's change. He could be so sweetly oblivious to his gift for winning people over.

Liza shook her head. "Amazes me how some men go apeshit over babies. I love Joan. But it's going to be a few years before she gets interesting."

Which was similar to what I felt: nice baby, but what can you discuss with it?

Kearney broke off the adoration. "Let's get our asses in gear. What trolley do we take to get back to your aunt and uncle's, Shirtsy?" And we went out toward the street.

Beyond the red and white umbrellas of the Bahnhof Cafe, a slender blue tram floated past. There were people outside, walking briskly, their eyes as calm as the umlauts in the shop signs along the shady, coffered facades of the Bahnhofstrasse.

It was Zurich, but, like everything else, not quite as I remembered it. Everything seemed so small and—after Rome and Milan perhaps—anal? The street was so civilly proportioned, it might've been indoors, and the people behaved much as I imagined people in a prestigious corporation to behave.

I looked ahead to see what Corey was making of this city I'd praised so lavishly. But Corey was walking with Kearney, and Kearney was back on the subject of babies.

"Earth to Joel. Earth to Joel."

Liza was walking beside me.

"You're certainly in a daze. Usually you'd be talking my head off by now."

"Sorry. I'm just. . . . Seeing you, your baby, seeing this place again. . ." I finished my explanation with a deep breath.

"I can imagine. We got here yesterday morning. And I must say it beats Mainz. No American servicemen for one thing. And I like Aunt Bertie. So sharp and energetic. And blunt. The way Gram used to be." She paused. "It makes me sad when I start comparing them."

I wasn't ready to talk about something so serious yet. I changed the subject. "You're looking good, Liza."

"Am I?"

Her surprise made me look at her more closely. "That's lipstick you're wearing?"

"A touch. I'm doing my hair different."

It was shoulder length now, with sheaves of it folded back on either side of her face, like fluffy, blonde wings.

"All part of the postnatal overhaul. But it feels so fake. I'd like to let myself go and become the fat frump I sometimes feel like. But Bob still thinks I'm beautiful," she sarcastically sighed. "And Bob must be appeased."

The sarcasm seemed to make it acceptable, for both of us.

We caught up with Corey and Kearney at the tram stop in time to hear Kearney say, "But she was gorgeous. I had thought—Liza's heard this, it won't embarrass her—I'd thought a pregnant woman would look clunky or out-of-date. Like a De Soto. But that's because I'd seen pregnant women only in the fifties, when I was a tot and everyone was pregnant. But Liza pregnant? Damn. She was as beautiful and curvey as next year's Porsche."

"Pregnant women will always look contemporary," Corey suggested.

"And now I'm back to my clunky sixties self."

"Hon, don't put yourself down."

"I wasn't putting myself down. I was making a joke. Sheesh." Liza rolled her eyes and handed out the fare cards Bertie had given her.

Our tram arrived and we stepped on. We skated through Zurich towards the lake and my half-remembered city pivoted in the windows: cafes and banks and flower stalls. It suddenly worried me that I wasn't more excited. I was going to see people I hadn't seen in four years, a house where I was loved, a place where I'd been gloriously happy. A happy adolescence is even more difficult to outgrow than a happy childhood, but I'd outgrown mine, eventually. Maybe I'd outgrown it too much and that's why I wasn't tumbling with emotion.

Kearney was telling about the birth, which he'd witnessed, while Liza half-listened with a condescending smile and Corey asked questions, as if he intended to be a father himself one day. It wasn't hypocrisy, only Corey's good manners and curiosity about people, just as it was good manners that caused him to hold his book—more Karl Marx—face down in his lap. But he must've been feeling dishonest, because, still nodding over Kearney's story, he turned to me and smiled guiltily. I smiled back at him, thinking only that his wire-rims were dusty and how I wanted to peel them off his ears and clean the lenses for him, but that would've embarrassed Corey in front of Kearney and Liza. I looked away and found Liza pinching her smile at me, as if I'd just done something cute.

Maybe this was why I didn't feel more giddy. I did not return to Kilchberg alone, but with this accumulation of people and changes, four years' worth. I hoped that Kearney wouldn't be obnoxious, that Liza wouldn't make a scene, and that my aunt and uncle would be utterly charmed with Corey Cobbett.

Through the white suburban door with the bright brass name plate, I heard *Schweizerdeutsch*. It startled me that I had to repeat it to myself before I understood: "He's here, Arthur. They're here!"

I heard the clop and shuffle of Aunt Bertie's shoes and couldn't decide if I should greet her politely or wildly.

The door was opened by a compact woman whose clenched teeth looked too big for her grin. "Jo-el!" she cried and lifted her arms. "They find you!"

I confused my greetings. When I stood like a man and let her hug me, it seemed cold, and when I cried, "Bertie!" squeezed her and pressed a kiss in her coarse white hair, it seemed sloppy and childish. And when I held her, I felt a terrible urge to kiss her all over, even feel her up, out of habit. Not that she felt anything like Corey. Her body was small and unevenly packed, like a badly stuffed chair.

"Right on the button, Bertie. That was their train," said Liza.

"And little Joan? Was she good? I said I sit with *Joanli*, but they say you must see her! So you are now uncle too, Jo-el. Like your Uncle Arthur."

Even Bertie had been seduced by the baby. But it was me she looked at, her eyes round with water that spilled when she blinked. A tear fanned out in the fine wrinkles of her cheek.

"Oh Bertie!" I scolded.

"Oh Jo-el!" she scolded back. "Here, here," she cried, flapping her hands at everyone. "No need to stand and talk away the day in the open door. In! Everybody in!"

Corey entered last, still wearing that half-pleased, half-invisible look people have at other people's reunions.

"You are...Coreeee! We have heard a great much about you. We are happy to meet you." She took his hand and firmly patted the back of it. "A boyfriend of Jo-el is a boyfriend of us."

Corey froze. He quickly glanced at me, then narrowed his eyes at Liza. Liza shook her head. Core and I had discussed this and decided there was no point in confusing the Swiss.

I wanted to think she could tell just by looking at us, but I knew Bertie better than that. "Not 'boyfriend,' Bertie. You mean 'friend,' don't you?"

"Ach. Mein Englisch." She swept her hand across her face. "Since Jo-el goes, I have no one to talk English at and my English goes to the dogs. Come. Put off with your rucksacks and we go see Uncle. You too, Coree. Boyfriend, pal, whatever you are. Our house is to be your house."

Bertie sent Liza and Kearney upstairs to feed and change Joan, then led me and Corey into the living room.

The pale, sunlit living room, with its French doors wide open on the garden, so that the room looked like a corner of the garden, or the garden another room. And there stood Uncle Arthur beside the chair he'd levered himself from when he heard us at the door, supporting his stick of a body with one hand on the chair's back. The same newspapers and journals were neatly stacked by the chair. It was as though he'd been sitting in that chair ever since I left and his unsteadiness was only a cramp from four years of sitting. But I knew from Bertie's letters that Uncle had been ill, that like Gram, he had a room on the first floor now, to save him from the stairs.

"Nephew," he said in gentle, croaking German. He held out a darkly freckled hand. "It's so good to see you again."

He gazed at me down his long, fond nose, his reading glasses perched on his speckled forehead. The little hair around his bald head seemed to sit on his ears like a laurel wreath.

"It's good to see you again, Uncle." I was disappointed with how nasal my German sounded.

"You might be too old to kiss me, but I'm old enough now to kiss anyone I please." And chuckling, he kissed me on the cheek.

"Here, Uncle. Sit down. Please don't stand on my account."

Arthur grumbled away my concern, but was lowering himself to his chair when he saw Corey. "Oh, and this is your friend. I'd forgotten you were bringing a friend with you."

Corey stood across the room, hands shoved shyly into his pockets. I wished I'd had a chance to get him to comb his hair back at the train station: He had a cowlick like a broken bird wing.

"*Ja. Hier ist mein Freund.* Corey Cobbett. Corey? *Mein Onkel*—I mean, my Uncle Arthur."

Arthur remained standing to shake Corey's hand. And very carefully, as if he'd been rehearsing it for weeks, Arthur said in English, "I am so pleased to meet my nephew's friend." He breathed a great sigh of relief and sat down. Arthur had a horror of speaking English, ever since the day he asked me if cows in America wore clocks.

Corey looked equally flustered; he knew no German.

"It's good to meet you, Mr. Scherzenlieb," he said a little too loudly. "It's an honor to be here."

When I'd translated that for my uncle, he asked, "And he's your roommate in New York? Good. I feel better about your moving to such a dangerous place, now that I know you'll be living with someone so large."

Which made Corey sound like a big dog. I looked at Corey and laughed.

"Come, come," called Bertie. "You have said your hellos. Now we must eat. We have been waiting dinner for you. Uncle must be starving. *Hast du Hunger,* Arthur? I wanted to give him his soup, but he said, no, no, we be waiting for Jo-el."

Corey and I smiled and waved at Arthur and he smiled and waved back as Bertie ushered us into the hall.

"Run upstairs, quick as rabbits, and have a wash-up. Go. Take your baggage. *Ach,* I am forgetting. Jo-el? You are in your old room, and Lucia has made the sofa in the office for your pal. Now go. Quick."

I led the way up the steep, familiar stairs, sniffing the veal that cooked in the kitchen, smelling floor wax and aged wood, the rich aroma of the old house itself. My worries had been groundless: I was overjoyed to be back.

We heard Liza and Kearney chatting on the second floor, the door to their bedroom half open.

"Quite a house," said Corey as we went up the next flight of stairs. "You never gave the impression that your aunt and uncle were rich."

"Now don't go sticking your nose up at it, Boy. Anyway, they're not rich. They're only middle-class. And Swiss." But by my standards of the past four years, they did seem rich, didn't they?

"I wasn't judging them. I like them. Very much. What was it your uncle said that made you laugh?"

"Oh, only that you looked like a faithful watchdog," I teased.

Corey laughed, trusting my uncle not to have said quite that, but liking the description anyway. He enjoyed being told he was simpler and more natural than he really was. Corey especially liked being compared to animals.

"And here's your room, Mutt."

The office, with the glass-topped desk where I'd done my homework, the engineering certificates on the wall, the glassed-in bookcase. The room had been perfectly suitable for the consultation work Uncle Arthur did after retirement, but a bit grandiose for a boy who'd used it only for a little algebra, a little chemistry and a lot of daydreaming. There was the glass door that opened on the balcony, where I'd done nothing but daydream. Nothing in my life had turned out the way I'd dreamed it. Thank God.

As soon as Corey dropped his pack, he picked up one of the books on the desk and flipped through it: a volume of metal stress tables. "So this is where you got your mathematics."

He was always doing that to me: my math, my motel industry, my *Decline and Fall of the Roman Empire*. I invited it upon myself. Not having been to college, I could be possessively pedantic about the few things I knew.

He closed the book and looked at the rest of the room. "Well," he said sadly. "They didn't put us in the same room after all."

"But we can visit." I opened the door that led into my bedroom. "All night long. We have this floor all to ourselves." And to prove it, I put my arms around him, snuggled my face in his chest and nibbled a button on his shirt. I felt him up through his clothes, just as I'd almost done with Bertie, just as I'd been wanting to do with Corey all week while we stayed in Italian youth hostels. "Oh, my big friendly dog," I sighed.

"Woof," went Corey.

Love, said Ed, our new roommate in New York, is regressive.

Joan gurgled at sunbeams in her bassinet beneath the open dining room window while the rest of us ate and chatted around the long white tablecloth. Bertie and her maid brought out veal, *spätzle* and peas; Arthur insisted on refilling everyone's wine glass. I talked about Italy, our one week in New York, Corey's new social work job, my lack of a job, Catherine's farm and, more shyly, Gramma Bolt's illness. Bertie asked how Liza and I were getting on with our mother. "Fine," I said and saw the way Liza looked at me. I asked Bertie about the cousins.

It was too soon for anyone to bring up what had happened to my father.

We went for a walk after dinner, at Bertie's insistence. She and Arthur needed a rest from this gaggle of Americans. Kearney unpacked the stroller and we took Joan with us. Wide-awake when we started, she quickly dozed off. She stretched out in the stroller with her lower lip curled under her big nose, like a dowager taking the sun. She had her mother's nose, and Liza had the strong, purposeful nose of Uncle Arthur. I was cursed with our father's weak nose.

"Drat you, Joan. Now's the time to be awake, not two in the morning," Liza grumbled.

We started out together, praising Arthur and Bertie as we walked the road that climbed the terraced slope above Lake Zurich. Kearney asked Corey about his summers with migrant workers, as an excuse to talk about his own work. They walked ahead of us while Kearney told army stories and Corey asked sociological questions.

The road twisted between nougat-colored houses and little yards stuffed with shrubs. I didn't remember the proportions and style of Kilcheberg looking so foreign. It was as precise and toy-like as an architectural drawing from the twenties. Far below, between the red-tiled roofs and steepling poplar trees, the lake glowed with the blues of a peacock's tail. Above us was the wooded slope of the Uetliberg. There was a clanging of cowbells in the distance. It was bright September and I had walked this route a thousand times when I went to the American school just outside the village.

Liza stopped to wipe the drool from Joan's shiny chin. She let Corey and Kearney get a little father ahead of us. "That stuff at the table about Mom not being pissed at me. You're wrong, you know."

I sighed. I was finally getting in touch with my past, but this might be my only time alone with my sister. We should talk. "I saw your dirty look. I still think you're being paranoid."

Liza answered with a lip fart and resumed pushing the stroller. "Maybe. But I do know this. Things aren't the same between Mom and me. She seems so distant now."

Liza's letters over the past year had been peppered with strange doubts and self-accusations, casually tossed in and never fully developed. I wasn't sure how serious she was about any of them. "Of course she's distant. There's the Atlantic Ocean." But I knew that wouldn't convince her. "She doesn't blame us for Gram. *Marat/Sade* had nothing to do with her stroke."

"Oh I know that. And I know Mom doesn't blame me. Consciously. But I can't help feeling she resents me. I mean, I'm over here and she's over there, and she's the one stuck with taking care of Gram, while she thinks I'm living it up in hog heaven over here. She must resent me. If I were in her shoes, I sure would."

"She doesn't resent you, Liza. She knows you have your own family now. She certainly doesn't think you're in hog heaven." I couldn't imagine life with Kearney to be heaven for any kind of animal.

"Yes. I do have my own family." She looked down at Joan. "So I hardly ever think about my old one. It's not like this is something I fret about all the time. Which is part of the reason I feel so guilty about Gram whenever I remember to think about her."

"That's only natural. We have our own life now and Mom has hers. We're adults."

"Hmmmm," went Liza.

"And you know how independent Mom is. Her farm, her vegetables, her chickens. She's talking about putting in some sort of generator, so she can be independent of the power company next. She's not going to resent us for following her example so well."

"Lady Walden's farm," Liza groaned. "I can't say I miss that." Thinking about the farm brought her back to reality. "Lord. After all those years resisting Mom and trying to find my own space—to feel guilty for succeeding? Okay, I know it's neurotic. Life is so strange. You feel weird about Dad, because he's a skunk, and I feel weird about Mom, who's so good. And Gram too," she added. "Poor Gram."

"But I don't feel weird about Jake," I said.

"No? After what he did to you?"

"That cheap, self-centered, irresponsible ham? What's to feel weird about?"

But Liza didn't laugh, which made me uncomfortable.

I quickly turned the conversation back to her. "But you're happy? The rest of the time?"

"To be sure. Which is why I feel guilty when I think of them. Quite happy. Or maybe content is the better word. Hard to say you're happy when you know this butterball is going to go off like a fire alarm at three in the morning. Do I seem happy?" she suddenly asked, as if doubtful.

I thought about it. "Well, content. More settled anyway. Less frazzled."

"I feel more settled. And content. Joan can be a pain in the bohunkus, but she does focus things. And keeps me occupied. I no longer have to choose between getting drunk with the officers' wives in the afternoon, or getting stoned with the enlisted men's wives."

"You still smoke grass?"

"Just once. Before I was pregnant. Don't look at me like that. I was bored!" But she giggled and lowered her voice. "I met this corporal's wife at the PX one day and we got to talking and ending up at her place listening to Joni Mitchell. And taking hits off her bong. Was fun. Weird as hell when Bob came home and I was still high as a kite. I gave him some bull about new diet pills."

"But you're happy now?" I asked worriedly. "Or content anyway?"

"I am. Joan's changed everything. She really has. I mean, I'm playing the guitar again because of her."

"Good." She'd given it up after marriage, along with painting and cigarettes.

"Well, I can't leave her alone, and it's not very exciting just to sit there and watch her grow. So, when I finish the housework, I pull out the gee-tar and strum and sing to her for an hour or so."

"'White Rabbit'?"

"Lord no. Tried it once and the high notes had her screaming. Just quiet, folksy things. She likes it. Just purrs and goos and watches me with her mouth wide open."

"Bob's not afraid you'll corrupt her with all those pinko folk songs?"

"Oh no. Bob's mellowed out. He really has. Okay, not as much as he could. But a lot. And he's a good father, Joel. You have to grant him that. A wonderful father."

The ground had leveled out and I followed Liza's eyes to the two men now far ahead of us. Kearney walked with his crisp, military stride, hands jabbing the air while he told a story. Corey loped beside him, hands in his pockets, eyes on the ground, nodding every so often. No matter how much Liza insisted on her happiness, I knew she couldn't be as happy with Kearney as I was with Corey. Her problems there had to be more important in her life than anything she felt about Mom or Gram.

"Your poor buddy," she sighed. "He must be getting an earful. I'm glad Bob's found somebody to talk to. He was afraid he'd be odd man out down here." She narrowed her eyes at them. "Doesn't Corey own any pants that fit him?"

I laughed. "He likes them loose." All his pants bagged in the seat; I found it sexy.

"I like Corey. I do." Liza watched the men a moment longer. "Don't get me wrong. Because I really do like him. But don't you ever find him a little, well...dull?"

I laughed at that too. Of course she'd find him dull. After living with Kearney, calm and reason would seem dull. "He's quiet," I admitted. "But he's not dull."

"I ask because he hardly says anything. Unless it's politics."

"Small talk isn't Corey's forte."

"Then he's the perfect match for you. You can do enough talking for both of you."

"I can," I said and laughed with her.

"I'm curious. I know it's none of my business. But we're brother and sister and can say anything to each other, can't we? Do you mind if I ask... Which of you's the man?"

I stared at her in disbelief.

"Bob says gay couples are made up of the one who... and the other who, uh, gives, I guess. The man's part."

"And Bob thinks I'm the woman?" My sister's ignorance threw me, but I was stung for a moment by the way Kearney treated Corey as a peer and Corey played along.

"Only because Corey's bigger and two years older," said Liza. "I defend you, Joel. I've told Bob it's just as likely you're the man. You've always been masculine, in your own Shrimp way."

I was finally able to say, "Bob's full of crap."

"Which is often the case. Then you're the man?"

"There's not a man and a woman. It doesn't work that way, Liza. Corey and I are equals. It's not like straight couples, where there's a dominant man and a submissive woman."

Liza's smile disappeared.

And I realized I'd said the wrong thing. "The way people *used* to see marriage," I explained, trying to undo what I'd done.

With her jaw strained forward, Liza muttered, "I wasn't talking about marriage. I was talking about fucking."

112

"Which is what I meant, too, only...Who does what in bed has nothing to do with who's...boss?" I couldn't get out of it. Anything I said about me and Corey became a criticism of her and Kearney. We were equals, they weren't and Liza had said she defended me, as if she thought there was something wrong about being the woman. I could make peace only be becoming explicit. "It's just semantics, Liza. If you mean 'anal intercourse,' just say 'anal intercourse.'"

"All right already!" She drew a deep breath and pretended no nerve had been struck. "So. Do you fuck Corey or does Corey fuck you?"

"Uh, actually, we're not into anal intercourse." Only then did I remember Joan. I looked down and found her sound asleep, lulled by the squeaking stroller.

"Then what do you do with each other?"

"Things." But to close the subject, I told her. "Mostly fellatio and frottage. You know, rubbing against each other."

"And that's all?" she said.

"It's enough."

"Very interesting." She thought about it moment. "But whew! Even gay men get touchy when their masculinity is questioned." As if that had been the cause of the tension between us.

We had come to the Kilchberg church, a stony Protestant thing with a walled cemetery beside it, a cemetery designed by Uncle Arthur. We turned the corner and found our partners waiting at the fork in the road. Both squatted on their haunches, a habit Corey developed when he talked to migrant workers, and probably how Kearney spoke to soldiers in the field.

"We're not as far apart as you think," Corey was saying. "My politics have nothing to do with envy or resentment or ideological cant. All I want is a return to community. The same sense of community that I bet is what drew you to the army, Bob."

Kearney heard us and looked up in embarrassment. He

113

quickly stood up, shaking his head and sneering. "I joined the army so I could express my real human nature. Kill, rape and plunder," he chanted, resorting to his old baiting. "Tough to feel much community with a pack of acid freaks and Puerto Ricans. No sir. My wife and daughter are all the community I need. Or can expect." He beamed at his wife and sleeping child.

Corey glanced at me sheepishly as he stood up. "We were waiting for you to tell us which road to take, Shirts."

"Let's go this way," I said. "I can show everyone the school I went to."

"Whoopee-doo. Shrimp's school," said Liza. "Let's see where you got so smart."

The school was half a kilometer beyond the church and we walked together, with no chance for further confessions or political proselytizing. We looked at the school from the road and didn't go in. Across a green field was a copse of trees with a brick house in it. On the other side of the road were the tennis courts, where two boys with headbands and long hair played.

"Looks more homey than my high school," said Corey. "Mine looked like a Sears and Roebuck warehouse. So what does it give you? Nostalgia? Regret?"

It gave me nothing, except surprise that it was so small. But the repeated bonk of a tennis ball on a fall afternoon made me suddenly think of Michael Something, the runty ballboy on the tennis team, one of my many short-lived friendships here. I had forgotten Michael ever existed. The kid had been even more of a misfit than I was, but if I had understood my brotherly interest in him and his timid courtship of me, I might've discovered sex much sooner.

Strange thoughts to have in the company of couples, and I was half of the happier couple.

"Hey, Boy. Your shirttail's out."

"Oh? You don't have to—"

I tucked it in for him, just to remind him and Kearney

what we were, and to give myself an excuse to rummage in his clothes.

Kearney turned around and tucked a blanket over Joan.

We had relatives instead of supper that night, a parade of kin whose visits brought out cheese and sweets from the kitchen, and bottles of wine from Arthur's bomb shelter. From the older folks came the usual insincere cries of how handsome I was and how much I'd grown—my body might've filled out, but I was still only five-foot-six. Most of their rapture went to baby Joan, who was set out to squirm on the carpet like a new pet turtle. Cousins my age looked bored, except Balz, who scolded Kearney for the My Lai massacre and the invasion of Cambodia. Kearney regretted missing out on Vietnam, but he listened to Balz with amused indifference, even when Balz said, "But now that you've forced that gangster Nixon to resign, perhaps you'll get your soul back." Corey came to Kearney's defense by saying that Switzerland, the home of Nestle's infant formula, wasn't exactly innocent, either.

In the end, only Urs and his wife remained. Arthur smiled sleepily while his youngest son pumped me about what was happening with "that sly dog, Jacob." Of all the relatives, only Urs was pleased by my father's new life, even envious. Ilsa finally succeeded in dragging him home and we could get to bed.

I tried to hurry things by helping Bertie clear away the food and dishes, but the others only sank deeper into their chairs. They watched the joyfully gurgling baby charge up and down the thick carpet on all fours. "Oh, Piglet. You are so out of sync," said Liza.

"Well. I don't know about the rest of you," I said. "But this cowboy's trudging off to bed. Been a long day. Hasn't it, Corey?"

Corey didn't look at me, but slowly stood up. "Yeah. I should be getting to bed myself."

"Yes! Bed! Everyone to bed!" cried Bertie, clapping her

hands. "We can play with the baby tomorrow. Arthur? *Schlaflei?* Everyone go. I will turn out the lights."

Joan began to cry as soon as Liza snatched her from the rug. The crying followed me and Corey up the stairs, then was muffled by a closed door on the second floor.

I went straight to my room, grabbed my kit and hurried into the bathroom. But instead of doing likewise, Corey only followed me from room to room, talking.

"Quite a day. Too much to process all at once. Did you have a good chat with your sister this afternoon?"

"Uh huh."

"I had an interesting talk with Bob. I think marriage has improved the old Kahuna. He's still all bluster and noise, but it's more transparent now. And I think he knows it's transparent." Corey leaned against the bathroom door and watched me. "I think being a father has brought out a side to Kearney we never knew was there."

"Uh oh. I knew it. Boy wants a baby."

Corey laughed. "It is the one thing I regret about being gay. But it's just as well. I'd make a miserable father."

I thought he'd make a wonderful father, but I wouldn't tell him that. It was a peculiar thing to wish for with Joan still howling on the floor below.

"How do you think your sister's doing?"

My mouth was full of toothpaste; I answered with a pitying lift of my eyebrows.

"Me too. I think marriage has been good for her. That sharp edge of hers seems to have softened a bit. Motherhood, maybe."

I spat into the sink. A stereotypical male view and I was surprised to hear it from Corey. He'd been talking too much with the husband. "She's making do. And she says she's content. But I still think she'd be happier married to someone else."

"Well, you've had a grudge against Kearney since our Boy Scout days."

"It's not a grudge. It's Kearney. They were never right

116

together. I saw them dating, remember? I only wish Liza had found someone she could feel as close and easy with as . . ." I smiled and stroked his chest—"as I am with you."

"Ah," he said and put his arms around my shoulders. "But we have to be fair to heterosexuals. They can be happy, too." He lowered his voice. "Uh, should I shave?"

But his chin felt nicely sandy, not scratchy. "Nyaah. But brush your teeth."

I hurried back to my room and sat on the bed to take off my shoes. The springs began to quack. I'd forgotten how noisy the bed was. The memory of trying to masturbate quietly here excited me, but I knew this bed wouldn't do, not with a house full of people below. I wanted to have the sex here, a gentle revenge on the room where I'd been so ignorant, but the sofa in the office was firmer, quieter. Prudence won out over fantasy, but I undressed here, to make my old room part of the event.

I poked my head into the hall. Corey had closed the bathroom door and ran water in there. I walked from my room to the office, the velvety air of the house passing through all my naked angles. I flopped backwards on the sofa and sprawled, a caricature of debauchery.

The sofa was wide and backless, a daybed actually, and I could smell its leather upholstery through the sun-baked sheets and blankets. The crying downstairs stopped. Then the toilet flushed and the bathroom door opened. I heard Corey clump into my bedroom, where he must've stood a moment, scratching his head. He clumped down the hall into the office, looking perplexed. He saw me and flinched.

"Expecting someone else?"

He laughed and quickly closed the door. "Well!" he said and took a deep breath. But instead of pouncing, he teased me, padding around the room, putting away his toiletries, winding up his clock, smiling to himself, stealing glances at me the whole time. "I'm setting it for seven. So you can get back to your room in case someone comes upstairs to wake us. Should I turn off the desk lamp? So you won't feel peculiar here?"

"I want to feel peculiar."

"Ah," he said and looked at me a moment longer before peeling his glasses off. His face was very blank and physical without the glasses. He came over and the sofa sighed beneath us.

I loved to start like this. Nakedness was power, but I could still tug and fold back Corey's clothes and catch something of that feeling from the first time three years ago, when we'd sat very still in his basement apartment in a trance that was broken only when I said, "Let's take off our clothes." We'd undressed each other that night, standing face to face, too excited to kiss or embrace while we did it. We kissed and embraced now, furiously, while we freed Corey from his clothes. It wasn't just the six days without sex that powered us, but six days in a foreign country, in Italy, where we were all skin and eyes, wine and sunlight, two alert bodies restraining themselves in crowded hostels. It had been wonderful to feel so richly horny again, to see Corey, so large and touchingly naked as he skitted back and forth in the cold showers, and not be able to touch him. I touched him now—his thick middle, flat bottom, his bulky shoulders —breaking off only to get at his underpants twisted around my foot and his ankle. Until I could stretch over him and enjoy that moment, when our fronts were bare and first pressed together, of pure present, of nerves steeped in smooth warmth, as if I inhaled ether through my skin. The moment passed, skin caught its breath and we could be conscious of what we did. I was so charged, I was afraid I'd finish in that moment, but I was able to continue, able to see Corey.

We seemed to take turns watching each other. Corey immersed himself in sex, more deeply than anyone could imagine when they saw him in the world. He closed his analytic eyes and surrendered to his body, only to open his eyes now and then, amused by what his body could give him. His sighs and moans were very close to laughter. Mine were more insistent, even deliberate, but sex is one time you can express anything you feel and I loved to take advantage of it.

"Oh, but you feel good," I said.

"Oh, ditto," he murmured.

When he enjoyed something I did to him, he promptly did it to me. We climbed up and down each other like monkey bars. We seemed to be the same height when we made love. We seemed to be all hands, then all mouths, then nothing but cocks. Our bodies continued to rearrange and random thoughts came to me, like the thoughts that come and go when you listen to a favorite piece of music.

The view of Lake Zurich from the balcony.

A landscape of skin and hair that I imagined with my hands.

The huge desk with eyeglasses I imagined watching us.

The boy who sat at that desk, receiving friends from school as if they were business associates. Or competitors.

If only I had known about this, I could've done it with Michael the ballboy.

I held Corey's head and pressed my mouth into Michael's mouth. Corey's chest could be Steve Bishop's, only Steve's would've been hairless and he wasn't going to get bored with me and join the school's drug set now that I had this to offer him. Corey's balls were Robert Rice's, only Robert's were smaller, the hair around them softer. And Robert thought I'd asked him here only to loan him back issues of *Fortune*.

There was nothing wrong about imagining others when I made love to Corey. The first time it happened— a new bellman with freckles, someone I'd trained after my promotion from night clerk to assistant manager—I was so worried I confessed it to Corey two days later. He wasn't threatened. In fact, he said it was perfectly natural, that fifty per cent of sex was fantasy and that he fantasized too, usually about me, but sometimes about other people. And he cited a few: the smirking, naked boy in Caravaggio's *Amor Victorious,* any of the elongated adolescents in a snapshot of young George Orwell and friends posed like Greek statues in knee-length bathing trunks, and, more embarrassingly, Ronnie Howard in *American Graffiti.* That my fantasies were about people we knew, and his weren't, didn't bother him. He seemed to understand, and, trusting in his understanding, I felt free to enjoy other bodies that came to me now and then. But it had never been like this before; there had never been so many people at once. Robert, Steve, Michael, Harry with the panda bear circles under his eyes, Kazuichi the Japanese boy who'd been left here to learn English—all came crowding into Corey until he was as densely populated as a city. The past that had failed to come to me all day was suddenly pouring through Corey.

He began to lift his hips to meet my mouth. Even there he could be one of the others, no matter how hard I felt it with my tongue, because this was the only cock I'd ever had in my mouth. "You want me to come? Like this?" he whispered, a breathless giggle.

But I couldn't let him finish yet. I wanted to keep us going, deeper, back to us again. I moved back up him and resumed kissing, drawing him back into his mouth and face. "God but I've missed you," I said. I could think of a dozen other people, but it was Corey I wanted and kissed through his smiles. I needed more, something that would carry us beyond my ghosts of missed opportunities into the hard, physical fact of us. I wanted to have him crowded inside me, extending me where I usually felt nothing at all. I took his hand, put a knuckled finger in my mouth and brought the hand down. He gingerly touched me there, then explored the tightness.

120

"Want to?" I became very solemn.

"Go inside you? I don't know if I can tonight."

"No? What if I went inside you?" Because, one way or the other, I wanted it to happen tonight. And as soon as I said that, it seemed even better to have Corey crowded with me instead of the others. "Okay?"

"Oh yeah. I'd like you inside me."

That was our language for it; neither of us liked the word fuck. I hadn't really lied when I told Liza we didn't do it. It was not so much a sex act as a symbol for us, a chance to be careful with each other. Corey could be so careful that he sometimes lost his erection, which didn't bother me; it was only a symbol and there were things I enjoyed far more.

"What can we use?" said Corey.

"Don't know." We did it so rarely, we'd come to Europe without anything.

"Let's not use soap again."

If Liza were awake, she might have some hand cream. I liked the idea of telling her who it was for, but Liza was asleep by now.

"I know. Yeah. Right back." Corey jumped up and wobbled around the room, reaching for his pants.

"Where you going?"

"Back in a jiffy," he said, covering himself with one hand when he zipped himself up. "Don't go away." He looked drunk as he stumbled out the door to the softly lit stairs, listened to the house, then felt his way down the bannister.

I felt funny having Corey get the stuff when I was the one who'd profit by it. On the other hand, it could be his way of taking an active part in this. Why was I thinking this way? Active? Passive? Straight roles had nothing to do with us.

Corey returned a minute later, sober now and a little self-conscious. He handed me a small porcelain dish with cherubs on the lid. The butter dish.

"I was looking for something like Crisco, but I don't recognize the labels here." He stepped out of his pants, stamping them to the floor. "But this'll do."

It'd be messy, but I liked the added twist. "Good Swiss butter. Sure. Now where were we?"

I wanted to get us sexually dizzy again and give the butter time to soften. Corey quickly returned to his sexual deeps, but it was difficult for me to get high again on kisses and feels when I knew where I was going.

When I thought enough time had passed, I turned off the light. Even as a symbol, there was something so incongruous about it, we needed darkness. The butter was solid and chilly. I kneaded some in my hand before I stroked myself with it. I smeared some over the space behind Corey's balls, slipping my finger into the parting of his cheeks, finding the spot like a wrinkled mole and easing one finger inside. It was like a bit of wainscoting that was really a door. Corey lay on his back with his legs hoisted up with his arms, quietly watching me.

He took me lying on his side, his back to me, one knee raised. It was a slow process, full of commands and requests, as if we were parking a truck. It wasn't like sex, but I had no trouble staying hard, even if I couldn't allow myself to enjoy it until the last inch at the base of my cock was safely inside him. I responded with a slight, impatient thrust.

"No!" Corey gasped and took several deep breaths. "Wait. It has to adjust to you."

"Sorry." It was frustrating to stay still when I could feel myself clenched inside him, feel my pulse there, feel nothing but myself. I ran my hand up and down his hairy front, trying to feel something besides the sweet pull in my cock. I found Corey's cock and stroked that.

"I think I'm ready. Can we roll over? Hold on." And with me clinging to his back, Corey rolled us over so that he lay on his stomach. He lifted his ass to see if I were still there. "Feel good?"

"Uhh!" I was angled into him, his bottom pillowed against his hips. "And you?" I remembered to ask. "How's it feel for you?"

"Let me just...ah. Feels good. Like being hugged from inside."

I couldn't see his face; it was like talking to him on the telephone.

"Why don't you wipe the butter off your hands. So we won't get it on their sheets." He passed me his undershirt from the floor. "And why don't you spread that under me? Just in case?" His lifted his hips while I arranged the shirt under his stomach. "Okay. Ready when you are."

I rocked on my hips, barely moving inside him. It felt good, frustratingly good, because I could already feel the finish of it approaching. I grabbed his shoulders, then his neck, his shaggy head, trying to make him more real before it was over. His muscle was locked around my base; it was only the vagueness inside him that did it to me. I pinned his arms to his sides. I made my strokes longer, trying to use his sphincter, but slowly, because Corey's body wasn't accustomed to this, but it could've been anyone or anything that clutched me.

Then Corey sighed.

I stopped. I wanted to jam my hand under him and work on his cock, so I could stay in him long enough for it to mean something. But Corey was rocking with me now and when I stopped, his pressure continued to ride me, out of my control. When I tried to press him flat, he only pressed back, with a twist that only hurried it along. I didn't want it tricked out of me while I did nothing, but I was afraid of doing anything passionate that might hurt Corey. The whole act was coming apart; our bodies didn't matter.

There was a final rush of frustration, and I came. I grabbed Corey's hips, seized the beat of my orgasm and thrust with it, furious with it. I was so determined to use it, I couldn't feel it, couldn't bother to cry out or even moan. I clenched my teeth and struck, and continued striking even when it was finished. I almost declared it finished by yanking out, when I remembered this was Corey. I had to withdraw slowly or I'd hurt him. Had I been hurting him? I stayed inside and sank against his back, frightened.

His body suddenly pitched itself up on one elbow so he could reach underneath and jerk himself off.

I held onto him while he shook beneath me. There was only a sickly ticklishness to being inside him now, and he seemed miles away. I hadn't hurt him, but the possibility stayed with me. It was the only thing worth keeping from the sex, now that I was finished.

But when we'd done this before, the five or six times, it was never our best sex. It wasn't meant to be. It was only our experiment, our chance to show we wouldn't hurt each other. I had expected something more from it tonight, something more from sex. I'd been waiting for this night for six long days, and lost it.

He went up on his knees and I slipped out of him. I felt very small and unnecessary draped over his back and kneeling behind him. I felt very alone.

I bit his shoulder, trying to make some kind of connection with him. I reached around to help him, but all I could do was hold his balls and feel the hurried beat of his hand. He was almost there and didn't need me, but I said, "Want *me* to do anything?"

He violently shook his head. It was raised now. He was supporting himself on one extended arm now. His broad back dipped like a bridge between his buttocks and shoulders. And then he came, in his usual deep, hoarse sighs, and it hurt me I couldn't see his face and the way his mouth blew into a grin when he came, like a slack sail swinging into the wind. It was like hearing him come with someone else.

He dropped to the sheets. His head was turned to one side and I saw his smile, his closed eyes.

I was annoyed he'd enjoyed it so fully. I climbed down

beside him, kissed his nose and said mockingly, "And your pal Kearney thinks *you're* the man."

"Yeah?" said Corey dreamily. He was still catching his breath. "Sort of sensed that. Maybe why I wanted. To do this tonight. That why you wanted. To do this?"

I'd said it only because it was the first taunt that came to mind. "Don't know," I admitted. But Corey was so matter-of-fact and unthreatened by it, and I'd been just as willing to have Corey fuck me. "But it might've given me the idea," I suggested. "Uh, I hope I didn't hurt you any."

"I might be sore in there tomorrow. But was worth it. It was so beautiful when you came."

He whispered it with such awe, I wished it were true.

I touched his warm face, his cool bottom. But his body didn't help. It had also been Michael's body, and Robert's and Kazuichi's, people who didn't exist. He was perfectly naked with me and I was disappointed it didn't mean more to me than it did.

"I guess doing it here was sort of exciting for you?"

"Sort of." Maybe that's what had made it so different tonight. I had come back here, so proud of the life I had found on my own, expecting to find that life in bed with me tonight. But we were more than this, more than two bodies that had sex. We were—

What were we?

I took a deep breath, hoping to get the smell of Corey's hair and soap and sweat, but my nose was too accustomed to us now to smell anything.

We were friends, partners. We were lovers, only neither of us liked the word: me because it sounded mushy and temporary, Corey because it had exploitative connotations. We lived together. We had come a long way together, too long for me to lie here wondering who we were. We were Joel and Corey, simple as that. For me to wonder about that was as goofy as picking up a spoon and wondering why it was a spoon, why it was this spoon and not another spoon, turning its very existence into a puzzle, a mystery. And yet, it was something like that which had spoiled the sex for me, as if I'd grabbed too hard at a spoon I was afraid might not be there.

Corey lay there with his eyes closed, lightly drawing circles on my back.

"Core? Do I always seem real to you?"

His eyes stayed contentedly closed. "Real? Very real."

"Seriously. Do you feel like I'm really here? Metaphysically."

It was the wrong word; Corey grinned. "You mean like, are you an illusion? Am I dreaming you? Is reality only a movie projected by God? Berkeley and all that?"

"Something like that. But not—"

"Well, I refute you thus," and he blindly kissed me on the cheek.

There are things you can't discuss with someone who minored in philosophy; they turn it into something they've studied. "But more real than that. More physical and strange."

The anxiety showed in my voice; he suddenly opened his eyes.

"I don't know how to describe it better, only... Do you know what I'm talking about?"

"Maybe. I'm not sure." He sounded worried. "I don't take you for granted. Is that what you mean? I care very much about you. You know that."

"I know. And I care about you. But it's not that." In his usual Cobbetty fashion, he was afraid he had done something wrong. "It's more..." I patted my hands around an empty space the size of a basketball. "More like—" What was it like? "When you stare at a word too long and it begins to look misspelled? Yes, like that. A word you use everyday and you find yourself looking at it so hard that it's nothing but letters. Until you have to look it up in the dictionary before you can be sure it's really a word."

"Hmmm." He sounded amused by it, not threatened. "And I'm looking misspelled to you?"

"Just tonight. And not just you. But things. Us." I was afraid I'd said something very terrible. "Haven't I ever looked misspelled to you, Boy?"

He seriously thought about it and I began to feel foolish.

"Now and then," he finally admitted. "But especially in the beginning." He sheepishly lowered his voice. "When I was *in* love with you. Before I loved you."

Corey was ashamed of the distinction he made between love and in love. It was like confessing he wasn't in love with me anymore, that he only loved me. That didn't hurt me because I didn't believe in his categories; I couldn't separate the two emotions in myself. I felt Corey separated them only to explain to himself the differences between his initial, difficult love for me, and the love that finally succeeded. I liked to think of his notion of two loves as an emblem of what we'd come through together.

"I love you," I said. "But I'm still in love with you, too."

"Yes. I know." He paused over his refusal to say the same. He was too scrupulously sincere to say it. "But I remember being with you and being overwhelmed with whys and whats and who-is-this-guy, especially when you were sleeping. It wasn't the bad doubting I used later. It was more like wonder and sort of exciting. I thought I was so rational and yet there I was, up to my nose in the ineffable."

"It is exciting," I admitted. "In an unnerving kind of way. But you can still feel it? Now and then, you said."

"Oh yeah. Like right now. Just talking about it makes me feel, oh, epistomologically spacey." He happily gathered me against his side, as if I were all that was needed to fill that space. "I'm sure you've felt it before too."

"Not like this." And not after sex. Sex usually answered any questions. But I was feeling better, now that we were talking and Corey didn't think I was crazy. Telling him I loved and was in love made my confusion easier to bear. I began to feel silly, as if I'd been fretting about something that everyone else knew how to handle.

"Maybe it's just your situation," said Corey. "We're over here, we just moved and aren't settled yet. You don't know what you'll be doing. Everything's so up in the air for you right now."

I smiled. "But I have you," I said. "You're all the situation I need."

Corey laughed. "No wonder you're confused. I'm misspelled to begin with. But my situation is better than yours. Because I have you."

"A ditz who has to ask if he's real?" I laughed at myself. "Uh uh. I'm the lucky one. I'm the one who got better than he deserves."

We teased each other and that settled everything. Insisting we didn't deserve each other proved that we knew otherwise. We could be silly together, confessing our faults—my sudden quirks, Corey's self-consciousness, my stub of a nose, Corey's big feet—until I felt good enough to let him go so he could shut himself in the bathroom. Corey needed a few minutes alone after doing what we did.

I thought about taking the butter dish back to the kitchen: It'd be difficult explaining its presence here tomorrow. But I sat there on the empty sofa with my arms around my knees, thinking about love. Because, without his body there to distract me, it was obvious what I'd been feeling. I'd said it myself: I was still in love with Corey. The fear or doubt or desperate whatever that had spoiled the sex didn't seem so bad to me now. I was still in love and my furious expectations had only been my response to something that had never explained itself away, never lost its power to amaze me. After all this time. I should be pleased with that. Shouldn't I?

Almost three years, and I could still surprise myself with my love for Corey, love for a guy, love in general. I had spent so much of my life being surprised by others. I preferred the surprises I gave to myself.

7

NEW YORK.

Manhattan.

Capital of the twentieth century, Corey mockingly called it.

I drew deep breaths each time I stepped into it.

Everything had been thrown up in the air. It hung above you—windows, stones, billboards—ready to fall, yet staying aloft a moment longer while you hurried beneath it.

Zurich now seemed as small as Williamsburg, and Williamsburg was remembered as an open-air living room. I waited for New York to become familiar, but the city was too vast and various. I kept dealing with it in metaphors.

Cross streets like vectors on a graph. A Cartesian product of a city.

Even the subway maps were abstractions. Manhattan looked like a whale lodged in the throat of the Hudson. I was inside the whale.

Or an amusement park. The subway stations especially, with their bare light bulbs, stained walls and sooty girders. They were amusement park funhouses with all the lights turned on. It was there you were most conscious of being in New York.

"City of gophers," muttered our roommate, Ed. "Everyone scrambling in the gopher hole of self."

Every morning, gophers filed down the stairs. There were no human voices, only the grim click of women's heels on concrete and, overhead, the continual sounds of taxi cabs drumming over the roof. Eyes hid themselves in newspapers, books, the shine of their own shoes. I was repelled at first by so many eyes straining not to see each other. There's the privacy of your own car in other cities, but here you had to imagine your own privacy. It was only out of courtesy that people made each other as invisible as the buildings that soared above them. Before I learned the rules, I saw the people.

A profusion of faces, stamped with character to the point of caricature: a cartoonist's notebook. They seemed grotesque at first, but my eyes adjusted to them. By comparison, people in Virginia seemed to have been innocent of face; I wondered how I'd been able to distinguish one person from another there. But here were so many faces that they began to repeat faces I had known. I found Zack Fuller, my boss at the Thomas Jefferson working the counter of a Greek coffee shop. Fisher from summer camp handled new accounts for Citibank. I frequently saw Uncle Arthur, once stepping from a cab at Lincoln Center with a beautiful blonde on his arm and later in a black hat and forelocks, reading a Yiddish newspaper. Liza was the receptionist in a seedy personnel agency, the girl whose cellophane smile crumpled when I pointed out the dead mouse in the corner.

October. A rustle of newspapers instead of leaves. You overcome the impropriety of looking at other people's faces by looking at their newspapers. The city is even laid out like a newspaper: long columns of print, with grey parks instead of photographs, five-story signs in place of headlines. The city left itself on your hands, like smudged ink.

A subway car like a collage of heads and newspapers. But now and then, on weekday mornings, you could look into the collage and find another pair of eyes looking back at you. You exchange a glance, that's all, and fade back into the wall of newspapers. You both have some-where else to go, but it's good to know that in this crowd of office workers, you are not alone. By the end of October I could recognize not only homosexuals who announced the fact in flamboyant clothes or the height of their boot heels or a touch of eye shadow, but those who, like myself, only needed to see another homosexual. I liked being part of such a community, even if it were only a community of the glance.

I glanced but the other glances were more furtive than they were on the subway, and this bar called Julius seemed like any other bar I'd ever been in, except for the complete absence of women. Everybody seemed to be talking and laughing; everyone noisily knew each other. And then I started seeing the guys, here and there, who stood alone and looked at nothing in particular, who focused on air, like people who know they're being watched. And I found the guys who watched them, not just glancing but staring straight at them, like hypnotists.

Corey came back from the bar with two bottles of beer. He'd brought me here so I could see one of the places from his summer in New York. A year after his first crush at Boy Scout camp, Corey came up here for the sole purpose of getting homosexuality out of his system; sexual thoughts were distracting him from his schoolwork. Corey could be so goofily rational. And he got it out of his system, fourteen times, with six different guys, but was pleased to find it back again by the next afternoon. He'd met five of those guys here, the sixth at a dance in a firehouse. I envied those fellows. I wished I'd been there and could have sidled up to a nervous but willing, oversized Southern boy in glasses, and taken him by the hand.

We only stayed long enough to finish our beers; the place depressed Corey. I found a strange sadness creeping over me while I played connect-the-dots with the stares that darted through the room. I rooted for a man who stared at a boy by the jukebox. When the watched boy turned and walked away, I felt sorry for the loser and relieved I'd never had to play this game. But something about the game challenged me: I couldn't help wondering how I would've done. I tried not to wonder too hard. Corey said that even when you succeeded, you often found yourself in bed with a jerk. I knew better than to cry over unspilled milk.

We were in the City of Homosexual Love, but how do you express your liberation when you've already found the one person you love?

A bright blare of brass. A prance of woodwinds and strings hurrying towards something wonderful. And the curtain rose on the inhumanly human voices. In the center of this newspaper city, there was opera.

The Magic Flute, with its Queen of the Night, noble hero and fool in feathers. I never knew anything so artificial could be so beautiful. Even with my German, the sung words were difficult to follow. It was the shifting emotions of voices and orchestra that did their work on me. I leaned against the standing room parapet and floated in music.

I'd come back from Europe with a sudden need for music. If my life were going to be up in the air in this city, I wanted to have music up there with me. I'd discovered classical music in Williamsburg, but this new need was more like the love I'd had for Broadway musicals on the radio when I lived with my father after the divorce. I might've gone back to that first love, if Broadway shows weren't so expensive and we weren't so poor after our trip. Neither of us had ever seen an opera and standing room was cheap.

Corey didn't enjoy it. He said his knees hurt and complained he couldn't follow the story. During intermission, he hunkered on his haunches in the dress circle lobby and scribbled notes on his program for a proposal at work. When it was over and I was floating down the stairs to the street, Corey was counting tuxedos and furs. "If only they didn't turn it into such a piece of conspicuous consumption," he muttered.

But he didn't criticize me for enjoying it and didn't try to dissuade me from going back. I wanted to go back and did, not always with Corey.

"Opera queen," said Ed. He'd seen it all.

I went every Friday, when I had to get up early anyway and could get to the box office in time to buy a standing room ticket for that evening's performance. *The Magic Flute, La Traviata, Carmen, Tales of Hoffmann.* I didn't keep track of the names of the performers, but I was there for the rush of music carrying a story, clarifying a story, raising story to pure emotion. Even in the dullest opera there were scenes or arias as exciting as my own emotions had been during crises, but without the complications now, or the responsibility. If only my life had been scored like an opera, with music announcing every change of heart, I might not have missed so much.

November. Bright sweaters and wool skirts were covered up with old winter coats and the subway became even shabbier. The meeting hall on lower Broadway stayed shabby, even when the people took off their coats and scarves and settled back on folding chairs for a lecture on monopoly capitalism. I watched a tiny pinfeather, leaked from someone's down coat, fitfully float in the drafty room. Even Corey was disappointed by the meeting, and said so while we rode the freight elevator back to the street. But he was determined to give this group the benefit of the doubt and said he wanted to go back the following Wednesday. He said he'd understand if I didn't want to go with him.

The following Wednesday I stayed home to read *Jude the Obscure.*

I was suffering a concussion of literacy, reading any novel that caught my eye, especially novels that had music in their words. I was surprised to find myself so interested in beauty, but, after all, I was a homosexual, and homosexuals are said to have an affinity for the arts. I was finally finding my identity. I read *Death in Venice* in preparation for the new opera premiering that month, but the line for standing room ran halfway around the opera hall that morning and I couldn't get a ticket. Every other Friday, for two months, I had had a ticket to the opera in my shirt when I stood in line at the unemployment office.

"Next."

It was fun to think I was probably the only person there who'd be going to the opera that night.

"Next."

We stood in a deep, high-ceilinged room downtown. Brown linoleum floor. Plate glass windows on the front and side. A huge warehouse with a neoclassical facade across the street. The light brown walls were bare except for a government-printed poster of a man who looked like Father from *Dick and Jane*. "Ask Yourself! Are You Eligible for the Benefits . . ."

"Next. Book please. Name please."

"Scherzenlieb, Joel."

"Have you been employed or offered employment at any time this week, Mr. Scherzenlieb?"

"No ma'am." Nobody in New York ever had any trouble with my name.

"Have you been actively seeking employment?"

"Oh yes ma'am."

"Sign here please. And here. And here." She initialed my little brown book, stamped the card I'd signed and tossed the card into the wire basket. *"Next."*

That was all they ever did.

Nevertheless, green checks for sixty-two dollars arrived in our brass mailbox every week. I was appalled at how easy it was for anyone to be paid for doing nothing. But when the checks continued to come, as regularly as money from home, I accepted them as something natural.

I stopped looking for work. The state had given me a gift of time and it seemed foolish to waste that time hunting for a job I didn't want. And there was a recession on. The newspapers on the subway said so. I became hopeful when I read that the federal government might step in and extend benefits from six months to a year. A year without work? In a year I could read a hundred novels and see maybe fifty operas.

I rode the subway home every Friday, satisfied that I'd done my job for the week. At Broadway and 110th Street I went up the stairs into winter sunlight and the broad sidewalk loaded with newsstands, bins of fruits and vegetables and the motley columns of people. There were always people on Broadway, no matter what the hour. I might've felt guilty with my unemployment if I'd felt alone, like when you stay home from school pretending to be sick and there's nobody there. But I was far from alone. "Don't these people ever work?" I wondered as I walked around them and with them. The elderly and retired took the sun on the benches out on the traffic islands. An occasional derelict shuffled along in shoes held together with masking tape. College students everywhere and, in greater numbers, students too old to be in college, but who wore the same sloppy clothes and shaggy hair and walked hunched over with intellectual preoccupation in a way that real college students never walked.

We lived in the shadow of Columbia University. From behind its granite walls and wrought iron gates, its presence permeated the whole neighborhood until, as Corey said, you began to suspect that even the shopping bag ladies lugged half-finished dissertations in their bags of wastepaper and clothes. Broadway was lined with bookstores that stayed open as late as bars, bins of books out front just as the grocers had bins of apples and oranges. Walking home late at night, you could look up and see book-lined rooms, airborne and visible through scrim curtains.

135

"But you don't understand. Godard is. . . . Godardian."

"Listen closely to the text next time. Jagger doesn't always say 'Angie.' Sometimes he says 'Andy.' Angie? Andy? Don't you see? The song's about androgeny. David Bowie's wife is only peripheral to it."

"Pyncheon's gone plastic."

". . . and was beautiful when we got back from the West End. Without getting heavy. She's a remarkably giving woman. But afterwards, when she was looking around my place, she asked why I had so many books in Hebrew. When I told her I'd dropped out of rabbinical school, she laughed. Turned out she's an ex-nun!"

I sat in the Hungarian Pastry Shop, around the corner from where we lived and across Amsterdam Avenue from where Corey worked. Corey was in one of the buildings on the cathedral grounds of St. John the Divine. He was meeting me here for lunch.

I'd become a regular here. It was where I spent most of my mornings while I waited for Ed to wake up and could go home and play his stereo. They had music here, baroque music and entertainingly baroque conversations. It was more a coffee house than a pastry shop. Students came and went, talking of professors and parties, but the real hard core were those students for whom college had only been a beginning. You paid only for the first cup of coffee, could refill your cup from the pots on the hot plate and stay as long as you liked. We sat there for hours with our books and our coffee, each a school unto himself. I saw the others leap at friends and acquaintances, anyone they could teach or be taught by, but I kept to myself and the day's novel. I could feel comfortable being alone, surrounded by so much cheerful noise. The white walls were hung with bright abstract paintings and little brass lamps with green shades.

Corey came in when I wasn't looking, but I saw him at the counter, frowning at the pastries while he left his order. He still wore that old army jacket, but under that was a corduroy sports coat, my best necktie and a white shirt that needed ironing. He'd had his annual haircut only last week and had gone from one extreme to the other. Surrounded by shaggy intellectuals and fluffy-haired college boys, Corey looked like a marine. He saw me and made his way around feet and backs to my table, without smiling.

"Hey there, Boy. How you doing?"

"Foul." He yanked off his jacket and slammed himself in a chair. "I wanted to finish the report on that Bedford-Stuy thing this morning."

"The daycare center," I said, so he'd know I cared.

"But do they let me work on that? *No.* Had to go to a tea and sherry reception for some bishop from Florida. Sherry. At ten in the morning? These damn New York Episcopalians probably pour sherry on their cereal!"

"I'm sorry. But at least you've kept your sense of humor about it."

"Hmmmph!"

"Well, as you've said, you can't expect a church to give up cocktails for Molotov cocktails."

"I never expected anything radical from them. Just a little amelioration and the chance for me to learn something about the real world. But they are so half-assed about everything," he hissed. "If they want to be a social club for Anglophiles, that's what they should be. Not sucker people like me into their churchy club with their ... Christ, the activist guff."

Two months, and Corey had nothing but bitter jokes for his new employer. He'd been skeptical when he took the job; you had to question the sincerity of a Northern diocese that had been running programs for migrant workers in Virginia when they had equally serious problems at home. But now that he was up here and involved in those home problems, skepticism had turned into outright condemnation that spilled over onto the religion itself. "Incense, vestments and altar boys. All the fun of the Roman Catholic Church, at half the moral price." Corey was used to the Low Church of the South. And, surprisingly, he was uneasy about the prevalence of homosexuals in the congregations here, and the clergy. "It's too easy for them. It's the Bloomingdale's of religion." Even Corey knew about Bloomingdale's. Ed had muttered something about Corey being a closet Christian, but Corey still insisted he was an agnostic, even to the people he worked with. He was an agnostic employed by the Episcopal church and yet he had no qualms about condemning the believers for their lack of belief. Corey liked to pride himself on his contradictions.

"But it's nothing new. I should be numb to it by now. How about you? I hope your morning's been better than mine."

"Just been sitting here reading, drinking coffee and getting smart."

He frowned again. "Brain must be turned on like a radio with all that coffee."

"I like feeling turned on."

"So." He adjusted his glasses and tried to look casual. "Have any interviews lined up for this afternoon?"

I knew that was coming. "No. I was going to read some more. Maybe go for a walk. What would you like for dinner tonight?"

"Shirrrts! You should be out looking for a job. You have all this time. You really should be using it to find something you really want to do. You can't collect unemployment forever."

"I don't intend to. When it runs out, I'll get a job."

"I don't want to nag you, but. This can't be good for you, Joel."

"Why?"

"It's not you. You've said yourself that you're happiest when you're working."

"I'll work when I have to. Don't worry, you won't have to support me."

"You know that that's not what I'm afraid of. It's just that I can't think it's very good for your mental health for you to do nothing but read and drink coffee for six months."

"Why not? You did it for four years, Boy."

And that stopped him. It always stopped him.

"Look," I said quietly. "For the first time in my life, I've got six months to do with what I please. If I want to spend it expanding my mind, I think I should be congratulated for my good luck, not scolded. It's not like I'm sitting around, popping bonbons and reading trashy novels, you know."

"I know," sighed Corey guiltily. "I'm not scolding you. I'm just concerned."

Having successfully defended myself again, I could be sympathetic to Corey. "The only thing that bothers me is that while I spend my time reading good books and listening to good music, you have to spend your time in that horrendous job."

"Not horrendous. Just frustrating. And disappointing." His eyes lost their focus as he thought about his own situation again, or mine.

"Consciousness is only an illusion created by the structure of language," said someone behind him.

He turned to look and turned back to me, smiling. "Ah, the lumpenintelligentsia."

"You're someone of a lump yourself, you know."

"I am," he admitted. "And I know I'm just as bad a bookworm as you are, although you seem to be getting a lot more fun out of it. But it's bearable only as long as you don't think of yourself as a stereotype. That's why this place depresses me. Action piddling away in words."

"I come here only for the coffee and the noise. A six-month vacation, Boy. That's all. A little learning, and then back to work for me."

The waitress with long, weeping willow hair brought Corey a glass of apple juice and two croissants segmented like beetles, with marmalade on the side.

He waited until she was gone before he said, "That's another thing I don't like about this place. It's expensive, unless you're willing to drink six cups of coffee. And the only food they have here is sweet. What're you reading today?"

Lolita, borrowed from Ed.

Corey looked disappointed.

"It's not pornographic. It's a beautifully written, serious book."

"I realize that. I've heard good things about it. But you're not reading the Ignazio Silone I gave you? You'd like it. It's Italian." Corey had been on an Italian Marxist kick ever since we'd been back from Europe.

"I'll get around to it. But Ed's always reading Nabokov and I had to see what it's like."

"Old Ed," said Corey. "Ed is strange. That's what I'm afraid we'll turn into."

"I thought you liked Ed."

"I do, but . . ." Corey smiled.

We talked over Ed while Corey fumbled with his croissants. Ed was an inexhaustible subject when we were tired of talking about ourselves.

Corey took only a half hour for lunch. Afterwards, I walked him back to work.

The cathedral grounds were like an English park, especially in the summer when the trees hid the brown tenements and gaudy Puerto Rican street mural on the other side of Amsterdam. But it was December now and the grounds were naked and incongruous. The cathedral itself, for all its size, looked squat. The archbishop had decided that it would be in bad taste to finish the planned steeples and towers while there was still poverty in the world. The uncompleted cathedral sat among the bare trees like a sagging stone circus tent. We walked around the Cathedral School to the fieldstone cottage where Corey worked.

"Oh, almost forgot. Bonnie in Accounting has invited us to a meeting of the West End Marxists tonight. Want to go? They're showing *Potemkin.*"

"We've already seen it twice."

"I wouldn't mind seeing it again. And Bonnie says that this group is more social and less abstract than the School for Contemporary Marxists downtown. Might be fun."

"I can't. Tonight's my opera night."

"That's right. It's Friday. What're they doing tonight?"

"*Tannhäuser*. Wagner."

"Ah. Well, I guess that should be interesting. You won't mind then if I go to this meeting with Bonnie?"

"Not at all. Why should I mind? Will you be home for dinner?"

"Hmmm. Starts at six. No, if you're going out, too, I'll just go straight down there after work." We were on the steps of the Offices for Charity and Development. "So. I guess that means I won't see you again until late tonight."

"I guess."

"I hope you enjoy your opera."

"And you enjoy your Marxists."

Corey had his hand on the door, but he didn't pull it open. He looked surprised by something.

"Does any of this feel funny to you?" he asked.

"Does what feel funny?"

"The two of us . . . going off in opposite directions."

"Autonomy," I said with a smile. One of Corey's words.

"Yes. I know. But . . . you're not pissed with me for nagging you?"

"No. I like your nagging. I'd be worried if you stopped. Still not going to skip *Tannhäuser* for your meeting tonight."

"I don't want you to. It's just . . ." A confused look in his eye, a smile floating in front of his confusion. He shrugged and touched me good-bye on my elbow. "See you later tonight, Shirts."

"See you tonight, Boy. Hope your afternoon goes better than your morning."

"Me too. Be good."

"You too. Bye-bye."

141

"Bye."

And the hobnailed door closed behind him.

I knew what he'd been talking about. It'd felt funny to me, the first time I went to an opera without Corey, but I'd grown accustomed to it. Corey was always slower than I was in sensing these things, and in understanding that they didn't matter. We should be able to have things we called our own, without having to force them on the other.

I didn't go back to the Hungarian Pastry Shop; it would've meant starting all over again and paying for that first cup of coffee. I went down our street of fossilized wedding cakes and into the wedding cake whose stone porch bore the name, "The Arden." Even our dusty lobby was like a cake, frosted with flowers and fancy cornices and cast-iron babies who'd become faceless under an inch of paint. The elevator didn't work and I had to walk up the five flights of stairs.

I undid two of the four locks and was able to push the door open. Which meant that Ed was still home. Our front hall was bare, except for the bicycle we'd never seen Ed ride, and as long and twisted as a passageway dug by ants. Twenty paces in, you finally walked past a few rooms: the grandmotherly living room on the right, Ed's cozy bedroom on the left, the rust-streaked bathroom on the left and, on the right, the big bare room where Corey and I lived. The hall ended in a sunlit kitchen. There, swigging Tab from a half-gallon bottle and glancing at the *Daily News* opened flat on the table, stood Ed, wearing his blue gingham caftan.

"Just get up, Ed? Beautiful day outside. Hey, do you mind if I play one of your records?"

Ed cringed the instant he heard my voice. We'd never seen him drunk, but he always behaved like a man recovering from a hangover. He raised a weary hand to signal "Hello," "Yes, I'm awake," "Go ahead and play a record," and "Leave me in peace," all with the same gesture.

142

It wasn't just me; everyone had the same effect on Ed. He seemed immensely old at thirty-four. His face was puffy and a bald spot mushroomed in his reddish-brown hair. His loose caftans gave the impression of a body like a half-deflated weather balloon. Eyebrows and eyelids bagged sadly around blue eyes that tried not to look at you.

But something about Ed made me want to tease him, which you could do by just talking to him. I enjoyed seeing how far I could go. "Would you mind a little Wagner at this hour?"

"Wagner?" he mumbled. "Didn't know I had any Wagner."

"You've got something called 'Wagner's Greatest Hits.' I assume it's Wagner."

He scratched his unshaved cheek with the bottle's mouth. "A natural assumption. Grrr. Must be something Sidney left over here."

Sidney was Ed's best friend, perhaps his only friend, a fortyish man who wore a hair piece and called Ed "Rita."

"Think Sid would mind if I played it?"

"You could serve pizza on it for all Sid cares about Wagner."

"Thanks, Ed. I'll try to keep it low. Oh, you were right about the Nabokov. I'm really enjoying it."

Ed closed his eyes and nodded, meaning "Of course," and "Why tell me?"

"There's tuna fish casserole in the refrigerator. You're welcome to heat up some if you're hungry."

"This is all the breakfast I need, thank you. Go listen to Wagner."

"Meet anybody interesting at the baths last night?"

"Joel. *Please.*" He raised his eyes to the tin ceiling: Why me? "I am trying to wake up. Play your music and leave me alone."

"Just being friendly, Ed," I said, grinning wickedly.

"I am not your parent. I am not your child. I am only the person you and your boyfriend share the rent with. This is the last time I ever rent to . . . Southerners."

143

"Okey-doke. See you later, Ed."

Ed was forever muttering that we were nothing but tenants to him. He let us use his books, his stereo, his dishes, even his sheets, but claimed it was only in the role of landlord. He seemed to expect us to use his experience too, the remarks about gophers and opera queens that he muttered as if to himself. But he refused to admit that we might be his friends. The notice on the bookstore bulletin board that led us to Ed had read, "Sullen male homosexual in twilight years has small room to let. Will consider someone similarly saturnine and withdrawn. Good situation for deaf-mute or Asian physics student." He'd never rented to a couple before and decided to try us, saying that we'd be leaving him alone because we had each other.

It was all a defense, of course, but exactly what Ed was defending wasn't clear. He seemed like a being from another planet to us. Or another era. Ed was gay, in his fashion, and he certainly wasn't in the closet. He worked as a waiter in a gay restaurant in Greenwich Village, on the night shift. He didn't have a boyfriend and never brought anyone home, but Sid said he often went to the baths after work. That word, "baths," intrigued me. I pictured the showers at summer camp, but on an urban scale, and hoped Ed would offer to take us there sometime. Ed never offered.

Ed's friend Sidney was everything Ed wasn't: noisy, flamboyant, campy, romantically maudlin. And he said that Ed was "your chronic Irish queen." But there was nothing queeny about Ed, except maybe his caftans. I was nervous when I first saw him in one; I thought he was wearing drag. Ed wore his caftans only around the apartment. When he went out, he trussed himself up in trousers and shirts that made him look like any other New York working-class drudge. I had been disappointed the first time I saw him in street clothes. The caftans were relics from Ed's years with the Peace Corps. He had a whole closet full that he had picked up in Tunisia and the Sudan. To hear Ed mention his time over there, you would've thought he'd just left the Peace Corps and that, like me, he was only taking a brief sabbatical before he returned. But Ed had resigned in the summer of 1969, five long years ago.

There were moments of sympathy when I felt Corey could've grown up to be Ed if he hadn't met me.

I put Wagner on the turntable and stretched out on the brocade sofa with *Lolita*. The living room was crowded with the furniture Ed's mother had given him when she sold her house in Queens and moved into a Catholic nursing home. Lace curtains and African wall hangings disguised the cock-eyed windows and flabby plaster walls that, in our room, were uncovered and obvious.

Ed eventually wandered in, eating cold casserole off one of his mother's souvenir-of-Atlantic-City plates. He didn't explain his change of mind, didn't acknowledge me or Wagner, but plumped down in his easy chair, ate and worked on the crossword puzzle from last Sunday's *Times*.

Humbert and Lolita arrived at their first motel to the tune of "Ride of the Valkyries." I admired Humbert, for both his craftiness and the intensity of his feelings. I was proud of myself for catching so many of the elaborate conceits and for knowing which lines were probably ironic. I read, confident that reading would make me a better person. Reading spoke to me through my pride. Music spoke directly to my emotions.

Up the red carpeted stairs they stepped, most often in twos, sometimes in groups, sometimes in furs and Brooks Brothers suits. There weren't as many fur coats tonight as there'd been last week at *Carmen*. Then the grand staircase had foamed with fur. You could shamelessly stroke the silky hairs as they swept past you, but not tonight. I was faintly disappointed.

145

I liked to arrive early, stand at the base of the double staircase that curved like the jawbone of a whale and watch the people ascend. Corey couldn't understand, but I didn't envy rich people or want to be one of them, no more than I envied or wanted to be one of the singers on stage. They were all part of the show. Even I could be part of the show, wearing my loosely knotted blue string tie that made me feel like a Belle Epoque aesthete. Because we were all rich by association here, a wealth not of money but of beauty and full-blown emotions.

Up they went to the tiers stacked above me, each seeking his or her level. Money didn't run from the top to bottom in the tall, layered foyer, but from the bottom up. Somewhere uptown, Corey was sitting in a rickety folding chair and probably listening to someone in loafers lecture about class structure. He should've come with me tonight and seen class firsthand. Unemployed, I had absolved myself of class and could enjoy it for the great masquerade it really was. But the show before the show did not excite me tonight the way it usually did. Perhaps it was the paucity of furs or perhaps I was getting jaded. Watching was not quite satisfying.

I wished Corey had come with me. Gay men here were always in pairs. And in abundance. There was no need for unconscious glances in search of fellow homosexuals. The male couples gravitated to the highest tier and I could see them way above me, posed along the railing of what was called the family circle.

The ten minute bell rang and I answered it. There was no rush for seats, but I raced up the steps two at a time, knowing the opera would offer the excitement I hadn't found in the audience tonight. I crossed the dress circle lobby, its walls padded in the red plush Corey dismissed as "whorehouse wallpaper." No, it was just as well he hadn't come with me. Corey didn't know how to enter the spirit of the thing.

Through the door and into the theater—

Space plunged in front of me. The floor swooped and the ceiling soared and the steep pitch of seats and steps at my feet almost pitched me into the air over the crowd far below. I tried to experience that pitch each time I walked through the door. There was a deep sweep of tiers on either side and, between them, a spacious dazzle of chandeliers, ivory walls and red velvet, all floating in the beehive hum of a thousand civil voices.

I was given a program and shown my numbered space at the partition behind the seats. I knew I should study the program, but I continued to glance and stare, taking in as much as I could. On my left was a Chinese woman with a libretto. On my right, nobody. On my far right, out in the row of box seats, ten doors suddenly opened at once and twenty men in black tuxedos sat down on the red seats. I almost always watched the first act without knowing exactly what was happening.

The chandeliers, like luminous strings of rock candy, had begun to sail up toward the ceiling, when a pack of men charged through the door behind me.

"Thirty-six? Thirty-six?" cried the one who seemed to be their leader, a fat man with a black beard, who was older than the others. "Ah yes, lovely thirty-six. Tis' here."

It was the empty space on my right.

"Pity. Full now. But there'll be empty seats at intermission. There's always empty seats at Wagner. The swine. I'd trade places with you, Gregory, if it weren't for my gout. Come, friends. We must get upstairs. Be tragic if we were locked out during the naughty Venusberg bits. Ta ta, Gregory. See you at intermission."

They hurried away, leaving behind a short, blond blur of a boy.

I scratched my shoulder with my chin so I could steal a look at him. He couldn't have been more than eighteen and the partition came up to his button nose. He pressed his mouth into the partition, brushed the hair off his forehead and forlornly stared into space. The boy looked so abandoned, I was going to offer him my program. But at that moment the lights died, the hive was silenced.

In the distance, the conductor raised his arms over a bed of tiny lights. The opera began.

The overture wasn't promising. There was a smugly noble, simple melody that sounded like something you'd hear at a high school graduation or in church. Even with the strings gliding beneath it now and then, the thing was a damn church hymn. I began to give up hope that *Tannhäuser* would be much fun. When suddenly, the hymn was replaced by a dance. A spritely little dance, with mice scampering on tiptoes. And with the mice, the strings began to breathe more deeply. Their heavy sighs sounded like either love or suffering: I could never tell with opera music. Whatever it was, it promised passion. An opera about passionate church mice?

And with the orchestra still describing dancing mice and heavy breathing, the curtain rose on an orgy in a cave.

The audience applauded. It was a stunning orgy. Pink men and blue women wove and unwove with each other on the floor around a throne. Red bodies embraced in ultraviolet grottoes in the back. When the music explained itself—the heavy breathing was sex, the mice pleasure—it no longer seemed silly, but drew me deep into the scene. One man, in the arms of a woman on the throne, didn't seem to be enjoying himself, but everyone else was and I enjoyed their display. It was intensely erotic, not like pornography, but like a pure sexuality where the skin and flesh were burned away. The scene pierced me and held me, for twenty minutes.

Then, with a change of lights, the grottoes dissolved, the nymphs ran away, the cave disappeared. All that remained was a winter hillside, a cross like a lone telephone pole and the man who hadn't been enjoying himself.

I usually loved the magic of scene changes, but as soon as this one was over, I was annoyed. I missed my orgy. A shepherd boy played a clarinet and a pack of monks marched in, singing that damn church hymn. My attention wandered. The boy beside me, his face ash-grey in the glow of the stage, looked very bored.

As soon as the house lights came up, I tore through my program. The love cave had been Venusberg, but it wasn't going to reappear. I knew I should be content with my twenty minutes of exhilaration, but once you've been moved, you want to be moved again, and more deeply and richly than before. That was the trouble with living for love and beauty: You're always left wanting a little more. I took my fickle appetite into the lobby to see if the audience had become more interesting.

"But you booed her? You actually opened your mouth and booed?"

"Of course. I love to boo."

"I don't dare boo. I wanted to boo. Scotto in *I Vespri*. I dream of booing Scotto. But I couldn't bring myself to boo."

I was at the railing, watching people gulp dessert and coffee in the restaurant below, when I heard the opera chatter behind me. I turned and saw the foursome who'd deposited the blond in Standing Room. The boy was with them now, standing a few feet away from them with his back to the railing, a hurt, distant look in his eyes.

"I once saw Scotto sing Glauce opposite Callas's Medea," said the man with the beard. "Callas, it goes without saying, sang poor old Renata right off the stage."

"I'd sell my soul to hear Callas."

"Your soul, dear Tom, could only buy an evening of Debbie Reynolds."

They ignored the boy completely. I didn't understand it. Because, in full light, I saw that the boy wasn't just blond, he was beautiful.

He slowly rolled his head from left to right, eyes seeming to see nothing. A sweetly vulnerable face was suspended between hard cheekbones. With one knee bent and his hips slightly canted, he had the perfect repose of one of those reclining nudes who gaze at you over their shoulder. Only he wasn't gazing at me or anyone. I could look all I pleased.

I stood only ten feet away, with my hands on the rail. The boy impatiently rapped on the railing behind him and I felt the vibration in the wood. The sensation tickled me like the Venusberg mouse music. I wished I could talk to the boy and offer him the kind attention he wasn't getting from his opera queen friends.

"Gregory?" The bearded man called the boy over. In a loud stage whisper he said, "I think that boy is cruising you."

Only when each of them, one by one, stole looks at me did I realize I was the boy.

"Never been cruised here," the beard whispered admiringly. "New York City Opera, yes. But never at the Met."

I turned and walked away as fast as I could. I hadn't been *cruising* the kid! I didn't cruise anybody; I was already attached. I'd only been studying the kid and feeling sorry for him.

I returned to my numbered space and tried to read the synopsis for Act Two. But Gregory's suede coat with a fleecy collar was still draped over the partition, proof that he'd be back. He was going to think I was hot for him. Damn conceited teenager. He'd been posing out there as if he expected somebody to take his picture. And what was he doing with that gaggle of older men anyway? Probably some sort of male courtesan.

The lights softly dimmed and Gregory still hadn't returned. I panicked, thinking I'd frightened him away. Poor kid. He didn't know what was going on. But while the orchestra was taking its bow, I felt him reappear. I heaved a sigh of relief and, then the annoying fear and curiosity started all over again.

This time the curtain rose on a bleak banquet hall decorated with shields. The program said there'd be a singing contest and I hoped the songs would be melodic enough to take my mind off Gregory. During a procession that I thought would keep his eyes on the stage, I looked at him again. His blond hair and pale face were as vague as fox-fire. There was a sudden glint of light in one eye that darted toward me. I quickly faced forward again, my heart pounding.

Dammit. Why was I feeling like this? I was obsessed with a shadow. Strangers had caught my eye and fantasy before, but only briefly, when I passed them on the street or saw them at the other end of a subway car. I'd never had to stand beside them through three acts of Wagner.

The singing contest started and I tried to focus on it. But the boy was like the famous pistol shot in the concert hall: His presence blew the opera away. The contestants seemed to be singing their songs, but these songs were as dull as sermons.

"How boring."

I turned.

It was Gregory who'd whispered. I heard him pull on his coat and saw him looking, not at me, but at the banquet hall. I faced the music again, as if I didn't care, and turned again in time to see him step back into the darkness, where he vanished.

I saw his shadow cross the seam of light that was the door. I watched the seam, waiting for it to wink open and shut and show that he'd finally gone. But the door stayed closed, for an infinite minute.

Was he still there? Was he waiting for me? Why the hell didn't he just leave?

There'd been so many missed opportunities in my life. I wanted to know if this were another.

The darkness snapped open and a blond head flashed across a red wall.

Seconds passed, as important and full as time in music, where the phrase that moves you most can be as brief as two heartbeats. Did he expect me to follow him? I wanted to follow, just to find out. Seconds gathered between me and my chances. The door had settled shut.

Tannhauser sang. My excitement began to subside and I'd be able to watch the opera in peace. Grabbing my coat, I raced out the door.

The lobby was red and deserted. The music behind me sealed itself up in the padded door and walls and I couldn't even hear my own footsteps as I hurried over the carpet to the railing. I looked down to see if the boy were on the stairs. I knew I was being a fool, but as soon as I was out in the silent light, I felt in full control of myself. I could choose to go home if I wanted; I hadn't enjoyed Wagner. Or I could choose to be foolish. There was adventure in being foolish, with no clear purpose in mind.

I saw the boy on the next level down, coming out toward the grand staircase from under my feet. I chose adventure.

I went down the stairs after him. When I reached the next level, he was already on the main floor. I wanted him to know I was here, and the carpeting still cushioned my steps, so I whistled a tune, the first one that came to mind. I swooped down the steps whistling, "The Ride of the Valkyries."

There was nobody else there but an attendant with an opera cape and broom, and the boy didn't look back to see where the whistling came from. He stood in front of the tall plate glass to button up his coat and smooth his hair. I saw my descent mirrored in the glass and the night outside, as if I were part of a high transparent mural. Gregory went out the door without waiting for me.

His indifference was a challenge. I had nothing to gain from this. I only wanted to talk to him, kick his indifference, perhaps throw him off guard by flirting with him. A conceited boy like Gregory needed to be thrown off his guard.

I was pulling on my coat as I hurried out the door into the cold, windy plaza. It was no good to whistle now, but my bootsteps on the pavement were audible enough. Gregory walked towards the street, beneath the bright arcade of the theater building on the right side of the plaza. We were alone in the plaza. I gained ground. Our steps echoed beneath the arcade, three of mine to every two of his.

Then, at the end of the arcade, Gregory stopped to read a poster.

I grinned excitedly as the distance closed. "Excuse me!"

He turned, without any hint of surprise or recognition.

I was terrified. My shout hung in my ears and I had to say something to give it a purpose. "Uh, you have any matches?"

The boy looked back at the ballet poster while he felt his pockets. "Terribly sorry. No."

"Perfectly okay. I don't have any cigarettes. For that matter, I don't even smoke!"

He nervously drew his head into his sheepskin collar. I'd broken his handsome repose. The need for public privacy here was so strong that just talking to a stranger could be an assault.

"Hey, didn't I see you at the opera tonight? Yes, I did!" I talked fast to get in as many blows as possible before he escaped.

"Probably," mumbled the boy, turned and walked away.

But I was right beside him. "Good first scene. In Venusberg. But after that, it failed to hold my interest. Do you get to the opera very often?"

The boy shook his head. He raced down a flight of stairs to the street, stopped at the curb and faced the traffic.

In a moment, I'd lose him. I had to give his shell one final hard kick. I stood in front of him and said the one thing I felt nobody had the right to say to a stranger. "I remember seeing you inside because you're so pretty. No, not just pretty. Beautiful."

But he didn't blush or groan. He didn't grimace and change the subject the way Corey did when I called him beautiful. He only turned his head, not out of shame but as if to give me a better look. Then he pretended to brush the compliment aside with a wiggle of his gloved fingers.

I was surprised. That sort of forwardness should've had him crawling out of his skin.

He glanced at the traffic, glanced at me again and looked bored. "I'm sorry. I'd love to talk. But I must be getting downtown. Which way are you headed?"

Was it an invitation? Opportunity was knocking in my ears. Opportunity for what, I didn't know, but I wasn't ready to release it yet.

"Downtown I guess. Yes, downtown. I wasn't planning to walk out halfway through Wagner, so I've got nothing else scheduled for the rest of—"

"I suppose we *could* share a cab," sighed Gregory.

He sounded reluctant, but I jumped at the chance. "Sure. Let's."

And with just a change in his stance, Gregory caused a cab to pull up in front of us. The back seat was huge and there was no chance of accidentally touching him. I'd never ridden in a cab in New York.

"Seventh Avenue and Tenth. Be in the left lane when you get there," said Gregory. For someone so young, he was remarkably at home in a cab.

We swung around a corner and the floodlit buildings and neon signs flew around me. There was a feeling of speed and space you never experienced on foot or in the subway. And a feeling of cost. I couldn't ignore the loud clicks of the meter up front.

"Oh, my name's Joel."

"You don't say."

"I'm a student at Columbia." I wanted to impress him, but Gregory only accepted it with a blasé nod. "Your name's Gregory, right?"

He nodded to that too, showing no surprise that a stranger knew his name.

"What do you do? Are you a student too or are you—"

"Does it matter?" he said wearily.

I told myself that I was riding downtown with Gregory only so I could continue needling him. But I couldn't concentrate, not with that damn meter ticking away. I had less than five dollars on me. And then it dawned on me that Gregory might not be gay. He sat coolly in the cab, oblivious to the possibility that I was pursuing him. I wasn't pursuing him, but I wanted him to think I was, but if he were straight, he wouldn't pick up on that and I'd seem like only an obnoxiously friendly stranger to him and not any kind of threat. What the hell was I doing anyway?

We raced through what looked like Times Square. It was too late to get out of it now. I resigned myself to enjoying this first ride in a taxi and wondered how I'd get home from wherever we were going.

"How far do you intend to go?" asked Gregory as he pulled his gloves back on.

"Oh, I'll just get out when you do. I can walk the rest of the way."

"Fine. Take the next left," he ordered the driver. "And stop halfway down the second block."

We passed Julius, where I'd been with Corey. That meant we were in the Village. I could find my way home from here.

"I'll take care of this," said Gregory as he pulled some bills out of his pocket. "I was going this far anyway. You don't have to thank me."

"Why thank you. Thank you very much," I said, combining gratitude with more needling. I followed him out of the cab and between the parked cars to the sidewalk. The buildings on this street were smaller and more eroded than the ones in our neighborhood. I was relieved to know I wasn't stranded in the middle of nowhere. "That's very kind of you," I said, as one last blow.

Another wiggle of gloved fingers. Gregory smoothed his hair, straightened his coat and gazed into space. "I'm stopping here for a quick drink. And you?"

I looked up. The sign said, The Ninth Circle Steakhouse, which sounded expensive and my adventure had gone on long enough. "I think I'll just mosey on home. It's been nice meeting you, Gregory."

Gregory looked straight at me. He tried to regain his repose while he pawed the sidewalk with a desert boot, then said snootily, "You don't want a drink before you go home?"

So he *was* interested. "I don't know. That opera made me sleepy." I could match blasé with blasé.

"I won't twist your arm. I just thought you looked thirsty. And this place is as good as any."

"Oh, all right. I guess I have time for one drink."

Gregory relaxed, then shrugged. He went up the steps and through the door as if it were only an accident that I was right behind him.

There was smoke inside, dark pine paneling and music. A fat thug sat at the door. A handful of old men conspired at the end of the bar by the window, but everyone else was my age or younger, and everyone was male. It was a gay bar. I'd been a fool to doubt my instincts about Gregory. The moosehead over the jukebox had a chiffon scarf in its antlers.

"You purchase your drinks here," said Gregory, pointing at the bar. "I have to check out something." And he strolled past the audience that lined the wall and down some stairs in the back.

I bought a bottle of beer and positioned myself against the wall to wait for Gregory. I assumed he was coming back. The wet label slid off the bottle and I realized how fidgety I was. It wasn't like being in Julius with Corey. There were lots of people here, but little talk. Only music and stares. I was nervous. A gangly redhead wearing platform shoes, a red football jersey and a sharktooth earring sashayed through the room; you could feel the network of stares tremble and snap, like a spider web strummed by a hand. Without Corey beside me, I couldn't help wondering if there were stares aimed at me.

So how had Corey done it? How do you begin to talk

to a stranger when both of you can't forget for a minute what it is that brought you there? Corey said he never went home with anyone unless he liked talking with them enough to sense that there was a possibility of love. Corey had risked love with six different people, fourteen times. He'd told me all about them, in bed after sex, when we were both satisfied and full of trust and could talk about pasts that hadn't included each other. The actor, the apprentice dock worker, the pansexual hippie, the student at Pace, et cetera: six people, fourteen times. All I had to offer was a history of misunderstood impulses, but I wasn't jealous of Corey. I envied him his time of promiscuity. It wasn't much, but it seemed like a beautiful excess compared to my past.

Gregory came back upstairs and went into the back of the room. He quickly scrutinized each face. Perhaps he was looking for me and had forgotten what I looked like.

How had Corey done it? I wondered. It seemed so complicated. I wanted to continue with this game, only to see if I could do what Corey had done.

Gregory walked towards me. He stopped a few feet away from me and stared, as if he'd never seen me before.

I was confused, but decided it was safe to walk over to him. "Hi," I said.

He smiled. I hadn't seen him smile all evening and he faced me now with a beautiful, flirtatious smile. "Hi there. How you doing tonight?" He didn't seem to know me and his smile was such a switch from his aloofness in the cab, I wondered if this were the same kid. Beautiful boys tended to blur together.

"Gregory, right?"

"Uh huh." He looked painfully edible.

I joked away my confusion with, "Dress circle, Ninth Circle. We seem to be running in circles tonight."

He looked me up and down and stared into my eyes. His eyes covered me.

"Ninth Circle? Is that the circle of the sodomites in Dante?" I asked.

"You from Texas?"

"No. Why do you ask?"

"Your little cowboy necktie." He reached up and ticklishly diddled my tie. "That's real cute. Makes you look like you just got off the bus."

His condescension annoyed me, but the feel of his fingers at my throat left me helpless. "Oh, well, uh, yippee-ky-yay," I said. "You look cute yourself, in that sheepherder's coat. You from sheep country?"

"You *did* get off the bus," he said with a coy smile. "This coat is a genuine Antartex. Want to feel it?"

We were antagonistically flirting with each other.

Gregory looked around while I felt his coat. "Circle's certainly full of trolls tonight," he sighed. "I'm so sick of the bar scene."

Then why did you come? I thought, but kept it to myself.

"No, nothing going on around here. I wonder if I should go ahead and go home."

Panic! And hope?

"You live near here?" I asked.

"I'm watching an apartment for a friend who lives near here. Stunning apartment," he said with a shrug. "I mean, it would seem stunning to someone who'd just gotten off the bus. I enjoy it as a change of milieu, nothing more."

"What's so stunning about it?"

"Come to think of it, you probably won't appreciate it."

"I can be very appreciative," I insisted.

He tossed his head and flipped his hair back and looked me in the eye. "I can't describe it in words. I would have to—"

The front door squeaked open and Gregory turned to look. In walked a man and a longhaired boy, in matching blue tuxes. Gregory checked them out and turned back to me.

"I guess I *could* show it to you," he sighed. "I'm not doing anything else right now."

"Sure. I'd like to see your friend's apartment. I'm curious about New York apartments." He was inviting me home with him? I was so surprised I wanted to postpone it long enough to get used to the idea. And he seemed so reluctant. "Let me just finish my beer. You don't want a beer while you're here?"

"You don't want anymore." Gregory pulled the bare bottle from my hand. His fingers were very small, soft and cool. "Come along if you're coming. I might change my mind."

It was opportunity. It was an experience. The smallness of his fingers excited me. I went with him.

He said nothing while we walked and, trying to make conversation, I said, "Oh, my name's Joel Scherzenlieb," thinking he might've forgotten.

But all Gregory said was, "Okay."

We didn't even shake hands, which I found odd. Shouldn't you at least shake hands with someone you've invited home for sex? Maybe there wasn't going to be any sex. Maybe he was only teasing me, just as I'd been teasing him back at the opera. I told myself I was going with him only to find out what his real intentions were. I wanted to have sex with him, but there was so much confusion and frustration mixed up with my desire it felt more like curiosity and less like lust. I was in full control of myself.

"Here," and I followed the little bastard into an apartment building whose glass and steel facade jumped out at you on this street of brownstones. The lobby was all mirrors and I couldn't help noticing how beautiful Gregory looked in contrast to me. Gregory avoided looking at me, even in the elevator.

I wasn't going to be made a fool by him. Even if he were beautiful, he was smaller than I was, more frail. If he had invited me home just to tease me, I would surprise him by pouncing and doing what I pleased with him, or doing enough to let him know who controlled the situation. But if he had invited me home for sex, had assumed that his looks were enough to get me into bed with him and that friendliness and simple courtesy were unnecessary, I could surprise him there too, by smirking at his advances, turning my back on him and leaving. I didn't need sex with supercilious strangers; I had sex at home.

Gregory unlocked a door on the fifth floor and we entered the apartment.

My first impression was that nobody had moved in yet. There was only a broad, glossy wood floor. But I saw a swollen black sofa at one end of the room and a chrome stereo with records jackets littered around it. The room was lit like an art gallery, with little spotlights along the ceiling aimed at the white walls. Only there was nothing on the walls, until I saw the black-and-white mural behind me. It was a giant photograph of a ruggedly handsome man in a perfect raincoat. I couldn't understand how anyone could live with nothing to look at but a picture that reminded me of an advertisement for raincoats.

Gregory hung up his coat without offering to take mine. "*That's* my friend," he said proudly. "I'll bet you never dreamed you'd be seeing the inside of *his* apartment."

He seemed to be referring to the advertisement. "Who is he?" I asked.

"Benedict?" said Gregory, expecting me to recognize him.

"Benedict who?"

"No who. Just Benedict. Benedict of Ford. Don't pretend you don't recognize his face, even if you don't know his name."

"Looks familiar," I admitted, but he looked like only any one of those unreal handsome faces that stare at you from magazines, billboards and the sides of buses. Those faces never really appealed to me because I didn't think they belonged to real people. "And this is his apartment."

"Actually, it's one of his lovers' apartments. But his lover lives in Tehran and Benedict's away on a shoot in the Yucatan, so I have it all to myself. I practically live here anyway." Coming home had made Gregory very chatty. "I'm like a brother to him and he doesn't like to go anywhere without me. The two of us really look great together, don't you think?" He stood in front of the mural. "He says he's going to arrange a photo session for me, which might lead to something with Ford. Who knows? Be a lot better than anything I could get with a degree from Parsons."

"That guy's gay?" I said, pointing at the poster.

Gregory cocked his head and smacked his lips pityingly. "Are you from New Jersey?"

"No. Switzerland."

"Sure," he said and, shaking his head, walked past me into what must've been the kitchen.

The apartment confused me and I had trouble remembering what it was I'd planned to do. I couldn't imagine myself pouncing on Gregory with his lover's picture staring into every corner of the room. And if Gregory had a lover, why had he brought me home? This was one of those cases where lover seemed like the right word, with its implications of someone keeping somebody, and even Gregory's lover had a lover above him. Where in the food chain did that put me?

I went into the kitchen where I found Gregory looking into a refrigerator that had nothing in it but four cartons of yogurt and a bottle of champagne. "You were right. Stunning apartment. Thanks for showing it to me."

"I still haven't shown you the bedroom," he said, looking at me as if he sensed I was trying to say good-bye. "As soon as I decide what flavor my mood wants, I'll show the bedroom."

"How about a bathroom? I'd appreciate seeing a bathroom right now." I thought I should use the toilet before the long subway ride home.

It was a difficult bathroom to think or even pee in. Everything was a glossy chocolate-brown and there were shelves and shelves of cologne. On the back of the toilet was a glass bowl with a single stalk like a crab claw stuck in it. One end of the green claw had burst open to reveal feather-like flowers inside. I focused on the wall and tried to think of something else.

When I stepped out, the first thing I saw was Benedict, glaring into the room with one hand on his hip, firmly asking me to leave. I heard the sound of a television from around the corner and followed it, assuming I'd find Gregory there and could tell him I was going. It was the bedroom, as spare as the rest of the apartment, with nothing but a television, a potted palm tree and a huge, low bed with a black leather bedspread, where Gregory lay naked.

I had to blink, because he didn't behave naked. He'd propped his head up on some cushions and was eating yogurt while he watched television. He had his legs spread apart and one knee raised and he was definitely naked. It lay in a puff of light-brown hair.

Without looking up, Gregory said, "'Modesty Blaise.' If I'd known this was on tonight, I wouldn't have let Ben's friends drag me to the opera. You should sit down and watch it. You might learn something."

There was no chair, so I timidly sat on the bed. The floor was strewn with enough clothes for a dozen people, but there was only one body opened on the bed. It was pure nude, with no dark hair to exaggerate the curves of the torso, just a faint down that was visible only where a tiny hair or two reflected the light. His stomach muscles formed a soft washboard and the thigh that lay flat had a long, shallow dimple in it.

I took off my coat, very slowly, as if he were a deer glimpsed in the woods and any sudden move might make him disappear. The phrase of music that moves you most can move you to utter stillness, and my mind was stilled even as my body changed. I slowly lowered my coat to the floor and waited for Gregory to finish his yogurt.

He rolled away from me to set the spoon and empty carton on the other side of the bed, his bottom sticking to the leather bedspread, then unpeeling from it, round cheeks rosy where they'd been sticking. He rolled back again, but stayed where he'd been, in the middle of the bed, without coming any closer to me.

Was he waiting for me to make the first move, or was he actually watching television? The apartment was very warm; perhaps this was only what he wore when he went to sleep. Now and then he giggled at the movie, as if he could follow it. If I were in his position right now, I'd have an erection—and twisted inside my pants, I did— but Gregory's cock lay lightly on its cloud of teased curls, a quiescent shade of pink, its head tucked back a tad in a collar of rumpled skin.

Then he shifted his hips, as if there were any need to call attention to himself there.

I decided to touch him.

I reached out with one hand, covered half the distance between us, then half the distance that remained, then half that, until I found my hand resting on his stomach.

He showed no surprise. His breathing didn't even change and he kept his eyes locked on the television.

I began moving my hand. I grazed the edge of his light-brown cloud. I moved a little deeper into it. His cock gained color and lost its loose collar.

Gregory suddenly looked down at himself, then turned and looked at me. "You don't want to wait until after the movie?" He sounded fretful.

I took hold of him and it stiffened.

"Oh. All right," he sighed. "If you like." And he settled back, but with his head still propped forward on the cushions.

I knelt over him, my work boots sticking off the bed. I used my other hand to stroke his chest and nipples. I bent down to kiss him. If handling his cock couldn't get him started, a kiss should, and I wanted him to kiss me with that mouth he was so reluctant to use in talking to me.

His eyes were wide open and he saw me coming. He turned away. "No. I'm not into that. But please keep doing what you're doing. I like that."

I continued, thinking it would only take a little more time, but he had a full erection now and he still seemed to be watching his movie. I wanted to go down on him, but he had refused to kiss me and I couldn't take him in my mouth without feeling I was humiliating myself. I was frustrated, but too aroused to do anything but obey him. I used my free hand to untie my boots so I could get my clothes off and at least feel him against me. One of the laces was knotted and I needed both hands. I let go of him.

"No, please. Don't stop. Feels so good. Oh yeah. Just keep it coming. Nice and easy. That's it." He finally looked at me, not out of gratitude, but because there was a commercial. My irritation must've been visible, because Gregory smiled pityingly, bit his lip, then reached up with both hands to undo my belt and fly. He yanked everything down and my cock sprang out. I could feel air all around it, and then his slim fingers. "Feels good, doesn't it? Yeah, nice and slow. It's not a race."

And for a few seconds, it felt good enough to seem to have been worth all the frustration. But with nothing to feel but the smooth run of his fingers and the trivial slip and tug of my own hand on him, I knew it wasn't going to take long. I hurriedly unbuttoned my shirt—I had to feel him against my skin—but I couldn't get my shirt off with one hand, only pull the front of my undershirt over my head so that it stretched across the back of my neck like a yoke. My thighs were still bound together by my pants. Our strokes were getting quicker. I shoved my pants and underpants down to my knees and scuttled forward to lie on top of him.

But it was too late. I was there. I closed my eyes and

gave in. It was all in my cock and no place else, but surprisingly good there. With nothing else to feel, I could even catch a faint tickle like urination.

Gregory had turned away and was gritting his teeth. He looked down at the couple of white dotted lines that crossed the black leather and ended on him. He made a face and wiped his hand on my thigh. "Very good. Now me." And he flexed his ass to get me going again.

It had all been in my cock and, now that that was gone, Gregory's beauty meant nothing to me. He closed his eyes and jiggled passively while I pumped him. Without lust, the act was as absurd as throttling a chicken neck.

"Okay. Tighter now. Put your other hand on my left hip. Yes, that's right. We're getting there."

The little bastard. This wasn't real sex. It was only masturbation by proxy. He thought he was too good to do it to himself. His hands lay at his sides, never touching himself or me.

"Faster now. Yes. On its way. Squeeze my hip. Okay. Watch me. Are you watching? Here it goes."

He sharply inhaled a few times, as if he were going to sneeze. Which was all that happened. The chicken neck tensed in my hand and sneezed three times.

I tossed it aside and turned my hand around to use his stomach as a rag.

"No. Don't." He reached behind him to a narrow shelf above the bed and brought down a canister of premoistened napkins. He passed me one and took out a handful for himself.

I wiped off my hands without looking at him. I knew it was wrong for me to hate him. It wasn't just the badness of the sex. Now that I had had my orgasm, it was difficult to imagine getting anything else from sex. Beneath all my subterfuges of combativeness and idle curiosity, this was what I had wanted from him all night. But now that I'd had it, it seemed like an utter waste of energy and feeling. Sex had never seemed like such a piffle.

Gregory came to life for a minute while he busily

165

dabbed at his stomach and groin and various spots on the bedspread. He stuffed the napkins into his yogurt container and held the container at me, so I could put mine in without him having to touch it. Then he lay back, raised his knee again and faced the television. "Oh good. We haven't missed the scene with Monica Vitti and the shoes." As if nothing had happened.

I stumbled to my feet and pulled up my pants. "I guess I'll be going now."

Gregory looked straight at me. "Going? Why?"

I untangled my undershirt and pulled it back over my head. "It's late and I have to be getting home."

"No. You don't have to go home," he chided. "There's nothing you have to do tonight."

"I have to sleep."

"Sleep here. I get up early. I was going to go to sleep when this movie was over."

He'd already proved to himself he was attractive enough to make an ass out of me; what else could he want? I sat down again, but only to retie my boot. "No," I said firmly. "I need to sleep in my own bed."

"Aw, come on. You're already here. Why not spend the night?"

I continued to tighten my laces.

Gregory had to take a deep breath before he could say, "*Please*. It's cold outside and . . . I don't want to sleep alone tonight. Please. As a favor to me."

"Sorry." I didn't know what to make of this. I'd assumed he'd want me to go and it should've pleased me to have him change like this and plead with me. Instead, it made me feel guilty. I picked my coat up off the floor.

"And it'll be good for you too. Big, comfortable bed. Hey, if it's this movie, I can turn it off. I've already seen it six times." He watched me put on my coat and became desperate. "If you spend the night, I'll let you fuck me. First thing tomorrow morning, I promise."

That made me queasy. I felt like I would never want to have sex again in my life, much less with him. He didn't want to be kissed, but he'd let himself be fucked? I felt queasily sorry for him and didn't know what to tell him. "Uh, thanks. But I really have to be going. It's not you. It's just that my lover doesn't know I'm out and I have to be getting home to him."

"Uh uh. You never said anything about a lover."

I disliked using that word for Corey, but it was the only one Gregory would understand. "I have one. And he's probably waiting up for me right now."

"So give him a call and tell him a lie or something."

"No," I said. "I can't do that." I stopped worrying about Gregory.

He made his eyes wide for me, a final plea. Then he sank back and groaned at the ceiling. "Okay. I've let you know how I felt about you. If you want to be like all the others, go ahead. I'm not going to whine and plead with you. All these neurotic people who've got this hang-up about spending the night," he hissed. "All they care about is *sex*. I've wasted a whole evening on you, and now I'm going to have to sleep alone anyway? Just leave. If you can't do me one little favor, stop torturing me and just go."

He was so adamant he made me believe I was the one in the wrong. "I'm sorry. I really have to be going. But that was fun," I lied. "Thanks. Hope to see you around, Gregory. Good night."

He folded his arms and pouted at the television.

Only when I was out in the hall did I remember how he had treated me. Nevertheless, I still felt guilty as I rode down in the elevator. And sad. And stupid. Outside, it was snowing. Rain would've been more appropriate for what I was feeling, but there was a hushed fall of white dots drifting beneath the street lights, dots that melted away the instant they touched the black pavement. It was my first New York snow and I looked straight up as it fell out of the darkness.

I tried to get my bearings. I walked west, into the neighborhood of bars where the taxi had dropped us off.

It was after midnight and men were everywhere, alone and in pairs, wandering in that steady fall of white that failed to accumulate into anything. Without looking at them, I knew they were gay. I wanted to cry out to them, "Don't. It's not worth it." I drew my head deeper into my collar and walked on until I found Seventh Avenue and walked down toward Christopher Street and the sub-way station. There were more men now, and more snow. The tiny lights of the World Trade Center were blurred by the curtain of snow. Wet flakes landed on my face and hair and seemed to fall right through me. It was as though I didn't have a body anymore. I was so depressed I seemed to be only a damp sadness swaddled in clothes.

I tried to distract myself by clucking over Gregory's coldness. He was the one who'd been the neurotic all evening, not me. I'd been perfectly justified in leaving. I tried to dispel my low spirits by telling myself I should be grateful he was such an easy person to abandon. I never wanted to see him again. There'd be no consequences. I mean, what if it had been wonderful? What if Gregory had been someone I wanted to know better? What if sex with him had been far better than sex ever was with Corey? And it occurred to me again that I had betrayed Corey.

It hadn't occurred to me during the pursuit or the sex. I thought of it only when I was feeling so depressed that the possibility of guilt couldn't make me feel any worse.

The subway station was painfully bright and full of murmuring men who'd just met each other. I stood away from them, at one end of the platform where gypsum icicles hung from a crack in the ceiling and the bare light bulb looked feeble and grey in the cold.

I tried to push all my sadness into the idea of guilt. But I was familiar with guilt—was I ever—and this didn't really feel like guilt. I mean, it had been so nothing, I couldn't bring myself to feel guilty about it. It was more like the sad stupidity you feel as a child when you've spent all your money on a toy that doesn't work. I had walked out on one of the masterpieces of Western music for something that had resulted in nothing but a soulful moldiness. If it had been good, then I'd have something to be guilty about. I'd made a mistake, but it had nothing to do with Corey.

I rode uptown in a subway car whose passengers looked as mournful as I did. Our street looking surprisingly like home to me, even with the coat of snow that was beginning to collect on the roofs of parked cars and the sooty cornices. I was happy to be going home to Corey. I wanted to tell him what had happened. I would tell him. He'd understand. He knew that I loved him and that a mistake like this had nothing to do with us. It would be as if we were having one of our usual conversations after sex, even though the sex had been an hour ago, and I'd had it without him.

The apartment was perfectly quiet. Ed was away at work and lights were on only in the kitchen, and our bedroom.

I walked into our room. The bulging, pockmarked plaster walls, the paper globe around the light on the high ceiling, my Mostly Mozart poster, Corey's wall map of the Eastern Shore, our deal desk stacked with books and, because there was no closet, the banged-up wardrobe with the anti-war sticker slapped on it by previous tenants; people lived here. I was home. A comfortable mattress lay flat on the wood floor and on the blankets lay Corey, reading a book and fully dressed.

"Hello there, Boy. Enjoy your *Potemkin?*"

Corey smiled, closed his book, kissed and petted me hello. "You should've gone," he said excitedly. "Had a very interesting twist this time."

"They played David Bowie songs while they showed it?"

"Somebody had snipped out the entire Odessa steps sequence. The scene with the baby carriage? So everybody started shouting, 'You skipped a reel! Where's the steps? We want our steps!' They turned on the lights, figured out that somebody'd run off with the whole scene from their print, and we sat there for fifteen minutes, reconstructing the Odessa steps from memory. Everybody. Real audience participation. There were people there who knew the thing shot by shot. But they weren't pious about it. They made jokes. This one older woman started mimicking all the faces in it. Was very funny. I was sorry when we finished and had to go back to just sitting there and watching the rest of the movie."

"Yes. You can get tired of being only a spectator," I said. Should I tell him?

"So how was your Wagner?"

"Nice beginning, but then it became slow and...long and..."

"Must've been long. It's almost one o'clock. But it was worth it?"

"It had its moments. But I am glad to be home." I took off my coat and shoes to lie down beside him. "There was this terrific scene at the beginning where..."

I only had to tell him about that first scene, because Corey was eager to talk about his evening. He had truly enjoyed it, not just the film, but the people there. They were of all ages and a variety of backgrounds, much more diverse than the sullen ex-student radicals Corey was familiar with from socialist groups here and in Virginia. There had been whole families there, even a socialist grandmother, and Corey made it sound as domestic and normal as a church picnic. "I'm going back next Friday and you should come with me, Shirts. You'd get a kick out of it."

"Maybe," I said. "Next week's *Don Carlos,* but maybe."

"I don't want to force you. But sometime. Okay?"

How like Corey: his pleasure in a human atmosphere, his insistence on giving me plenty of room. No, it would only be cruel to disturb his contentment and trust by telling him what had happened tonight. And I hadn't really

170

done anything with Gregory; I hadn't even taken off my shoes with him.

"Two more pages. I just want to finish this chapter," said Corey.

I snuggled into his chest and asked him to scratch my back while he read.

He seemed as real to me as a house, and Gregory as unreal and inconsequential as a dream. I decided to keep my mistake to myself, a private, inconsequential, bad dream.

We made love the next morning. It was Saturday and we had a long, leisurely breakfast in the diner around the corner. I enjoyed weekends and the chance to have breakfast with Corey. We nosed around in bookstores that afternoon. Corey looked both intellectual and hunky in a bookstore and I had to restrain myself to keep from hugging him.

Monday, I finished *Lolita* to start the novel about Italian communists that Corey had been pushing. Corey was reading Gramsci, but he knew better than to recommend anything but novels to me.

By Wednesday, I had enough distance to think calmly about what had happened on Friday. It seemed rather comic now: the blind pursuit, the games of indifference, the neurotic restraint of the sex. The sex seemed especially funny: our only handshake, one that had taken a detour through a pair of genitals. I tried it with Corey that night, but his hand was as familiar as my own and we ended it all over each other.

I was alone all day Thursday. Ed spent the day with his mother; Corey went to Brooklyn and didn't come back until late that night. I started thinking about Gregory, without the sex. I was idly curious about him. I mean, what kind of person was he to have been like that? How old was he? I decided he had to be older than eighteen. I didn't want to see him again, but I was curious about his life. Who was he? Was he typical of the gays I glimpsed on the subway or at the opera or of the staring throngs I'd seen that night at the Ninth Circle? Was sex with Corey *always* better than the sex these people had?

Friday night, Corey went to his West End meeting and I left for the opera. On the trip downtown, an opera played inside me: a singing of nerves and an excited soar in the orchestra pit of my stomach.

Standing room again, in a fashion.

I stood at a rakish angle against a black wall in Julius.

Not the Ninth Circle, where I might have run into Gregory, but Julius, where the volume of conversation and the relics from its days as a speakeasy—the photographs of Thirties celebrities and racehorses on the sagging wall, the sawdust on the floor, the framed citation from Walter Winchell over the bar—made it easier to pretend you weren't there for sex.

I was curious. And it wouldn't hurt. Just one more time. I knew there was a good chance I wouldn't meet anyone and that nothing would happen tonight. But I hoped something would happen.

No music compared with the excitement I felt when I contacted someone with my eyes, received a smile and fearfully crossed the room to speak to him. The fear was the best thing about it. Overcoming fear each time was a glorious accomplishment. I loved making the first move. And it was fun to remake myself each time I tried to make someone new.

"Hello. How you doing tonight? Oh, I'm fine too. Joel. And you? Come here very often, Ted? Kind of deserted this early. I think we're the most interesting people here. Oh, I'm an assistant stage manager with the opera. And you?"

I knew exactly what I was doing. I wasn't fooling myself. I had made an art out of fooling myself in the past, but I knew I was in the wrong here. And knowing you're bad deepens an experience, makes it more interesting.

172

Great Expectations
Lolita
Tannhauser
*Gregory—MM. Prettiness corrupts, absolute prettiness
corrupts absolutely.*
Bread and Wine
Don Carlos
*Ted—good K, bad S, med student. Like a medical
examination. Literary. Calls me boy Mme. Bovary.*
Madame Bovary
"The Conformist"—with Corey
Rigoletto
*Topher—Southerner at Pratt. MM, S, no K. Loves
Fellini. Bathtub in kitchen. Cat named Hotpoint.
Long ride to Brooklyn.*

That winter I kept a notebook where I listed books read, operas heard, movies seen. It gave me a feeling of accomplishment when I could finish something and write it off with its name. I couldn't resist the temptation to include the names of the people I'd slept with. I added a few details to jog my memory, but kept the details cryptic in case Corey stumbled on the notebook. I could always tell him they were people I'd met at the Hungarian Pastry Shop. And I noted the operas I skipped, in case Corey's memory was better than mine.

I was only being prudent, not guilty. My Friday nights

had nothing to do with Corey; they didn't take away from the fact that I loved him. And they didn't hurt our sex. They did the opposite. I was afraid at first that I'd be bringing these new bodies home with me, that there'd be even more people infesting Corey when I made love with him. But Corey was never more solidly Corey than on those nights between Fridays. I was never more keenly aware of how Corey's shoulders fit my hugs, how the room of his mouth fit my mouth or how thickly his bones were padded with Corey. I couldn't feel bad about that.

And he had done this himself, fourteen times. Whenever I worried too much about the rightness of it, I told myself I'd do it only fourteen times, until my experience matched Corey's. It was only accidental that Corey had his experience before we found each other, and I was getting mine afterwards. Corey had the benefits of college and a bit of sexual experimentation. I could afford only the sex. I joked with myself that I was going to night school. But it really was educational. I learned about French literature, Italian movies, Manhattan rents and what other people did for a living. I wondered if I should spend a couple of my fourteen times with women, just to broaden my experience. But I didn't know how one went about meeting women in this city, and guys were so available. I learned to avoid the Gregorys.

Sentimental Education
Radio City Christmas Show — w/Corey
Tosca
Matthew — fat, friendly actor involved in project that will make him rich sometime next week. Much K and S. Cockroaches. Many cockroaches. Rabbits.

K was code for kissing, and there were enough people who disliked it to make kissing worthy of comment. "Rabbits" was not code for anything, but two very real rabbits named Flopsy and Mopsy who limped loose

174

around the apartment while their owner and I had sex. It was odd glancing over the notebook afterwards and seeing these encounters summed up so briefly. But once you have them home and undressed, strangers only have personalities of what they'll do or won't do in bed.

Maurice (the novel, not a person)
The Magic Flute (I told Corey I loved it so much I was seeing it again)
Brad—Black bank teller. Wants F but settles for S.
Skin like silk stockings.
Another Country

Dear Joel,   *Jan. 1975*

I should have written sooner, but with sick Gramma and chickens sick too, I never seem to have the time or desire. Decided I better drop you this note to at least wish you a very belated Merry Xmas before more time passes.

The winter's been miserable and seed and fertilizer prices threaten to go through the roof for the spring. At least there's no lines again at the gas stations. The Co-op is not renewing the lease on the land this year, but I'm going to take out a loan and plant it myself. I don't mean to bring up a sore subject, dear, but if you haven't found work by the spring, there's plenty for you to do down here.

Thank you for the presents. You're right, there's nothing I need right now (short of miracles and a tractor), but the mysteries for Gram were a nice thought. No, I don't know if she's read them, but I don't think it matters. The living room is her room now and she sits there all hours smiling into an open book. She was "reading" your German grammar the other day. But she seems content. I miss her advice and criticism, but she's as content as a baby and we can't begrudge her that. Thank God for Medicare.

Books and opera seem to be all that's on your mind right now, Joel, and while I have nothing against the arts, I really think you should be doing something. Recession or not, there must be jobs up there, if only you set your mind to finding one. I don't want to sound like a nagging parent, but New York must be awfully boring without a job.

Things are tight, as you know, so I send you only my love and best wishes. If you write your sister, please let her know I'm mad as hops at her for her not writing. Not a peep since she saw you in Switz. I feel I'm barking at the moon when I write her. Your father sent me a large photo of himself and his resume. I don't know if it's the stinker's idea of a Xmas present or if he's asking me for a job.

Take care, dear. Say hello to your friend for me. Do you ever hear from that little theater gal you were seeing? Tardy Merry Xmas and a Happy New Year.

Love, Mom X

The X that made her sound like a Black Muslim was her symbol for a kiss. I wrote Mom X at least once a month, guiltily. I had a better understanding now of Liza's paranoia about Catherine and Gram. It had been different when I was down there, when I had seen Mom and Gram every week, grown accustomed to Gram's illness and seen there was little I could do for her, except visit her. But now that I was away, I could think about Gram as she'd been before the strokes, and her condition became strange to me again, painful. Someone had died, without really dying. I felt sorry and guilty whenever I thought of her, then guilty for not thinking of her more frequently. There was nothing I could do with my guilt except write to Catherine, and tell myself I should go home to help in the spring.

Liza wasn't writing to me, either. The Christmas card they sent, addressed to me and Corey, had been written by Kearney. I assumed Liza was busy with her daughter and marriage.

Corey joined the West End Marxists. He grew accustomed to the idea we could have independent lives without our life together being thrown into question. He was surprised and pleased one Sunday when I stood with him on the windy corner of Broadway and 110th, collecting signatures for something—I could be more forward about it than he was—but he didn't expect me to make a habit of it. His sole worry about me was that I was still on unemployment.

The green checks continued to arrive in the mail all winter. My list grew. I read novels with the tipsy, grinning alertness of someone undressing their first partner, and approached people in bars with the intellectual pleasure of a reader searching for a title he had only heard about.

> *The Red and the Black*
> *La Forza del Destino*
> *Saul—D.C. lawyer, midtown Hilton, Jewish, poppers,*
> *F! Room service snack and invitation to visit him in*
> *D.C. but he leaves for baths when I go home.*
> *Crime and Punishment*
> *Ragged Dick*

Ragged Dick was a play.

A ticket came in the mail one day, accompanied by a note scrawled in red pencil: "Son, thought you might like to see how the old man's progressed." No explanation, no return address or phone number. The address of the theater printed on the ticket was a side street in the village. So Jake was in New York.

And my first reaction was to be indignant that he'd sent only one ticket, as if Corey didn't count and I lived alone. He knew about me and Corey. Catherine had told him, out of anger, as proof of how he'd ruined his son by not sending me to college. Catherine had been so angry after Jake's announcement she wasn't always logical, and it had been several months before she learned to accept Corey as my "friend." But Jake knew about us and had even referred to "your European honeymoon" in his last card, which meant Bertie must've written to him. I hated to have him mocking us like that, but I hated it more when he ignored Corey's existence.

Corey wasn't at all offended. "You haven't seen each other in almost three years. He probably wants some time alone with you."

"I don't even know if he wants to see me. He wants me to see *him*. And his *Ragged Dick!* Which sounds like a live sex act. Don't look at me like that, Boy. It's only my father. It's not like this is someone I care about, one way or the other. It just bothers me he didn't include you. I'm tempted not to even go to this thing."

But I went, alone. I was curious—calmly, grudgingly curious. And I had nothing to fear from seeing him again.

It was the first week of March, but there was still snow heaped along the curbs and deep pools of black water trapped at the street corners. The theater was in a large clammy basement on Grove Street. Behind the woman who took my ticket was a plasterboard wall covered with photographs, and a photograph of Jake. He wore a tight, calibrated smile in a face that was unnaturally sharp and in focus, even his pores in focus. He was surrounded by younger faces just as unnatural, but those people belonged to their faces, while Jake's looked like a mask. I began to remember the person who'd worn that mask. I waited for his photograph to wink at me. It had been easy enough for me to joke about Jake when my only contact with him were his postcards, but now I was going to see him again. I made fun of my confusion by telling myself I should've brought rotten eggs to this play.

The play began. Jake walked out on stage in a loose black suit, arguing with someone in a passionate fury I'd never heard from him in real life. He looked smaller than I remembered him, but maybe that was only because the actor opposite him was so fat. His hair was dyed black and he had a slash of black make-up under each eye. He fumed about his place in history. It was five minutes before I realized *Ragged Dick* was another Watergate satire, and that Jake was playing Nixon.

Except for the hair receding over his temples, he looked nothing like Nixon; he made no attempt to sound or move like Nixon. He sounded like Jake with a temper, and moved like an upset businessman. Everyone else in the cast clowned shamelessly, but Jake remained perfectly serious, as if his Nixon were the one man who wasn't in on the joke. I wanted to think it was bad acting, but he still exuded a subtle authority and you couldn't help feeling he knew exactly what he was doing. He was trying to make you feel sorry for Nixon. I resisted. Like everyone else, I'd enjoyed hating Nixon for the past year and a half, but hatred gets old. It was difficult to keep up.

I had admired my father for the longest time, up until the day he palmed me off on my mother. And even then I couldn't hate him cleanly. He was my father; he did important work in the world. He wasn't James Bond or anything like that, but he selflessly gathered intelligence for our country. Even Catherine had to respect Jake when he had the C.I.A. behind him. When he showed up at the farm and loitered there, the habit of respect was still strong enough to choke my love for Corey, for a time. It was only after the night I saw the light that I heard about Jake's grand announcement: his fond farewell to government service. He'd been wanting to quit for a long time, had been saving up for it for two years, but hadn't known what else he could do with his life, until *Marat/Sade*. Even when I heard all that, I couldn't hate him. I was too much in love to want to hate anyone. And, after all this time, Jake's behavior finally made sense. He'd only been saving money, cutting expenses, one of which was his son. It was almost a relief to learn it was something so crude and simple.

But here he was tonight, gnashing his teeth and cursing a tape recorder. I couldn't pretend, like people did with Nixon, that I'd distrusted the man all along. I didn't want to hate Jake now. Hatred made him too important. But what did that leave me with?

I stayed in my seat when the play was over. I wanted to leave, but knew I shouldn't. I went down front and asked a stagehand if there were a back door to the dressing rooms. No, the only way out was through the theater. I wouldn't put it past Jake to invite me down here and then quietly slip out the back. He hated scenes.

Actors came out and departed. Then Jake came out, head bent down, looking more alone and preoccupied than the others. He wore a turtleneck and a Greek fisherman's cap.

I waited for him to see me. When he didn't, when he kept walking and didn't even look for me, I panicked and called out, "Jake!"

He looked up. His face snapped to attention. "Joel? That's right. I plumb forgot. Lad! How you doing?"

He wasn't Nixon now. He was definitely my father. I cursed myself for calling out while I let Jake shake my hand.

"Slipped my mind it was for tonight, the ticket I sent you. Wasn't sure you would make it. Uh, short notice and all. But you came. Great. Thanks for coming."

"Was curious," I told him.

"Yes? Was hoping you might be." He looked vaguer than his photograph, larger than he'd looked on stage. "So?" He nodded at the stage. "What did you think? Not much of a script, I admit. Shallow. Full of cheap shots."

"I didn't like the play. But I thought you were okay."

"Yes? Really? No, you're just saying that to be polite."

Why couldn't he leave it at that? "No. You were interesting. You were trying to make people pity Nixon, which was different."

"Just . . . pity?" he asked worriedly, and thought about it. "Hmmmm. What I'm aiming for is sympathy. Something the director and I worked out. He assumed, because of my age, I would identify with Tricky Dicky. Ho ho. Nothing could be further from the truth. But he does have a point. There's a little Nixon in each of us. If you could break through the defensive derision, you'd have a great American archetype. Should be the plummiest role an actor could have today. A cross between Willy Loman and King Lear? Mark my words, ten years from now, when this scapegoat business is forgotten, a great actor is going to give us a Nixon who'll move audiences to tears."

It annoyed me that my idle remark could release so much chatter from him. He seemed to think he was talking to a friend. And he spoke with such childish exuberance, without a trace of his old irony. Irony had made him seem like he knew far more than what he told you, but now he told everything and it was nonsense. His hair was still dyed dark for Nixon and he wore jeans. He looked like an old liberal.

I fought back by ignoring his speech. "How long you been in New York? I thought you were still in California."

"Long story. Came back East, oh, two months ago? You have to be anywhere, lad?"

"Is it that long a story?"

He missed my sarcasm. "No. Not long at all. It's just I haven't had dinner yet and wanted to grab something. You're welcome to join me."

I was still curious. I wanted to see who he had become, and who he might be to me now. "Sure. I've got nothing else planned."

Out on the street, Jake told about his decision to come to New York. California was nice, but it was all commercials and extra-work for television, with none of the intellectual charge of the New York theater scene. His agent—a former colleague—put him in touch with the Off-Off Broadway people who were doing *Ragged Dick*. The show was Equity but the pay was miniscule. He was taking classes at Herbert Berghof and trying to get into one taught by Stella Adler. He was staying in a loft in Soho with another old C.I.A. colleague, a man who'd quit over Vietnam and now wrote pulp spy novels.

"You'd be surprised over all the little ins I have. There's this bohemian network of former operatives, old boys like myself who've bacheloored themselves for the sake of the company. And I'm sure my resume gets the response it does because I had the gumption to include both the O.S.S. and 'Forty-nine to Seventy-one, work with a Federal agency whose name cannot be disclosed, Zaire, Angola, Thailand, Cambodia.' People call you in just to see what a former C.I.A. man looks like."

I remembered a time when I could fawn all over Jake in hopes of being let into his life like this. Now he probably spoke to anyone like this. The idea hurt me.

"I don't have to tell you how much I've enjoyed the turn of events in Angola. They've approached me twice, begging me to come back and work with them. Gave me no end of pleasure to tell them they could jump in the lake. If Kissinger and his stooges hadn't ignored us four years ago, treated us as idiots, I might still be with them. Well, I'm glad to be out of that snake pit. Ah, here we are. The restaurant with awnings."

There was a small restaurant on the corner, fogged windows hung with shaggy plants.

"Cheap and mixed. Gays and straights both, so neither of us will feel out of place."

"Not important." I was confused by his acknowledging my homosexuality so casually.

"My director took me here while we were working out my part. I suspect he's gay, but it's something we haven't talked about. We get along surprisingly well."

What was he trying to say? If he wanted to put me at ease, he didn't succeed. I sat with my back to the rest of the room, so I wouldn't check out the men. "So. Since you've been in the city for two months, how come you didn't get in touch with me?" I wanted to taunt him with that.

"Oh, you know how it is. There's things you intend to do, but . . ." He shrugged. "And I didn't know if you'd be on speaking terms with me, lad."

He already knew, and could blithely accept it. He had a conscience like Formica.

"You didn't want to take a chance?" I said. "You would've had nothing to lose."

"Not true. Being an actor has made me very sensitive to these things. I'm not sure how I would've handled the rejection."

I couldn't believe he'd said that.

"Okay," he admitted. "You're right to be dubious. I burned a few bridges to get where I am and won't pretend I lose sleep over it. But a man can't help feeling a certain fondness for... the ashes of his life? And you must admit. Much of what I burned were things we're well rid of. Before any of us could be free."

"A regular Abraham Lincoln," I said.

Even that failed to hit. "Only the Abe Lincoln of myself. I don't think we can pretend any of you were ever my slaves."

Oh no, massa, no. But the truth was: no. Or if I'd been a slave, it had only been in my own head. He'd done me a great favor by self-destructing.

A waiter came and took our orders.

"But. Enough about me. Actors can talk about themselves until the cows come home. And mighty strange cows at that. But how are you doing? You like New York?"

I said I did.

"You doing anything with your acting?"

"I was never serious about that. I don't have the narcissism it takes to be an actor."

He only smiled. "Then you're back to your old vocation of making money. Well, somebody's got to do it." Subtle, but he was finally responding to my digs.

"Wrong," I said. "I'm unemployed."

"Oh? I'm sorry." He made his eyes look sorry. "I guess this recession takes its toll on all of us. But I'm sure something'll turn up, lad."

"Nothing to be sorry about. It's the best thing that ever happened to me. I collect unemployment and spend my time reading. I'm reading the books I would've read if I'd gone to college," I said pointedly.

"Uh huh." He looked away. "And are you still with

. . . ? I'm sorry, I can't remember your lover's name."

"Corey. *Of course.*" He asked only to elude my point, but it annoyed me he thought we might not be together. "Only we don't refer to ourselves as lovers."

"You mean you're just friends now?"

"No. We're what we always were. It's just that we don't like that word."

"Why not?"

"It sounds mushy and exploitative and . . ." It embarrassed me trying to explain and Jake's opinion meant nothing to me. "It's just the wrong word for what we are."

"So how do you refer to yourselves as a couple?"

"I don't know. As us?"

"Interesting. Very interesting," said Jake. "We've burned almost everything. Even the words. But I'm glad to hear you're still together. Whatever you call yourselves."

My life with Corey was none of his business; I was not going to say anything more about it.

"Oh. Speaking of couples, I hear you saw your sister in Kilchberg."

"Yes. What? Did Bertie write to you?" I hoped Bertie gave him hell.

"No, Liza told me in a letter. She said you had a very nice visit."

"*Liza?* Liza wrote *you!* She doesn't write to the rest of us!"

"Only one letter," he said sheepishly. "Back in November. And not a very friendly letter at that."

"That's good," I said. "But why write you? What did she say?"

"Odd things. It wasn't the most coherent letter I've ever read. But the upshot of it was . . . she blamed me for failing to provide a good model. Of a husband and a father." He paused, as if I might disagree. "Now, I know I failed you financially, and for that I'm sorry. College was regrettable," he admitted. "But I don't see how failing to provide a good model could ruin anyone's life. Do you think I've ruined your life?"

"No," I said, reluctantly. "You certainly made it difficult. But no, I like my life. Although what I have, I have no thanks to you."

"And I don't expect any thanks. Although, there are days when I think I did you kids a big favor by getting out of the way. You'd understand if your grandfather had been alive when you were born. My papa, and I loved him. But the man was a little king. His family was his little kingdom and his alone, which was why he left Switzerland as soon as he got married, so he wouldn't have to compete with his own father. A benevolent tyrant, and he loved us, but... he left me with a superego the size of the Matterhorn. Duty to country, duty to family, duty to.... I spent fifty years climbing out from under that mountain. I like to think I've spared you kids all that. But we fathers are in a no-win situation. Damned if we do, and damned if we don't. Uh, this came out in therapy. I went into therapy, you know. For my acting."

He sounded so reasonable, and yet.... "Then it's Grampa's fault that you're an asshole?" There. I'd finally said it.

He stopped. He lowered his head and smiled. "No. I'm much too old to blame my father for my mistakes. I'm a self-made asshole, thank you. I mentioned him only to give you an idea of what the alternative was."

But there was no pleasure in hearing him plead guilty when he did it so easily.

"But getting back to Liza," he said before he looked at me again. "She said her life was ruined. Her life, her marriage, her attitude towards men. All ruined because I failed to provide a good model. Which hurt. A little. You can see why I had my doubts about getting in touch with you." He wooed me with a look.

He was no more worried about Liza than I was. He'd brought her up only so he could explain himself to me, gradually, without having to confront my feelings about him. I ignored his look. "Liza seemed content when I saw her."

"Yes. I wanted to ask you about that. Did she seem like somebody whose life had been ruined? Or was she only dramatizing for my benefit?"

"She loves her baby. She even loves Kearney. No, she seemed content." I refused to give him the pleasure of letting him think he'd ruined anybody's life.

"Well, we all like to dramatize now and then. But I wrote your sister, did a full mea culpa, because I thought that's what she wanted. Fathers can't help feeling different towards their daughters, because daughters are... because they're women, I suppose. But I told her, no matter how bad things were, her life wasn't ruined. Nobody's life is ruined until they're dead. I'm certainly proof of that. I reminded her she's young, and if life with Bob weren't peaches and cream, she could always follow the example of your mother and grandmother."

"And she said?"

"I don't know. She never wrote back. Which is what leads me to believe she was only dramatizing. And getting in one last blow at me. But I suppose we all have one score or another to settle with our parents." He knowingly lifted his bushy black eyebrows at me.

I didn't know whether I should punch him in the nose or burst out laughing. I too had a score to settle with my father, but Jake wasn't that father anymore. He was someone else, a clown who'd never betray you because he was too transparent to inspire trust in the first place. He thought he was being so clever, so seductive, admitting that he'd done wrong. All his psychology: To know all is to forgive all, and Jake had forgiven himself completely. I wanted to forget his wrongs, because to dwell on them meant he had really had some say in the shaping of my life. And yet, there was still this obligation to do or say something that might make my existence register on his smug, slick surface.

186

Our food came and while we ate, I called him an ass-hole again, several times, once for referring to "The Three Graces" and later for calling the farm "Tara." He admitted his error each time and it never made a dent in him, but, strangely, it made me feel less uncomfortable with him. We were there until midnight.

"I'll take care of this. If you don't mind my 'sneer money,' as your mother once called it."

"Don't be an asshole," I told him. "I'll let you buy me a cheeseburger." I followed him up to the cashier.

Staring at the register, refusing to look at us, was my pal, Ed.

"Ed! Hey! Small world, isn't it?" After my father, it was good to see someone I *knew*.

"Hello, Joel." Ed didn't look up. He must've known I was here all along. "Whaja have?"

I told him and said, "He's paying," nodding at Jake. "This is Ed. Our roommate. I had no idea you worked here, Ed. I always pictured you in a nice place."

"That's $4.65," said Ed.

"And Ed? This is my father."

"Father?" Ed looked up. He stared at the dyed hair and eyebrows while he took Jake's money. "Right," he said and quickly counted the money into the drawer. He was as uncommunicative here as he was at home.

Jake headed for the door, pressing his hand over his mouth.

Ed looked into my eyes. "Corey home tonight?"

"Where else? Nose buried in something Marxist, no doubt." I glanced at the door, wondering why Jake hadn't stayed to charm another stranger. "Well, gotta run. See you in the morning, Ed." As a final friendly taunt, I added, "I'll have to come here often. Now that I know where you work."

I found Jake outside, chuckling and shaking his head.

"Yes, Ed is weird," I admitted. "But he's a good guy under his gruffness."

187

"Didn't you notice how your friend was looking at us? Your friend in there..." He grinned at me. "Your friend thinks you're cheating on Corey."

"What!" I panicked and stared back at the restaurant.

"He thought I was your date. Or you were mine. I *am* the older man."

I stared at Jake.

"That is rich. A city where a father can't have dinner with his own son without people assuming... Ho ho. I should be upset, but it is funny."

"Ed thought that?" Me and Jake? "No, Ed didn't think that."

"It read in his face. Sorry, but it is funny. I trust it won't create any problems."

"It won't create problems. Corey knows where I am. Corey won't presume anything." And only then did I realize that Ed didn't know, and that I wasn't laughing at something I should've found very funny. But Jake was laughing, so cool he wasn't fazed when someone assumed he was his son's lover?

"But you know what they say," I said, as matter-of-factly as possible. "Gay men do to each other what they wish their fathers had done to them."

That stopped him.

It stopped me too. I couldn't believe I'd said it. Brad the black had told me that two weeks ago and I'd treated it as only a perverse joke. But to say it to my own father? I'd grabbed at it as one last brick to pitch at his composure, nothing more. And it had the effect I wanted.

He looked horrified. He couldn't speak. He had trouble looking at me.

I kept a straight face. I appalled myself, but, like kids grossing out each other in the lunchroom, I wanted to burst into giggles. The idea of Jake naked was akin to gopher guts and boogers.

He swallowed and attempted to smile.

And I burst out laughing. It wasn't nervous or deliberate but a spontaneous explosion of laughter that cleared away everything. "The look on your face," I cried. "Don't you know a put-on when you hear one?"

"Then—? Oh? Oh." He could smile again, but still looked unnerved.

"You're safe, Pops. Rest assured." I slapped his back and continued laughing. "I'm not even *attracted* to older men. I've never wanted to go to bed with you. You're safe. You're nothing to me but an ex-father."

"Well, uh, good. Good." And he promptly regained his composure. "And you'll always be my...ex-son?" He thought about that a moment before he decided it wasn't such a bad thing. "You worried me for a moment. We all know about fathers and daughters, but fathers and sons is something I still associate with picnics. Ho ho. No, I'm still the uptight heterosexual, I'm afraid. My re-acculturation hasn't gone *that* far."

Already he could recover with a joke and an explanation, but that didn't bother me. For a moment, I had finally gotten to him. I continued to get the giggles every time I remembered the look on his face while he walked me to the subway station.

"I'm glad we got together tonight," he said at the top of the stairs. "Been very interesting. For both of us, I think."

"Oh yeah. It's been interesting all right. How much longer you going to be around?"

"At least until June. Longer if I can get into a decent play or break into the soaps. I'm afraid you haven't gotten rid of me, lad."

He pretended it was a joke, but it was a joke. Jake was an old family joke. You could be fond of him the way you could be fond of old, repeated jokes. We gave each other our phone numbers. We even shook hands.

"So give me a call next week."

"Or you call me," I told him.

But on the ride home, without Jake there to be laughed at, I wondered about my laughing. Was that what had worried me about him, that I'd been in love with my

189

father? I had been in love with him, in a way, but with his authority and approval, not his body. His authority was gone now and I was free. I wished he'd kept a little authority, for the sake of decency, but I felt good being able to laugh at him. To laugh at your own mistakes proved that you'd outgrown them.

I described the encounter to Corey as a comic episode, only he had trouble seeing the humor. His refusal to help me turn it into comedy annoyed me.

"Don't look so solemn, Boy. It didn't depress me. I enjoyed it."

"I wouldn't have enjoyed it. Incest, even as a joke... ugh. And all his self-serving psychologizing and worming? I'd hate to see my father make himself so pathetic."

"Yes, you would think that," I said. "The guy who does his laundry *before* he goes home. So your father won't think you're a slob."

Corey freely admitted he was hung up on his father. They didn't see eye to eye on anything—Mr. Cobbett had said he'd move the family to Australia if Bobby Kennedy were elected—but Corey still wanted the man to think well of him. Fathers were sacred to him. But not even Ed's misunderstanding could tease a smile out of him. "We better clear that up with Ed. Suspicions like that can be poisonous."

"Don't be a jerk," I told him. "If Ed wants to think the worst of me, let him. Dirty minds have dirty thoughts. I'm going to act like I never dreamed he could suspect it." I only meant it as a way of mocking Ed, but after I said it, I felt as if keeping that suspicion in the air was also a way of getting back at Corey for refusing to help me laugh at my father.

The next day was Thursday, Ed's day off, and he was alone with me in the apartment all afternoon. He never mentioned last night, but his refusals to look at me seemed more deliberate than usual. He couldn't mention it, because that would betray his claim that we were

190

nothing but tenants to him. I took perverse pleasure in letting him stew in his misunderstanding. He shut himself in his room when Corey came home.

"Hello, Shirts," said Corey when he came into the kitchen. He put his arms around me and hung onto me for several seconds, then released me and shuffled into the bedroom. He returned to the kitchen without his coat or necktie.

"Bad day?" I asked.

"Yeah. Strange day. Hey. You want to eat out tonight?"

"I've got dinner almost ready."

"Oh. Okay." It didn't seem to matter to him one way or the other. "What're we having?"

"Stew."

"Good." He went to the built-in sideboard and pulled out dishes and utensils. "Afterwards, you want to go out for a drink or something?"

"Sure. How come?" Once home, Corey preferred to stay home, isolating himself with a book or, sometimes, me.

"I don't know. I just feel like doing something trashy tonight."

It was just like Corey to think that going out for beers could qualify as trashy, but Corey did it so rarely.

"Something the matter?"

"I'm just bored with being so high-minded and puritan. Where does it get you? Nowhere. I need some beer and noise, have some fun and stop thinking about political crap."

I was glad to hear him talk this way. It wasn't that I was morally intimidated by his political concerns, but there were times when I felt excluded by the satisfaction he got from them. It was good to know that Corey too could be dissatisfied.

"Sure. Be fun," I told him. "What brought this on? They kill one of your projects at work?"

"No, work was the same stupid round of paperwork and handshakes. It was my lunch with Rosa Blum that put me in this foul mood. That woman from the steering committee of the West End Marxists?"

I served the stew and we ate while Corey told about his meeting with Rosa Blum. She had arranged the meeting to talk to him about the possibility of drawing him deeper into the organization. Corey hadn't known there was anything deeper, had thought the group was only one, homogenous, democratic unit. It wasn't, and Blum wanted Corey to be part of the cadre at the center, on one condition: She wanted him to improve himself. "A little kindness or civility, and she might've convinced me. But no, she berates me!" he said, feeling hurt and angry when he remembered it. "'We've discussed this among ourselves and we think you're much too aloof.' They accused me of thinking I was better than the people around me Aloof? There's many things wrong with me, but aloofness isn't one of them. There's nothing wrong with being reserved."

"But don't you know, Boy? Reserve is bourgeois," I teased.

"Not bourgeois. Just good manners, that's all. Reserve, aloofness, shyness, whatever it is, I'm still not going to go into group therapy to cure it."

Which is what Blum had suggested: that Corey join a Marxist therapy group that met every Wednesday.

"I like the way I am. Basically. I don't want to have to remake myself in order to conform to somebody's narrow idea of how a good Marxist should behave. I don't trust psychology anyway. When people can't improve the world around them, they settle for improving themselves, and I expected much better from a group of Marxists. The whole business bothers me. That they have this secret elite at their core? I trusted them and thought I knew who they were. But now? It's soured me on them. I don't know anymore. It's the kind of thing that makes me want to turn my back on politics altogether." He smiled at the idea, then laughed. "Maybe I should follow your example and become an opera buff."

I laughed with him, until I remembered my operas.

"Goodbye Marx, hello Mozart!"' said Corey.

"But you don't like opera," I nervously reminded him.

"No," he admitted. "And it might be too much work for me to learn to like it. But right now—"

The buzzer went off like a klaxon.

I flinched, recovered, leaned back in my chair and pushed the button on the voice box. "Who is it?"

"Desire's sweet remorse," sang a voice downstairs.

I buzzed him in and shouted down the hall. "It's Sidney!"

There was a groan from Ed's bedroom.

I turned back to Corey. "You're not serious, are you? Because, if you are, tomorrow *is* Friday, and I guess I *could* pick up a ticket for you too. If you're serious." I was almost clenching my teeth.

"Tempting, but...no. I really should go to tomorrow night's meeting, just to see how I feel about it. Maybe it's not them, maybe it's just Rosa that's put me off. I shouldn't be so sensitive about it."

I was relieved; at least one more Friday night was safe.

"Talking about it makes me feel guilty for being soured by it," Corey continued. "I get empty courtesies from the church. And rude toughness from people like Rosa. If only you could put one inside the other. That's all I want. Politics that're tough but polite," he said, smiling at himself.

We heard Ed at the front door and Sidney's deep meow. "Rita, darling. Kiss-kiss. I remembered this was your night off and wanted to drop by to...oh, hello boys!" he crooned when he saw us at the end of the hall.

"Hi Sid," I called back to him.

Ed tried to usher Sid into the living room. "They're in the middle of dinner right now. We should leave them—"

"I won't *eat* your tenants, Rita. Adore your caftan," he told Ed over his shoulder and clopped down the hall towards us.

Ed was right behind him. "Come on, Sid. They don't

193

need you pestering them." He usually wasn't so concerned about protecting us from Sidney. And the truth of the matter was we liked Sidney. It was me Ed wanted to avoid tonight.

"We've finished dinner," said Corey. "There's some stew left, if you're hungry."

Sidney sniffed at the pot on the stove. "No, thank you. I had a single lima bean at home and am quite stuffed already." He moved the pot to the back and climbed up on top of the stove. "Oh good. Still warm. And how are Ariel and Caliban this fine evening? Mammy Rita providing all the comforts of home?"

Sidney was wearing cowboy boots tonight, a fur jacket and a loud Hawaiian shirt. He had an artificial tan that, on his glossy face, looked more cosmetic than healthy and gave his skin the appearance of a glazed doughnut. Sidney was vain about his looks, but even more vain about his ability to make fun of that vanity. We knew his thick, black hair was a toupee only because he had peeled it off one night and passed it around the room.

He sat daintily on the stove and looked around the kitchen. "Don't you have anything for a little drinky in this dump?"

"Only Southern Comfort," I told him.

"Ugh. I'd sooner drink maple syrup. You Southerners drink the most hideous things."

"We don't drink it. You gave it to us as a housewarming gift, remember?"

"And there's still some left?" Sid howled. "Well! I see some gifts go unappreciated. Okay, nothing for me to do but drink it myself. Rita, could you pour just a teensy glass of that candied booze for me?"

"Come on, Sid," muttered Ed, unable to bring himself to look at either Corey or me. "Let's go into the living room. I think we're interrupting a serious conversation."

"A serious tête-à-tête? Nobody's serious anymore. What could you children find to be so serious about?"

"Politics," said Corey with a guilty smile.

"Oooo. Deep. That's what charms me about you, Caliban. You are *so* sixties. No, not sixties exactly. Thirties. Positively thirties."

"Sid? The living room?" Ed pleaded.

"Speaking of politics," Sid said grandly, "I discovered last night that I'm something of a political personage myself. Did you know that I am *the* politically correct role model of young gays in the seventies?"

Corey and I laughed.

"I am," Sid insisted. "And I must say it surprised me too. But that's what I was told last night. By a fascinating man named,"—dramatic pause and lowered eyes—"Michael." He looked down at his bony hands and pretended to be puzzled that they were both empty. "I distinctly remember asking for a drink. Or did I?"

Ed gave up. He squeezed past Corey to the sideboard and thrust a glass and bottle at Sidney, then stood with his back to the sink and looked out the window.

"Très merci," Sid said and filled his glass. "But the dish on Michael, since everyone is clamoring to know... Cheers, darlings, ugh—Michael is lean, butch and beautiful. Well, not nearly as butch as he thinks he is. One of those male secretary types, in truck-driver drag. And a gay activist. Well! Nobody's ever called me a politically correct anything before. 'Flattery will get you everywhere,' I told him. But he was absolutely sincere. I think,"—he raised his chin and romantically flared his nostrils—"I'm in love."

"You met him at a gay activist meeting?" asked Corey.

"At the baths. Only Michael made me feel like we were *at the barricades!* And there I was, *Liberté* with the bare tits, like in that painting, leading you children on to freedom, liberation and wild promiscuity."

"So what makes you a model?" asked Corey. "Your lack of, uh, inhibitions?"

"That. And the fact that I'll fuck anything that wears pants."

"Promiscuity is politically correct?" I asked.

Ed glared at me and tried to secretly shake his head at Sidney.

"So says Michael. 'You have shown us the way,' he told me. 'You are our ancestor.' Still not sure I like that part. Makes me feel like I should be in a museum. But yes, because it's man's nature to hop from bed to bed. And we mustn't go against Mother Nature, must we? Just imagine. Me. A politically correct role model."

I was above politics, but it amused me to think that my Friday night activities might be just as political as Corey's. I looked at Corey. He was as amused as I was.

"Bullshit," said Ed suddenly. He cut his eyes at me and Corey. "That's not what you believe, and you know it, Sid."

"I confess it threw me for a loop. All this time I've thought of myself as a pariah because of my, shall we say, excesses? But it's nice to be told that I'm only doing what the rest of you should be doing, that I'm more in touch with my true male self. Promiscuity! Breaking the chains of monogamy!" He thrust his fist in the air. "Breaking down race! Breaking down class! Promiscuity *is* the Revolution!" Sidney smirked and shrugged. "Or so says Michael."

"You going to see this Michael again?" asked Ed pointedly.

"Touché. Yes, I do want to see him again," he admitted. "Oh do I want to. But it is a conundrum, isn't it? He liked me because he thought I was a model fairy. But if I go chasing after him, heart in my hand, he'll see that his model fairy has little clay feet."

Ed nodded knowingly. "See? You're not really promiscuous. You want what everyone else wants. It's just that you try and fail more frequently."

"That's a tacky way to put it. But yes. It's true. And it gets to be such a bore, Rita. One grows tired of falling in love with every guy who drops his drawers. And that's why this thing appeals to me. Freedom from heartache. Even if it does go against my instincts." He turned to us and explained, *"This* is why I come to Rita. So he can remind me that we're both much happier being miserable."

With a sidelong glance at me, Ed said, "I'm certainly not one to throw stones at promiscuity—"

"Miss Stall Seventeen at the Everard? You're certainly not."

"And I'm probably more promiscuous than you, Sid. Because I have no delusions of love."

"Do I hear the Irish queen keening in the wilderness?"

"But it's a second-best way of life!" Ed barked. "I'm not going to fool myself and turn it into an exemplary way of life. Because it's no substitute for committed, long-term relationships!"

His sudden fervor took us all by surprise. For an instant, I forgot that Ed didn't know, that he only thought he knew. Then I remembered I didn't have to feel guilty. I found Corey innocently smiling at me.

"Who said anything against Ariel and Caliban?" said Sid, noticing Ed's embarrassed refusal to look at us. "I wasn't trashing the newlyweds. Michael *did say* that monogamous couples weren't quite honest. Dupes of the status quo or something. But even in my greenest envy, I can't believe that. I adore the spectacle of other couples."

Corey became flustered and said, "Well, Shirts and I are very lucky."

Ed looked at him pityingly.

I felt uncomfortable, then annoyed with Corey.

"Luck and being from the provinces," sniffed Sid. "But I do admit that I envy you. Oh young, requited love. But 'fess up, boys. Don't you sometimes envy me? For my wild and sensuous life?"

"Not really," Corey apologized. "I mean, I did it myself for a while and . . . it was fun. It was. But there's no comparing sex with somebody you don't know to . . . somebody that you care about and really know." He looked at me sheepishly. It was difficult for Corey to say such things in public.

197

"Then you've been out trying a few taste comparisons?"

Corey only laughed. "No. It's something we both know from memory."

"Pity. I wouldn't mind giving either of you a chance to compare your warm, giving intimacies with a little meaningless tricking. But, if wishes were horses..." He winked at me.

And Corey laughed even harder.

There was a subtle smugness under Corey's embarrassment and it irritated me. Corey had appointed himself our spokesman and his presumptions sounded thin, stupid and oppressive to me. I felt myself siding with Sid.

"Well, adultery *is* the only drama in bourgeois life," Corey teased back.

"Bourgeois?" said Sid. "Are you calling me bourgeois?"

"He's quoting an Italian," I said. "It isn't original," and then realized I said it only because I wanted to strike back at Corey some way.

"I see. Well I should know better than to argue with a Marxist. They come up with the most radical quotes to justify the dreariest, most conventional behavior. Ed's right. You *are* a closet Christian. Neither of you are *ever* tempted to come out of your house and play?"

"No," said the fool. "Shirts and I are enough for each other. But thanks for the offer."

New pain rose in Ed's face and he turned away again and faced the window. His misunderstanding no longer amused me. If Corey weren't so unconscious, so innocent, he would be as pained as Ed was.

Sid sighed and shook his head. "I sometimes wonder if the two of you are really homosexuals. You seem like two nice boys who're only posing as homosexuals. To make yourselves seem more interesting."

"We're gay all right," said Corey, still smiling at me.

"Pshaw, I say. Or if you are, you're suffering from the

delusion that it, *and* socialism, are as American as apple pie, Caliban."

"We just don't let our sexuality dominate our lives," Corey announced.

And that did it: I rebelled. "Aren't you going to ask me? There are two of us, you know."

Corey looked surprised, then guilty. "Sorry. I was only speaking for myself." He nodded at me, as if to give me permission to speak.

I glared back at him and demanded, "Ask me what I think of promiscuity."

"Yes, Ariel. What do you think?" said Sid playfully.

"I think it's great."

Ed spun around.

Corey only cocked his smile at me.

"Why do you think I go to the opera every Friday?"

And Ed slammed one foot against the floor. "I see it again and again!" he shouted at the ceiling. "They move to New York to save their relationship! They think all they need is a little excitement! And the excitement destroys the relationship!"

Sid and Corey stared at Ed. And Ed looked down, realizing he'd jumped the gun and that I hadn't confessed anything yet.

Suddenly, I couldn't confess. Ed's outburst frightened me and I realized that what I wanted to say was too deadly to be said only because I was irritated with Corey. My irritation died and I wanted only safety.

Sid turned his diabolical smile back to me. "And why do you go to the opera?"

Corey was confused, over Ed, then me.

"Oh—" But a complete denial, a shrug and a muttered "Nothing" would only make everyone suspicious. Trying to look comically blasé, I said, "For the action in the men's room."

Puzzled looks; I panicked to think they might believe me.

"Of course. Lots of action in the men's room at the Met. Especially during Wagner. Good lightning. Spotless floors. I really should invest in a pair of kneepads, because those floors are hard." I had to invent more and more details, desperate that they see I was joking, dammit. "And I restrict myself to men in tuxedos. the cumberbund's a nuisance, but a man in a tux is going to be clean. That's something you can count on."

And Corey finally began to laugh.

Sidney caught on, slapped his knee and howled, "What an active little imagination our Ariel has! The face of an angel. The mind of a slut. And all this time I thought butter wouldn't melt in his mouth."

I faked a mischievous grin and heaved a sigh of relief.

Only Ed didn't laugh. My joking appalled him and his mouth fell open when Corey laughed. But even with my escape, his misunderstanding still frightened me. It was too close to the truth. The joke had gone on long enough.

"Yes, we Scherzenliebs have a gift for the bizarre. I get it from my father. Who you met last night. Ed."

Ed snapped to attention.

"I hope not," said Corey. "Some of those things your father said last night would put even Sid to shame."

Ed looked straight at Corey. "Joel has a father?"

"No, I climbed out from under a rock," I told him. "Of course I have a father. Don't you remember? You met him last night."

Ed stood there like a man whose pocket had been picked.

And Corey fell back in his chair. "I get it," he said. "Now I remember. Shirts told me that you—"

"I didn't think it. It was my father who thought it." I had to appear completely innocent.

"Whoever." He chided me with a glance. "*Somebody* thought you didn't think Jake was Joel's father. Shoot. Now I get it. No wonder you thought there was something dangerous going on."

"Ohhhh!" went Sidney, his eyes suddenly wide. "Rita thought? Ohhh!"

"We're sorry, Ed. Joel or I should've cleared that up for you. But really. That was Joel's father."

Ed suddenly recovered with a shiver. "What's everybody babbling about? I don't know what you're talking about."

"For shame," said Sid wickedly. "You dirty old man, you." He turned to me. "Rita's been thinking that your daddy, Ariel, was really...your sugardaddy." As if he thought I might not understand.

I laughed a little too hard, like someone pretending it was the first time they heard an old joke.

Ed shifted angrily inside his caftan. "I don't know what you're talking about," he insisted. "Why should I even notice who he was with? Father, grandfather, I don't care. None of my business." He was too proud to admit his mistake, and too proud to admit he'd been concerned. "Come on, Sid. The kitchen's too small for four. If you're here to see me, come and see me and stop flirting with my tenants." And Ed marched out of the room, caftan fluttering behind him.

Sid sat very still on the stove. "Uh oh. I think we hit a nerve. Poor Mother Rita. All heart and pretending not to be involved. I better say good-bye to you boys or he'll never speak to me again." He climbed down, winked at us and went off to the living room.

"Shoot," said Corey. "I'd forgotten all about that. You shouldn't have let it gone on as long as you did, Joel. It was cruel to play Ed along like that."

"It wasn't deliberate. I guess I forgot it, too."

"Really? Well, if I forgot it, I suppose you could, too. Poor Ed," he sighed. "Nice to think of him watching over us like a guardian angel." But he had to smile. "A nearsighted guardian angel. I hate to admit it, but it is kind of funny. Don't you think?"

"Hysterical."

"You should probably be more careful about the stories you tell Sid. I think he half-believed you about the Met rest room."

"You mean you didn't?"

Corey laughed and began to clear the table.

The danger had been cleared away; I was safe. But safety didn't feel good to me. I watched Corey cheerfully splash himself and the floor as he washed the dishes. I'd almost hurt him in the presence of others and yet there was no gush of love or good will that sometimes comes when you decide to protect someone. I resented the need to protect him. I resented my own cowardice.

Corey sang while he washed.

Take heed you forces of oppression,
Your bloody end is drawing near.

It was a song he'd learned from the West End Marxists, and the combination of those ruthless lyrics with his oblivious innocence made him seem like a perfect idiot. My sister had been right. Corey was dull. He had no imagination, no idea of just how bad other people could be. An outsider might admire that kind of innocence, but I felt trapped in it. I was trapped in his trust but was too much of a coward to kick my way out.

"If you're not going to let it dominate your life," I heard Sid sing to Ed in the living room, "then where's the fun in being queer?"

Corey and I were alone. But even without spectators, I could not bring myself to tell Corey the truth. I blamed it on cowardice and loathed myself as much as I loathed Corey. On the other side of the airshaft outside the kitchen window was another kitchen exactly like ours. A boy and a girl sat there, eating dinner and talking. Other couples, any other couple, seemed more genuinely a pair than we were.

Corey finished and faced me while he dried his hands and wrung out the front of his shirt. "Funny, but I feel much better now than when I came home. You don't still want to go out for a drink, do you?"

"Not really. No."

"Me neither. Nothing like a few minutes with Sidney to satisfy your need for trashiness. Then you won't mind if we spend a quiet evening at home?"

"I won't mind."

But he wanted to go to bed early; that dangerous conversation had awakened nothing in him but a wish to make love. I told him I wanted to read. He accepted, but sat up to read and wait for me to get sleepy. But Corey had to work tomorrow and I didn't; I could read much longer than he could. I read *The Counterfeiters* until he was fast asleep and only then did I lie down beside him. The feel of his bare legs beneath the blankets was very sexual, but I could wait until tomorrow. Tomorrow was Friday.

Julius gradually filled with bodies.

When I arrived at eight, there were less than twenty people. I stood in the back of the elongated room, where I could take in all my possibilities. A heavy oak bar ran half the length of the room, with cast-iron beagles along the foot rail and, above, guys having after-work drinks with friends. I was the only one in the primary cruising area: an open space away from the windows and around the jukebox. At my back, the wall turned a corner and there was a deep, narrow alcove furnished with a few tables, but only couples sat there and I didn't have to check it out. The black walls above the tables were chalked with graffiti: "John Loves Bill," "Lou and Dave Now and Always," "I Never Met a Man I Didn't Like." The jukebox played "Lady Marmalade"; it always seemed to play "Lady Marmalade." I leaned against the cigarette machine and quietly drank my beer.

Early arrival betrayed eagerness, but I had no qualms about appearing too eager. I had to be home by midnight and naked eagerness speeded things up. A few fellows at the end of the bar stole glances at me, then went back to their conversations. A kid who sat alone looked at me over his shoulder, but immediately faced forward when I looked him in the eye.

I adjusted my expression so I'd appear alert, friendly and curious. It was a point of pride with me not to play the faintly bored, sleepy-eyed Narcissus. I'd never thought of myself as handsome, but had discovered at Julius that I did look young, which passed with some people as a kind of handsomeness. I could use that, but was too proud to invite stares by acting like a beautiful young dummy.

An older man at the end of the bar turned around on his stool and faced me, but continued to talk to the man beside him. He was much too old for me, but his gaze was easy and amiable. His horn-rimmed glasses added to his look of openness. I quickly looked away, but felt that was rude. I looked back at him and apologetically lifted my eyebrows, signaling I was sorry but that he wasn't my type.

He promptly jumped off his stool and walked over.

That killed his chances immediately. Young or old, I had a fetish about being the one who made the first move.

"Hello there. I'm Al." He confidently held out his hand, as if this were a private party and he were the host. "And you're . . . ?"

"Joel," I said and shook hands.

With his eyeglasses and a slight gut, he looked like a high school chemistry teacher. No, Al was too old for me and he'd made the first move, but I didn't want to be rude and was willing to talk to him for a few minutes.

"You look like you're in an awfully good mood tonight, Joel. Something good happened to you?"

"Not that I know of. But yes, I guess I am in a good mood."

"Which is rare in this city. And rarer still to have the

confidence to show it. I think it shows strength of character. You must be a very strong person, Joel."

I knew what he was doing but enjoyed being told I looked happy. "You look quite happy yourself tonight, Al."

"Well, I am. Miserable March we're having, but it's warm and friendly in here. I just spent two months in Los Angeles. It's good to be home."

I could feel the sexual undertow in the way he leaned towards me and looked at me, but I wasn't intimidated. Sex with him would probably be quite comfortable and friendly. It was too bad he was old enough to be my father, because...

Was that why I was holding back? I considered it, considered Al. I certainly didn't want to go to bed with Jake, but there was something neurotic about refusing to go to bed with anyone who reminded me of my father. I was curious. I wanted to test my limits. After all, that was part of the reason why I was here every Friday night: to explore my limits. I'd already slept with a fat person and a black; I should experiment with someone older.

He was telling me about Los Angeles and the concerts and operas he'd attended there. He was a music critic. Well, I certainly liked music.

But he had made the first move. If I were going to be in control, I would have to say or do something that would put his easy approach in the shade.

I rested one elbow on the cigarette machine behind me and lazily swigged my beer, trying to look as cocky as possible. Then I looked him in the eye and said, "I think you're cute, Al. You very horny tonight?"

He suddenly looked suspicious.

I couldn't understand his reaction, so I made myself clearer. "Would you like to go to bed with me?"

And he drew back!

His friendliness vanished and he was suddenly all armor and antennas, looking me up and down. And then, an expression of sternness dropped over his face like a visor. "What's your game, buddy?"

"Game? I'm just being horny and friendly. What's wrong?"

He shook his head. "You certainly looked innocent enough, but ..." He snorted at himself and tried to be civil. "I'm sorry, son. I'm sure you're a good kid and I don't mean to sit in judgment on what you're doing. But it's a point of pride with me never to pay for it."

Pay for sex?

"In fact, this is the wrong bar for you. What you want is Cowboys and Cowgirls uptown. Or even Ninth Circle down the street. They try to discourage hustlers here."

"But—"

"Good luck, son. Nice try and no hard feelings." He smiled and shook his head and returned to his stool at the bar, ten feet away. He wagged his thumb at me to point me out to his companion, who laughed.

Well, I hadn't really wanted to go to bed with him anyway. But it hurt me that somebody could think I was a prostitute. I tried to enjoy the joke that I'd been turned down because I'd offered myself too readily, but the sting stayed with me. I had to leave the cruising area and move to the front of the bar, where Al couldn't see me.

One slow beer later, I still hadn't made contact with anyone else. People grew choosy as Julius filled with competitors. Al's accusation stayed with me and I couldn't help seeing the bar as a marketplace. The usual feelings of community and generosity were replaced by an uneasy suspicion that we were all sexual commodities, intent on buying each other. I'd acquired more of Corey's socialist thinking than I pretended.

I stood there, trying to make generosity flow again for the sake of a beefy fellow who leaned against the brass rail at the window, the logo on the glass printed on his face by a street light outside. Then Al walked past, with the kid from the bar who hadn't been able to return my gaze —" ... play some Saint-Saëns for you and you'll see that serious music can be just as exciting as the New York Dolls or . . ."—and I was free to return to my post at the cigarette machine.

There were more people in the back now, but mostly circles of friends who sexlessly chatted together and showed no interest in the faces around them. But on the bench beside the jukebox was an interesting guy with shoulder-length hair, a goatee and a walrus moustache. He noticed me, but seemed unable to make up his mind whether to cruise me or one of the guys displayed along the opposite wall. I was trying to make up my own mind on whether I wanted to kiss someone through a moustache, when I followed one of the walrus' indecisive glances to check out my competition. It was a boy my age but slightly taller, with a pale, bristling moustache of his own, a red sweatshirt with a hood and bright white painter's pants. The walrus had good taste. The boy had wavy brown hair, pink cheeks and full, crooked lips. I mentally shaved him and he became very cute and collegiate. We were drinking the same brand of beer. He surveyed the room, noticed me looking at him, but let his eyes travel past. Then his eyes snapped back to me. He stared. It was more a stare than a cruise, but everyone had their own style.

And I was interested. I tested his interest by calmly staring into his stare and his stare never wavered. I checked behind me, afraid I was only standing in a crossfire of cruises, but it was definitely me he was cruising. I smiled and started across the room towards him, thinking, "Sorry, Walrus." My heart raced as I walked the boy's stare like a tightrope.

He broke into a grin. It was wonderful to be received with such gratitude. With a grin instead of gay bar cool, he looked familiar, like someone I already knew, but then half of New York looked like people from the past.

The boy suddenly held out both hands and cried, "Shirtsy!"

I stopped. Except for Kearney, nobody had called me Shirtsy since—

207

"Don't you recognize me?" Hands still extended, he bent down, as if I might recognize him if he were shorter. "From Virginia? From Camp Wolf?"

"I"

"It's Wyler!" he shouted. "Wyler Reese!"

That twerp bastard, Wyler? He talked as if I should be overjoyed to see him.

"Wow! *Wow!*" He was bobbing and grinning, gesturing at me with both hands. His joy looked brash at Julius. "Too much! This is too fucking much!"

I slowly took in the fact that this was Wyler Reese, from summer camp, who had whined and bullied his way through my summer, who had called anyone shorter than him "queerbait," who had called me queer. Last of all, I took in the fact that we were both in a gay bar.

"See. You were right!"

"I was?"

"You know. That I was gay, man! I was hiding it like crazy, couldn't even admit it to myself. But you knew. You saw right through me, didn't you?"

But I couldn't remember thinking Reese was gay.

"And now," said Reese proudly, "I've come out." Which was a bizarre thing to announce when you were dressed gay and standing in a gay bar.

"Well, good," I told him. But what was good about discovering that you and an old enemy have something in common? The only clear impulse beneath my confusion was to tell Reese to drop dead and walk away. But he was so shockingly happy to see me, I couldn't bring myself to do it. "You visiting New York?" I asked.

"Hell no. I live up here. Since this summer. I finished at V.P.I. and Barclay's Bank snapped me right up. And I grabbed it, man. Wanted to be in the Apple. Where the action is." He looked over Julius to show that this was the action he'd come for. "This your bar, Shirtsy?"

"I come here now and then. Is it your bar?" If it were, I'd have to find another bar.

"Nyaah. I'm a Ninth Circle man. More pretty faces. But things don't get going there until later, so I like to drop in here and check out the meat. Too much yak here, not enough action. Sure the hell glad I came in tonight. I still ain't believin' this is you."

"Me neither."

"Should've known you'd end up in New York. Birds of a feather, huh? And you haven't changed a bit, Shirtsy. When I saw you over there, I thought I was flashing on the past."

I didn't like being told I hadn't changed in five years. "But you've changed, Reese. I still can't recognize you. That moustache."

"Yeah, my Marlboro Man 'stache. That's to show that just because I'm gay I'm no wimp. I'm surprised you don't have one, too."

"I don't have the lip for it." Neither did Wyler and he might've been attractive without it. Or maybe he would've been attractive if only he weren't Wyler. "And I don't like moustaches anyway," I insisted.

"I've changed in other ways too, man. Like, I found out what I wanted in life."

But even with his moustache, even with my memory of who he was, I could feel something clouding my awareness of him. "Which is?"

"Hey man!" he laughed, as if it were perfectly obvious. "Dick!"

This was the guy who'd called me queer behind my back. I looked into the idea of having sex with him and it was like peering over the edge of a cliff, stepping back even as you feel the space below drawing you down.

Wyler froze his eyes and smiled at me as if he were feeling something similar.

"You have a lover?" I asked, hoping he did and that that would be the end of this.

"Nyaah. Not now. Did, in Blacksburg, but he got freaked when his parents found out and threatened to disinherit him unless he got married. The jerk. He was my roommate senior year and *loved* to give head. And now the wimp's married. You got a lover?"

But Wyler had known Corey and it'd be wrong to tell on him, especially when it was Corey who'd "defended" me that night. "Not at the moment."

"Yeah, you need a lover when you're in the sticks. But can be a real bitch up here. Cuts into your fun. I'll bet you know how to have fun."

"Now and then," I muttered. I was thinking about Corey's contempt for Wyler, then my own contempt for Wyler, but that only increased the temptation to fall.

"Hey. Awfully loud in here. You want to go someplace quieter? Where we can talk over old times."

Old times with Wyler Reese: what a disquieting thought. But I knew that wasn't what he wanted. "Where did you have in mind?"

"You live anywhere near here?"

"No. I'm all the way up on the Upper West Side. Way up. Maybe we should just go to a coffee shop near here." Maybe a half hour of conversation with him would remind me who he was and draw me back from the cliff's edge.

"No sweat. Or, if you like, I live just on the other side of Union Square. We could walk over there. I could show you my Manhattan pad." He tried to be casual about it, but had to moisten his lips to keep them from sticking together. "You game?"

The desire that didn't shine like desire, the temptation that weighed on me like an obligation: This was something we had to do and I knew it. I let myself fall. "Oh, okay."

"Okay? Great! Then let's get out asses out of here, Shirtsy."

His joy didn't fool me. He had to be feeling the same somnambulism of desire I was feeling. He couldn't forget how I had once hated him or how he'd once hated me. Sex was going to be our way of settling old scores with each other.

210

Out on the street, the last of the banks of snow left by the snow plows was melting, revealing a winter's worth of cigarette butts, wrappers and blurred newspapers. I resented having to do what I was doing and wanted to walk to Wyler's apartment without talking. But I had to talk. The silence was too strange. I asked him what he did at Barclay's.

"I'm with their computer section, designing programs and stuff. Good bucks too and they're going to get better. I already got my own secretary. See, I'm their Fortran whiz kid and they want to keep me. Top of my class at Tech. Hey! I'll bet you had no idea I was smart."

"No I didn't," I said honestly.

"Had to keep it a secret at summer camp, but I'm a math freak. I love the stuff and it led straight to computers. Didn't want it to show at camp because I thought it wasn't cool to be smart. Or masculine to be smart. I was so hung up about people thinking I was queer I didn't want them to suspect I was intelligent. Fucked up, huh?"

"Very," I said. "And now you're gay and in computers?"

"Oh yeah. Play the nerd when I'm at work with the breeders—they think I'm Mr. Straight Arrow at work—then stud like crazy on the weekends. It's like having two lives, man. I've come to terms with myself and can be smart, masculine and gay, all at the same time."

Except for the homosexuality, he hadn't really changed that much. He spoke with the same slangy noisiness he had used five years ago, as if his social self had locked at age seventeen while the rest of him had plunged into computers. If only his speech had changed, I could pretend he was another stranger like all the others.

"But gays *are* smarter than straights, as a whole. And the straights pick up on it. Look at you. You never made it a secret that you had smarts. So everybody *knew* you were queer."

"Not everybody," I said, thinking of myself. But I

211

didn't want to think of myself or my past, didn't want to even correct Wyler's stupid assumption. "Where is Barclay's anyway?"

"Down in Wall Street. Right in the heart of nerd country."

Where, at one time in my life, I had wanted to be. And Wyler was a math wizard, something I pretended to be but knew I really wasn't. If I had had my wishes, if everything had worked out as once planned, and my homosexuality still been able to come to the surface—because homosexuality was a certainty even if nothing else was—I would've become someone like Wyler? With college and without Corey, I could've become Wyler. It was a frightening thought. I wanted to feel superior to him, but was intimidated by his success at being what I had once wanted to be.

"What biz are you in now?"

"I'm unemployed," I said, wanting to be proud of it, wanting to dissociate myself completely from the kind of life I had so luckily avoided.

But Wyler was only envious. "Oh yeah? You collecting benefits? Must be great. I'd love to be on unemployment. Fuck my brains out every night of the week instead of saving it up for the weekends. Does it get boring doing it all the time?"

"Uh, I pace myself." He made even casual sex seem bad. His very existence was like a criticism of my life. And yet, I still walked with him around deserted Union Square where the bare trees clacked together in the wind and there was nothing on the street but Wyler and the occasional wad of paper that blew past us. Wyler was cheerfully dense to the fact, but this was only something we had to do, nothing else.

We came to a dingy row of brownstones in the east 20s and entered one.

"A real hole," said Wyler as we went up the stairs. "But it was as close as I could get to the West Village. That's where I really want to live. Just a hardon away

212

from Christopher Street? That way I could hook two or three people a night. That's how I like to live my life. I work hard and I play hard. I got my name on a few lists over there."

He unlocked a door and turned on the light in a bare, narrow room. It was only one room, with a refrigerator and stove fitted into a wall, a card table and a sofa bed. The bed was still opened across the room and there were orange plaid sheets tangled on top of it. The sofa bed looked brand new and I'd seen the insides of enough gay New York apartments to recognize designer sheets. But everything else about the apartment was squalid and a pair of underpants hung like a trophy on the arm of the sofa.

I wanted to get it over with as quickly as possible. I didn't even wait to take off my coat. I grabbed Wyler and attacked his face with my mouth.

He held on tight, almost inhaled my tongue. His moustache felt like pubic hair. He pulled back to catch his breath and say, "I still ain't believin' this, man." He ran his hands through my hair. "Feels like a fuckin' dream."

Or nightmare, I thought. I released him so he could pull his sweatshirt off. Beneath it he wore the faded shirt from a Boy Scout uniform.

"One minute. Before we get going.'" He went over to the bed, dug behind the mattress and pulled out a Band-aid tin. "Indulge in a little smokey-smokey?" he asked, flourishing a joint.

"No thanks. But you go ahead." I threw off my coat and paced the room while Wyler lit his joint. There was a metal grate over the only window, making the place feel even more like a cell. He had certainly stripped his life down to the essentials. Two stacks of green computer print-out sat on the card table with a loose-leaf notebook and a skin magazine. I picked at the magazine. The pages stuck together before popping open to a mouth fellating a cock. And I remembered something else about Reese: How, during that first long winter at the farm, whenever

213

I masturbated and wanted something violent, I imagined forcing Reese to do this to me, as a way of humiliating him. I had wanted to humiliate someone—it was the only way I could express my homosexuality—and my imagination had chosen Wyler Reese. His paranoid assumptions about me had been more important than I cared to admit. "On second thought," I said, "let me try some of that."

I'd smoked dope only once, with Liza the night before her wedding. It hadn't done much for me, but I hoped it might simplify my feelings toward Wyler. The first toke only burned my throat.

"This is gonna be great," said Wyler, sitting on the bed. "Took me five years but I'm finally doing it." He took the joint from me and sucked on it. "So tell me," he said from the back of his throat. "How many did you score with at camp?"

"Score with?" I said hoarsely.

"Yeah. We were keeping track, me and my crowd. Like we were obsessed. So we knew about you and Bryant, and you and... what's-his-name, the weinie."

"Weinie?"

"You know. Mr. Clean. Cobb or... Cobbett! Yeah. Kahuna overheard us once and called us liars. Threatened to put his boot up our 'sweet A.'"

"Kearney did that?" That surprised me more than Wyler's idea that I was actually doing anything back then.

"Yeah. But I think the great Kahuna had the hots for you himself. But your tentmate, Bryant. You made it with him, didn't you?"

My timing was delayed. I burst out laughing at the notion that it was me Kearney was interested in; it was my sister he was trying to meet. Kearney? Me? Bryant? Wyler's imagination had turned Camp Wolf into a continuous orgy in the woods.

"Yeah. I knew it. He claimed you didn't, even when he had nothing to hide anymore. Summer after the summer you were there, I got the wimp drunk one weekend and took him skinny dipping in the James. He played it real dumb and pretended not to get the idea. But when he did...! Started in the water, ended up on the raft. Still light and nobody around for miles? Whew! But he was real uptight about it afterwards. Didn't want to do it again. Was afraid to even be alone with me, the wimp! Was too chickenshit to even admit he'd done it before. But I can't believe he spent the whole summer in your tent without you putting the moves on him."

Poor nervous, homely little Bryant, I thought, and took a deeper drag on the joint, seeds bursting like tiny fireworks. Poor deluded Reese, I thought and began to unbutton my shirt.

"You and Cobbett I know about. Because I heard him in your tent after that time we went to Claremont. I think about that and feel so fuckin' envious. Damn but you had balls." He drew on the joint and suddenly blew out the smoke before he inhaled it. "Oh shit!" he cried. "That night! You remember riding back in Fisher's car?"

"Sort of," I said. I stopped unbuttoning my shirt. But Reese had been passed out on the ride back.

Wyler was breathless, pink and grinny. "Five of us drove in? And I got crocked? And on the way back, you started feeling me up?"

I remember that night, but I'd never laid a hand on Reese. I'd been disgusted when he passed out and sank down and his leg touched mine.

"Oh Jesus. I started it. I was pretending I was drunk, sliding down so I could push our legs together. But I didn't know what to do next. I was scared shitless. And then when you put your hand on my knee, I just about shit in my pants. You saw right through me, Shirtsy. You knew all I needed was a good hump. But I wasn't ready to handle it yet. Damn but I was a jerk to run away."

For a moment, I believed him and thought I'd remembered that night all wrong. But Corey and I had told each other the story of that night several times. It was Wyler who remembered it wrong. "No," I said. "I don't think I put my hand on your knee."

215

"You did. Probably the sort of thing you did so often you didn't even think about it. But I remember every move that night. Here, let me show you."

He grabbed my belt and pulled me down so I was sitting beside him.

"Okay. Pretend we're in the car. No, you can't look at me. You have to look straight ahead at the road. Cobbett's sitting on the other side of you, remember."

I looked to my left, where Corey would've been sitting, and saw the poster of Mick Jagger on the wall. At camp Reese used to tell people that he had Mick Jagger's lips. "Where's the joint?" I asked. I thought that might help.

"I put it out. We didn't have grass back then, just beer. And we're driving along, and the top's down, and I'm smashed, but not as smashed as I pretend I am. Nobody's talking. There's just the wind and the road. And I slide down, gradual like. Until I had my leg against yours." He leaned back, supporting himself on the bed with his hands, then pressing his leg against mine.

The pressure was definitely sexual.

"There. But then I jerked back, just a tad. Because I was scared."

But I was the one who'd jerked back, knocking my knees against Corey's.

"Then I let my leg fall back, until I was touching you again,"—it did— "and more road goes past, and more road."

There had been stars overhead that night, wheeling a little with each turn of the road. My feelings of hatred for Reese came back to me, but hatred, coming to me through five long years, seemed changed. Any emotion that had lasted that long was indistinguishable from passion. It certainly wasn't love but, in terms of sex, it served love's purpose. I couldn't distinguish the excitement of hate from the excitement of sex or grass.

"Okay. I let my leg stay like that for miles. And then, you put your hand on my thigh."

216

I did and his thigh's warmth poured through his pants into my hand. The touch of a hand was the dramatic event it had been five years ago. "But I didn't do that," I said.

"You did. And I was sweating bullets."

Corey had done it to *me*. Maybe Wyler had seen it and confused his memories: His past was such a tangle of fantasy and wishful thinking. I moved my hand up his thigh.

"No. You didn't do that."

"What stopped me?"

"I rolled away from you, like I was drunk." But he didn't roll away. He looked down at my hand. "I was such a dumb shit back then," he moaned. "I keep playing and replaying this scene, wishing I'd done it right."

"And? What should you have done?"

"This." He clapped his cold hand over mine. "Happened a year later, I could've done this." And he brought my hand up over his crotch, which had a little fist inside.

I braced my other hand on his knee and leaned in to kiss him.

"Uh uh. Not yet," he laughed. "We're in Fisher's car, remember? Cobbett's sitting next to you, and Fisher and Yo-yo are sitting up front." He scooted up the bed toward the mangled pillows. "Have to wait until we get back to camp."

I quickly untied my shoes.

"All the time getting hotter and hotter the more we think about it."

I kicked off my shoes and came up the bed after him.

"And then, when we get back to camp . . . you ask me to your tent, not Cobbett," he spat.

I lunged at him. His legs opened. His arms went around me and he kissed furiously.

"Oh yeah, babe. This is what I've been waiting for . . . Do you think anybody can hear us? No, they're all asleep in their tents by now. What a tongue you have. No, let me do that for you. Great. White skivvies. None of that faggy color stuff. Let me just . . . Oh wow. Look at that dick. Dreamed of seeing it with a bone. Dreamed of taking it like . . ."

Up close, he didn't have to be Wyler Reese anymore, if only he'd stop talking. He could've been anyone met in a bar, anyone whose lips were full, whose body was smooth and lean inside their clothes. But he continued to talk between kisses and sighs, going in and out of his Boy Scout fantasy, never letting me forget that this was Wyler, so that all my kisses and embraces were charged with my hatred for Wyler. He shut up only when he took me in his mouth, but that was where I'd put him in *my* fantasies, and it was wonderfully sordid to watch him boastfully make eyes at me while he showed off with his tongue. Undressing him was like a prolonged, tender murder.

"My dick okay? I know it's crooked, but that's because —oh? Oh yeah. You really know what you're doing."

I could turn my symbols inside out so that even when I sucked him I was humiliating Wyler.

He pulled away to pluck a white tube from between the sofa arm and mattress. "See? Was worth the wait, wasn't I? I've caught up with you, haven't I?" He squeezed clear jelly into his hand and reached down to me. "I love touching your dick. So soft and hard. Here. You do me. Get me ready." And he gave me the tube and stretched his legs apart.

He wanted me to fuck him; that was even better than anything I'd imagined with him.

"We're hot together, aren't we, man? That's it. Go inside with your finger. Uh huh. This is gonna be fanfucking-tastic, babe." He rubbed jelly around my balls, then beneath them to my anus. I tricked somebody I didn't like into sticking his finger up my ass. "Yeah? Yeah? Oh, okay."

But I hadn't said anything. I'd squirted too much jelly into my hand and was wiping the excess on his cock.

"First, I've got this." His hand went back behind the mattress and came back with what looked like a bottle of

218

nail polish. "Be prepared," he said. "Even got poppers. How you want to do this? You want to go first?" He unscrewed the bottle and passed it to me.

I'd tried amyl nitrate with Saul the lawyer last week, but maybe my nose had been stopped up or maybe it was because I was having an orgasm at the time, but it hadn't seemed to affect me. I put Wyler's bottle to my nostril and breathed deep.

My heart began to race, but it seemed only like a continuation of sex and grass. And then there was a rush in my head and I thought I was going to pass out. I seemed to pass out, only I was very conscious of an abrupt, passionate embrace with Wyler, and then Wyler's stunned face overhead. He shook his nose like a dog who'd sniffed something sharp. My legs were up on his shoulders, my heart was pounding and there was an odor of dirty socks in the room: the poppers. I became frightened when I thought I was having a bowel movement. And then I realized Wyler was fucking me.

Not exactly, because he wasn't moving in and out, but he was definitely in, still catching his breath and blinking his eyes, then brushing his cheek against my calf.

I didn't think he should be there. Saul had coaxed me into being fucked, but Saul had been behind me and he was a complete stranger anyway, so it didn't really mean anything. I wasn't sure what it meant with Wyler, but I didn't like it. Corey wouldn't like it. That I was using our symbol with Wyler Reese. Corey went inside me so rarely and yet I had allowed our opponent in.

Then he began to move and there was a dull ache between the choked pulses of my heart and anus, a vague ache that seemed half-imagined. I surrendered myself to the punishment. I suddenly felt I deserved the punishment. For betraying Corey. And I'd almost begun to enjoy being punished, when Wyler suddenly frowned, then gasped, then yelped, then sank down on his knees and was still.

"Shit," he muttered. "Sorry. I usually last, I really do.

But I'll make it up to you. See if I don't." He gently lifted me up and just as gently eased out; my anus breathed. He rolled over on his back and raised both legs in the air. "Now you make me make toeprints on the ceiling. Okay? I'll make it good for you, I promise."

Angry with him, I entered much too quickly. He winced and I wished he were face down so I wouldn't see his face, and then wished I weren't in him at all, because this was for Corey and me, no matter who was doing it to whom. But once I was in, it felt too good. His face relaxed and I decided it was safe to start fucking.

"Hmmm. So this is what you like," he sighed.

"Uh huh." But moving didn't bring me close to orgasm the way it did with Corey. Being fucked had hollowed me out, or maybe it was because this was Wyler, but I held onto his legs and methodically pumped him.

"I don't do this with just anybody, you know. I like being topman."

I thought he meant he was uncomfortable, so I nodded at the amyl nitrate bottle on the sheets. "You don't want to use some of your stuff?"

"Uh uh. High enough already. Knowing it's Shirtsy's dick inside me."

I was trying not to look at him, but had to look when he said that. I was frightened to find him staring back so intently. Our eyes locked for a moment while I wondered what he was feeling. I fucked harder, determined not to care what he felt. He rocked himself into my strokes, as if he actually enjoyed it, and he had his hands on my hips to keep me at it. Then he closed his eyes and sweetly tucked his lower lip under his front teeth.

And I came, loudly, beautifully, not caring if the thrusts hurt him or not. Until I laid my head on his chest and died.

His arms fell around me. Instinctively, I wrapped my arms around him. He breathed deeply, warmly. Very gradually, tenderly, I pulled out of him, then lay there in his warmth.

When I opened my eyes, I found the face of Wyler Reese in my arms. I waited for the last wisps of sexual smoke to clear. So I could see who I was with and how I felt towards them. Because sex changed people. It changed me. Sometimes there was friendliness, sometimes cool civility, sometimes outright hatred once the need was used up and there was nothing left to explain why you were in bed together. But that was how it'd been with strangers and Wyler was somebody I knew. It was difficult to say what he was to me now. I was grateful to him for sex that had been positively cacophonous with feelings of hate and joy, guilt and pleasure, and so good it seemed to have burned up all my hatred for him. I felt as if I had no skin.

The wide mouth on that flat pan of face looked as innocent as Howdy-Doody. How could you go to the trouble of hating such a face? Annoyance, yes, but not hatred. My hatred now seemed to me to have been as clumsy a piece of sexual theatrics as Wyler's Boy Scout charade. I tried to atone for it by asking, "How you doing?"

"Blissed out," he purred. "That was dynamite." His eyes remained closed.

"But you'd already come," I reminded him.

"Yeah. But it was your getting off I wanted to see. That was so beautiful it was like it was me."

His flattery made me uncomfortable, so I passed it back to him. "You were pretty good yourself. You've had lots of practice, huh?"

"Yeah. I've been around. But it was all like I was only getting ready for this."

More theatrics, I decided and countered with, "There's nothing wrong with your penis, Wyler. It's a fine penis."

"But it's not nearly as beautiful as yours."

We seemed to be fighting each other off with flattery, only Wyler's sounded less self-conscious than mine.

"Jesus," he sighed. "Say the more you dream about it, the more of a letdown it's gonna be. But this was a dream come true."

221

"Oh? Well," I said nervously, "I'm sure you've had better."

He opened dazed blue eyes and looked up at me, but couldn't keep his eyes open. "Oh Shirtsy," he whispered. "Shirtsy, Shirtsy, Shirtsy. Went apeshit for somebody only once in my life. Took me going apeshit before I knew I was queer. And that was over you, Shirtsy."

I almost leaped off him, but his arms pinned me to his chest. I grabbed for an explanation, something that would make what he'd said mean something else, but all I could say was, "The grass really helped with the sex. Good grass, right?"

"You made me know I was queer. Soon as you were gone, man, I knew I'd been in love with you. Took me six months to accept it, but I was in love with you back there. And now, here we are again. And I was ready for it. 'Bout time, huh?"

I had skin again and it was trapped in Wyler's embrace. I didn't want to believe that Wyler had once been in love with me. No, it was the Boy Scout camp that obsessed him, not me. "Oh, it was probably just adolescent lust," I said. "Maybe I was the first guy you ever had sexual feelings for,...." but that didn't sound much better. "No. You weren't in love with me. You were probably just... regretting, oh, regretting that you never had the chance to do something you wanted to do. It's like Oscar Wilde says. We regret only those things we didn't do. I know I do." I knew I was babbling.

Wyler wistfully smiled. "You ever regret that we never got it on at camp?"

"No. In all honesty, Wyler, no."

"That's cool. Yeah, you probably had so much dick to choose from down there, I was no great loss," he said sadly. "But I'm a better fuck than any of them, aren't I?"

"Yes," I said, "but..." It was his whole fantasy about me that I had to demolish before I could be free of him. "In all honesty—and I should've told you this earlier. But

222

I never got it on with anybody down there. Not once. I didn't even know I was gay back then."

He opened his eyes and grinned. "You're just saying that to make me feel better."

"Honest! I was just as dumb as you were. Not even that night with Corey. We just lay on our cots and talked."

"Uh uh. I ain't believin' that. But thanks for saying that. You just want me to think I didn't fuck things up back then. But it doesn't matter to me anymore. Now that we've found each other again."

Nothing I said could wake any sense into him. He could barely keep his eyes open, but I felt trapped in those eyes. There was a strange sense of deja vu, but none of my other encounters had ever looked at me like this. What I feared was that Wyler wanted to be in love with me again. I should've felt insulted, but it made me uneasy, and there was that sense that I'd been through this once before.

"You like living in New York?" he asked.

"Very much," I said, leaping at an innocent subject.

"Yeah. I like it. But I get lonely during the week."

"Well, maybe we could get together for coffee or dinner sometime during the week." What was I saying? I didn't want to strike up a friendship with Wyler.

"New Yorkers are weird. Even when you go to bed with them, they won't give you the time of day," he said sleepily. "I need a good Southern roommate."

"If I know anybody who's—"

"You like where you're living, Shirtsy?" His eyes were closed and he was smiling.

"Yes. I do." It frightened me that he could lay himself out so openly.

"Just an idea. Sleep on it."

"But," I had to say it to him as bluntly as possible, "I'm not able to think of you like that, Wyler."

"Like what? I'm not saying we should be lovers. Just

roommates." He was so matter-of-fact about it, he didn't even bother opening his eyes.

"But . . . I'm not even sure I like you."

"No? But you loved fucking me, didn't you? Oh yeah. You loved it as much as me. Fucks don't lie."

But mine had been powered by hatred. And now that hatred was gone, I felt nothing but a worried pity for Wyler. Arguing with him was like trying to argue with someone who was talking in their sleep. "Where's your bathroom?"

"On the right. In the hall," he murmured. "Don't take long."

I quickly sat up and saw the foreign apartment around me. I'd sat up naked and finished in enough foreign apartments to realize it was getting late and I should be going home. It was a relief to know that there was someplace else I had to be.

"You can use my robe," he said. "In case there's somebody out there."

But I pulled on my own clothes, with my back to the bed, waiting for him to ask what I was doing before I gave him some story about why I couldn't spend the night. He said nothing. I put on everything but my shoes before I turned around to look at him. With a smile on his face and completely uncovered, he lay there like a piece of dough waiting to be baked.

"Wyler?" I whispered.

But he was asleep. Sweetly, deeply, conveniently asleep.

With my boots in my hand, I tiptoed to the door. I didn't even turn out the light, for fear of waking him.

The subway station at Christopher was homey and familiar. This was where, every Friday night, I could safely think about what I'd just done. There was usually damp regret, but that was only the biological aftermath of sex, and I had learned it was as temporary as an itch, and about as moral. But tonight's regret felt different.

There'd been no regret during my long, hurried walk

back to the West Village—I wasn't sure what other subway would get me home and had felt the need to return by my usual route—only a feeling of escape and relief. My escape seemed so easy I decided I'd put too much importance in the encounter, that it wasn't really any different from the others. But here, safely underground, I did not feel as perfectly alone with my biological mood as I usually did. For one thing, I had never had to sneak away like that. I'd parted with other partners on the mutual understanding that once was enough and we were finished with each other. Leaving Wyler like that, I felt as if I'd left something undone. As if I'd left his stove on. I was sorry I hadn't at least pulled a blanket over him. After all, whatever the motivation, the sex had been exciting.

Poor Wyler. He thought he'd once been in love with me. He couldn't be in love with me now. I decided I'd only been flattering myself by imagining that. But even out of Wyler's embrace and safe from his eyes, the idea of his love, whether in the past or in the present, still made me uneasy, still filled me with the fear I'd been here before. Or maybe it was only the feeling of being buoyed back into the past that unnerved me. It did strange things to one's sense of reality.

A train arrived and filled the station with a wall of painted windows and open doors. All I had to do was step in and sit down; the train would carry me back to reality. I wondered if I should find a new bar, where I wouldn't run into Wyler, then if I should stop going to bars altogether. Every Friday night, on my way home, I entertained the notion of becoming faithful again.

The train sat for several minutes at Times Square. I saw the electric moon of a clock out on the platform: It was after two. I'd never been out so late before, but thought I could trust Corey to have already gone to bed. It was good to be going home to Corey. I could forget last night's annoyance with him and be grateful that he was there to go home to. The doors shuddered closed; the girders raced past like trees.

And I understood my deja vu. I'd had sex with someone who'd been in love with me without my knowing it.
Like the morning after my first sex with Corey, when I
was on my motorcycle, racing the trees on my way back
to the farm.

But that was a happy memory and Corey's love had
meant something to me, even back then, before I understood it. Wyler's love seemed like nothing but an emotional misunderstanding; it should've amused me. I didn't
understand why it should make me uneasy that Wyler's
love felt like a parody of Corey's. Everything happens
twice, said Corey or Marx, once as something real, and
then as farce. This was definitely the farce.

I amused myself by pretending that everything was
going to repeat itself. I would arrive home and find Jake
there, the guilty conscience that would postpone my dis-
covery of happiness—but I'd seen Jake two days ago and
he was incapable of being anyone's conscience. Weeks
would pass, various complications and then, on one confusing night, I'd discover I was in love with Wyler Reese?

No way. If that was what worried me, I was crazier
than I thought. And yet, I couldn't help remembering
how good the sex had been. The farther I flew from the
scene of it, the better it looked. I had loved hating Wyler.
Did I hate loving Corey? No, I didn't hate my love, but I
did feel confined by it. I could never selfishly let myself
go with Corey as I had with Wyler. And not just sexually,
but in terms of my day to day life with him. If only I
could put one inside the other...

But no, I wasn't going to fall in love with Wyler.
There was nothing to be afraid of there. I'd merely been
reading too many novels and real life did not work itself
out in such neat, ironic patterns. I was in an associative
mood tonight, that's all. Earlier, I'd seen Wyler's life as a
parody of mine. The world was a funhouse mirror.

I'd stopped worrying about it by the time I climbed the
stairs in our building. It was all too complicated, this living for sex and love. What I needed was a good, safe

hobby. Or a job. I fished out my keys and started matching them to their locks.

I was still fumbling with the patented safety lock when the door began to snap and pop on its own.

I backed away.

The door creaked open. There stood Corey.

My stoicism collapsed. I was terrified to find him facing me, wide awake at three o'clock in the morning, wearing a stern mask of sadness. How did he know?

"Boy! What're you doing up so—"

He cut me off with a raised hand, then stepped aside and nodded me in.

Worry about something hard enough, and it won't happen. But I hadn't been worrying about this tonight. It hadn't even crossed my mind. Suddenly I wanted nothing from Corey but that he be ignorant and smugly trusting again. "Almost three, Boy." But he couldn't possibly know for certain. "I hope you haven't been worrying about why I was—"

"Ssssh!"

Unless he had found my list and the entries that had been growing more explicit. My heart raced.

He led me down the hall, but Ed was at work and we should have been able to talk anywhere in the apartment. The mere sound of my voice must cause him pain.

I loved him; I did not want to hurt him. And worse, I did not want to lose him and hurt myself.

Corey stepped into the living room and stood there, looking at something he wanted me to look at. His sadness did not look as stern as I'd remembered it seeming at the door.

I followed his look to a baby on the sofa. The baby was longer than my niece Joan, and even in sleep seemed more humanly expressive than Joan.

I touched ground again and drew a deep breath. It was this sleeping baby that worried Corey. It wasn't me at all.

This baby?

227

9

THEN A HAND with blunt nails tucked the blanket around the baby's plump leg. The hand raised a silencing finger across the pinch-lipped smile of my sister.

"Liza!"

"Sssssh," she went and shared her smile with Corey, who stood there with his hands in his pockets.

Relief became joy—for a moment. Then confusion set in.

Joan slept on her stomach, faced turned out and little fists balled, silky hair feathered around her bony head.

Liza's hair was almost as short as her daughter's. The frame of angel wings had been shorn and her hair was level with her jaw. She had ears again. Her face looked as sharp and spare as a knife and I blinked twice before I realized she wasn't wearing make-up. Her hair needed brushing; her eyes needed sleep. I stepped towards her to kiss my sister hello.

The floor creaked under the carpet.

"Ssssh!" She held up her hand while she studied her daughter. "In the kitchen," she whispered.

Liza lifted a guitar from the chair beside the sofa—the guitar bonged faintly when it touched the floor—and turned the back of the chair against the sofa. She wedged a sofa cushion on its side so that Joan was boxed in all around.

What was she doing here? Our silence made her presence more dramatic. I found myself expecting the worse, almost hoping for it.

"Okay," she whispered, shooed us out into the hall and gently closed the door behind her. "The little dickens doesn't know what time it is. Jet lag. Well. Hello there, Shrimp," and she gave me a hug and a kiss on the cheek.

I was excited, confused, but all I could manage to say was, "This *is* a surprise."

"I'm full of surprises," said Liza. With her arm across my shoulder, we followed Corey to the kitchen.

"I'm putting on some tea," said Corey. "Not sleepy. Might as well be alert. Anyone else want tea?"

"Well," I said. "Well! What a surprise." I deliberately grinned to hide my confusion. But I was happy to see her, happy because she was my sister and happy because I'd been fearing the worst for myself, only to find my catastrophe upstaged by this. I couldn't help feeling that Liza was here because of a catastrophe of her own, but one that I approved of. "It's terrific to see you, Liza, but . . . what brings you to New York?"

"You," she said. "What else?"

I glanced at Corey to see if he knew yet, but he watched expectantly.

"We really threw Corey for a loop," she said. "He came home and found us sitting on your front stoop."

"Yes. I was coming home and heard wailing," said Corey. "Like cats. I thought it was only cats, which sound like babies to me anyway. But it was Liza with Joan, crying her heart out."

"Joan crying her heart out. Not me," said Liza cheerfully.

But Corey wasn't trying to be funny. "I just wish she'd told us she was coming. You should've called us, Liza. I don't like the idea of you and Joan out there in the cold."

"We were both bundled up. And it was only an hour or so."

"Still. You should've called ahead. What if we'd gone

out of town for the weekend? New York at night is not a good place for a mother and child."

"I can take care of myself," said Liza, not at all annoyed by his chiding; apparently they'd already been discussing this. "Don't be so motherly," she teased. "Corey always such a mother hen, Joel?"

She seemed so calm and cheerful, I had to doubt what I was hoping. Not only did my wish seem groundless, but it was perverse to wish such a catastrophe on your own sister. But the question would not go away. "Then, Bob's not with you?"

Liza shrugged. "Nope."

"Then, uh, where is he?"

"Off with the boys on maneuvers. Once a year, a bunch of them go off with the Dutch and Germans to play 'army' for a month. Shooting missiles into the Baltic."

"Then, you're here on vacation? Alone?"

"Vacation? Yes. Kind of. Me and Joan." She looked as if she were bursting with a joke she couldn't wait to tell.

Corey glanced at me and I realized he wondered what I wondered, but had been waiting for me, the brother, to find out.

She reached into her pocket and brought out a freshly opened pack of cigarettes, shook one out and stuck it into her smile. It took her two matches to light it. I hadn't seen Liza smoke a cigarette since the night before her wedding.

I could no longer play innocent. "Uh, Liza?" I passed her the ashtray. "Have you, uh... *Have you left Bob?*"

She met my eyes with hers and was ready to grin or break out laughing. Then she took another long drag from her cigarette, lowered her eyes and solemnly said, "I think so."

"Oh, hell," moaned Corey.

"Oh Liza," I sighed, as sadly as possible, but all the time thinking, *I knew it, I knew it!* with a joy I knew wasn't right.

230

Liza squared her shoulders and proudly smoked her cigarette. She seemed to gain strength from our response; we made what she'd done more real to her. "Took me four miserable years to do it. But I finally did it."

"What happened?" I asked.

"What happened? I woke up. That's what happened."

"Yes, but what did it? Did he hit you or you got into a bad fight? Did you find out he was seeing other women?" I asked.

"*Nothing* happened. Bob's been what Bob's always been. And I woke up to the fact that that's not what I want in life."

"But...?" But I agreed with her. I'd never believed Kearney was right for her.

"But you don't just leave someone out of the blue!" said Corey. "There wasn't a fight or something that set it off?"

"No. How could there have been a fight? Bob's been on maneuvers for four weeks."

"Just out of the blue? Nothing triggered it? You just got up and left him?"

"Yes!" said Liza, growing impatient with our failure to understand.

"But you were happy together!" Corey cried. And he caught himself, realizing how vehement he'd become. He looked to me to continue the questioning, but before I could ask anything, he broke in with, "Weren't you? Okay, I can imagine Bob's not always the easiest person in the world to live with. But you have something together. Don't you? Three years of marriage and a baby? That's something, isn't it? I don't understand how you can walk away from that...*for no particular reason.*"

Liza angrily cut her eyes at Corey and addressed me. "The reason is that it was wrong. Right from the start. One long lie. And for four years I've been trying to make the lie true by lying to myself. No more. I finally woke up. And nobody's going to shame me because I woke up."

"Nobody's trying to shame you," said Corey apologetically. "I just find it too—I find it too abstract to believe. You loved each other for three or four years."

"Sheesh. And I thought you two, of all people, would understand. You're not exactly a conventional couple yourselves, you know. You're following your hearts. Can't you understand me following mine?"

"I'm not talking about being conventional," said Corey. "I'm talking about the love you had."

Liza gritted her teeth. "But the love we had was conventional. All the approved lies. Yes, Bob loved—*loves* me. Like a ton of bricks. And I played along with that. For four long years. Ever since we met. I compromised, I played along, all the time thinking that it was this game that was the real thing. Like my doubts were nothing but neurotic tics and cowardice and excuses. Joel knows this. Joel's heard it all before. It doesn't surprise *you* that I've done what I've done."

"No," I said. "It doesn't"

"Well, I finally admitted to myself that it was the doubts that were real. And it was love that was cowardly."

I nodded knowingly and felt a deep sympathy for my sister, a sympathy that seemed to originate in righteous satisfaction for what I'd achieved with Corey.

Corey brought two cups of tea to the table and sat down between us. "Please. I admit I'm in the dark here. I'm only your brother's . . . partner. And I'm sorry if I've been speaking out of turn. But out of the blue like this. It goes against everything I've ever thought about the two of you. Okay, I do tend to romanticize marriages and the like." Beneath the table, his knee brushed against mine.

And only then did I remember that I had no cause to congratulate myself and Corey.

I reached over to cover Liza's hand with mine. "But why now, Liza? I understand. Sort of. But after all this time, what happened?"

She shrugged. "I woke up."

"Nothing special brought it on? Nothing like... Bob seeing other women or something?" My mind kept coming back to that only because it seemed like something Kearney was capable of. I realized I could be talking about myself.

"No. And I'm glad it wasn't, because that would've put me in the position of the Injured Woman," she said sarcastically. "No, I know it sounds like nothing, but..." She drew her hand out from under mine to light up another cigarette. "He was gone. Was plain as that. Bob was gone for four whole weeks and I finally had room to breathe and think straight. We've never been apart for that long the whole time we've been married. Oh, the first few days I missed him. As usual. But then I got used to it and found myself feeling more... relaxed. It was like I'd been keyed up for three years and stopped noticing it because it'd been so constant. I found myself doing things I usually didn't do when Bob was around. Little things, like letting the apartment to go to pot while I sang all afternoon. Getting my hair cut. That fluff-bunny look was such a hassle. I know it doesn't sound like much, and it isn't—it shouldn't be. So, couple of weeks go by and I'm quite content doing what I please. And then I start realizing, 'Bob'll be back in a week.' And then, 'Bob'll be back in a few days.' And I could feel myself getting all tensed up inside, knowing I had one day less before I'd have to go back being the way I was. It was awful." She laughed. "Dreading his return was way out of proportion to the little bit of happiness I'd had while he was gone. Four days left, then three days, and I got so tense I started getting sick to my stomach. Literally." She laughed again, callously this time. "I was literally throwing up! Honest. And it finally dawned on me. 'Elizabeth,' I told myself, 'you don't have to live like this. There *are* alternatives to being miserable.' I was very cool and rational about it. Was not hysterical in the least. Spoke to a lawyer yesterday. JAG lawyers can be as bad as chaplains, always siding with their fellow officers, but he gave me the info I needed. About divorce and custody. I went straight from there to the bank, then into town to buy my ticket. And then I went home. To sleep on it. So I could prove to myself it wasn't any whim, that it really was something I had to do. When I woke up this morning, I knew it was the right thing and nothing Bob or anyone else could say would've made me feel differently. I took Joan with me to the airport in Frankfurt...and here I am," she said proudly, "smoking cigarettes in New York City."

Corey pinched his eyebrows over the story, not sure how to react to it.

"And how do you feel now?" I asked. "You still feel like you're doing the right thing?"

"Yes," she said automatically, then admitted, "Oh, I am scared. Who wouldn't be? I don't know what's going to happen. But I can be happy being a little scared, considering what the alternative's been. Might be more difficult if I were alone, But, having you, Brother..." She smiled wistfully.

I liked being counted on. "You'll go on to Virginia and stay with Mom and Gram?"

"Well..." Her face darkened and she looked at Corey's tea. "I don't think I'm quite ready to do that yet."

"Oh Liza. You don't still think Mom's got a grudge against you?"

"There's that," she admitted. "And I feel a little raw right now."

"Come on. Be practical. Where else can you go?"

Liza picked at the chipped Formica on the table's edge. "Here?"

"Here! But Liza, we—" I looked at Corey, but he was as surprised as I was. "We'd love to have you, but...And Joan? I don't think—" And yet, I did have a responsibility; I didn't want to say no.

"I know it's a lot to ask. But it'd only be for a few days. We can sleep in the living room. For a few days, Joel, a week maybe. While I catch my breath and get my head together."

Corey was thinking very hard and serious. "I think we could convince Ed," he said.

"I don't know." I liked the idea of Liza staying here. "I'm just trying to be practical about it. It'd be different if you had no place else to go, Liza. You could stay with us as long as you liked. But Mom's got a whole house down there. She'd be happy to have you. She'd understand. She's been through this herself, remember?"

"Which is why I'm not ready to go down there," she said sharply.

"But why?"

"Because I'm not ready to deal with her gloating."

"What'd she be gloating about? That you're getting a divorce? That's nothing for anyone to gloat about. Catherine least of all."

"No. She wouldn't gloat out loud. But it'd be there. Under all her sympathy and understanding, there'd be hints of 'I told you so, I told you so.'" She imitated our mother with a nasal voice that was purely imaginary. "And I couldn't deal with that right now. I'd react against it. I'd start defending Bob. And the next thing I knew, I'd be going back to him. No, I've thought this through and Mom's the last thing I need right now."

"You couldn't admit you made a mistake? To Mom?"

"Not to Mom. Not yet anyway."

"There's some cribs in storage at the Cathedral School," said Corey. "They're never used. I'm sure they'd let me borrow one."

I knew how Corey's mind worked. He'd set aside all his skepticism about Liza's decision so that he could play the part of the Good Samaritan.

"Just for a week or so. That's all I ask, Brother. You won't have to worry about feeding us—"

"I wasn't thinking about that."

"—or supporting us. I've got a little money left. And I could maybe earn a little money while I'm here."

"Don't worry about that. I don't think you're going to be here long enough to get a job."

"I thought I could sing."

"This is New York, Liza. You've got to be awfully good to get a singing job somewhere."

"Then I'll sing on street corners. You see people doing it in Germany all the time."

"I don't think that'll be necessary." I presumed she was using it only as one last argument to convince me. But I was already convinced. I wondered how far my unemployment would go with two more mouths to feed and if maybe now was the time for me to get a job. Corey wasn't the only one who wanted to be a Samaritan.

The phone in our bedroom suddenly rang, muffled by our closed door.

Corey stood up. "Who the hell can that be? What time is it anyway?"

"After four," I said as I stood up too.

"Oh shit," said Liza. "I'll bet that's Bob."

The phone rang again, but Corey and I only stood there, staring down at Liza.

"Must be morning over there," she explained. "Bob probably just got home and found my note. Probably looking for me."

"Your note?" said Corey. "You mean you didn't tell him you were leaving?"

"Does he know you're here?" I demanded.

"Uh uh. Told him only that I was taking Joan back to the states. Didn't tell him where."

Corey and I stared at each other. We were the ones panicked by the desperate ringing in the next room, while Liza remained calm.

"So don't tell him I'm here, okay?"

"Why not?" said Corey.

"Because I don't want to talk to him."

Liza seemed to know what she was doing; we didn't. We obeyed Liza.

"You talk to him," I told Corey. "You're closer to him. He'll trust you."

"No. You're the better liar."

236

I didn't like being told that, but Corey was right and the phone was still ringing. "And you're not here?" I asked Liza as I went for the bedroom door.

"And you haven't seen hide or hair of me!" she called out.

When I opened the door, the ringing sounded as shrill as a scream. I knocked the receiver out of its cradle before I picked it up. I would pretend I'd been asleep. "Hulla?"

"Hello? Shirtsy? This is Bob Kearney." Quick and blunt, from halfway around the world. "I'm calling to find out if you know—"

"Wha' time is't?"

"Ten in the morning here, so it must be the middle of the night over there. Look. I know I've woken you up. But I wouldn't be calling unless it were an emergency. *Have you seen Liza?*"

"Huh? Liza? No, Liza's living in Germany. With her husband."

"Come on, man. Wake up. This *is* her husband. This is Bob Kearney. *Calling* from Germany."

"Oh?" But I felt cruel playing the sleepy fool with him. "What's up, Bob?"

"What's up is that—Liza's gone! Joan too. And I'm calling to see if you've seen or heard from her."

"No. Not a peep. She left without telling you where she was going?"

"Nothing. Only..." His long distance crispness began to break. "Came home at six this morning. Been up north on maneuvers for four weeks, and came home to an empty apartment. Nobody there. Nothing but a note taped to the tv set."

He sounded so forlorn and confused, nothing like the vindictive husband I'd been imagining. "What did the note say, Bob?"

"Got it right here. Been clutching it ever since I got home and been calling all over base, trying to find someone who might've talked to her or—*Dear Bob,*" he read. "*I am sorry to do it this way, but it is the only way. I have*

237

taken Joan with me and returned to the States. Please don't think it was something you did. It was me. It has always been me. We are wrong for each other and no amount of love can ever overcome that undeniable fact. I am sorry to have to hurt you like this, but there is no alternative after having hurt myself for so long. But sometimes we have to hurt others in order to save ourselves."

I could see part of the kitchen from where I sat, but only Corey had leaned back far enough for me to see him. Liza was hidden in the corner.

"And then she goes on about what she took out of our checking account and what to do with her possessions and . . . custody of Joan." There was a long pause and a low, cold roar in the line. "And she finishes by saying her mind's made up and I won't be hearing from her again until she gets a lawyer."

"Then she's left you."

"Seems to be the size of it," he muttered. "Yes dammit! She's left me!"

"I'm sorry, Bob. I really am." I did feel a little sorry for the man. "I wish there was something we could do for you, but you know Liza. She's always had a mind of her own."

"What bothers me most," he continued, half to himself, "the thing that's knocked me cockeyed is I never saw this coming. No arguments or sulks. Nothing. She's been happy as a clam ever since we had Joan. And now this?"

"Maybe she's been hiding some of her feelings?" I suggested.

"Uh uh. I know her feelings. Know them all too well. I wonder if she's flipped out. I was gone too long and she had some kind of nervous breakdown or something."

"No, Bob. I don't think—"

"Liza gets anxious when she's alone. She's anxious anyway, like about her old lady. But it really gets bad when she's alone. I wonder if having me away for so long at a stretch, she panicked. Went off the deep end. She got so

238

panicky she had to run home to her family? Damn. How could I have let this happen? If only I'd seen it coming! I could've taken some precautions!"

"You can't think that, Bob. Liza has her reasons, I'm sure—I haven't seen her, but I know my sister. If she left you, it wasn't because she went crazy."

"But I'm worried about her! And if she's gone crazy and is out there somewhere with my baby girl...No, you're right. I have no grounds for thinking that. But I've got to find an explanation somewhere. And thinking she's crazy makes it easier for me to forgive the bitch. Hey, I call her a bitch now only because I'm angry. She's pulled the rug out from under me, Shirtsy. But I don't want to be angry with her. Because I still love her. She's left me up to my ears in shit, but I still love her."

I had to end this conversation. Kearney was getting nowhere and I was being drawn into his pain. "If we see her, Bob? If she does show up in New York, is there anything we should tell her for you?"

"Yes. You can tell her to call me. There's nothing I can do to her over the phone. I don't want to hurt her. I love her. If there's problems, she and I can work them out. We've worked them out in the past. Tell her I love her and I'm not going to give up either her or my daughter without trying to do something to save us. But it's her I want to talk to, not some asswipe lawyer. Can you tell her that? And phrase it more kindly, will you?"

"If I see her. Have you called Virginia yet?"

"No. I was going to call them next. Just figured she would've passed through New York and thought she might've talked to you."

"Your call is the first I've heard of it, Bob. I'll bet she's gone to Virginia. Or is on her way down there. But Bob? It's four-thirty over here. And Gram's very sick, you know. So could you wait a few hours before calling them?"

"What? Oh sure. Sure. Yeah, she probably is with her

239

mom. Okay. Thanks for being an ear, Shirtsy. I'll let you know what happens." *Click*. He finished so quickly, I knew he was going to call Virginia immediately.

I returned to the kitchen. "Whew!"

"Thanks, Shrimp," said Liza with a thin smile. She offered me a cigarette.

I shook my head and collapsed in the chair.

"Very awkward?" asked Corey, concerned for me.

"What is it you're supposed to tell me?" asked Liza. "*If you see me.*"

I gave her the message.

Liza nodded. "Poor Bob," she sighed and sipped her cigarette. "He's going to add up quite a phone bill before this is over."

Her nonchalance annoyed me. I was torn between sympathy for a sister and pity for a husband, but my sister showed no pain at all. "So it didn't upset you to hear me talk to Bob?"

"Not at all. Surprisingly. Made me more confident that I *am* doing the right thing."

"But you left without telling him?" said Corey. "You didn't even wait until he was back and you could tell him to his face?"

"Bob read me your note. That you taped to the tv."

"Yeah, well I had to put it somewhere where he'd see it." But she knew that wasn't what we were questioning. "You don't think Bob would've let me walk out the door with Joan if he were there, do you? No sir. Not that he would've used force. Bob's never laid a hand on me, not even the times I've taken pokes at him. Nope. He would've pleaded, promised and apologized. Lose his temper maybe, but then be so damn remorseful about it he'd make me feel like I'd drowned a kitten. And what's sickening about it is that none of it's a put on. All of it would've been perfectly sincere."

"But you won't talk to him now? Not even on the phone?" asked Corey.

"No way. Because he'd pull the same crap on me there.

And by sheer persistence, the dope would talk me back into his arms." Liza looked at both of us, recognizing that she was losing our sympathy. "I know what I'm talking about," she insisted. "I know that if I talk to him, he'll make me feel guilty and confused and I'll be right back where I started from. He'll promise me this and promise me that and mean every desperate word of it. And we start all over again and after a few weeks things slide right back to the way they were. And I slide with them. Just because it's too much trouble to fight it. It's as much me as it is him. But it's not right that I have to get hurt and angry in order to hold my own with Bob. He does it naturally, without even having to think about it. But I have to feel pain before I can work myself up to do anything about it. It's too draining. I don't have that kind of energy. So it's compromise, compromise, compromise. With me always paying. And me getting nothing in return, but that sad-eyed love of Bob's that hangs on me like a wet blanket. I've been paying for four long years now and I'm bankrupt. I stopped existing, except as Bob's Wife. So when he was gone for a month and I could exist again—" She grimaced and shook her head. "This probably all sounds crazy to you because both of you are men and you can hold your own with each other. Without having to strain."

"You see it with same-sex couples too," said Corey.

"But not us," I quickly added.

"No, not us," said Corey.

"Good. Might be good therapy for me to spend some time with a couple who are equals. Help me screw my head on straight."

Her compliment felt unearned and my uneasiness caught up with me again. But no, whatever our problem was, we weren't Liza and Kearney.

"It's been a long day, guys. I am zonked."

"How do you want to work this?" said Corey. "There's my sleeping bag in the closet. I'll use that tonight and you and Joel can share the bed."

"No!" Liza laughed. "I don't want to sleep with my brother! And I won't break up a set. No, *I'll* use the sleeping bag and sleep in the living room. Where I can keep an eye on Joan. You two keep your bed. And when we get the crib, I'll take the sofa."

Corey gave her his sleeping bag and I gave her a flannel shirt to sleep in; she'd remembered all Joan's things but forgotten some of her own. She kissed each of us on the cheek and said, "Thanks for trying to understand."

Alone in our own room, in the calm silence that followed, a sense of contentment stole over me and Corey. Neither of us mentioned it, but it was definitely there as we quietly undressed for bed. We were helping someone. And no matter what else had happened tonight, the failure of one couple made our existence as a couple seem more real to me.

"So," I said as I pulled the blankets up around our shoulders. "What do you think?"

"Only that... oh, I'm not sure what I think yet. You mean if Liza's doing the right thing or not."

"That. And the rest of it. Her staying here for a few days."

"That part I like. Appeals to the Boy Scout in me."

"Aha! I thought so."

"Still, I can't believe it's really over with them. Can you?"

"Don't know. I never felt he was really right for Liza."

"Yeah, but... three years of marriage? That's as long as we've been together. And a baby to boot? No, I can't help feeling that she'll stay with us a week or so, work out her problems on her own and go back to Bob."

"I hope not."

"No? Maybe you know better. You're her brother. But I can't help hoping they do get back together. Maybe it's because I identify with Bob."

"Don't be a jerk, Boy. You don't identify with Bob."

"I don't want to. But I do. A little."

"You're nothing like Bob," I insisted.

The front door clattered open and shut and we heard Ed dragging his feet down the hall.

"He's certainly late tonight," said Corey. "I was hoping he'd come in while we were still in the kitchen. So we could clear it with him about Liza."

"Do it in the morning," I yawned and snuggled into Corey.

"Hey? Why were you so late tonight? Must've been after three when you came in."

"Me? Oh, uh—" It was only panic's habit and Corey sounded curious, not suspicious. "You know Wagner." Was it Wagner I was supposed to have heard tonight? "Didn't let out until almost one. And I was feeling so high I wanted to walk home. I guess I dawdled."

"No problem. Only you couldn't have chosen a worse night for dawdling. Never sure what I should say to Liza. I wanted you to get home and take over."

"Sorry I was so late, Boy. It won't happen again." I kissed his unruffled forehead.

"It did add to the suspense," he said. "You sleep well. I think we're both going to need it."

"Uh huh. Probably sleep until noon," I sighed.

And we adjusted the covers again while we untangled ourselves from each other and settled down back to back. Corey immediately fell asleep, but I just lay there, feeling his warmth behind me and thinking. I didn't brood or fret. It was only a quiet turning over of thoughts.

Liza and Kearney.

Corey and me.

Me and Wyler. Me and a half-dozen other partners of no weight or importance.

But what happened with me had nothing in common with what was happening with Liza. The little stabs of conscience that had punctuated our conversation did not cut very deep. They were only pokes reminding me that I had to be more careful. And I would be more careful. Tonight had shown me how this sort of thing could get out of hand.

243

I coolly acknowledged the dangers. But beneath my conscientiousness was another feeling, an emotion that seemed to have nothing to do with my thoughts and yet kept those thoughts aloft, like a current of air. I was frightened by my sister's pain and Kearney's confusion. I did not want anything like that to happen to us.

It was so late now it was becoming early. The black silhouette of the building framed in our smudged window was growing windows of its own, grey cornices and the sharp cage of a fire escape. The sky above it grew lighter. Our own room grew around us, bare as ever, but grey now, with its high ceiling disappearing into shoals of shadow above us.

I was glad my sister was here. I fell asleep, soothed by thoughts of domestic order and normalcy.

At seven o'clock, I was awakened by screaming from the next room: Joan.

At eight, Catherine called. Yes, Bob had phoned in the middle of the night and if we knew what in Sam Blazes was going on . . . I passed Liza the phone and she passed me the baby.

"Just take her, Shrimp. She won't break. Mom? Good morning. I'm sorry the stinker called you in the . . . Oh? . . . Uh huh . . . Uh huh . . . *Uh uh.* No . . . I can't just yet, because . . . Mom! Will you let me talk?"

I lugged Joan over to our bed and plopped her down beside Corey. He was still half-asleep, propped up on one elbow while he watched Liza on the phone and this baby on our bed, trying to remember where they'd come from.

Joan was delighted by the bed. It was low enough to seem like part of the floor and yet so soft and smelly. Her fine hair was combed forward, like the hair of a man trying to hide a bald spot, and the legs of her orange overalls were unsnapped and flapping. She tried standing up, but the mattress was too soft. She keeled over backwards and landed on Corey's stomach.

"Oof!"'

"Dada!" she cried and lunged for Corey's face.

I was miffed she'd called Corey Dada and not me.

She began gibbering to herself and slapping Corey's face. I took advantage of her preoccupation to pull on my pants. I didn't think it was right my sister or her baby should see us in our underwear.

"I'll come down there, Mom. But not just yet. I have to—Joel. Don't let her do that. She's at the age where she doesn't realize she's hurting other people. Play 'Where's Baby?' with her—Please, Mother. I know what I'm doing and the time's not right to ..."

Corey suffered Joan's beating with closed eyes, a smile and an occasional wince, as tolerant as a family dog. I pulled her off him and sat her down on the mattress. "Where's baby?" I sang.

She didn't get it.

I threw the sheet over her head and tried again. "Where's baby?" She cooed under the sheet, then I pulled it off her and she burst into giggles. "There she is!"

We played until her mother was off the phone.

Liza took Joan into her lap and finished snapping her overalls.

"So what's the word?" I asked.

"Oh, she wants me to come straight home," muttered Liza. "Says she'll hire a lawyer for me down there. But I told her: I'm not coming home until I'm good and ready."

"She wasn't upset?"

"You know Mom. She skipped the hysterics and went straight into the nuts and bolts. She said we would talk about it when I was there."

"So when do you think you'll go?"

"When I'm good and ready," she repeated, peevishly.

Joan wiggled in her lap and reached for Corey. "Dada!" she gibbered.

"Keeps calling me Dada," said Corey, flattered and amused.

Liza didn't even smile. "Babies this age aren't very discriminating when it comes to fathers. Any large hairy object will do."

It was Saturday, but Corey and I couldn't go out for our usual leisurely breakfast. We ate at home, because of Joan. I went down to the bodega around the corner for eggs, bread, baby food and disposable diapers. It was the closest store, in the middle of a Puerto Rican block on Amsterdam, and I'd been there many times, but had never noticed the items advertised on the store's sign, done in paint, as if they were the neighborhood's only absolute necessities: *Tabaco, Biero,* Pampers.

Breakfast was an unappetizing affair, with Joan in Liza's lap letting mouthfuls of runny egg spill down her chin and spatter her bib. After breakfast, Liza gave her a bath. She usually bathed Joan in the evening, but there hadn't been enough time last night. She considered using the kitchen sink, which was certainly deep enough, but it was still full of dirty dishes and we'd lost the plug. Liza decided to use the huge claw-footed tub in the bathroom, even though it meant she had to scrub it first. There was a coat of green and grey dinge at the bottom that had never bothered us when we used the tub for showers. Joan stomped up and down the bathroom while her mother scrubbed. Joan was just learning to walk and there were so many things here to grab for support: pipes, the toilet, my knees, her mother's stooped shoulders. I intervened only when she discovered that pulling on the toilet paper could make the dispenser spin like a top. Liza filled the tub with two inches of water and began to undress Joan. Corey and I stayed in the doorway and watched.

"What're you gawking at, guys? I'm only going to wash a baby." On her knees, with her shirt tail out and her sleeves rolled up, Liza looked very tough and self-sufficient.

"I was the youngest," said Corey. "All this is new to me. I find it fascinating."

Liza lifted the naked baby who looked so pink, cheerful and edible and lowered her into the deep white dish of the tub. Joan's eyes grew wide. Then her mouth grew wide and she began to howl.

"Oh, Piglet," Liza sighed. "You're supposed to have outgrown this. It's just like your tub at home, darling." She brushed a little water on her daughter's chest, but Joan sat there, screaming.

I looked down the hall, afraid the crying might wake Ed.

"Your tub scares her," said Liza as she lifted Joan out. "Only one thing to do. I'll have to get in with her, so she'll know it's okay."

Joan leaned against the tub and stopped sobbing. "Mama?" she cried and pointed when Liza began unbuttoning her own shirt.

"All right, guys. Shoo. You can be voyeurs with my daughter, but I draw the line at putting on a show myself. Don't fret, my little neurotic. Momma's getting into the big, bad tub with you."

Liza closed the door on us and we returned to the kitchen.

"Fascinating," said Corey. "Absolutely fascinating."

"I think it's going to be more than we bargained for."

We'd finished cleaning the kitchen when Liza came out, wrapped in a towel, carrying her clothes in one arm and towel-swaddled Joan in the other. Joan was talking: gibberish, but arranged in sentences, as if she knew the tune of speech even if she didn't know any of the words yet. "Really?" Liza answered her. "You don't say? What was that? Could you repeat that?" They went into the living room and Liza pushed the door half-shut with her foot.

A minute later, Ed's door opened and out tromped Ed with a face like a fallen cake.

"Ed? You're certainly up early. Uh, not yet eleven."

"Couldn't go back to sleep," he grumbled and went for the coffee. "Had the worse dream. Dreamed I was back in Tunis. With the Unesco Mother's Helper Program. And I

247

was locked in a room full of veiled women and squalling brats. Not something I care to relive."

Corey and I looked at each other while Ed looked for the sugar.

"Oh Ed," said Corey. "Before we forget... Joel's sister arrived last night. You won't mind if she stays with us for a few days? Will you?"

"Will she play Alice Cooper records nonstop and hog the bathroom all morning, blow-drying her hair?" Which was what Ed's cousin had done when she stayed here.

"No. Not much chance of that," I said.

"Then why should I care? But if she's going to sleep on the sofa, make it clear to her that in the afternoon the living room is mine. And I hope you've warned her not to expect more than a grunt or a nod from me."

"We'll warn her," I assured him.

Just then, there as a joyful shriek from the other end of the hall, and a naked baby staggered out of the living room. Joan hurried to the wall, caught herself on it, pushed off and lurched across to the opposite wall. She faced us, threw her arms in the air and shrieked again, before landing on her bottom. Liza ran out in panties and bra, scooped Joan off the floor and whisked her back to the living room. "You little showoff, you're going to catch cold." She butted the door shut behind her.

"Oh yes. One other thing," I told Ed. "She has a baby."

But Ed was still staring down the hall.

"A well-behaved baby," I lied. "And it'll only be for a few days."

"Joel's sister left her husband," Corey quickly explained. "And she needs a place to stay for a few days, Ed, before she goes home to Virginia. We know it's an inconvenience for you, but we can't abandon a mother and child, can we, Ed?"

"Extraordinarily well-behaved baby," I said.

Ed slowly turned his head and glared at us.

"For a few days?" asked Corey.

"Open a kindergarten!" Ed cried. "Why should I care?"

We had spooked Ed one time too many; I couldn't look him in the eye.

"What do you expect me to say? *No? Out they go?* I'm stuck with you, which means I'm stuck with them, but your relatives are none of my business, and all I can say is that if I find baby puke on the upholstery, *you're* the ones who'll pay to have it dry-cleaned!" He grabbed his coffee and stomped down to his room, muttering, "Families. Southerners. *Babies.*"

"Thanks, Ed. I hoped you'd understand," Corey shouted.

Ed slammed his door behind him.

"Uh oh," I said."

"He'll come around," Corey insisted. "Give him a day or two to adjust to the situation, and his old Peace Corps altruism will reassert itself. I hope. Anyway, who can resist something as innocent as a baby?"

Ed could, but he managed to do it only by avoiding contact with Joan all weekend. He was grudgingly civil with Liza when he met her, but carefully avoided meeting Joan.

The rest of us were dominated by Joan that weekend. When Joan was awake, we couldn't talk or even think for two consecutive minutes without having to do something for Joan or worrying *why* we hadn't had to do something for her. I gave in and, just to have something to do, let Liza teach me baby procedure. She had me changing a diaper while Corey watched from a distance. And it was a disgusting business, but only slightly dirtier than sex and not nearly as messy as butchering a goat.

By Monday, Joan had loosened her hold—on the others. Corey went to work. Liza ran errands: first to Western Union—it'd been decided that she should telegraph Bob and let him know that she and the baby were safe, without letting him know where they were—then to a Legal Aid office for interim advice, and then, if there was time, to a couple of folk clubs, just out of curiosity. Uncle Joel stayed at home with the baby.

I was glad when Liza came home and I could get out, even if it was only to buy groceries. Liza had learned what she needed to know. She'd forfeited any claim to alimony by running out on her husband, but she said she didn't want anything from Kearney. New York divorce laws were impossible and the lawyer said her best bet was to file for divorce in Virginia. If she wanted custody of her child, she was right to keep Joan with her now, but the husband could file for temporary custody if it looked like the wife were in an unstable situation. An unemployed brother and his homosexual lover would not be considered stable by a court of law, and the lawyer suggested she go straight to her mother in Virginia. And, because it was 1975, there was only one folk club in all of New York. With so many pros out of work, there was no hope for novices like Liza.

So there was nothing to keep Liza in New York and everything to justify her going home to Virginia. But Liza remained quietly adamant. Not yet. A week, maybe two weeks. Time to put her head in order. "I know it sounds neurotic as hell, but you'll just have to bear with me. I'm not going to face Mom until I know where I stand. I didn't pop out from under Bob's thumb just so I could go crawling back under Mom's."

"Come off it, Liza. You were never under Mom's thumb. She doesn't have a thumb."

"On you it was probably light as a feather. But not for me. Anyway, I'm perfectly safe here as long as Bob doesn't know where I am. And my 'unstable' situation." She made mocking quotation marks with her fingers. "Although I think you and Core are a damn sight more stable than most of the couples I know."

Not even in my first weeks here had the city seemed so threatening. I was out on the street after sunset, with Joan strapped to my chest. She was getting too big for the harness and she threw me off balance every time she squirmed around to look at something. She kicked her feet against my thighs as if she were spurring a horse; she tugged at my ears as if they were reins. I had to be stoical about it while I gave my full attention to the potential dangers that surrounded us. Would the man carting a box of oranges run into us? Were the two snarling derelicts going to pitch their empty wine bottles at each other as we hurried past them? I covered Joan's head with my hands. Could I get across Broadway without running before the light changed? I was unnervingly alert to everything around me, but only as possible threats. My senses were stretched in all directions. I saw the black on roller skates, radio clutched to one ear, when he was still a block away and warily followed his snaky waltz up the sidewalk until he was safely past us.

If I'd known it was going to be this bad, I would never have ventured out with Joan. But Corey was at an Episcopal banquet tonight and Liza was down in the Village again, singing for dimes and quarters. I wanted to see how Liza was doing. I almost turned back at the subway entrance, but resentment kept me going. I had not been out of the apartment in two days. I hoped that by showing up in the Village with Joan, I could not only check up on Liza, but maybe shame her into dropping this singing nonsense.

Joan cried when the station trembled and a train roared out of the tunnel like a beast with yellow eyes. She stopped when we got on, but remained petrified all the way downtown. I sat down and could relax. "That's right," I cooed to her. "Not nice to torture your uncle. Only selfish little egotists hurt the people who're taking care of them. Now you be nice or Uncle Joel might forget himself and throw you under a bus, sweetkins." You can say absolutely anything to a baby, as long as you say it sweetly. I often used that ploy to simultaneously vent my frustrations and soothe Joan. A woman sitting beside us looked horrified.

We got off at Christopher and immediately heard singing. I climbed up the stairs toward a voice that cracked and croaked like a broken radio. I was relieved to see it wasn't Liza. A motherly woman in a turquoise dress stood at the red, spotlit wall of Village Cigars and sang "Old Man River," while the tape recorder she held on the palms of her hands played music for "The Impossible Dream." She was indulged by an audience of protective homosexuals. We were on the gay side of Seventh Avenue.

I'd forgotten that this was where we'd be. It had only been a week and a half since I'd last been down here, but the place felt different to me. Although it was a weeknight, the fellows were out early, seizing advantage of the prematurely mild weather. The men who filed into Christopher Street and past the proud singer were dressed for spring; short jackets showed off the tight curves of their jeans. I wanted it to please me, this suggestion of bodies shaking off their winter cocoons, but a week of Joan had warped my mind. The buds in the front of jeans made me think of the way Joan's diapers bunched between her legs.

"Dada?" said Joan, reaching for a man with a beard and glitter eyeshadow.

I turned away before she could grab his gold earring. "No stupid. Not your Dada." I stood on the corner, puzzling over my lack of sexual interest and wondering where Liza might be.

On the other side of Seventh was the little park where I'd expected to find her. The park was deserted, except for the jumble of drunks and junkies on the benches outside the iron fence. The park's trees, sidelit and backlit by the street lights around it, were still bare except for the rows of balled-up pigeons roosting on the branches.

Then there was a pause in the roar of trucks and taxis down Seventh. The singer in turquoise had finished her song and was lightly, lightly applauded. And above the patter of hands, I heard another song echoing in the distance. Traffic and madwoman resumed in unison and the distant song was lost, but it seemed to have come from the bay of narrow streets that fanned out to the right of the park.

I carried Joan across to the heterosexual side of Seventh, where people were still straggling home from work or straggling home with groceries. And there, just before the supermarket, a small crowd lingered along the curb, facing the locked doors of a savings bank. On the steps stood Liza, furiously singing.

One pill makes you larger
And one pill makes you small
And the ones that Mother gives you
Don't do anything at all.
Go ask Alice
When she's ten feet taaaaall.

She sang with her shoulders thrown back and her eyes fixed on the high cake-slice of building across the street. Her voice was strong and clear. Her hand snapped across the steel strings and the guitar resonated like a pipe organ. The strap around her neck was taut; the unclipped ends of her silver guitar strings quivered with sparks of light.

"Mama!" went Joan.

"Sssssh," and I stepped behind a parked van so we could watch Liza without distracting her.

She closed her eyes for the ecstatic high notes, but even when her eyes were open and focused above the audience, you could see her joy. She took such pleasure in her singing that I stopped resenting her. I could bask in my sister's pleasure and envy it happily, until Joan yanked at my nose and once again said, "Dada."

Had Liza left Kearney to sing?

"Thank you, thank you," she said, breathless and grinning when she finished the song.

Her audience applauded and a few people shyly stepped forward to toss coins into her open guitar case before they moved on. A dozen or so people remained, all wistful, all Liza's age or slightly older, with the exception of a fat, clerkish man in his fifties who'd settled himself on the hood of a car. He had the look of a lecher who was going to sit there for hours, eating my sister with his eyes.

They were *all* men, except for a pair of women in leather, and the wistful looks suddenly stopped seeming like innocent nostalgia. No matter how much pleasure Liza was getting, she had put herself in a dangerous position here. I came out from behind the van as Liza tuned up for her next song.

"Hey there, Sis."

She looked up, startled. "Joel? What are you doing down...? What the hell did you bring Joan down here for?"

"Mama!" yipped Joan.

"Joan missed her Mama," I said, lifting Joan from below so she could get to Liza's collar and hair. "So I brought her down to see you," I said sweetly.

"Oh Piglet," she muttered and made kissing noises while she tugged her hair out of Joan's fists. To me she snarled, "For crying out loud, Joel, I'm sure she's missed me before. Couldn't you have just given her her bottle or a graham cracker?"

"She missed you," I repeated. "And I wanted to come down here anyway, and make sure you were all right." At my back, I heard a rustle of annoyance from the spectators.

"Doing fine. Or *was,* until y'all showed up."

Joan stopped reaching for Liza and began to cry.

"I think she wants you to hold her," I said, unbuttoning the straps that held her in.

Liza glanced desperately at the people behind me, but climbed out from her guitar strap. "No thanks to you," she muttered. "Here." She swapped her guitar for her daughter and jiggled Joan until the crying stopped. "Where's her hat? You shouldn't have taken her out without putting a hat on her. It's not *that* warm."

The two women in leather came up, dropped some money in the case and stood there admiring the baby. The horsey one looked embarrassed but her petite friend, who wore brown lipstick, said, "What's her name?"

"Joan," said Liza, smoothing the baby's hair.

"Joan!" crowed the woman. "How perfect! I'm glad it's not Gracie, but Joan is perfect. After Joan Baez?"

"No, not really," said Liza with a faint smile. "But does work out that way, doesn't it. Doesn't it, Joan? Doesn't it, Piglet?"

The women stood there with smiles and folded arms, but behind them, the men were leaving. They weren't going to hang around to pick up a woman with a kid, I decided.

"Come on, Jackson," said the horsey woman. "Let's go. Enjoyed your singing. Nobody sings those songs anymore."

"Maybe we'll catch you on our way back from the Duchess," said the other. "Bye-bye, Joan. Bye-bye." She wagged both hands at the baby. "Joan? I love it!" she laughed as they walked away.

"Lesbians," I explained.

"I'm not blind," Liza muttered. "But they liked my music and that's good enough for me," she said defensively. "I hope *you're* happy. You've scared off the audience that took me an hour to build up."

"Hey honey! Sing us another song!" Only the lecher remained, still perched on the car hood.

"Show's over," I told him, hoping it were true.

But the lecher didn't budge and Liza only glowered at me.

"Creeps," I whispered. "It's not a good idea for you to be down here alone, attracting all these creeps."

"I don't attract creeps. I attract people who like my songs."

"Bull."

"Bull yourself. Or when they are creeps"—she nodded at the man on the hood—"I can take care of myself. Stop being so god damn paternal, Shrimp."

"I'm not being paternal. I'm just trying to look out for you."

"I can look out for myself, thank you."

"You should be looking after your daughter."

She pinched her mouth and glared. "You jerk. Don't go pulling that on me, jerk, when I've spent the past twelve months—Jesus, Joel! You take care of her for a few crummy hours and you think that gives you the right to call me negligent!"

I hadn't intended to say that; it just popped out. "No. I don't think that. I just think that you've got better things you could be doing, instead of coming down here where you're vulnerable to every creep who comes down the block."

"Asshole," she spat, then glanced around.

We were being watched, not only by the lecher, but by everyone who walked past. People in New York will argue about the most intimate things in public, but Liza wasn't used to that.

"I won't talk about it here. You have a bone to pick with me, we'll pick at it at home."

"Fine," I said more amiably. "So let's just pack up your guitar and go home."

"No. I'm not ready to go home. You go, and take Joan, and I'll meet you back there in an hour. She's going to scream bloody murder now that she's seen me, but you have nobody but yourself to blame for that."

Before I could stop her, she'd snatched her guitar back and thrust Joan at me. I had to take Joan or we would've dropped her. "Come on, Liza. Why can't you come home now?"

"Because I'm just getting into my stride. Another hour and I'll be able to pick up some real money."

"Okay. Then Joan and I will wait for you."

"Jeez, Joel. Just take her home. You'll distract me and . . . *she doesn't have her hat.*"

"If you're so concerned about Joan's hat, then come home."

Liza paused, then slung her guitar back on. "I won't be blackmailed. You're the one who forgot her hat." She resumed tuning up her guitar. "It's not like you have anything else to do," she muttered. "She's your niece. It's not going to kill you to spend a little time with her."

But before I could protest that that had nothing to do with it, Liza launched into "Don't Think Twice It's All Right."

One of those screw-you-I'm-leaving-you songs and Liza began it with a nasty note of bitterness. But she accompanied it with a gentle patter of plucked strings that seemed to soothe Joan like a lullaby. Joan was heavy and I sat on the cold steps to hold her in my lap.

People stopped to listen. Liza turned to face them and the song began to soothe her too, becoming less bitter, more bittersweet. She seemed able to lose her anger and defensiveness in this song, discipline her feelings in the act of performing them.

But when she finished the song, her annoyance returned when she said to me, "If you're so hot on hanging around, why don't you make yourself useful and count the take."

I did. Along with two scraps of paper with compliments and phone numbers scrawled on them, I counted close to twenty dollars in her case, which irritated me. It was difficult to disapprove of something that was so profitable. And it was difficult to stay angry with my sister while she sang. She had a performer's aura of invulnerability. I felt a little silly and superfluous sitting at her feet while she sang and all these people stopped to listen to her. I might've given in and taken Joan home, only my pride was involved and I didn't want to admit to Liza that she was right.

Liza sang "The Night They Drove Old Dixie Down," "Song for David," "Will the Circle Be Unbroken?" and "Diamonds and Rust." Even with me and Joan behind her, men still stopped to listen. All were Liza's age or older. People my age and younger only rolled their eyes scornfully and hurried past the anachronism. One of the drunks from the park wandered over, stood beside Liza, clapped hands and hummed, trying to pass himself off as part of the act. Liza and her audience ignored him until he gave up and staggered off, mumbling, "jiveass white shit —doan wanna sing no white shit anyway." The fat lecher remained loyal and one or two men watched with flirtatious grins, but Liza was right about most of them: They were there for the songs. There were more women now, too, and that had a civilizing effect on the situation.

I remained alert to trouble. I could at least do that. I'd watched the pushy drunk like a hawk, making sure he didn't get too close to the guitar case. Then I saw a man moving back and forth outside the ring of spectators. He seemed to be checking us out and I wondered why. He was in the shadows, so I couldn't see his face, but when his silhouette passed between us and the display windows of the bookstore across the street, I saw his short haircut and wondered if he were a plainclothes cop. I didn't know if what Liza was doing were legal or not. Then the man came forward, shouldering his way through the people in front. He brought an awed grin into the light from our doorway. It was Jake.

He stood squarely in front of Liza, but she sang over everyone's head and didn't see him. He saw me and Joan, performed a little dumb show of surprise—waving hello, pointing at Liza, pointing at Joan, grinning and shaking his head. He folded his arms and stood there, waiting to be seen.

Liza finished her song and promptly adjusted a string, without seeing Jake.

Jake stepped forward. He quietly walked up to her, without opening his arms or even his mouth.

Liza only sensed someone approaching her and instinctively stepped back before she looked up. Then she saw who it was, and froze.

"Kitten!"

Liza held her breath; Jake his grin.

"Hey mac!" cried someone in the crowd. "Bug off! Let the lady sing!"

"Kitten?" Jake repeated. "What're *you* doing here?" He

waited for a response from her, then quickly turned to the audience. "This is my *daughter!* Who I haven't seen in three years!"

Liza looked to me for help, but I'd already warned her that Jake was in New York. She faced me while she cut her eyes at Jake, a corner of her mouth attempting a smirk.

"And *this!*" exclaimed Jake as he went for Joan. "This is my *granddaughter!* Who I've never seen before!" He lifted her an inch from my lap and promptly lowered her again. He was playing to the crowd and I thought the actor in him had triumphed over all human feeling, until I caught the frightened look in his eye. He turned his petrified grin back to Liza. "Aren't you going to say hello to your old man?"

"This bum for real, little lady?" It was the lecher who was being so protective. "Want me to give him his walking papers?" He slipped down from the hood.

She glanced at the man, at the spectators and the movement of her eyes broke her trance. "Oh no. He's for real. *He's for real everybody!*" And having to come to his defense made her smile at Jake, boldly.

I waited for her to lash out at him. I might've forgiven Jake but I looked forward to Liza attacking him.

"So? Liza?" he asked, getting more worried.

And Liza strained her neck muscles—a here-goes-nothing gesture—closed her eyes and hugged him.

The guitar was caught between them. Jake looked more startled than ever. I was surprised and disappointed.

And then a joker in the crowd applauded, and everyone applauded.

Liza blushed and stepped back. "Fancy running into you down here. You old fart."

"Well, my theater's only a few blocks from here," said Jake trying to hide his confusion. "I was on my way home from a cast meeting—no performance tonight. And I heard someone singing. I am flabbergasted! Never expected to see *you* in New York. Almost didn't recognize you,

Kitten. It is you?" He had never been at such a loss with me, but he was certainly at a loss with his daughter.

The crowd was breaking up, shaking heads and telling each other, "That's New York for you." Even our lecher departed, with a mournful sigh.

Liza watched them go and took off her guitar. She looked at me with an expression that could've meant anything from "You win" to "What am I in for now?" Her letter to Jake had blamed him for everything, and yet Liza had not been impressed when I told her Jake was in the city. She'd said she might see him, if the mood hit her, but it seemed to have had very low priority on her long list of maybes. She studied him hard, trying to make up her mind about something.

"Yes, I was walking down Grove and I heard singing," Jake continued. "I only wanted to reconnoiter. But every girl I hear bussing on corners makes me think of you, Kitten. Even though I've never heard you sing. Imagine my surprise when I saw that it *was* you. Although, if your brother hadn't been with you, I might not've recognized you. Hello there, lad."

"Hi Jake."

"Uh, your singing sounded very good, I thought."

Liza had been watching him as if she were actually listening. Then she raised her chin and said, "I've left Bob."

Jake closed one eye. "What's that?"

She heaved a sigh of relief and continued. "I've left Bob and I'm divorcing him. That's why I'm here in New York. I'm on my way to Virginia to divorce Bob."

"Oh?" said Jake, "Oh! Ohhhhh," trying one response after another, before choosing sympathy. "I'm sorry to hear that. Terribly sorry." He looked sad.

"Don't pretend to be surprised, Jake. Just seems like nobody in the family's ever had very good taste in men. Except Joel."

He was too busy thinking to even smile at the joke. "No. Can't say I'm at all surprised. I was hoping the two of you would be able to work something out, but...

260

Divorce does seem to be the family tradition, doesn't it?"

"And it's a good tradition," said Liza. The longer she was with Jake, the more confident she became. The bad tradition is that we marry such men in the first place."

Jake only mumbled. "Maybe, but... uh, you never answered my letter."

"What could I say? Doctor, cure yourself? Or however it goes."

"I've learned by my mistakes, Kitten. I hoped you could learn from them, too."

"Don't flatter yourself. I'm not following in your footsteps. My mistakes are original. And Jake? Could you please cut it out with the Kitten?"

"That's right. I forgot. Sorry."

I seemed to have come in on the middle of a private conversation. Liza seemed surprised by how easily she could handle Jake face to face. If she realized this with Jake, why couldn't she realize it with our mother?

"Say," said Jake. "This is probably not the best place for a family reunion. We must look like a family of gypsies out here. Would you like to go somewhere where we could sit down and talk? Uh, have you eaten yet? My treat. Joel and... the baby too."

"Her name's Joan," I told him

"Of course. Well, this is the first time I've ever seen her." He laughed.

"No," said Liza. "Better not. It's past Joan's bedtime and we should be getting home. No, tonight's not a good time."

But once Lisa understood she had nothing to fear from Jake, maybe she'd understand the same thing about Catherine. She could overcome her doubts and go home to Virginia, if those doubts were really what was keeping her here. It was a gamble, but I was willing to take it. "I'll take Joan home. You go talk to Jake."

Liza looked skeptical, but she was obviously tempted. "No. Joan'll scream bloody murder all the way home. I can't do that to you, Joel."

"You were willing to do it to me a half hour ago. Go ahead. I won't mind."

"I'm sure Joel can handle it," said Jake. "You won't mind a little babysitting, will you, lad?" He was dying to talk to Liza.

"Why should I mind? Been doing it all week. No, you two go have a dinner and chat somewhere and I'll take care of Joan. Even give her a bath before putting her to bed, if you like."

Liza was puzzled by my determination that she talk with our father. "Well...okay, Jake. If you're so hot on talking, I guess we can talk. But don't think you're going to talk me out of a divorce."

"Why would I even try? That's none of my business. I just want us to catch up on each other, that's all."

"All right. We can catch up," she said and put her guitar in its case. "I'm sure I won't be out too late, Joel. But you will take care of Joan?" She leaned forward, as if to kiss Joan or me, but smiled instead and muttered, "You were right. Meet all *kinds* of creeps down here."

"Just go!" I laughed. "Go! And good luck."

Liza frowned, annoyed I was making it so important. "I'll take the guitar. Weighs a ton with that change, but you'll have your hands full as it is."

"Thanks, lad. See you later." Jake looked very pleased with himself and, as they walked off, almost put his arm across his daughter's shoulder, but thought better of it.

Joan stared as her mother walked off with that strange man. She closed her eyes and howled. Liza looked back, her hand over her mouth, and for a moment seemed torn between being a mother and being a daughter.

"Go!" I shouted. "We'll be fine!"

Joan screamed in my ear all the way home and I was unable to give much rational thought to whether or not anything would come of this.

I was running her bath when Corey came home. Joan had finally cried herself out and was happily wrapped in the nest of pink toilet paper she'd unwound from the roll.

"Should we be letting her do that?"

"She's having fun. How was your banquet?"

"The usual churchy decadence. Two deacons got very drunk and were camping it up like queens. Innuendoes about an organist and his organ. And then they did a can-can dance." He leaned against the door jamb and watched me fill the tub. "Liza's not home?"

I told him what had happened. He made faces and could laugh only late in the story. But he agreed that it might be good therapy for Liza to talk with Jake. "Don't get me wrong. It's a joy to have them with us, and I'll miss them when they're gone. But it worries me that your sister's still here. It's as if she didn't know what she wanted."

"A divorce. That's what she wants," I said while I unwrapped Joan from the tissue and clothes.

"I guess. But she's taking her sweet time in getting it. Oh, I don't know. I shouldn't judge. It must be awfully difficult what she's going through. But it's so alien to me: marrying the wrong person and then having to divorce them. You need any help?"

"Nope. We're doing fine."

But when I set Joan down in the water, she started howling again. She was now able to sit alone in our tub when she could see her mother peering over the high white wall. Apparently she didn't trust me. I lifted her up, sweet talked her until she stopped crying—"You little neurotic; oh yes, you are"—but when I lowered her again, she resumed screaming.

"Maybe it's the wrong water temperature," Corey suggested.

"Water's fine."

She was all screaming mouth and bulging cheeks.

"What now?"

"I guess I just let her howl and get it over with as quickly as possible."

"But it's traumatizing her," said Corey. "She's scared. Must be like sitting in an open sarcophagus."

"Okay. What do you suggest?"

"Well, I'm thinking maybe one of us should get in with her."

I swung Joan out of the tub. "Fine. Get into the sarcophagus, Boy."

"No. You better be the one. You're her uncle."

"What does that have to do with it?"

Corey bashfully lowered his eyes. "Sounds crazy, but ...I couldn't be comfortable being naked with a child I wasn't related to."

"That's silly! She's one year old. Be like taking a bath with your dog!"

"What can I say? Yeah, it's silly, but... If you insist, I guess I could put on my bathing suit."

I laughed at him. "Here. Hold her," I said and stood up. "Such modesty. I'll show you. Nothing sexual about it at all." I quickly pulled off my clothes and sat down in the three inches of warm water. Corey passed Joan back to me and I placed her between my raised knees.

She looked from one knee to the other, as if they were the arms of a chair, then patted the strange water with her hand. Her pink and white plumpness made my body look surprisingly grey and hairy. That body should've been more frightening to her than the high walls of the tub.

"See. Nothing child-molesterish about it."

But it did feel odd. It was strangely pleasant to share nakedness with this small animal who was smooth enough to seem human. I immediately used a washcloth on her, before Corey's fears could suggest anything to me. But the sensual feeling that stole through my skin wasn't at all sexual. It was more general than that, more an end in itself. There was so little of Joan to wash that it hardly seemed worth the trouble, but I found myself taking great pains with the tiny cups of her ears, her puffy legs, the puckered faces on her knees and elbows.

"Eeek!" she shrieked and splashed me. She indulged in high-pitched mouse squeals for the sheer pleasure of hearing her own voice. She splashed me again, harder.

I turned away and found Corey, still in his coat and tie, sitting on the edge of the bathtub. He watched us with that handsomely intent look of his.

I liked having him watch us, but couldn't resist teasing. "This why you wanted me to do it? So you could gawk?"

"Not consciously," he said without losing his composure. "But you do look very beautiful together."

"Uh huh. I hear you."

"And I was just thinking that maybe you've found your vocation."

"What? This?"

"Not your vocation exactly. But something that maybe gives you a feeling of satisfaction?" he timidly suggested.

"Uh uh. No way. Ow! No, stupid. *Not* a toy." I tucked myself under my testicles so she wouldn't be tempted to grab it again. "Here. Play with Mister Duck. You're as bad as Liza," I told Corey. " 'You're not doing anything, Brother. You can play Mother.' As if playing Piglet's mother were a treat. Quack, kid. Who says quack quack?"

"But you love her, Shirts. Anyone can see that. The way you baby her?"

"Of course I baby her. What else can you do with a baby? Shut your mouth, Joan. A fly's going to fly in." I gave her face a swipe with the washcloth and she wrinkled up her mouth and nose. "Here, Boy. You want to adore her, you can adore while you dry her off."

Corey gingerly accepted her. He was best with babies in the abstract, and when they were freshly washed. But I didn't really scorn his wrongheaded admiration. I didn't take care of Joan out of love, but love *was* a habit I'd developed towards her while having to take care of her. I liked having that love recognized.

Corey made halfhearted clucking sounds while he poked Joan dry. She began to look uneasy, so I started talking to her as I stepped out of the tub.

"Now don't you feel better? You little piglet. Oh yes you are. You're the little piglet. And what does the piglet say? What does the piggy say?"

"Oink, oink," answered Corey.

"I wasn't asking you, I'm asking her. Who's the clean little piggy? Who's the clean little piglet?'

Bundled and hooded in towels, Joan giggled and pointed at me.

"No. Not me. You. You're the piglet." I put my arm around Corey's waist so I could get in close enough to press my nose against Joan's. "Youuu. You're the clean little piglet. You have to know how to speak their language," I explained to Corey.

Only my backside was wet, but I was dripping on Corey's good dress slacks. He didn't complain or step away. He held Joan up so that her towel-cowled head was level with mine and his eyes swung back and forth between me and Joan. Then he kissed Joan on the forehead, and me on the cheek.

We were making love when Liza came home—just me and Corey—and I didn't hear about her dinner with Jake until the next day.

"I still don't get it," I told Liza for the hundredth time. "If you can be with Dad and not feel intimidated, what makes you so sure it's going to be any different with Mom?"

And Liza repeated what she'd been repeating all day. "Because Jake is only Jake, but Mom is Mom. Can't we just drop this?"

We weren't losing our tempers. We couldn't. Liza was feeding Joan her dinner while I cooked spaghetti for ours. In addition to disrupting normally civilized behavior, Joan's presence could temper potentially uncivil exchanges as well.

Corey was present, too, pressed into service as a high chair. He held Joan in his lap on a sheet of newspaper spattered with custard and pureed beef. Joan could be as unreasonable as her mother.

"Hmmph," went Liza. "That was a dirty trick, you pushing us together like that."

"Don't blame it on me. You wanted to see him, too."

266

"Was curious. Wanted to see what the old fart was like now, that's all. But you wanting me to practice on him so I'd be able to face Mom . . . ?"

I'd already confessed to her that the idea had crossed my mind.

"Is it such a hassle, Joel, having us around, that you'll pull tricks to get rid of us?"

"Wasn't a trick. And it wasn't why I did it. Was just a possibility that crossed my mind, Liza. We enjoy having you here, hassles and all. However . . ."

"Yes? Here," she told Corey, pushing jar and spoon at him so she'd be free to deal with me. "See if your luck's any better than mine. However? Yes?"

"I just think—and Corey agrees with me—that you're in a very vulnerable position here. And it worries us that you're prolonging it."

"I've told you why. And if I can't make it any clearer, I'm sorry. Shows how little you respect me, Joel, if you have to resort to tricks. *Male* condescension."

"Hold the spoon above her head," she told Corey. "If you can get her to look up, she'll open her mouth. But you have to move fast."

Corey cautiously waved the spoon over Joan, like a magic wand. He was staying out of this argument.

"See," said Liza, "I know all about tricks. And I've tried pulling them on myself in the past, and look where it's gotten me. No, Joel. Things like this have got to be confronted head-on."

"But you're not confronting it, Liza. At least, not that we can tell."

"You don't know! I'm not about to start issuing bulletins every five minutes on my state of mind! But I'm confronting it in my own head. It's a slow, private process. It's like what they say about painting: That for a painter, *not* painting is sometimes part of the act of painting. Well, *not* thinking about it is part of thinking about it."

"Well, yes. Maybe. But in the meantime, Liza, you're in a very vulnerable position."

"What's so vulnerable about it? Bob's on the other side of the ocean and even if he had a lawyer over here, nobody knows where I am. Look. I'm not leaving my husband to go back to Mother. I need this vacation from authority. Which is why it annoys me, Shrimp, when you play the Great White Mother."

I threw the wooden spoon at the boiling spaghetti. "If I'm playing...!" Hot water peppered my hand and I shook it. "If I'm playing Mother, whose fault is that? You're the one who's stuck me with Joan and made me feel like a god damn parent!"

"There! You do resent having us here."

"I don't! I don't even resent getting stuck with Joan! But if you're going to stick me with responsibility, don't act so indignant if I feel responsible for you, too!"

Liza folded her arms and scowled.

"Or would you rather have me like Jake? That's what you have to choose from, Liza. You can have people like Jake, who're mildly interested in what happens to you. Or you can have people who really care. Like me. Or Catherine."

"Or Bob!" spat Liza. "This is exactly what I'm trying to escape from. I'm sick of being cared for. It's jail, Joel!"

"The way I care about you is nothing like Bob's. And Mom's wouldn't be, either. Do you hear me trying to stop you from singing in the streets? I don't like you doing it, but it's your life and I won't interfere."

"Then what do you call bringing Joan down last night?"

"I was lonely," I said, which I knew was half-true.

"Oh yeah?" said Liza, thinking she knew the other half. "You don't like my going down there because it means you have to sit with Joan."

There was a return of last night's suspicions. "Okay," I admitted. "That's part of it."

"Don't let him fool you," said Corey, nudging Joan's mouth with the spoon. "He loves being with his niece."

"And what's the rest of the reason?" said Liza. "And

don't give me that malarkey about me being vulnerable down there. Because you saw. I can take care of myself."

"Okay," I said. "It makes me wonder if maybe that's *why* you're staying here."

"To sing on street corners? Jesus, Joel. You're as stupid as Jake."

"Well, it makes more sense than waiting to get up enough courage to face Mom. I don't know. Maybe you have fantasies about being discovered or—I'm not saying I believe it. But it did cross my mind."

"Jeez, Joel, you talk just like Dad."

"Jake asked you that?"

"No. He assumed that. Went into this crazy talk about realizing that *we* were the kindred spirits in the family. That we were the artists."

"Are you?"

"Crap, Joel! You've heard the way he talks. Gave me the creeps to hear him dragging me over to his side like that. The selfless, struggling artist. Sacrificing everything to his art. If I believed that, I'd be painting. Singing's just a hobby. It brings in a little money, and it makes me feel good. And if I were serious about it, I'd be doing it in Virginia. Where people don't know yet that the sixties are over."

"Yes. No market in New York. I'm glad to hear you feel that." I was feeling embarrassed for my suspicions, and relieved.

"Oh, I've considered it," said Liza. "I have my day-dreams just like everybody else. But I've been singing just to give myself something to do. I'm not going to come to terms about anything by sitting around here staring at my belly button. And singing does make me feel good about myself."

"I know. I could see that. Which was why I couldn't really try to stop you."

"It does," said Liza. She wiped Joan's mouth off, lifted her from Corey's lap and set her on the floor.

"But Jake sees himself as an artist?" asked Corey.

269

"Like you wouldn't believe. He has this line of bull about the artist as outlaw. Anything the artist does is justified, so long as it benefits his art. Murder, robbery, neglect of family. He told me all that because he assumed I was leaving Bob to sing, just as he dumped us to act. Which really gave me the creeps, having him think I was doing what he did."

Joan sat on the linoleum, chewing and pulling at a back issue of *Mother Jones,* and I stepped around her to get the spaghetti pot over to the sink. "He give you his bit about *his* father being a tyrant and how we should be grateful he was so loose with us?"

"Oh yeah," she sighed and grinned. "And it was all I could do to keep from laughing in his face. Although, he does have a point. But...poor Jake. Poor, flaky Jake."

"Off in his own world," I said.

"To be sure. But you're wrong about his not caring about us. He does, from a distance. And he especially cares about what we think of him. Kept harping on that letter I wrote. I had to come right out and tell him that I had better things to do in Germany than sit around hating him and that I wrote that letter just to let off steam. It was more convenient to hate Jake, who was on the other side of the world, than to hate the person in the next room." She stopped to think about that person, frowned and shook her head. "And you? You used to hate Jake frontwards and backwards, and for good reason too. But he talked about you as if you were old friends. What do you feel about him now?"

"I never really—" But Liza had been there and I had genuinely hated my father. "Yes, I did. But now...hard to remember what all the fuss was about. Just a foolish man. It was only coincidental that he was our father and that we expected fatherly things of him. But after talking to him last week, oh, I don't know. The hatred seems to have been all in my imagination."

Corey listened to us and sadly nodded. "You're making

me feel very naive. For having conventional parents who I didn't have to have mixed feelings about."

Liza and I looked at Corey, and then at each other, like two adults sharing their surprise over something said by a small child.

I laughed and wagged my finger at Corey. "You? Who gets broody every time he has to go home on a visit?"

"Only because I resent having to clean myself up," he guiltily admitted to Liza. "And because I know I'll have to watch what I say about my 'roommate.'"

"Boy's folks still don't know," I explained.

"At least they pretend not to know; they sent both of us Christmas presents. But, courteous Southern son that I am, I won't confront them with it. Unless they ask."

Liza and I smiled our conspiratorial, superior smiles at each other.

Our phone rang; Corey jumped up to answer it and escape all this sudden attention.

"But going back to question one," I began.

Liza groaned.

"Maybe this thing with you and Mom is all your imagination."

"Maybe it is. So what? I still have to handle it in my own way. Your pushing isn't going to help. Another week. Maybe two. I just ask you to respect me enough to—"

"Hello?" went Corey in our bedroom. He deliberately greeted the caller loud enough for us to hear, "Oh, *Bob*. How you doing, *Bob?*"

Liza grimaced and rolled her eyes. "Again?"

It was Kearney's fourth call this week, but we stopped to listen anyway.

"No, sorry, Bob. She hasn't passed through here again. At least not that we know of."

Liza's telegram had included its place of origin, so we had had to tell Kearney that, yes, we'd talked to Liza, but only briefly on the phone, when she had called us from the airport on her way through New York.

"Yes, well, if her mother's not giving out the information, Bob, I don't see what Joel and I can do. Catherine hasn't told us either." Corey carried the phone out into the hall, where we could give him signals on what to say. He still lacked confidence in his lying. "Yes, Joel's here. Would you like to speak to him? No, we're not going anywhere tonight. Why?" He squinted, then shoved his glasses up his nose, his eyes growing wider. "Here? What do you mean you're...? *In New York?*"

Liza froze. Then she glanced at me, at Corey. She looked hard at Corey.

"Well, Bob. So you're in New York. Well." He looked at us, pleading for advice. "Yes. We should get together. Since you're here. Tonight? I don't know if tonight's...."

I hurriedly nodded at him. It didn't seem real that Kearney could be here, but I knew we couldn't do anything that might make him suspicious. And that immediately gave me an idea for what we had to do.

"Uh, sure. If you're here only for one night, yes, tonight it has to be. Where you staying? We could come down and meet you there."

I shook my head and pointed at our floor.

"Or, if it's better for you, I guess you could come up here." And hearing himself, Corey suddenly shot a look of surprise at me. "Yeah? Well? Where are you now? I suppose I should give you directions on how to find us."

I continued to nod to keep Corey going. He kept looking at Liza.

But Liza showed no response to what we were doing. She had sunk back in her chair and folded her arms across her chest. I heard her foot tapping beneath the table.

"Okay then. Well. I suppose we'll be seeing you shortly. Can't promise anything, Bob," he said, still watching Liza. "But if... All right. See you then." He hung up and his face remained blank.

"Oh damn," Liza groaned. "Damn, damn, damn. That stupid fool's come after me? Of all the arrogant... Why can't the dumb bastard leave me in peace?"

"Calm," I said. "We have to stay calm."

But she was far calmer than I thought she'd be. "They must've given him leave. How the hell did he manage to finagle... And why in blazes did you invite him up here?" She glared at me. "What makes you think I want to talk to the bastard?"

"Yes, why?" said Corey. "I did what you told me only because I didn't know what else we should—"

"Dammit, Joel. Is this another one of your tricks?"

"Quiet. Both of you. I know what I'm doing. Okay? How long before Kearney gets here?"

"He's out at Kennedy, but he's rented a car. Half hour maybe? An hour?"

"Okay. First things first. Liza? Do you want to see him?"

"Hell no! What makes you think I'd want to see that...? If that bastard thinks he can hunt me down like a... jackrabbit—"

"Okay. Then we have to move fast. We've got to hide your clothes and all your things, then you take Joan to the coffee house around the corner and wait there."

"Why?"

"Because Kearney's coming. And if you don't want to see him, we don't want him to know that you're here."

"Then why did you have me ask him up?" said Corey.

I was losing patience with both of them. *"Because,* until Kearney sees she isn't here, he's going to suspect she is. So we have to ask him up, act like nothing's the matter, play dumb and get him off our backs once and for all. You want him to think you might be here?"

"No. But I didn't come to New York to play hide-and-seek with the bastard."

"It's your choice. The bastard's here now and you can either face him or hide. If he can't find you, maybe we can get him to go back to Germany."

"You don't know how stubborn the bastard can be."

"Suit yourself." But I was annoyed with her for resisting a scheme I was quite proud of. "You want to stay here and deal with him, fine. All I'm doing is offering an alternative. Do what you want."

Liza slowly stood up, but then only stood there, nodding and sneering and looking around the kitchen, as if the room could tell her what to do. Then she saw the half-empty jars of baby food on the table. She snatched them up and threw them into the trash can. "Come on, Piglet. You and I are going bye-bye."

While Liza bundled up Joan, Corey and I folded the crib and stashed it in Ed's room. Ed was at work and we could put Liza's suitcase and guitar in his room, too. But those were the easy things. There was baby debris everywhere: squeeze toys, bottle nipples, extra pacifiers, tiny, mouse-like socks. We combed every room, collecting everything that indicated the presence of a baby.

We walked Liza and Joan to the door. "Here goes nothing," she muttered. "And one of you will come down and get me when he's gone, right? Just be careful what you say to Bob. Bob's lots of things, but one thing he isn't is stupid."

"Maybe I should go with you," said Corey.

I shook my head. "He knows you're here. And he trusts you more than he trusts me."

Liza drew a deep breath. "So we're really going through with this."

"Unless you want to stay and see him."

"Cram it. If you're doing this, Joel, to test me...if you're pulling this so I have to hurry up and make my decision—"

"Liza, I'm doing this because the jerk's here and this is the only thing that might get rid of him. Trust me."

"Oh I trust you. Don't have any choice, do I? I better go or we'll run into him on the street. I'm in your hands, Joel. Good luck."

"Bye-bye. Bye-bye," I called to Joan as Liza carried her down the stairs. All Joan knew was that something out of the ordinary was happening. She looked pleased and excited by it.

274

"What happens if Bob wants to spend the night?" asked Corey.

"Come on, Core. Give me a break. I can only worry about one thing at a time. I don't know. We'll tell him Ed's bringing ten people home for an orgy or something."

But now that Liza was gone, I was very nervous. We went back to Ed's room and rearranged Liza's things so Kearney wouldn't see them if he demanded we show him the room. We made another quick inspection of the whole apartment and I realized that the living room smelled strongly of baby. It wasn't just my imagination. There was a definite, sweetish sour odor of milk, talcum and drool. Corey sprinkled some of Ed's cologne on the carpet and I felt better.

We returned to the kitchen. I threw out the cold spaghetti and started over. "So Kearney won't think he's interrupted anything."

Corey sat on his hands and grimaced. I assumed he was only nervous until he said, "I know this is the wrong time to bring this up, but... I wonder if we're doing the right thing. Hiding a man's wife and child from him."

That threw me; he'd helped me prepare the apartment as if he were in full agreement with what we were doing. "Come on, Boy. We've been doing it all week."

"I know. But lying on the phone is one thing. Going to all this trouble and then lying to the guy's face is something else. We're really getting in over our heads on this. And I can't help wondering if, by doing this, we're *pushing* your sister into a divorce."

"Liza had her choice and she took it. We're sticking by her decision, that's all."

"But giving her that choice, putting it in those either/ or terms? That forces the issue, don't you think?"

I had gone to all this trouble for the sake of my sister. I did not like having doubts cast on my role as her protector. "Are you gong to play along while Kearney's here? Or are you going to be moral? Because if you're going to

275

be moral and analytical about all this, then maybe you shouldn't be here after all."

Corey looked pained. "I didn't mean to suggest that. I want to stay. I don't want to be excluded from this. And I *am* with you. It's just that I have my doubts and needed to express them. For the sake of my conscience."

"Boy," I sighed. "Come on. This isn't the time to be . . . Lionel Trilling. We've chosen our course of action and we've got to stick with it. No point in even thinking about it until after it's over."

The blare of the buzzer ended all moral questions.

10

"HELLO, BOB. COME on in. You found us. No trouble parking, I hope? Joel's back here in the kitchen. We were just about to sit down to supper."

Robert Kearney walked down the hall, Corey right behind him. We'd left all the doors open, to show we had nothing to hide, and Kearney stopped to peer into each room. He kept his hands in his pockets and tried to appear casual. I'd expected him to arrive in a rage, or with a great noisy pretense of friendliness. But all he said was, "Nice place you have here."

"Uh, kitchen's straight ahead."

"Hi, Shirtsy." He greeted me with a weary nod and stood there, studying the white cabinet, the yellow linoleum, even the stamped tin ceiling. There was nothing feverish or suspicious about his glances. He looked like someone trying to remember what it was they were looking for. His eyes were bloodshot and there was a day's growth of blond sand on his face. He wore civilian clothes, but his shoes were military black and spit-polished.

"Hello, Bob," I said with quiet sympathy and offered him my hand.

"What? Oh." He shook my hand—his grip was hard, his palm clammy—and continued to look at the shelves.

Corey looked with him, afraid we'd left something out.

"Don't you have anything to drink around here?"

"Sure!" said Corey, relieved. "Well, uh, only Southern Comfort."

Kearney made a face. "I shouldn't be drinking anyway. But yeah. Could you give me a glass of that?"

Corey nervously poured and passed the glass to him. "You look exhausted, Bob."

Kearney sniffed at the stuff, found a chair at the back of his knees and sat down. "Haven't racked out in forty-eight hours. Can't say I was sleeping all that good before then either."

"Too upset?" said Corey.

Kearney sipped and closed his eyes. "What do you think?"

I had never had to deal with a laconic Kearney. I told myself that he was probably more dangerous like this, but he seemed sad to me, pitiable. "Have you eaten yet?"

"Crap on the plane."

"Then have some of this," I said, placing a plate of spaghetti in front of him. I could at least be kind to Kearney. Somehow, being kind made me feel better about what we were doing to him.

Kearney eyed the spaghetti as if there might be some sign of Liza in it.

I quickly served our plates and Corey and I sat at the table and busied ourselves with the salt and pepper. For a long, difficult minute, nobody said a word.

Kearney ignored the food, turned sideways in his chair and leaned back against the wall. He held his glass and stared off.

In the kitchen on the other side of the airshaft, two guys were laughing and drinking beer with a girl whose shirt was unbuttoned.

Kearney said, "You have to ask yourself if it's worth it. Breaking your balls to protect these people."

Corey hadn't noticed what Kearney was looking at. "You shouldn't talk like that, Bob. Although it's to be expected you're angry with Liza."

"Liza?" Kearney didn't seem to know what he was

talking about. "Oh yeah. Liza. Yeah, I'm angry with her too. That's what's made me angry with the whole damn world." His tone was flat and dry, anything but angry. "All the way over here, the airport in Frankfurt, the damn plane, the airport here...asswipe clerks, bimbo stewardess, everyone...every person I saw I thought, 'You saw them. You helped them. You're all in this together.' It's crazy, I know. But there's part of me that says you're all against me. All of you." And he singled me out with his eyes.

Corey looked at me worriedly.

"We're not the enemy, Bob. Corey and I want to help you. But we don't know any more than you do. Our only contact with Liza was that phone call from the airport."

"And she never told you where she was going?"

"Back to our mother." I quickly added, "But not straight away. I think she wanted to visit some friends first."

"What friends?"

"I don't know. Friends from college, I guess."

Kearney shook his head. "She doesn't have any friends from college. The only people she's stayed in touch with are you, her mother, her father, and those relatives of hers in Switzerland. She doesn't have anyone else to go to."

"Maybe she's at Catherine's now. When did you call there last?"

"Yesterday. And Liza still wasn't there. Or so she claimed."

Corey sat up and rubbed his palms against his pants. "Bob? Aren't you looking at this the wrong way?"

"What way? That everybody's lying to me? What else should I suspect, when my wife and daughter just vanish."

But Corey was genuinely sympathetic; he seemed to have found a way to help that wouldn't compromise his honesty. "You talk like Liza's been kidnapped. But she's made this choice of her own free will—so it seems—and of course it's painful for you, but I don't see how there's anything you can do but abide with her decision. The world hasn't taken her from you. She's done it herself."

Kearney looked away and pretended not to listen.

"And if people are covering for her—I *mean*—" Corey quickly caught himself. "If, say, *Catherine* is covering for her, it's because Liza wants her to. Wherever she is right now, Liza's made or making her own decision, and there's nothing you or us or anyone can do to make it for her. She's not some piece of furniture people can capture and recapture from each other."

"She's still her mother's daughter," Kearney muttered to himself. "And her mother's never liked me."

"How do you know she hasn't stayed in touch with anyone from college?" I asked. "You can't see *all* her mail."

"I did," he said. "And she saw all mine. Because we were close. We were *that* close!" He slammed his glass down so he could hold up his index fingers side by side. "We knew *everything* about each other. We were part of each other! And then to have her go and fuck me like this?"

"You must not have been all that close after all," I said.

"We sometimes miss things," said Corey more kindly. "When we're happy."

"Although you'd have to be asleep to have missed something like that in Liza," I cruelly insisted.

Kearney looked straight at me, stunned. Then he collected himself and said, "No. I won't accept that I've been asleep for three fucking years. Because it was too damn good, too damn real." His teeth were bared, but his eyes began to water. "Three years of happiness. Three years of knowing that no matter what a dead-end shit hole my life in the army was, I did have a family. I did have one solid rock to stand on." His words bubbled through the moisture collecting in his throat. "I'm not going to be talked out of that, dammit! Something's changed. I've got to find out what it is and fucking fix it!" And he slapped the table. Jarred loose by the blow, a single tear rolled down his cheek.

Corey picked up a napkin and timidly pushed it toward Kearney.

There was a moment before Kearney saw the napkin and understood it; he grimaced and turned away. "Yeah. The bitch can make me cry." He shrugged, then angrily sniffed up the tears in his nose. "That's what she's done to me! Because I love her. Even now. She's my fucking life! And I'm not going to sit by all candy-assed and helpless while my whole frigging life just walks out the door." He glared at Corey. "That's where you'll never understand me. I won't just abide." He sneered. "Abide with her decision, huh? I fight for what I want. Abide is for when it doesn't matter. When you're just playing a game. You get bored with the game, you just quit. But this ain't no game. This is love. The kind that, when you lose it, you lose everything. You just want to blow yourself away."

He turned from Corey's sad face to my stony one. But even I was feeling pity for Kearney, more for his ignorance than for his pain.

"Shit," he said and sank back in his chair. "I'm wasting my breath telling you people this. You don't know what the fuck I'm talking about, do you? Real love is like a foreign language to you."

The sad look disappeared from Corey's face. "Our love is just as valid as yours," he said sharply.

More valid, I angrily thought.

"Oh yeah? I know how you people live. Yeah, you live like couples and pay lip service to love, but if there's somebody on the street who catches your eye, you'll jump into bed with him without thinking twice about it. I've heard all about the gay scene." He sneered. "That isn't love."

"But *owning* someone," I sneered back. "That's real love, huh?"

Kearney only folded his arms. "It figures. Yeah, this is what I expected. Fags *would* serve up the same kind of crap you get from women's lib." He pointed his finger at me. "Look! I never owned her. If anybody owned anybody, she owned me."

"We may be faggots," said Corey, trying to keep his temper. "But we're faithful to each other. Our love is much closer to yours than you want to admit."

"Oh yeah? Yeah?" But Corey's firm tone forced him to change his line of attack. "You don't have any kids though, do you?"

"No," Corey admitted. "And that's the only difference."

"Not the only difference!" I said.

"Its a big difference!" said Kearney. "Damn straight it is. Because it's not just her walking out on me I have to abide with. It's her taking my daughter with her. My own flesh and blood, dammit!"

As gently as possible, Corey said, "The courts try to be fair. They'll arrange some sort of joint custody."

"I'm not interested in any joint custody crap! I'm not going to screw up my kid with a broken home. Look at how divorce screwed up Liza. That's what did it. Made her so afraid of love she runs away from it."

I wanted to shout at him: It's not love Liza's escaping from, but you, you son of a bitch. But we weren't gaining anything by being angry with him. We should be convincing him we were his friends, throw him off guard and throw him off my sister's trail. I tried to eat, but the spaghetti had cooled. Nobody was eating.

"Children aren't china," said Corey. "And I don't think a divorce does nearly as much harm as . . . as an unhappy marriage that stays together. Joel wasn't irreparably damaged, and I don't think Liza was, either."

"But we have a good marriage! It isn't unhappy." Kearney shook his head. "Anyway, I might be old-fashioned, but I don't call homosexuality being in *mint* condition."

I took a mouthful of cold food to stop myself from saying anything.

Corey kept his temper, too. "Well, *I* didn't need a divorce to become gay."

"Yeah, well..." Kearney abruptly dismissed it with a swat of his hand. "I'm not here to argue about how you live. What you do is of no concern to me. All I'm saying is that no daughter of mine is going to grow up without a father."

"When you find her," I said calmly, "what're you going to do, Bob?"

"What do you think? I'm going to talk sense to her." He looked at me and wheels began to turn inside his face. Perhaps he was realizing that anything he said here would find its way back to Liza, because he suddenly became civil. "Talk sense to her. That's all. I'm not going to threaten her or bully her. Let her know that I love her, and remind her that she loves me. And we both love Joan. And then find out what went wrong and arrange to fix it. Hell, if it's army life she doesn't like, the army don't mean shit to me anymore. I can fucking retire," he laughed. "Compared to her and Joan, the army don't mean diddly-squat. And I won't hold this over her head, either. You can count on that. Once this is all squared away, I will *never* hold it over her head." He hopefully arched his thin eyebrows at me. "You can tell her that much, can't you?"

"I could," I said. "If I were in touch with her."

He clacked his tongue, but stayed calm. "You're sticking with that, huh?"

"Because it's the truth."

"Bullshit. You know where she is. I know that you know and don't think for a second that I don't. Yeah, yeah," he said before I could argue. "She's your sister and blood is thicker than water. But it's not me you're hurting, Shirtsy. It's her. In the long run, it's going to be her."

"You think she's going to miss you?"

"I do, as a matter of fact. But that's not what I'm talking about."

His confidence frightened me. "What then?"

"That's for me to know and you to find out. Or for

Liza to find out. Because it won't mean shit to you. But it'll hurt Liza. If I don't find her."

Joan, I thought, and custody. But, as Liza said, he would have to find them before he could resort to that. "I'm sorry, Bob. But if she doesn't want to see you, there's nothing I can do about it."

He rubbed his whiskered mouth with his whole hand, then turned to Corey. "And you, Cobbett? You sticking to this line of bull, too?"

Corey had to clear his throat before he said, "Yes. Because it's true, Bob. But I think you're making things unnecessarily hard on yourself doing it like this. I understand how you feel, but you should see if maybe the lawyers can—"

"She's at her mother's, isn't she?"

Corey stopped, thought and said, "If she has any common sense, that's where she'd be."

"Uh huh, uh huh." He turned back to me. "Y'all's old man's here in town, isn't he?"

"In New York?" There was a flash of panic because the question took me by surprise, but Kearney obviously knew and all I could do was nod.

"Then I think I'll go see him."

"He doesn't know where she is, either," I said much too quickly.

My panic pleased him. "Oh yeah? Maybe not. But I'll bet he knows *something*. And he's been in my shoes himself. He'll know what it is I'm going through. What's his phone number?"

What would Jake do? Would he cover for his daughter? Would he side with the husband? I didn't know and my first reaction was to prevent the meeting.

"I could give you his number. But he's not there right now."

"Where is he, then?"

"In a play."

"What time does he get home?"

"Midnight maybe. Maybe later."

284

"Okay. Then I'll just hang around here until midnight and we'll give your old man a call." He leaned back in his chair and smirked knowingly at me. "If you're so sure he doesn't know anything, then why don't you want me to talk to him, Shirtsy?"

"I don't care if you talk to him. He's at the theater now. That's all." But it was obvious Kearney was determined to talk to Jake, even if it meant waiting here all night. And Liza couldn't bring Joan home until Kearney was gone.

Corey caught my eye and bit the corner of his lip.

"This theater's down in Greenwich Village," I said. "Um...if you really want to talk to Jake, I could take you down there." It seemed the only way. If I were there, perhaps I could make sure Jake didn't give us away.

"Tell me where it is and I'll go down there. Alone." Kearney didn't want to stay here, either.

"That's the problem," I explained. "I'd recognize the place when I saw it, but I don't remember the street or the name of the theater. Just some cellar off an alley somewhere." It would be dangerously complicated, but I couldn't think of anything else. "I'll take you down and you can meet with Jake after the show."

Kearney was suspicious and undecided. "This better not be some kind of wild goose chase."

"I wouldn't do that." I laughed nervously. "I know you'd beat the shit out of me, Bob," I added, resorting to flattery.

That seemed to make him feel better. "All right. Take me down there. Sooner I see your old man and get what I want out of him, the sooner I can get down to Virginia."

"And that's where you think Liza is?" asked Corey timidly. "In Virginia?"

"Yeah. And you know she's there, don't you?" Kearney watched for a look that might give away what Corey knew.

But Corey only said, "Then why do you have to talk to her father?"

285

"Because the old man's been in my shoes. And because it's good strategy to secure your bases behind you. I'm not leaving any stones unturned. Okay, where's the latrine in this place?"

I showed him, taking one last look at the bathtub to reassure myself that Joan's duck wasn't there. I went back to Corey, grimaced at him and held up the fingers I'd crossed for luck.

"Do you know what you're doing?" he whispered.

"Not yet. But if it's a disaster, I'll try to get away and call. Wait a little before you go and fetch—"

The toilet flushed and I hurried back to the hall with my coat.

"Come on, don't have all night," said Kearney.

"Good luck!" Corey shouted after us. "I hope things work out. One way or the other."

Kearney didn't say a word as we went down the stairs. I realized I'd put myself in a situation that might turn into a trap. If things went wrong, if Kearney wanted to break my arm, there'd be nothing to stop him.

The street out front was unnervingly empty. Kearney's car was double-parked and there was already a parking ticket under the wiper. He pulled the ticket out, balled it up and tossed it.

"You're not worried about the police?"

"Car's rented," he muttered. "What can they do to me? Get in."

He hadn't even bothered to lock the doors. I got in beside him, shut the door and the trap became very real.

Kearney raced downtown. Cabs blew their horns at us, brakes screeched behind us and I repeatedly pressed an imaginary brake pedal against the floor, but Kearney remained as cold as a stone. I wondered if he drove like this to shake me up, but he seemed to have forgotten I was even sitting beside him.

"Certainly seem to be in a hurry, Bob. Play won't be over for another hour."

"I want to finish with this fucking city soon as possible."

"You're not planning to leave for Virginia tonight, are you?"

"Damn straight. Get there first thing in the morning, while they're still asleep." And he caught himself; he hadn't meant to tell me that. "I find out you've warned them, and they've had time to bury my family somewhere, your ass is grass, Shirtsy. You hear?"

"You don't have to worry about me," I said. "I want to keep out of this mess."

"Damn well better keep out of it. Nobody's business but mine."

"I guess they didn't give you much time off. The army, I mean." It might be useful to know exactly how long we'd have to hide Liza. "Is that why you're in such a hurry?"

Kearney drove as if he hadn't heard the question, then said, "Unlimited. Until it's settled. Yes sir, Uncle Sugar understands. The army looks out for its own," he said, but bitterly. "I got leave that's un-fucking-limited."

My heart sank. It wasn't going to be as simple as I had hoped: covering for Liza until Kearney had to return to Germany. Maybe he wouldn't come back to New York after tonight, but that didn't seem likely. We would have to think of something else. But first things first: There was still the problem of this meeting with Jake. As we got closer, I became more afraid of the bond that must exist between divorced men.

I took my time in recognizing the street where the theater was. We drove in circles until I decided not to press my luck any further. "I guess it is this one after all. Yes, there's the theater. I recognize the stained glass window on the brownstone next to it."

Kearney double-parked again. I told him to lock the doors: If his car were stolen, we wouldn't be able to get him out of New York tonight. My mind had never been quicker or sharper and I could think of a dozen things at once. I came up with a method for dealing with Jake.

We stood on the sidewalk by the sandwich board outside the theater and the stairs that ran down to the door. I cocked an ear and listened. "Yes, play's still going on. Should be over shortly."

"*Ragged Dick?*" Kearney pointed at the poster. "What kind of damn show is this?"

"Nothing pornographic. Just Watergate and all that."

"*That's* porno. What's your old man doing in crap like that?"

"Actors have to eat. Now, if I remember right, this place has a stage door out back. The cast usually comes out that way, but he might, if he's got friends in the audience, come out this way. If we want to catch him, one of us should stay here while the other goes around back." I paused, weighed Kearney's suspiciousness and went ahead with my gamble. "I know where the stage door is. So why don't you wait here."

Kearney narrowed his eyes at me.

"I know where the door is, Bob, and it's just as likely he'll come out this way."

"You trying to pull something on me?"

"Bob. Don't be so paranoid. I only want to make sure we don't miss Jake. If you want to cover the stage door, fine."

He was still hesitating when we heard muffled applause from below.

"Play's over," I said. "One of us better get back there or he might get away."

"Where's this fucking stage door?" he demanded.

"Around the block and up the alley," I said. I didn't even know if there was an alley. "You'll bring him back here when you find him?" I shouted after him, but Kearney didn't even turn around. He hurried down the tree-lined sidewalk of that street that was as well-lit as a movie set.

I waited until he turned the corner, then charged down the stairs and into the theater.

Nobody watched the door and the grinning, groaning audience was already pulling on coats. I jumped on to the low empty stage where a stagehand was scooping chunks of cream pie into a dustpan. I asked him where Jacob Scherzenlieb's dressing room was.

"No dressing room, pal. But you can't go back there. Cast'll be out in a few—"

"I'm his son," I said. "Family emergency," and I plunged into the curtains where I heard voices babbling. I found myself tangled in black curtain, groping and punching at it until I finally reached down and threw the curtain over my head. I came out in a space packed with men pulling off neckties and suits.

"Jake?" I called. "Jake Scherzenlieb?"

They looked like businessmen stripping for a gym class, a mass of white shirt tails, elbows and boxer shorts, but someone shouted, "Present," and a face streaked with cold cream turned around.

"Joel! Son! What a surprise." He shouldered his way through emptied sleeves and flicking neckties. "How did you like the show tonight? We've added slapstick."

"Didn't see the show. Look. Dad? Something's come up." I automatically looked behind me, in case I'd been followed. "Kearney's in New York."

"Kearney?" He didn't seem to know the name.

"*Bob* Kearney. *Liza's* Bob!"

"Oh *him*. Oh? He's followed Liza to New York? Oh boy," he groaned, but with no more feeling than what anyone would show over the bad luck that had fallen on a stranger.

"Dad. We don't have much time. Kearney's outside and he wants to talk to you."

"Me? Shouldn't he be wanting to talk to Liza?"

"He doesn't know Liza's in New York. And we don't want him to know."

"Ah. Now I'm beginning to get the picture. You're hiding her from him?"

"Yes. And Kearney wants to find out what you know."

"I see. Hmmmm." He looked faintly hurt. "And you'd like me to sneak out without him having a chance to talk to me."

"No. I want you to talk to him. But I don't want you to let on how much you know."

He was surprised by the request, smiled at it, then looked very serious. "Okay. What should I know. Brief me."

I was so relieved I could've kissed him. "You don't know a thing. You haven't seen Liza. You haven't even heard from her."

"I think I can manage that. Because I *don't* really know what's going on with your sister. But why won't she see him? If he's come all the way from—"

"Too complicated. He's out there waiting for me. Oh, and look, don't let on that you've just seen me."

"You don't have to tell me my job, son. I've made a career out of deception, remember?" But he said it while he shifted his eyebrows over other thoughts. "You really trust me with this?"

I didn't have any choice but to trust him, but I said, "Yes, Dad. I do. I trust you."

"Well—" His smile returned, larger than before, a warm, satisfied smile. "In that case, I can't very well let you down, can I?"

"Thanks, Dad. I knew we could count on you." I gave his shoulder a squeeze and took off. "See you out front."

I jumped off the stage and ran up the aisle. Of course we could trust him; all we had to do was let him know what was going on and make him part of it. Outside, Kearney was nowhere in sight. This just might work after all.

A minute later, Kearney wheeled around the corner in a furious walk. "Where's this goddamn alley!" he shouted from five doors down.

"You mean you didn't find it?"

"Goddamn right I didn't find it! Damn thing doesn't exist!" He charged toward me, fists coming out of his pockets, but I calmly stood my ground.

"Oh it exists, but you have to know where it is. Doesn't matter though. One of the actors just came out and he said the stage door's blocked up with sets or something. Everybody's coming out this way tonight."

"Yeah? If you're fucking with me and he's slipped past you—" He stopped a woman coming up the stairs. "Is Liza's fa...is Mr. Scherzenlieb still in there?"

It was Pat Nixon, the only woman in the play. "Jake? Oh yes, Jake's still in there," she said, lowered her head and hurried away from this lunatic.

"See? Trust me, Bob. I've got nothing to gain from screwing you."

He was confused enough now to be embarrassed by his anger. He shook his fists loose and waved his hands at himself. "Okay, okay. I'm being paranoid. But who wouldn't be in my situation?"

"I understand. And you haven't slept in a couple of days. Of course you're going to be edgy." His physical presence could still worry me—he was larger and stronger and there was still violence there—but I now felt I could handle him. All I had to do was keep him so confused he couldn't think straight.

Finally, Jake came out. He played the part of the surprised father, and then the surprised in-law, to perfection. "And *Bob's* with you? Bob! What brings you to the Apple? And where's Liza? Didn't she want to come down and see her old father?"

Perhaps it was only because Kearney had an automatic respect for his elders, but Jake's arrival had a peculiar effect on Kearney: He became calmer, more civil, and none of it seemed fake. "Hello, Mr. Scherzenlieb. No, Liza's not with me on this trip. Which is what brings me to New York." He straightened up and became very brave about it. He told Jake his story.

"Oh. I didn't know." Jake shared a shocked look with me. "I'm terribly sorry to hear that, Bob." He looked terribly sad and sympathetic.

"Then you haven't heard anything from her. Damn. I was hoping you had."

"Sorry. Not a peep. But then, I *am* the black sheep of the family. Nobody tells me anything." A wan smile for his son. "Where is she now?"

"That's it. I don't know."

"Oh boy. Oh boy." Jake shook his head and laid a hand on Kearney's shoulder. "I've been there, Bob. Must be very rough for you."

"Can I buy you a drink? Dad?"

The Dad startled us both. They hadn't seen each other since the fateful night of the cast party and there'd been no communication between them. Kearney had been shocked by Jake's decision to quit something as manly as the C.I.A. to become an actor. But in his time of need, Kearney respected the man and treated him as a father, something nobody else did.

"Wellll . . . ?" went Jake.

"Yes. Let's go have a drink," I told him. "Bob feels that everyone's against him and I think we should let him talk it out of his system." Perhaps, together, we could convince Kearney that Liza wasn't in New York.

"All righty. A drink sounds good. Where should we go, lad? I'm the newcomer here, you're the native."

But all I knew down here were gay bars. And I realized that that would be perfect. A gay bar would confuse Kearney utterly. "Julius?" I suggested.

Jake laughed. "I've walked *by* there a few times, but can't say I've ever had reason to go inside. But okay. Lead the way, son."

"I don't want Joel to give you the wrong impression," said Kearney as we walked. "I am short-tempered, but I'm not paranoid. I'm not. I'm having to consider all the possibilities, that's all. You know how it is. When people don't look you in the eye, you get suspicious."

"I know," said Jake, looking him straight in the eye. "I doubt that I can be of much service, Bob, but I'll be happy to lend you an ear. So tell me. What happened? I presume she felt you were neglecting her. That's how it started with Catherine and me."

We walked together and Kearney told Jake everything he'd told me and Corey, only in a more orderly manner now, without those disruptive bursts of hurt or anger. He presented himself as a patiently suffering, reasonable man, too strong for anything like vindictiveness or rage towards a runaway wife. Jake acted very understanding and sympathetic, so sympathetic I worried that he was being won over to Kearney's side. But when we got to the bar and Jake held open the door for us, he gave me a wink. Jake's insidious wink was wonderfully reassuring tonight.

Kearney took two steps into the Julius and froze.

There were a dozen people inside, but not one of them was a woman. And beside the jukebox were two men who were crawling over each other like puppies.

Kearney's arms went out from his sides, as if he were preparing to run.

Jake came up from behind and gave him a pat.

Kearney jumped, spun around and glared at my father.

"Well, it *is* New York," chuckled Jake as he looked the place over. "Nobody bats an eye. Hmmmm. Interesting place. Looks like an old speakeasy. Let's grab a table in the back and see if... hey, Bob. Don't look at me like that. Ho ho. This place was Joel's idea, not mine."

"Sorry," I said, restraining my smile. "It was the only place I know down here. It's not *too* gay, is it?" I congratulated myself on the cruelty of this stroke.

Jake laughed at Kearney's frightened stare. "Joel's idea. No, no, I've never been in here, Bob. Haven't changed *that* much. I still prefer *les femmes.*"

Kearney blushed. "I wasn't thinking that. Dad. No, Dad. That's not what I was thinking, Dad."—repeating the word as if to explain to the whole bar his relationship with this other man. And people were watching us, but only because we were such an inexplicable threesome. Still, with his crewcut and shoulders, Kearney could pass for a very butch number. I hoped somebody would make a pass at him.

Kearney edged toward the tables in the alcove in back. There was an empty table at the front of the alcove and Kearney sat behind it, on the bench along the wall, drew a deep breath and tried to get back to what he'd been saying. "It was the way it came without warning. That's what hurt. You want to kick somebody in the teeth when they hurt you like... not that I want to hurt Liza!" He hadn't meant that to slip out. "I don't. No. I can forgive her. I have. Already." He tried to look calm and reasonable, but succeeded only in looking wooden.

Jake gave me a disapproving glance as we sat down. This bar was a bad idea if it were going to release Kearney's demons. He politely exchanged the subject. "So you're on LMD?"

"Yes, sir. With an, uh, open extension."

"Extension. Surprising. In my day, all they allotted you was four days. You were expected to see a lawyer, arrange your divorce and return to duty immediately. Difficult to fit in a haircut in that time, much less a reconciliation."

"Yes... well, the Army's more humane about these things now," said Kearney, still nervous.

"What's an LMD?"

"Leave for Matters Domestic," said Jake. "Divorces, funerals, et cetera."

"Anybody want a drink?" asked Kearney. "I'll buy if you fly, Joel." He was afraid to approach the bar lined with homos and I was happy to take his ten dollars.

When I returned with the drinks, Kearney was trying to explain away his earlier burst of anger. "Don't get me wrong, Dad. I don't want to hurt Liza. I just want to make things right with us, that's all."

"I understand," said Jake. "Initially there's a feeing that you've been stabbed in the back. Initially."

"Exactly!" cried Kearney. "That's exactly what it's like. My situation must be identical to what yours was. Stabbed in the back?"

"Maybe. But it was a feeling that didn't—"

"You're giving yourself heart and soul to a good cause —the army for me, the uh, agency for you—and the people you're doing it for pull the rug out from under you? They dump you?" He was so excited to find a kindred spirit he forgot his nervousness.

"Yes. Well..." Jake lowered his eyes. "I believed that myself. For a time. But in my heart of hearts, I knew I wasn't in the company for my family's sake. I was there for reasons of my own. Self-esteem. Ego. The power trip, as they call it, which I remember only all too well myself."

"Yeah, sure, when you get down to the basics, of course I'm there for myself. Only—" He suddenly shook his head. "No. Not really. Not when I'm doing nothing over there but sit on my butt and babysit a pack of pot-heads. It's no picnic, Dad. If I didn't know I was doing it for somebody, I would've gotten out years ago. Okay, there's days when it's hard to believe that something like one's country is real enough to be worth protecting. But I do have my family. There's days when they're all the country I have, but that's enough to keep me going. Until this." He covered his eyes with his hand. "And it is like being betrayed, like being stabbed in the back."

Jake scratched his head. He didn't know how to deal with this kind of confident self-righteousness. "And you really don't think you've neglected your wife? Liza, I mean."

"What? Oh no. Not at all. Doted on her. Dote on Joan too. Hell, I've never been one of those husbands who spends all his free time at the officers' club, acting like he was still a bachelor."

"Hmmm. If that *is* the case, then your case is very different from mine, Bob."

"I've been a good father. And a good husband."

"Have you? See, I wasn't. And once I was able to admit that, divorce became plain common sense. I would've been a bastard to try and stop it. And not just a bastard, a fool. Because I realized that, well, I'd never really wanted the responsibility in the first place. It was a job I did badly, and a relief to have it taken away from me."

When you don't know what to tell the other person, tell him about yourself; only I wasn't sure how much of it was true and how much was only being said for Kearney's benefit.

Kearney didn't think any of it was true. He squinted at Jake, like a man trying to pick up something too small for his fingers. "You mean you could just . . . ? Uh uh. I can't buy that. You couldn't have felt that way!" he insisted. "No, that's just what you told yourself to make it easier. And you didn't feel that way. I know you didn't, because you went to the trouble of getting custody of your son here."

"Oh, *that.*" Jake softly chuckled to himself. "I'm sure Joel could bend your ear on the results of that debacle." He looked at me fondly, but turned back to Kearney before he could register my reaction. "Yes, I'm afraid that was more circumstances than the results of a burning desire on my part to keep a finger in the family pie. If Catherine had had her druthers, she would've gotten 'em both. But the woman was too damn proud to take any money from me. Even child support. And too practical to think for a minute that she could provide for both of them. Soooo, we decided that it was only fair that we take one apiece."

"Then you really did flip a coin?" I asked.

"Ho ho. No. That was just my little joke. Which nobody ever laughed at. No, it just seemed natural for me to take the boy and Cat the girl. Presuming that men

296

know all about boys and women know all about girls. A false presumption as it turned out."

He wasn't guilty about it, only mildly sheepish, and perhaps sheepish only because he was telling Kearney something he had never really talked about with me.

It didn't surprise me that a decision so important to my life had been arrived at so carelessly. And I was already feeling benevolent towards Jake simply because he was following my wishes. But I might've suffered a rebirth of my old anger, if Kearney hadn't been there.

He squinted harder than ever at Jake. His upper lip curled above his teeth. He suddenly jabbed his head at Jake. "Are you putting me on?"

"No. Why should I be putting you on, Bob?"

"But that's... that's..." His teeth were bared, his mouth half-open, the skin around his eyes crimped in pain. "Isn't that awfully callous?"

"Yes," Jake sighed. "I admit it does sound a trifle cold."

"Cold? It's—" He looked left and right, searching for someone with whom he could share his disbelief. And all he saw was Julius. "It's unnatural!" he cried.

"Well, unconventional maybe," said Jake with a nervous smile.

Kearney collapsed his back against the wall, his eyes locked on Jake. "You really did it like that?"

"I did."

"Without putting up any kind of fight? Without any feeling of love or responsibility or duty?" Disbelief was turning into indignation. "All you felt was relief?"

"Yes, Bob. In the end that's what I felt," said Jake. He had to turn away from Kearney just as he'd turned away from me.

"Jesus," Kearney hissed to himself. "And I came to *you* thinking I could get help or advice?"

"I told you, Bob, I had no advice to give."

"I can't understand how a man could have so little feeling for his own family. Damn. And yet you can talk about it as if you were proud of it?"

"I'm not proud of it. I'm proud only that I can now admit to myself what I felt." Jake glanced at me.

I wanted to defend him, but didn't know how. I agreed with all the accusations; the only thing wrong about them was that they came from Kearney.

"But the selfishness of it. That just floors me. Hell, if you could wash your hands of your own family like that? Your own fucking family? Damn! No wonder Liza's so screwed up."

Jake straightened up in his chair and tried to look wise. "You're young," he said. "You might be a father and a captain and all that, Bob, but you're still very young. I know. Because I had the same beliefs myself when I was your age. But you don't know half of it yet. When you've experienced some of what I've experienced—"

"Bullshit. I'm not like you and nothing's ever going to make me like you. Thank God. I'd kill myself before I ever let my family go the way you did yours. Because my family is *me.*" He angrily shook his head. "No. Even if I lose Liza, I'm not going to lose my daughter."

My cloud of mixed sympathies dissolved and I remembered what I was here for. "You want to get custody of Joan?" Our fears had not been mere paranoia after all.

"Damn straight, I do. Because I love that kid. Enough to lay down my life for her."

"But Liza loves her, too," I said, before I remembered I wasn't suppose to have seen them. "Doesn't she?"

"Then she'll have to choose, won't she? If it's this fucking freedom-to-find-herself she wants, she can fucking have it. I can't lock her up in a cage. But if it's Joan she wants—"

"If you can't have Liza, then Liza can't have Joan?" Jake frowned. "That's awfully dog-in-the-manger, Bob."

"*You* might see it like that. Yes. You *would* think that's what it was. But I love my child. And if I need to use my own daughter to slap some sense into Liza, I'm sorry but that's the way it has to be. And if sense can't be slapped into her, I'll at least be able to save Joan from her screwed-up mother."

"But it'll be up to a court to decide who gets Joan," I said.

"Yeah? And who do you think they're going to side with? A good father and husband who's serving his country? Or a woman who runs off for no reason at all and is so flipped out she won't let her husband know where she is?"

"If that's the case," I said, "why don't you go back to Germany and let a lawyer take care of all this? Couldn't they put out a warrant for Liza's arrest?" I was sure Kearney was fooling himself about the prejudices of the court, as long as we could get Liza back to Virginia. "Let the courts get Joan for you."

"Shit," said Kearney. He sneered at me and shook his head. "You don't understand at all what I want. Both of you. You're both too far gone in your selfishness to understand me at all."

There was a long pause and Jake said quietly, "You want your wife back. *And* your daughter."

"Bull's-eye," said Kearney, but Jake's sympathetic tone surprised him and he suddenly became quieter, sadder. "Yes. That's what I want all right. And if I have to black-mail that girl to her senses, so be it. I'll chase her halfway around the world if I have to, like she was the fucking Holy Grail. Because that woman is my life. I ain't shit without Liza."

Jake downed the rest of his scotch as if it were a deep breath. "I'm sorry for you, Bob. I truly am. Those are beautiful sentiments. But very dangerous sentiments."

"Sentiments? Principles!" cried Kearney. He glared at Jake and contemptuously shook his head. "If you hadn't crawled so far up your own asshole, you'd understand that."

Jake thought for a moment, then quietly took his coat off the back of his chair. "Sham a few emotions on stage

299

and you recognize the sham emotions in real life. No matter what people tell you you're suppose to feel." He slowly stood up.

"You *would* believe family's all sham. Makes it more disposable, doesn't it?"

"It's not worth bleeding yourself white over. I better be going, Bob."

He was running away. Jake did it with dignity, but not even the parting shots could disguise the fact that this was an escape. I had certainly seen him do it often enough in the past.

"You going to be staying with Joel for a few days?"

"Hell no. I'm getting out of this pesthole as soon as possible."

"He's leaving tonight," I said.

"Ah. Well in that case, we probably won't be seeing each other again. I'm sorry you can't see my side of it, Bob. All I can say is that I hope things work out. To everyone's satisfaction."

Kearney only snorted.

"Joel? Son? Talk to you sometime during the week, I guess." He winked at me, then departed.

I was sorry for the abuse he'd taken. "Thanks Dad," I called after him.

But what was I thanking him for? The meeting had been a disaster. It'd done nothing to lay Kearney's suspicions to rest and had succeeded only in muddling my feelings about my enemy; alongside Jake's enlightened indifference, Kearney's passion seemed less clearly evil.

It was just as well that Jake had deserted me.

"Shit and double shit," Kearney muttered to his glass. "No wonder Liza's a mess. Old man like that? Never understood how she could talk about her old man with so little respect. Now I know. People like that, no wonder the country's going down the toilet."

"Can I get you a cup of coffee, Bob? Long drive down to Virginia."

"Coffee? Yeah. Better have some coffee." He looked

up at me trustingly. Jake had made even me look good to Kearney.

I was glad to get away from him, if only for a minute. But the end was in sight, if only for tonight. Get some coffee into Kearney, get him on the road and out of town. Then we could catch our breath and plan our next move.

The bartender gave me the coffee in a paper cup and I made my way back toward the alcove. Halfway there, I saw Kearney suddenly shield his face, as if he didn't want to be seen. Someone was cruising him, I thought. I hoped it'd make him uncomfortable enough to want to leave immediately.

But a body suddenly walked past me, going straight for Kearney. I saw only the back of a sweatshirt with a hood, then heard the sweatshirt sing out, "Kahuna, man! Wow!"

I lunged for the corner behind the cigarette machine.

"I don't believe it! This is too fucking much, man! I never thought I'd see *you* in New York. And here? Far fucking out!"

The table was at the front of the alcove, almost level with the wall I pressed my back against. Wyler Reese's back was to me, but I could watch Kearney's shocked face slowly acknowledge that he knew this person. How could I have been so stupid to forget I might run into Wyler here? He was the last thing I needed tonight.

Wyler threw his shoulders back and proudly said, "Guess what? I came out too."

Kearney just sat there, one hand covering the bottom half of his face. Then he spotted me against the wall, watching him through the empty bottles and glasses that sat on top of the cigarette machine. I put my finger to my lips and shook my head.

"But hey! What am I telling you that for? I mean, look where we are, man! But you too, huh! I can't believe it. The camp stud himself. That camp was nothing but one big closet. You know, I always thought you might be one, too."

301

"One what?" Kearney forgot me. "Get out of here. I'm married."

Wyler laughed. "Then what're you doing here? Oh I know. You're writing a book and you're here for research. But hey. It's cool. I won't tell a soul, Kahuna. Your secret's safe with me. But wow, man. Can't get over it. The great Kahuna too."

There was nothing playing on the jukebox and Wyler always talked too loud; I could hear every word.

And then Wyler started talking in Kearney's old pidgin English. "Kahuna want dick. Much dick. Dick good. Kahuna love dick."

Kearney tried to bear with it, but his temper finally snapped. "Will you shut the fuck up and leave me alone! I'm no faggot. I'm married!"

"Hey, man. Stay cool. Just happy to see you, that's all."

"Well, I'm not happy to see you. An asswipe back then and you're still an asswipe and I don't have time for asswipes dammit! So get lost. Unless you want my boot shoved up your sweet A. Go give somebody a blowjob, or whatever it is you people do in a place like this."

But instead of being frightened away, Wyler sat down. "Easy, man. Hey. I know what you're going through. I've been there. Coming out can be really tough. But nobody's out to get you. We're all your friends here, babe. I know exactly what you're feeling. And if you're married, hey, must make it doubly tough."

Kearney glared at me, so hard I was afraid Wyler would turn around and look. I was prepared to duck down behind the cigarette machine, but Wyler was too busy offering understanding.

"It's a ticklish business. Not just coming out, but coming out in one piece. I mean, some people lose it all when they come out. Like, you remember that wimp back at camp, Shirtsy? Joel Scherzenstein? He's gay. You once said he wasn't, but he is. But he came out D.O.A. Stillborn, man. A real cold fish."

Kearney was suddenly interested. "You're in touch with, uh, Shirtsy?"

"In touch? I was in that mother's pants and up his ass, putting him through changes like you wouldn't believe. A week ago. We were eating each other up with spoons, man."

"Did he say anything about a sister visiting him?"

"Shit no. We had something going and the mother wouldn't even give me his phone number."

Kearney looked disappointed.

"But I'm on to that little bastard's game. You see him, Kahuna, watch out. He might look innocent, but he is one ball buster. I mean, I was almost in love with him, all last week. Came in here every night, hoping to see him again. I asked around. And you know what? People knew him. They knew who I was talking about. Runty dude who walks like he's bowlegged, in here every Friday night. Never goes home with the same person twice. Never. And get this. A couple of people heard he was hustling. Can you dig it? That wimp, a hustler!"

Al, the chemistry teacher, certainly had a big mouth. But if Wyler thought I was a prostitute, perhaps he'd steer clear of me.

Kearney, however, was suddenly interested again. "This was recent?"

"Like last week. But sounded to me like it's been going on for some time. Something you see all the time up here and I wouldn't have even brought it up, except that you knew Shirtsy. But that's what you got to watch out for, Kahuna. There's people who, when they come out, leave their hearts behind. See, I've kept my heart, and heartless pricks like Shirtsy like to break off pieces just to watch it bleed. But I wouldn't have it any other way. Keep your heart, Kahuna. And watch out for the pricks. Hey, you haven't happened to have seen him in here tonight, have you?"

I frantically shook my head at Kearney.

303

"Nope. Can't say that I have. But I'm just passing through."

I was relieved, and surprised. There was an amused gleam in Kearney's eye when he glanced at me again.

"Yeah? Oh, feh—I'm glad to be finished with the creep. Shouldn't even be wasting my breath on that little mother. But hey. What're we talking about him for? We should be talking about you. Kahuna in Julius. Wow! Who'd ever picture it? So tell me. Who did you score with at camp?"

Kearney calmly stood up. "Time for me to go, asswipe."

"Hey, don't go. We got a lot of catching up to do. If this place is a bummer for you, we could go somewhere else. Want to walk over to my place? I got a real Manhattan pad now and it's only a few—"

"Nope. Getting late and there's nothing more I have to say to a nerd like you, Wyler." He looked at me, then the door catty-corner from my wall, me again, the door.

"Aw, Kahuna. Don't be so touchy. You don't have to worry about me putting the moves on you or nothing. Even AC/DC, you're still big bad Kahuna to me. I wouldn't dare—"

That was all I heard before I went for the door. Kearney patiently suffered Wyler's pleading until I could get away.

Kearney came out to the street three minutes later, alone. I stood in a dark doorway on the other side of the street and watched Kearney turn and turn in front of Julius' dingy stucco wall. I considered letting him look, but that would only feed his suspicions. And he apparently trusted me now, enough at least to cover for me with Wyler.

"Over here," I called and stepped out of the shadows.

Kearney walked over. "Let's go," he said. "I'm giving you a lift back to your place."

"That's okay, Bob. Subway's near here. Thanks though."

"Shut up. You're getting a ride."

"In that case..." It didn't sound trusting, but I walked with him. "Still a twerp, isn't he? Coming out certainly didn't help Reese. Still a twerp, and still stupid. Imagine him thinking me a hustler. And thinking you were gay?" A little flattery wouldn't hurt. "The guy's blind. Lost in his own little world."

Kearney said nothing, kept walking, then said, "Cobbett know you're cheating on him?"

I looked straight at him. He was watching my face as we walked, waiting to see how I would react.

The question, his look; I almost tripped. I quickly recovered and calmly said, "Oh sure. We have an understanding. Which means it's not really cheating."

But it was too late. "Bullshit," said Kearney and he faced forward again with a wicked grin.

"It's true. It is. Corey and I do have an understanding. We believe sex has nothing to do with love. No matter how it might look by hererosexual standards. And"—I attempted a little laugh—"I don't do it for money. That's a misconception of Wyler's. We are just as appalled by the idea of prostitution as anyone else is." But I knew that Kearney hadn't taken hold of this as just another cause for moral disgust. He'd found a weapon.

"Bullshit," he repeated. "Even if you are giving it away for free. I wonder what old Cobbett would say if he knew."

I choked. "But—but he does know. And he does it, too. A little."

"Uh uh. I don't buy that. Queer or not, Cobbett's still the good little Boy Scout. Faithful and loyal and true. While you run around this pesthole, jumping into bed with anything that has a prick."

"Corey *talks* monogamy, when straights are around. The way he did with you. Because he thinks straight people wouldn't understand."

"Oh yeah? Okay. I'm curious. Like to talk to him about it. Maybe learn something." And his malicious playfulness gave way to raw contempt. "Like how he can dip into an asshole when he knows it's had Wyler Reese's slimy prick up it."

I hated him for that, but panic remained stronger than hatred. Kearney's obscenity made what I'd been doing seem far worse than it had ever seemed before. How *would* Corey react?

"Suit yourself, Bob. It's a topic that still embarrasses Core and he'd rather our straight acquaintances didn't know. But, since that blabbermouth Reese spilled the beans... Oh, Corey will probably just blush and say something like—I don't know—just that a little sex on the side can never hurt a partnership that's based on true love and understanding. Which is what we have." Which I hoped was true.

"You think so? Well, I think Cobbett doesn't know a fucking thing about it. And when he hears, it'll wipe him out. Be like a stab in the back. And, friend, I know exactly what that stab is like. Got no qualms about seeing someone else share the experience. If I were you, I'd be doing my damndest to get on my good side, so I'd keep my mouth shut."

He had his weapon and there was only one thing he could want it for; I had to escape before he could use it. We were in front of the stairs to the subway. "I'm taking the subway home after all. I don't like your attitude, Bob."

But before I could step away from him, Kearney grabbed my arm. "No way, fucker. Not when I've got you by the balls. You run off now and I'm walking straight to a telephone."

He dug his fingers between the bone and muscle of my arm. We were in front of the newsstand by the subway entrance and there were plenty of people. Nobody looked twice at us.

"He won't believe you," I said.

"Oh no? You want to find out?" He threw my arm

back at me, confident that what he knew was enough to hold me. "Okay, smartass. Where's Liza?"

I rubbed my arm as if that pain were my only concern. "I told you. I don't know."

"Cut the shit. Don't think you can fuck over my life without me doing my damndest to fuck over yours. She's in Virginia, isn't she?"

I shrugged unconvincingly and said, "If you're so sure she's in Virginia, why're you using threats to get what you already know?"

"You been dicking me all night. Sticking me with that asshole who calls himself your father, sticking me in a fag bar, playing dumb about that bitch sister of yours. But I'm not going to be dicked, smartass. I've been playing your game all night, now you're going to play mine. Your old man don't know shit, but you do. You know where she is, don't you?"

"Yes," I said.

"Okay," he said and waited for me to finish. "Yeah? Come on! I'm not going to stand out here all night with my thumb up my ass. *Where is she?*"

I guiltily looked at my feet. "How do I know you won't talk to Corey anyway? Just for spite."

"You don't, do you?" cried Kearney triumphantly. "You don't, except I don't give a fuck about either of you. You can live your shitty faggot lies until your cocks rot off—I don't care. Wouldn't waste a breath on you. So long as I got what I wanted."

There was only one answer I could possibly give him. I drew a deep breath and said, "She's with her mother in Virginia."

"Yes!" said Kearney.

It was too easy. He'd given me the answer himself and I'd delayed only while I considered the results. And to make the lie more believable. But there was no relief with the lie, no satisfaction when he swallowed it so willingly.

"There. Wasn't so hard stooling on your sister, was it?

In Virginia, huh? See. I knew it all along," he said, grinning and nodding, totally pleased with himself. "Just had to hear it from you, Shirtsy. Damn. Why've I been pissing my time away in this hole when I knew all along she was in Virginia?" he muttered to himself.

The cause for panic gone, I was free to feel nothing but my anger. "You just wanted to practice your bullying," I sneered. "Before you bullied Liza."

"Bullying? Bullshit. I was up front with you. You were the ones who started dicking me, before I even thought of dicking you. Dicking?" He laughed at the word. "Hear that? But dicking's what it's all about for you people. You *like* getting fucked. Shit. I've been talking to you people in the wrong damn language." He was so pleased with his victory, he was joking. "Come on. Give you a ride back to that shit hole apartment of yours."

"No. I'm taking the subway."

"No skin off my nose. Just wanted to show you there were no hard feelings. But the sooner I get out of here and down there, the better."

"What makes you think I won't warn them you're coming?"

And that shook his confidence, for a second. "Because you're too smart to do anything that stupid. Not when I've got you by the balls. Damn. You'd probably like *that* too, wouldn't you? By the throat then. And I do have you by the throat, Shirtsy."

He did, and yet I had lied to him anyway. His gullible confidence did not make me feel superior; it only supported my fear that he was absolutely right and that I had cut my own throat. I had gained us a day, maybe two. But Kearney would be back. Intent on recovering Liza. Intent on destroying me and Corey.

"You're not going to get her back," I said. "Even when you find her."

"That's what you think, fuckwad. Just you wait. Nighty-night, Shirtsy," he sarcastically sang at me and swaggered across Seventh Avenue, without bothering to look back at me.

I watched him go, then stumbled down the stairs to the subway. Almost immediately, my mind began to replay what had happened. The future frightened me; I could only think about the past, trying to isolate where I'd gone wrong, as if I could go back in time and fix it. Because it had almost worked. If only I hadn't taken Kearney to Julius. If only... but I'd been so full of myself and it'd seemed like such a cute stunt. What an idiot I'd been. All that blithe, flashy promiscuity: It'd been nothing but a harmless toy for me. But because Kearney used it as a weapon, I now saw it as a weapon. How would Corey see it? I didn't know. I didn't want to know. I contemplated the subway tracks and saw a lone black glove lying between the ties. The white tile walls began to glow, then dance with the light of an approaching train, and I shifted the blame to Liza. Blaming Liza, I stepped through a door and sat down.

If only we hadn't let her into our household. Her vulnerability had become ours. What she was doing here seemed more gratuitous than ever. Her refusal to see the husband she was divorcing was absolutely pointless, but it was because of that neurotic refusal that I had made my own life open to attack.

And only then, while I sat numbly on the train that lurched uptown, did I think of telling Kearney the truth. It hadn't crossed my mind when I was face to face with his threat, but it came to me now and seemed perfectly sensible. And beneficial too, because such a confrontation would force Liza to make up her mind, once and for all. It wasn't too late. I could call Virginia in the morning, confess and apologize to Kearney, make sure that Corey would never know. . . .

But no. It was not something I could consider for very long. I recognized how cowardly it was. And that frustrated me because, except for the cowardice involved, it was a perfectly justified course of action. I still didn't know exactly what it was we were protecting Liza from, but I would continue to protect her. Even if it meant that Corey would learn the truth about me. I liked myself for rejecting cowardice and, because I could like myself again, I realized it must be the right decision.

But Kearney would be back. In a day, maybe two. Kearney would be back.

When I opened the door, I heard the voices in the kitchen. I turned the corner and saw Corey, then Liza at the table. And with them was Jake.

"And here he is," Jake hollered. "The confidence man himself. And all in one piece? No broken bones or slivers of bamboo under the fingernails?"

"Hey, Shrimp," Liza said, looking at me gratefully.

I tried to smile. I was puzzled to find them in such good spirits. And Jake was with them. "What're you doing here?"

He laughed. "Didn't know if you were going to get out of there alive. Ho ho. Just joking. Sorry if I seemed to run out on you, but I saw I wasn't going to convince Bob the sky was blue, so I thought I'd be more useful coming up here to spread the alarm and see if I could be of help." He beamed at me, then at his daughter.

It should've been nice to know that Jake hadn't abandoned me after all, that he wanted to help us. But he could be of no help to me.

"So what happened?" asked Corey. "You have any trouble after your father left?" He was more serious than the others, more concerned about what I'd been through. He pulled out a chair for me and, after I sat down, laid a warm hand on my knee.

"Nothing much," I said. "Nothing really."

"And where's Bad Bob now?" asked Liza.

"What? Oh. On his way to Virginia. Where he thinks you are."

"Lord. Lord! Poor Mom." But Liza was chuckling as

310

she shook her head. "What's she going to do when she finds Bob on her doorstep? Fit to be tied."

"I trust she still owns that shotgun," said Jake.

"To be sure. A load of rock salt in his butt might make Bob see the light."

Their lightheartedness made them seem as callous as children. I covered Corey's hand with mine, studied our hands before they vanished and said, "Liza? I hope...I hope this is what you really want. Because we're all in it now. Up to our necks."

Jake laughed. "That's what I've been telling her. Damn well better be what she wants. After all, she's made me a traitor to my class. Yes, sir, my loyalty to my daughter has made me disloyal to the holy order of jilted husbands." But he showed no regret, basking in his regained position of family importance.

"Aw, Shrimp. Don't look so worried." Liza grinned and squeezed my shoulder. "Jake's been telling us how wonderful you were. Sneaky? I never knew how ingeniously sneaky you could be. And that asshole deserved every trick you could cook up. Coming after me like I was some kid who'd run away from home. Keep him guessing, I say. And taking him to a gay bar!" she howled. "Lord, but I'd love to have been a fly on the wall. Old uptight Bob must've had a cow!"

I winced. "But he'll be back. When he finds you're not with Mom, he'll come straight back. Out for blood."

When I looked at Corey's face, he raised his eyebrows sympathetically. He saw only that I was worried, and still trusted me enough to believe I deserved sympathy.

"We know that," said Liza. "We're taking a few precautions about that."

"Called your mom," said Corey. "And we warned her that Bob might be on his way down. She's none too happy about the whole business. I can't say I blame her. It's not fair to dump something like this in her lap."

Jake waved Corey's objections aside. "Cat'll know

what to do. She might not have dealt with the likes of Bob before, but Cat's a firm believer in the institution of divorce. Uh, your sister was careful not to mention to her that *I* was involved."

"But the important thing," said Liza, "is that I'm taking Joan over to Daddy's tomorrow."

"We figured that Bob was so appalled by my unnaturalness that he'll avoid me like the plague. Liza and Joan can stay with me a few days. Until Hurricane Bob blows back out to sea."

"I told them we'd miss Joan," sighed Corey. "But it does make sense and it was inevitable anyway. Liza's decided that, soon as Bob's out of the country, she's going down to her mother's."

Liza frowned, avoided my stare and shrugged. "Yup. Playing hide-and-seek tonight was fun all right. But it's too dangerous to keep playing it. Custody and all that."

Corey added, "Jake told us about Bob wanting custody."

"So you'll get us out of your hair after all, Shrimp. I'd hop on a bus tonight, only we might run into Bob down there. But we'll just lay low until that bastard gives up and goes back to Germany. Then it's bye-bye New York, hello Mother and guilt." She grimaced. "But I'm so pissed at him now, not even Mom could make Bob look good to me."

"Oh," was all I could say while I wondered why this couldn't have happened sooner, before Corey and I were involved. But it was too late now. A day, maybe two, and Kearney would be back. Not knowing exactly when only made it more threatening. But at some indefinite moment, he would tell Corey. Unless I told Corey myself. I could at least have control of when it happened. And I could frame the story in love, apology and mitigating circumstances. Or no, there had been no mitigating circumstances, it had all been me and it would be cowardice to say otherwise. But yes, I would tell him, before Kearney did.

I waited to feel good about that decision too. I didn't; I couldn't shake the feeling of fear and uncertainty that continued to open beneath me. Jake and Liza continued to plot and prattle, selfishly confident that everything was fine.

"You really think this extended leave thing is a crock?" Liza was asking.

"Sure. No such thing. New Action Army or no, brass doesn't care if a captain's happily married or unhappily divorced. In fact, they prefer they'd be divorced. No, this extended leave business is a bluff. He'll have three days, then fly back to Germany. You can take my word for it."

Just enough time for Kearney to do his damage. In their confidence, Jake and Liza had abandoned me.

Finally, Jake went home, telling Liza he'd be by first thing in the morning. He would borrow his roommate's car and it'd be easier that way than carrying Joan and Joan's paraphernalia downtown by subway. For tonight at least, we were safe from Kearney. Liza kissed me good night, congratulated and thanked me again and went to bed.

"Pretty rough?" asked Corey while we undressed.

Do I tell him now?

I couldn't. My mind was still fresh with Kearney's use of what I'd done. I could tell myself, shout to myself above the din of my fear, that what I'd done was not really all that terrible and that it was only Kearney's use of it that made it seem so. I should wait until tomorrow, when my fears had subsided enough for me to see clearly.

"Kind of rough," I said. "Kind of complicated."

"You beginning to feel a little sorry for Bob?"

"Sorry!" It was as if Corey had shoved me away with his hand. "For that bastard? He's every bit the son of a bitch Liza's been saying he is. Anyone who could thre—" But I couldn't tell Corey why the man was a bastard, not yet.

"Yes. Well. I imagine he's striking out at everything in sight. Sounds like he certainly lit into your father. But you have to understand his position. He feels like a rug's been pulled out from under him. Of course he's going to say rash things."

Dammit, Corey. You're sympathizing with the wrong person, I thought.

But I was too frightened to contradict him. All I could do was get into bed with him and try to find some comfort in the way he held his arm under my shoulder, in his assurances that in just a few days we could go back to being the way we had been.

Corey left for work the next morning, just as he always did.

Shortly after ten, Jake arrived with the car.

I helped load it with crib, guitar, Joan and all the other things that had seemed to take up so much space in our apartment for the past week and a half. The car was an old maroon Cadillac, a broad boat of a car, and Liza's things disappeared into its deep interior as if into a black hole.

Joan sat on her mother's lap and reached in vain for the rubber doughnut that had been set on the dashboard. Liza rolled her window down to say goodbye. "Okay. You'll call me the minute you hear anything from Mom or Bastard Bob?"

"I'll call. Probably call you before then, just to find out how you're doing."

"They'll be fine," said Jake and he started the car. "Braxton's loft is as big as a playground. Joan can have her run of it."

"She's not old enough to run," I said.

The purr of the engine caused Joan to look around excitedly. She pointed at me. "Bye? Bye?"

"That's right, Joan. Bye," I said.

"Bye, Shrimp. Enjoy getting a well-deserved rest from us."

And they pulled away, leaving me on the curb with my hands in my pockets. I watched the car glide through the morning shadows and sunlight of our street, until it turned left on Broadway and was gone.

Upstairs, our apartment had a ghostly silence to it. It wasn't a real silence—Ed snored softly behind his closed door; outside the closed windows a soprano was singing her way up and down the scale—but it felt like silence. I wandered from one empty room to another, waiting to feel glad that I was alone at last. But I didn't feel glad, only lonely. My own family had abandoned me. I knew how maudlin and foolish the thought was, but it persisted. Joan had been such a nuisance for the past week and a half, but I still expected to catch sight of her out of the corner of my eye. I was disappointed each time I looked around and saw only a bare patch of floor.

I had something more important to worry about, but wasn't sure how best to worry about it. To think about that only made me more sorry that Liza was gone, because Liza was probably the one person in the world with whom I could talk about it. She could help me put it into a clear perspective. But even if she were here, I doubted that I could tell her. I was afraid she'd think I blamed her and that I'd brought it up only to convince her to surrender herself to Bob. I didn't want her to think that.

To give myself something to do, I looked through my desk drawer for Jake's number, so I could have it by the telephone when I needed it. I found it right away, scrawled on the program of his play. In the back of the drawer was a green spiral notebook where I had entered all those names. I flipped through it. The names and remarks didn't seem to mean anything to me. Kearney's threat, detached from his anger, now seemed less real too, like something I'd only read somewhere, just as these names seemed like things I'd only read about, not done. I knew all were more real than that.

The dry rubber band on a packet of letters had broken and envelopes were spilled across the bottom of the drawer. I absently stacked them together again while I waited for the phone to ring. Most of the envelopes were addressed with my mother's compulsively neat handwriting. I saw my name in Aunt Bertie's jittery, illegible hand. Then I turned over a letter from Corey. Catherine's handwriting and Bertie's were as real to me as their voices, but not Corey's. When you live with someone, you don't have much opportunity to write to them and Corey and I had written to each other only during those summers when he had worked with migrant workers on the Eastern Shore. I tugged out the folded sheet of yellow legal paper. The handwriting, in pencil, had none of Corey's clumsy ease, but was as tight and tiny as something scribbled by a mouse.

Dear Joel,   *July 15, 1972*

*   The farmhouse they've given us is still without electricity. I am writing this by the hissing light of a Coleman lantern. There are five of us at the table, all writing letters and slapping mosquitoes. The black dots edged with red are not misplaced punctuation, but dead mosquitoes. The water spots are sweat, not tears, but I do miss you in my fashion.*

*   We've been busy building more bath houses. During the day I am blank and one with my hammer and saw. I also drive the van that picks up the children for the ad hoc daycare center we've set up. One cannot think about anything when one has a gaggle of black and Hispanic kids babbling at one's back. But I miss you at night. Carnally, of course, but more conversationally. I like the people I work with, but there is nobody here to whom I could say absolutely anything. I have no pride with you and feel you have none with me. With each other we can say absolutely anything. This is one of the advantages of having been through what we've been through together. We are cured of romantic pride.*

*   I feel foolish going on like this, saying the things that shouldn't have to be said. But as we know, I've always expressed myself badly. Seeing each other only every two weeks I don't get the chance to complete my incomplete thoughts the way I do when we're together every day. I'm referring to "Can Karl Marx find love and happiness in the arms of Andrew Carnegie?" You were half-joking and I only an-*

swered the joke half. But we are different and it is a mystery that we should be together, a mystery I respect rather than one I want to solve. In the beginning I was naively drawn to you because I thought you were a blank slate upon which I could write the imaginary person I thought I could love. You cured me of that, accidentally but justly. You are your own person and I wouldn't have it any other way. What's the point of attaching oneself to someone who's only a projection of one's own imagination? On my own, I would be as smug and self-righteous as some of the people I'm working with. Alone, you would be one of those types mired in self, ambition and resentment. But together we form quite a remarkable person. I don't know how deep our ambitions or politics run, if they are truly us or only the clothes we wear at the moment. But perhaps our politics give us the difference that gender gives heterosexual couples.

Bath houses might seem a Victorian obsession, but the prevalence of skin diseases, especially impetigo . . .

I scanned the final paragraphs down to the promise of coming home next weekend and the closing—"With friendship as well as love, Corey"—then laid the letter down.

Three years ago, and yet I clearly remembered my feelings the day I received it: awe for such a practical, genuine assessment of our love.

The letter gave me no comfort now. How innocent we'd been back then, to harp on our political differences. I had no politics, even then; the "Andrew Carnegie" remark was only an obsolete image of myself, a joke. And Corey wasn't Karl Marx. He hadn't even read any Marx when we had finally connected and he had begun his drift leftwards only after I had moved in with him. *I* had radicalized him? In a way. Maybe with desire domesticated, he had to look elsewhere for something to dream. Unrequited love was replaced by unrequited politics. Love had changed his handwriting too: tightened it up, made it smaller and neater.

These thoughts of Corey's were three years old, and yet he had never articulated his love more clearly. Rereading it, I saw that all he articulated was what we would've been without each other. He believed in my love and all he could describe were the things love had overcome.

Perhaps all he loved was my love for him. Was there anything about me worth loving except for the fact that I loved Corey? Self, ambition and resentment. Throw my love into question and there would be nothing left for Corey to love. If only he had said he loved my face, or my intellect, my wit, even my body, I could feel I had something that might survive this crisis. But all he loved were our differences.

I desperately toyed with the absurd idea that nothing could be more different than infidelity. Perhaps my confession would only add to my appeal. I had hurt him once and it had bound us together. Would this additional hurt make the tie doubly binding? But that was only words and I couldn't believe them.

The telephone rang and I snatched it up. "Hello?"

"Sitting right on top of it, weren't you? Feeling guilty about sending Bob down here with that cock-and-bull story about your sister hiding down here? You should be."

"Kearney's already come and gone?" I asked in a panic.

Catherine's voice was quick, compressed and angry. "Oh he's come all right. Like a bat out of hell. But I don't think he's going anywhere for a while. He's up in Liza's old room. Out like a light."

"What happened, Mom? You didn't knock him out, did you?"

"Hmph. Would've liked to knock him out. Would like to knock the daylights into each and every one of you, the way you've been handling . . . no, he's sleeping."

"Sleeping?"

"Pulled in two hours ago looking like a zombie. Said his piece, didn't make much sense, didn't believe me when I told him Liza wasn't here and went looking all

over the house and barn for her. Then he went back up to
her room and the next thing I knew, he was face down on
her bed, dead to the world. I couldn't wake him with a
stick."

"Ah," I said and again, "Ah."

"Well?" she demanded.

"Let him sleep, Mom. He hasn't slept in a couple of
days and he's probably real tired." If he slept all day, it
would give me until tomorrow to—

"What makes you so concerned for his welfare all of a
sudden? You sent him down here!"

"Did he give you much trouble?" I contritely asked.

Catherine sighed. "No. He was too bushed and befud-
dled to be anything more than a pain in the neck. To *me*.
I've handled enough crackpots in my time. But I don't
have the time for this kind of nonsense right now, Joel!
I'm alone down here with your grandmother. I'm two
weeks behind on getting anything planted. Your grandmother's had another relapse. I don't have the energy to
coddle a crazy son-in-law!"

"Gram's sick again?"

"Oh, your grandmother's always sick these days.
There's so little difference between her being well and her
being sick again... I don't have time for your sister's fun
and games! The minute Bob wakes up, I'm packing him
back into his car and sending him back to you. He's your
problem, not mine. I don't appreciate being saddled with
him."

"I'm sorry, Mom. I know it wasn't right for us to involve you—"

"I'm not saying I don't want to be *involved!*" Her indignant protest was automatic. "Your sister's problems
are my problems, whether I like it or not. But I can't be
of much help to her when none of you are telling me
what's going on up there."

"Didn't Liza call you last night?"

"Yes. Big deal. She told me Bob *might* be headed my
way. Never hinted to me you told Bob that this was

where she was. He was so sure I was lying to him that he did everything but look under your grandmother's bed. The only way I could deal with him was to convince him that you were the one who was lying. Sorry, Joel, but I had no alternative," she said without remorse.

"I'm sorry, Mom, but I didn't have any choice either. And he already believed she was with you, no matter what I told him."

"Is your sister there? I want to talk to her."

"Uh, no. She's out at the moment."

"Convenient of her," Catherine muttered. "We would've all been spared this if that little stinker had come down off her high horse and come straight to me when she left Bob. He's talking custody, you know."

"I know."

"And not making a helluva lot of sense either. I frankly told him he doesn't have a snowball's chance in hell of getting custody of Joan, but he seems to think he has some trick up his sleeve."

"Did he say that?"

"No. He just talked around in circles about love and custody and I couldn't get a word in edgewise. Have Liza call me the minute she gets in."

"Sure. Uh, do you think that's safe? Won't Kearney hear the phone ring? Mom, is there any chance he can hear you now?" I asked worriedly.

"I just checked on him and he's out cold. Going to sleep for hours."

"Could you just let him sleep, Mom? Please?"

"I have no intention of waking him up. He's going to be madder than a wet hen when he finds out I've let him sleep half the day away, but I don't want to go near him. He seems to be in one all-fire hurry to find Liza though. As if every minute counted. You have any idea why?"

"Really? He told us he had all the time in the world."

"That's what he told me too. Maybe he's just impatient. But don't worry, I intend to let him sleep."

320

"I'm sorry we had to do this to you, Mom. I am, but could I ask you for one more—"

"I don't resent being put upon, Joel. I'm just mad over the way you and your sister have gone about it. And I just want to let you know I'm mad."

"And you have a right to be mad," I conceded. "But can I ask you one more small favor, Mom? The minute Kearney leaves, could you call me?"

"I'll call. You need time to hide Liza?"

"That and . . . other things. I'll have Liza call you when she comes in. I hope all this hasn't disturbed Gram too much."

"Oh, Mother's too out of it to be disturbed by anything. I envy her. Right now, I'd like to crawl into bed beside her and forget everything."

"I am sorry it had to happen right now," I insisted.

"But when it rains, it pours," groaned Catherine. "Good-bye, dear. And be careful. I seriously doubt Bob's crazy enough to do something like kidnap the baby, but you never know. Be sure to keep an eye open for that. Okay. And I'll give you ample warning when he leaves here."

"Thanks, Mom. Bye now." But when I hung up all I could think about was her remark that Kearney was acting as if every minute counted.

Perhaps Jake was right after all. Perhaps Kearney had only three days in which to settle with Liza. He had started his leave yesterday, which meant he would have to be back in Mainz tomorrow. And he was wasting today in sleep. Maybe, just maybe, Kearney would run out of time and go straight back to Germany, without time to do anything in New York but change planes. It seemed like only a faint possibility, but I grabbed at it. There was now a chance I wouldn't have to tell Corey after all. The situation was no longer totally hopeless.

I dialed Jake's number. Liza and Joan had just come in and I told Liza everything Catherine had told me.

"Ooo boy," moaned Liza. "Poor Mom. I'll never hear

321

the end of it once I get down there. Gram *very* sick?"

"I don't think so. It sounds like only more of the same. I wouldn't be too worried."

"That's good. I'm glad not to have that on my conscience too. *You* certainly sound like you're in a better mood than you were an hour ago."

"Do I? I wasn't aware I was in a bad mood earlier," I lied. "How're you doing?"

"What do you mean, how'm I doing? You only saw me an hour ago."

"I miss you," I said.

"Hmmph. I guess I better be phoning Mom. You remembered not to tell her where we were?"

"I remembered. I only told her you were out."

"Okay. Talk to you later, Shrimp. Bye."

I went out to the living room and put Vivaldi on the stereo. I enjoyed my new feelings of hope. Beneath those feelings, I could still acknowledge that Kearney's sleep might mean nothing more than a few extra hours of safety, but emotionally I felt as if I'd been saved. I stayed home all day, reading. It had been days since I'd opened a book, but I started *Salammbo* that afternoon. Ed woke up, asked where everyone was and seemed disappointed when I told him, despite his grumbling, "Now we can have some peace and quiet around here."

The afternoon passed, and then the evening, without a call from Catherine. Corey came home, but it was an eight-hour drive from Virginia to New York and there'd be plenty of time for me to tell him, if Catherine called. The black phone stayed silent and Kearney slept and hope began to seem less like hope and more like the ability to see into the future.

"You're certainly affectionate tonight," said Corey.

"We're alone!" I whispered. "If we wanted, we could run around nekkid!"

We didn't, but we did go to bed early.

And when we were finished and still splashed with each other, Corey suddenly cradled me hugely in his arms, one beneath my back, the other under my bottom, leaned down and gazed at me, as if he had something important to say. He didn't say a word.

It was as if he knew he had me back again.

I woke up happy and remembered Kearney only when I saw the clock. It was already noon. And Catherine hadn't called. Even if Kearney had left during the night, Catherine was up before six and she would've called us if Kearney were gone. Eight hours away, in that cock-eyed farmhouse, Kearney was still asleep. His three days were almost over and he would have to fly back to Germany within the next couple of hours. My hopes had been justified, my fears imaginary. I had slept through the crisis only to wake up and find it past.

Corey was just waking up, too, which meant it was Saturday and he didn't have to go to work. Neither of us had had full night's sleep over the past couple of days and we needed the extra hours. Only now did I realize that yesterday had been Friday, my day at the unemployment office. My chief worry this morning was that I would have to go down there on Monday and give them a more plausible story than the fact that I'd simply lost track of the days.

I wanted to go out for breakfast, which we hadn't done in two weeks. But I knew that we should stay by the phone, for form's sake. We dawdled around the apartment, took leisurely showers, ate a very late breakfast and, in general, tried to reaccustom ourselves to the shapelessness the hours had once had before Joan and Liza took them from us.

It was after three and Corey was in the bedroom, reading Michael Harrington. I was in the kitchen, reading more Flaubert and waiting for the coffee water to boil. When the buzzer for the door suddenly blasted through everything.

The peace that had seemed so real crashed, even before I knew who it was.

I pressed down on the button to speak and listen, but could only listen to the low-pitched buzz of air downstairs and a rasp of shoes scuffing against the foyer floor.

The intercom blared again.

I was finally able to croak, "Whozzit?"

"Bob Kear—"

My finger slipped off the button and cut him off.

"Oh damn," said Corey coming out to the kitchen. "He's back again? Great."

"Do I let him in?" I said. The only solution I could think of was that we not let him in. "We could pretend we're not home."

But Corey thought of Kearney's return as nothing more than an inconvenience. With Liza and Joan hidden away, he thought we had nothing to fear from Kearney. "No, we can't do that to him. He's going to be royally pissed off, but there's nothing we can do but face the music. I think we can handle him. There's two of us. Here. You're only going to make him madder," he said, pushed my hand away and pressed the button that unlocked the door.

It would take two minutes for Kearney to walk from the front door up to our floor. I had counted on eight hours in which to make my confession.

"Kearney's trying to blackmail me," I said quickly. "But if I tell you myself, he won't have anything to use."

Corey turned and faced me, looking merely curious.

I drew a deep breath. I'd hoped I'd break into tears when I told, but there wasn't enough time and I spoke too quickly to cry. "I love you, Corey, and I'll always love you, but I've slept with some other people." I was shocked by how quickly I said it. "Only a few. A couple, that's all, and it was only sex. I never even got their phone numbers, Corey! You could hardly call it sex in fact, because... But Kearney found out about it and he's trying to use it against me to find out where Liza is. I know I shouldn't have done it and I know I should've told you, but

324

I never had the opportunity. Or no, *of course* I had the opportunity, but I didn't know how to do it because I didn't know how you'd react and...I love you dammit! And all those other guys didn't mean a damn thing to me."

His mouth was open with his jaw drawn back so that he looked both ill and stupid.

"But Kearney's trying to blackmail me with it!" I insisted. "He said he'd fuck us over for fucking with him, unless I told him where Liza was. But I didn't tell him." I tried to sound proud of not telling him. "It was blackmail and I couldn't do that to Liza and there was the principle of the thing! Blackmail. Which is worse than anything I did, even though it meant you having to find out in the worst way about... And it was right I didn't give in to him! Isn't it? Isn't it, Corey? Say something, Corey. Don't just stand there. Please say something!"

His mouth began to close. "But when?"

"The nights I went to the opera. See, I got bored with opera, too, just like you, Corey. But not all the times I went to the opera, only since Christmas. I can't even remember how many times, it was that unimportant to me, and I never did it with the same person twice because that would've been unfair to you. I never even spent the night with them! You're the only person I ever wanted to spend the night with, Corey!"

There was a violent knocking at the door.

Corey didn't hear. "I still don't... Bob was going to tell me?... unless you showed where Liza was? Which is why you're telling me now?"

"I wanted to tell you. I've felt bad for not telling you, but I was scared and then I stopped doing it. I haven't done it in *weeks*. I don't know why I did it, but I've gotten it out of my system. That's all it was, something I had to get out of my system. Had nothing to do with you or us. Dumb, huh? Idiotic and selfish, right?"

Again the knocking at the door, and Corey not so much nodding as letting his head drift up and down.

"Because I *love* you, Boy. I do. More than anything else in the—"

But his empty face frightened me. I turned and raced down the hall toward the knocking door. I wanted to let Kearney in and give myself pain I knew how to handle.

II

I FLICKED BACK the lid on the peephole. His un-
shaven face was huge and swollen in the fisheye lens; the
distorted body beneath it tapered like a tail. The walls
curved around him.

I undid the bolt, turned the knob.

The door flew out of my hand, kicked open by Kearney.

"Fuckwad!" He grabbed my shirt at the neck and drove
me against the wall inside the door. "You're going to get
everything I promised!"

The back of my skull hit plaster.

"Jerked me off for the last time, faggot. No more
games." He kicked the door shut behind him and held me
against the wall. His anger was not at all wild, but hard
and steady. The face spikey with blond stubble was op-
pressively close to mine.

I punched at the face. I had no room to swing and felt
my fist only tap his jaw.

"Piece of . . . !'

He grabbed my arm before I could hit him again, spun
me around and gripped me in a headlock. He had my arm
twisted up behind my back.

"You want to play like that? We can play like that.
Fuckwad."

But I hadn't done it to stop him. I'd hit him knowing
what would happen. I wanted it to happen; it would be
like throwing myself into a fire.

"Want me to bust your ass, don't you? I'd love to mop your ass all over this pesthole." He wrenched my arm up towards my neck. "Where's Liza?"

"Don't know!" I shouted, my head and back bent backwards around the pain.

"You want me to shove this arm down your throat? Where is she?"

Then I heard footsteps coming down our long hallway, then, "Hello, Bob."

Kearney relaxed his grip and I saw Corey.

He stood a safe distance away from us. My first thought was that he wanted to stand there and watch Kearney beat me.

Kearney laughed and let go of me. "Your boyfriend's the one who wanted to play rough. I was only defending myself. You going to brain me with that thing?"

Only then did I see the empty bottle Corey held like a club. He was pale. His teeth were clenched. He breathed again, but still gripped the bottle. "You want something from us?"

"Damn straight. I want to know where my wife and kid are."

"Bob, they're not here."

I stood between them, shaking the pain out of my arm. We stood still, but were each fired with adrenaline.

"All right. I can see that." Kearney looked down the hall and put his hands on his hips while he tried to regain his breath. "I'm not here to hurt anyone." He looked nastily at me, then smiled. "I'm just looking for my family. Still looking. You're not going to invite me inside and let me sit down?"

"I would've two minutes ago," said Corey.

Kearney became worried. He hadn't intended to lose his temper, not if he were going to use his weapon. He covered his eyes with his hand and contritely said, "Look, Cobbett, I just lost control, that's all. I don't have a thing against you. And if I'm pissed at Shirtsy here, that's only because he lied to me. I wouldn't have laid a hand on him

328

if he hadn't taken a punch at me. But I'm exhausted. I've been going up and down the whole East coast like a damn yo-yo. You can at least let me sit down for a few minutes, can't you?" He thought his contriteness was convincing, but he was exhausted and incapable of hiding anything. His eyes were red, his voice slightly hoarse.

Corey looked at me, tapping the bottle against his thigh.

"Let him sit down," I said. "I don't care." But I wanted him to stay, long enough to do what I'd told Corey he had threatened to do. I wanted Kearney's crime to upstage mine.

Corey continued to look at me, not Kearney.

"I won't lay a hand on anybody." A sinister smile as transparent as glass. "Trust me."

Corey finally nodded. "Okay. We'll let you rest for a few minutes. Back here."

The sunlight in the airshaft shined through the smudged kitchen window. Kearney sat at the table and lowered his head, as if exhausted or guilty. But he slyly watched me from under his eyebrows.

I stood in the doorway. Corey went to the stove and turned off the water that had almost boiled down to nothing. "You want some coffee?" he muttered.

"Nope. Just want to sit. This chair's all I need for now."

We waited, saying nothing. I felt that Corey wanted to get rid of Kearney so he could deal with me. I tried to catch signals of what he was feeling, but Corey's face, usually as open as a book, was closed shut.

"Drove all this morning," said Kearney. "The night before that too. Feels like I've been bouncing around like a pinball ever since I got here."

"Yeah. Well," said Corey. "I'm sorry we can't help you."

"You really don't know where my family is?"

"Can't say that I do."

"And not even Shirtsy here knows? Frankly, I find it

hard to believe you don't know where your own sister is, Shirtsy." He folded his arms and leaned back. "Should I remind you of our little talk the other night? Come off it, Shirtsy. You can tell me."

I had nothing to lose now; I could at least be bold. "No."

His smile tensed cruelly. "You're not going to tell me? Not even with your boyfriend right here with us?"

"I won't be blackmailed, Kearney."

His smile broke and his eyes went blank for an instant. He drummed his fingers on the table, glancing from me to Corey. "Give you thirty seconds to think about it. Thirty seconds," he said, jabbing his finger at his wrist-watch.

"What're you talking about?" said Corey.

"Shirtsy knows. Don't you, Shirtsy? Don't you!"

I said nothing.

"Shit!" He shoved his watch hand into his pocket. "I'm not bluffing dammit. If you're counting on my sense of honor, Shirtsy, you've got another thing coming to you. Because I don't have any honor anymore."

I answered with a shrug.

Kearney looked queasy when he saw he was actually going to have to use it. He shot one last look at me, then turned to Corey. "Yes, sir. Yes, one hell of a family we've gotten ourselves messed up with, Cobbett. These Scherzenliebs. They'll stick it to you every time." He was building up to it, not for effect, but to gather the momentum to actually say it.

"You trying to say something, Bob?" Corey's eyes met mine. Accusingly?

"Have to admit that... yes, I am. I'm shocked that Shirtsy can just stand here and listen to this, but..." He stabbed me with his stare; his determination to hurt me made it easier for him. "I tell you this as a friend, Cobbett. Friends should confide in each other, no matter how shitty the dirt. But you'll never guess who Shirtsy and I ran into the other night. You remember a little nerd named Wyler Reese? From Camp Wolf?"

"Reese? Yeah, I remember him."

"Ran into him in this gay bar Shirtsy took us to. Shirtsy thought he was being real slick taking me there. Thought I couldn't handle it. But it backfired on you, didn't it, Shirtsy? Because I ran into an old friend of his. And did he give me an earful about what your little boy-friend's been up to, Cobbett."

Corey remained stone-faced, only there were ticks of confusion in Corey's eyes when he heard Reese's name.

"Aren't you curious about what he had to say? Well, I'll tell you. As a friend. Seems your little pal's become quite a fixture at this bar. Getting quite a bit of action there. In and out of beds like a rabbit. And he must be pretty hot stuff, because Reese had been in his pants and was dying to get into them again. Well, it shocked me. I'd always heard that gays lived lives of shameless promiscuity, but thought the two of you were an exception. You told me so yourself. A happy, faithful couple. But. Seems like your buddy is just another buddy-fucker, Cobbett. My heart bleeds for you. I know what it's like to be shafted. Liza's never been unfaithful to me, but... comes down to the same thing, doesn't it. We've both been shafted, friend."

Corey listened coldly, a look of discomfort stealing over his face. With Kearney? I didn't know how it affected him to hear my confession immediately echoed like this.

Kearney slowly stood up. "That's all I had to say. Only reason why I came by. See, I feel more rested already." He turned to me, hoping to find a ruin, and was surprised to find me so calm. Then he smiled again, assuring himself that my stoicism was only fake. "Yes. Shitty business. But we shafted husbands have got to stick together, Cobbett. Reese was telling me Shirtsy's made quite a name for himself in this bar. The rumor is that he's some kind of male whore. Now, I can't imagine anyone paying for sex with Shirtsy, but that's the rumor." Another contemptuous look at me and he added, without even pretending to be sincere, "Hope I haven't created any problems speaking out like this."

Corey stared at him over the bent bridge of his glasses.

"Guess I should be going now. Leave you lovebirds alone to hash out your differences."

Corey suddenly said, "You really disappoint me."

Kearney sneered exultantly at me, before he realized Corey was speaking to him.

"You've been getting a raw deal, Bob, and I *had* sympathized with you. Even now, I try telling myself you're upset, you're not responsible for your actions. But what you're trying to do to Joel and me"—he became more heated—"is bastardly behavior. It really is. It disgusts me. That is real shit, Bob."

"Don't blame the messenger for the bad news, Cobbett. Well, I didn't expect to be thanked."

"What you're trying to do to us . . . You're a real pig, Kearney."

Relief flooded me, hearing Corey take my side, but died just as quickly. What else could he say to Kearney? His attack on him had nothing to do with what he might feel towards me.

"Sorry you feel that way, Cobbett."

"What I feel is that you've put me in a difficult position. Because with all our disagreements, I always thought you were a decent, moral person. You're so choked up with hatred, you can't even . . . And I feel partially responsible. Because I've been helping to hide them from you. But now? God, there is no way I could help put you back in touch with her. You're capable of anything now. And I'm going to do my damndest to protect Liza from you."

The tone threw Kearney. His gloating slowly gave way to anger until, when Corey mentioned Liza, Kearney snapped. "Don't think I haven't known all along you knew where my wife was. And don't go pretending you were ever my friend, because you weren't. I was only too glad to make your life as much of a hell as mine is. You deserve it."

"The only thing that hurts me is your behavior, Bob."

"Oh yeah? You think so? Try telling yourself that the next time you hang your mouth on a piece of meat *you know's* been through the sewer."

Corey stiffened.

"Going to be poison, Cobbett. And I'm only too glad to be the one who poisoned it for you."

Corey looked at me while he searched for a way to strike back. "You didn't poison a damn thing. I tell you this only so you don't go away thinking you've accomplished something. But you haven't told me a damn thing I didn't know already."

Kearney bit his lip. "You're shitting me," he insisted. "You didn't know."

"Sorry, Bob. I knew. All of it."

He angrily turned on me. "So you ran straight home and told Daddy, huh? Bet you cried your little heart out. Can't believe your ass hasn't been kicked out into the street," he spat.

"I don't know how it was with you and Liza. But our partnership is based on more than just . . . sexual possession."

I drew a deep, hopeful breath when I heard Corey say that.

"Bullshit," Kearney whispered. "Bullshit," more to himself than to us.

He suddenly looked totally helpless standing there in the middle of the kitchen, eyes freezing when he recognized he was too helpless to even hurt us.

"Bullshit!" he cried, knocked a chair over and kicked it across the floor. "Candy-assed . . . !" He knocked the jars and shakers off the table. "Like punching shit! There's nothing to hit!" He wheeled around and swept the boxes and cans off the top of the refrigerator.

Corey backed up toward the window; I stepped back from the door. But nothing was being thrown at us. Kearney didn't even look to see where we were.

"Immoral! Heartless! No fucking way I can even hurt people like..." He grabbed the table and flipped it over on its side. Something glass popped. "Punching at turds! I only get covered with shit!" He crushed a box of sugar with his heel, then threw himself at the cabinet and the shelves stacked with plates. But his foot caught on something, a table leg, and it threw him off balance and tossed him toward the wall. He hit the wall with his shoulder, then caught himself with both hands before he slipped to the floor.

He stayed like that, leaned against the wall, one hand on the cabinet, his other hand and his face pressed against the yellow plaster. His shoulders began to shake. "Fuckers," he sobbed. "All of you. Fucking unnatural, heartless fuckers. Am I the last fucking human being?" He kicked at the underside of the tabletop beneath him, but there was no force in his kicks now. "You shits. Damn every last one of you."

A door down the hall popped open behind me. "What fell?" Ed moaned.

"Nothing, Ed. Sorry," I said automatically. "Go back to sleep."

His door slammed shut.

The voice from the hall caused Kearney to lift himself away from the wall and look around. His eyes burned. "Really dying to use that, aren't you, Cobbett?"

Corey had picked up the bottle again.

"Can't wait to bash my skull open, can you? Or do you want to fuck me with it? Yeah, that's what faggots want most, isn't it? To fuck a *man*. Bring me down to your level. Which is what this is all about, right? You might be telling yourself you're doing this for Liza. Bullshit. You're just out to fuck me. Because you can't stand the idea of a real man in this fucked-up family. I'm the last good man and you hate me for that. You want to see me take it up the ass, one way or another."

"Get out," said Corey. "Or I'm going to call the police."

"The police? You think I'm afraid of the police? The cops are on *my* side, asshole."

Corey was taken aback, but said, "Call them, Joel."

"I'll be gone before they get here," said Kearney. "Don't think I want to waste any more of my time wading in whaleshit. And don't think I'm running away either. Because the cops and Uncle Sugar are my ace in the hole. But I'm not going to use them until I have to."

He's gone crazy, I thought, seeing his old arrogance return.

"I'm finished with you, but I'm not finished with Liza," he crowed. "So don't think it's over. Out of my way, asswipe." He shoved me aside and swaggered down the hall.

Corey and I stared at each other while we waited to hear the door slam.

But behind me, the footsteps returned; I quickly turned around.

Corey hurried over to the doorway.

Kearney walked right up to me, hands on his hips again, eyes looking at the floor.

"Okay. You won this round. Only because you're too empty to feel a damn thing." He drew himself up and locked eyes with me. "But there's something else I came here to tell you. Yeah, something else, and I should've told you right off instead of getting swallowed up in your shit," he hissed. He raised his chin and looked down at me. "Your gramma, Shirtsy..." But he faltered, looked away and had to brace his shoulders before he could go on. "Your grandmother's dying. The doctor gives her forty-eight hours."

"No she's not. She might be sick but she isn't dying."

And Kearney looked as disgusted by his own lie as we

were, but he stuck to it. "I was down there. I saw her. I heard what the doctor said." He tried to hide his disgust by speaking coldly, as if from a great distance.

Corey shook his head. "You're that desperate now?"

Kearney ignored him. "You tell your sister I'm willing to take her down there. No questions asked. And once we get there, I'll leave for Germany. Alone. If that's what she wants."

"You really expect us to believe you?" said Corey. "After all this?"

He had to close his eyes to finish. "Tell Liza my offer. Tell her I can get her down there in plenty of time. I'll call you in an hour and you tell me what she says." He turned and walked quickly toward the door, as if running away from his own lie.

I thought a moment, then followed him down the hall. "If it's the truth," I taunted, "and such an ace in the hole, how come you didn't use it until now? Liar!"

He didn't turn to face me, but kept going until he was out the door.

I slammed the door behind him, locked it and watched him through the peephole. The tiny figure, silhouetted against the stairwell window like a black stick, hurried down the stairs. He was so burned up with his obsessions that he didn't even know how to lie anymore. But when I turned away from the door, I found not a home made safe again, but a place that felt foreign and unreal to me, as if there had been a fire that had burned away everything familiar.

I found Corey leaning against the refrigerator, hanging on to it with both hands, his forehead slanted against the white enamel.

I laid a hand on his shoulder, then embraced him from behind. He let me hold him for a few seconds, then suddenly said, "I better call Liza and let her know Bob's back," and slipped out of my arms.

I stood there, the stroke of his leaving still vibrating between my arms. The kitchen was in pieces. The spikes of the table legs stuck out into the room. There were cans all over the floor, a crumpled mustard jar that bled yellow and a dinner plate that was broken clean in two.

What had happened—it felt like it should be over. But it wasn't. It had just begun.

I uprighted the table while I waited for Corey to return. I picked up the dented cans and used a dish towel to pick up the worst of the glass, the mustard, the sugar and listened to hear Corey make his call. I heard nothing from the next room. Finally, there was nothing more I could do here. I made my way to the bedroom.

He sat in the chair at the desk, his back to the door. He sat hunched over so that his blue shirt was pulled taut across his shoulders. He ignored the phone beside him.

I started to touch his back, then didn't. "Did you get Liza?" I asked.

"Line's busy," he muttered, but didn't turn around to look at me.

I stepped around his chair until I stood in front of him, but he didn't look up at me. I lowered myself to the floor and sat at his feet. Timidly, I laid a hand on his knee and looked into his eyes, trying to ask with my eyes what he was feeling.

"Judge and you shall be judged," he said.

My throat went dry. I could only whisper, "Corey? Do you want to condemn me?"

The vague eyes suddenly solidified, focused on me. "No," he said in surprise. "How could I? It's *him* I can't condemn, because it's partly our fault and . . . I'd never judge you like that, Joel. Black and white like that." He rubbed his chin against his shoulder, remembering something. "I can't say I *like* us right now. Either of us."

"What you said in there? Did you really mean it?"

"Which?"

"About sexual possession?" Or had it only been for Kearney's benefit?

"No. I meant it. It is what I believe. It is," he insisted. "Something like that could never damage what I feel towards... And when you consider the source, when you consider his intentions, be *reprehensible* to let him do what he was trying to do. He can't hurt what I feel for you."

There was the beginning of a sense of relief, only I felt it hadn't been earned yet.

"We should feel free to play, if we want to. Yes. I believe that." He addressed the air above my head and only seemed to be arguing with himself, without forgiving me.

"That's all it was, Core. Playing. I always came home. I never saw anyone twice."

"And we *are* male," he declared. "I think there's something in male biology that needs this sort of thing. It's just the way men are, gay men especially."

I wanted that to mean safety too, but it was all from principle, everything he said; I didn't know what emotions Corey tried to shape or restrain with those principles.

"How many guys?"

"Five. Six? If you give me a minute, I can remember exactly and tell—"

He cut me off. "No. The numbers aren't important. One or a hundred, it doesn't matter how..." His face pinched shut around it. "Just so difficult for me to imagine any of it. You telling me, then Bob telling me—I haven't had time for it to sink in. But it happened? It really happened?"

"Yes. I'm sorry, Corey. But it did happen."

"But I felt like we were always together. Even when we were in different places. I feel now like we've hardly seen each other. The whole time we've been in New York."

"We *have* been together. I've always been where you thought I was. Except those five or six Friday nights."

"Did you enjoy it?" he asked sharply.

"No, I... not really."

"I wish you had. Because I could understand that."

"I enjoyed the chase, I guess. But the sex itself was

never anything special. There was never anything to say to them afterwards. Like there is with us."

He didn't seem to hear me. "You said Wyler Reese was one."

Someone he knew, someone whose image could make it real. "Yes."

"What's he doing in New York?"

"Works in a bank."

"Then he lives here. Then you see him around. Now and then?"

"No, Corey. Only that once. And him too. I went to bed with him only out of curiosity. To see if he'd changed, and he hadn't. You were right about him. He is gay, but just as much of a jerk as ever." I began to panic, thinking of Corey thinking of me and Reese. "Doesn't that prove something? If I can do it with someone I don't even *like*?"

"*Who* you did it with doesn't matter to me. Shouldn't. No. I just make an ass of myself by asking," he muttered to himself. "Feel like an ass already, for not knowing. I must sound like some possessive old queen."

It hurt to hear him hurting himself with words. "Don't say that. You *should* be asking—"

I stopped when I met his eyes. There was a contraction of pain in them, as if the very sound of my voice angered him. It frightened me to see him finally finding his anger. I had no right to speak to him.

I turned away and laid my cheek against his knee. I waited, hoping the gesture and my silence would cool his anger towards me.

He sat very still and said nothing, for a long time.

Outside the window, the fire escape hung on the other building like an iron frown. A tortoiseshell cat floated on tiptoes up the iron flight of stairs. She paused at the top, then sat on her haunches and busily, sweetly, licked herself clean.

You only want it to be over. You only want the anger to come and be done with, regardless of the consequences. And you grow so used to your fear that you doubt its sincerity, because you can still notice something as trivial as the cat outside.

And then, on the back of my neck, I felt Corey's hand fall. I waited for him to squeeze my neck and give my head an angry shake, but the relief of knowing he had finally found his anger was too strong for me to want to resist him.

But then, there was an amplified crackle of fingernails scratching my scalp.

I turned and looked up at him in surprise.

"What hurts," he said sternly, "is that you never told me."

Here it comes, I thought, but he was scratching my head as a way of reassuring me that he could still love me. I could submit to his anger knowing that there would be something on the other side of it.

But then he shook his head, tried to smile and said, "Here. I feel funny having you down there like..." He helped me to my feet and I stood there, which felt funny to me because it felt too casual.

"I feel bad about you not knowing. But I didn't know how to tell you. I wasn't keeping it a secret to hurt you."

"We can't hide things from each other. Not something like this. They can only come between us, alienate us. I mean, right now, the thing I still can't get out of my head is: Why didn't I know? Why didn't I even suspect it?"

"Because it had nothing to do with you. Or no, I mean, nothing to do with my love for you." I stood there like a boy being reprimanded by his father. "Corey? Do you think you'll forgive me?"

"Forgive you?" He looked startled. "That goes without saying. Of course I forgive you."

I was startled by how automatically he said it.

He saw the disbelief in my face and added, "I forgive you because I love you. I'm not sure how much I like you right now, but I do love you."

"Even now?"

340

He looked perturbed that a profession of love wasn't enough. "Yes, even now, because I know you meant no harm. You said it yourself. You were only playing. You're young, you're male. You never told me and that was wrong. I can get angry about that."

But he didn't sound angry. "Then why can't you show it?" I pleaded.

"I thought I was." He thought about it a moment. "What did you expect me to do? Jump out the window? Throw you out the window? You tricked a few times. So what? If you'd become involved with one of these people I might feel threatened. Maybe. But I can't feel threatened because you went out five or six times and did something we should've talked about letting each other do anyway."

It was what I had wanted him to say, and yet it didn't feel right. I had tensed myself so tight in preparation for his anger that there was almost a feeling of loss.

"You've confused me," he said. "And that hurts. But you've confused me before. We *began* with you confusing me, remember? But I swallowed my hurt back then and found I was very happy. This confusion isn't nearly as bad as that one."

He was right and yet it didn't please me the way it should've. It was as though he could not be angry with me because he thought I didn't have the moral intelligence or will that made me worthy of anger.

And the telephone rang.

We looked at each other, waiting for the one to whom this conversation meant the least to pick it up.

"Probably your sister," said Corey.

I reluctantly picked it up. The voice at the other end was breathless, precise and urgent.

"We just found out. Gram is dying. I have to get down there, Joel. I can't stay here. Joel? Are you there? *Joel. Gram is dying.*"

I was looking at Corey. "Kearney talked to you? How did he find out where—?"

"I can't give a damn about Bob now. I've got to get down there."

"Liza, he tried feeding us the same line of bull too."

"What're you talking about? I haven't talked to Bob. I've been talking to Mom."

"And Mom told you...!"

"Joel, listen. Gram is dying. They give her a day. Maybe two. I have to get home before it's too late."

I turned to tell Corey, but he already understood.

"I've let this go on for too long. There's too much I've left unsettled with her. I always thought that there was time. But there isn't time. I have to see her before she dies. So she'll know I care."

"She already knows, Liza. She doesn't hate you." Our grandmother was dying. Of course. It had only been a matter of time. But she had certainly chosen the wrong time. "Anyway, you can't go down there now. Kearney's bound to show up. He knows about Gram."

"I can't let Bob matter to me now. It's important that I see her. I have to." But she didn't sound hysterical. All emotion had been channeled into this dangerous decision.

"Liza, we don't know what he'll do! He talked like he's got something up his sleeve and... He's crazy, Liza. He's capable of anything." He hadn't been lying to us after all; he was even capable of using someone's death to get what he wanted. "Dammit, Liza. Kearney's going to use it as a trap!"

"Joel. She's your grandmother too. Don't you feel any of what I'm feeling right now?"

Her accusation angered me, when everything I said now was out of my impulse to protect Liza. "After all we've been through for you, Liza, for you to go down there now would be like throwing it away."

"I won't be able to live with myself if I didn't at least make the effort to say good-bye to her."

I looked to Corey for help or advice. I saw him listening with his lips parted and was plunged again into the tension Liza's call had interrupted. "Kearney was here," I told her.

"Screw him! I can't worry about that shit at a time like this."

"He made us an offer concerning you. I'm supposed to relay it to you."

"Like what?"

If Liza were determined to throw it away, I was willing to give her the means to do it. I described his offer, sneeringly, so that there'd be no doubt what I thought of it.

"Was going to have to take the bus," she said to herself, and hesitated.

You stupid woman, I thought. You'll end up right back where you started, with nothing to show for it but the mess you've made of our life. "Okay then. What do I tell him when he calls back?"

Silence, and then, "What d'you think? Tell him to go fuck himself. I'm not taking his help, not even now."

I was ashamed that I had doubted her. "Okay. But he's sure to show up if you go down there. Maybe he'll have a lawyer with him, maybe he'll try to take Joan away by force. *We don't know*. But you're playing right into his hands if you go down there."

Liza sighed. "I know. I realize all that. It's just that... No, I can't continue to hide up here when I know that someone I love is down there dying. I have to do what I have to do."

"What's Mom say?"

"Oh, Mom's too upset to be any help right now. She says I should be there, says both of us should be there, that the burden shouldn't be all hers. But then she chewed me out again for not coming down there right away and said I'd be an idiot if I came down now. And then a minute later, she tells me I should come down anyway, that if Bob showed up, she'd deal with him."

"What if I went down? I could go down for both of us."

343

"Thanks, but that's not the point, Joel. This is my—What? Just a minute, Joel." Her voice moved away from the phone and I heard her conferring with someone.

"She's being irrational," I told Corey. "She wants to go down there today, Kearney or no Kearney."

Corey sadly shook his head. "I'm sorry, Joel. About your grandmother."

"Yes, well. She's been sick. It was only a matter of time," I heard myself say.

"Joel?" A new voice entered my ear.

"Hello, Jake."

"Bad timing, eh? But death gives extensions only in movies, and Mrs. Bolt was never a good chess player."

I hadn't realized how much my grandmother's death should mean to me until I heard my father being so callously cheerful about it.

"But look. I think I've come up with a scheme whereby your sister can have her cake and eat it too. I gather from her end of the conversation that you're not too sympathetic to her whim either."

"No. I know what she's feeling. I just think it couldn't have come at a worse time."

"Well, the Three Graces were close. I can understand it myself, even if it does jeopardize her situation. You can't argue with the heart. But I think we can finesse our way around the Bob problem."

"How?"

"When Bob calls back, tell him Liza says yes to his offer."

"But Liza just told me—"

"She says yes, but she won't be able to leave until tomorrow morning. Tell him there's something she has to do or . . . make up something. You're as much a hand at the plausible lie as your old man is. Meanwhile, I'll borrow Braxton's Cad again and I'll drive Liza down there tonight. You're welcome to join us if you like. But that'll put us in Charles City in the wee hours of the morning, just about the time Bob's realized he's been duped. Liza can spend a few hours with her grandmother, and we'll be on our way back to New York by the time Bob arrives. So? You think my scheme might work?" he asked proudly.

"*Sounds* good, only I've lied too many times to Kearney. He won't believe me."

"Good point. Maybe if he heard it straight from the horse's mouth...Liza?" Another conference and Jake came back. "Okay. If you can't convince him...have a pencil? Have him dial 676-1007 at, oh, six o'clock sharp. It's the phone booth down on the corner and I'll make sure Liza's there. It's a number I keep handy, for sticky situations. Old habit of mine. Okay, you got that? We'll tell him that Liza'll meet him at your place, tomorrow at eight. Liza requests that you tell him he can talk to her only if all else fails. But I'll be getting back in touch with you before six, soon as I get clearance on Braxton's car. He's out at the moment. You want to ride down with us, lad?"

"Yes, I guess I should go down there, too. Yes, definitely. I want to go with you."

"Good. Be a nice little reunion for all of us. Okay, I'll call back before six, you can report on the Bob problem and I can give you an approximate time when we'll be swinging by to pick you up. Roger-dodger? Okay, lad, roger and out. Everything's going to work out fine."

I returned the phone to its cradle and tried to block the tune of Jake's professional chatter from my head, so I could focus my thoughts on my grandmother. That was what should be important to me right now: her death. But thinking about her only brought me back to Kearney. I suddenly realized why Catherine hadn't called to warn me of Kearney's departure; she'd been too busy with Gramma Bolt's dying.

I thought about calling Catherine, to show my concern, to ask for details, to see if the grief in her voice could help me feel what I knew I should be feeling. But I didn't know if she and Gram were still home or in a hospital, and if they were home, Catherine would be in no position to listen to my trivial sympathies.

"How you doing?"

I was standing at the desk with my fingers still touching the phone. Corey's voice was the one that now seemed faraway to me. "Jake has a plan," I said.

"You're going down there with them?"

"Yes. Tonight."

He must've felt the pressure of my solitude, because he remained in his chair, made no move to offer a consoling arm or embrace that would only have gotten in the way of what I was trying to feel right now. I was grateful to him, until I remembered what had been interrupted.

"I never knew your grandmother when she was...at her best. But from everything you've told me, she must've been a remarkable woman."

A well-meaning remark, but contrived only to fill the silence.

Death, even one so many miles away, should've made what was happening in this room as inconsequential as a children's quarrel. I couldn't think about both things at once but when I thought about one, I felt I did it only to avoid thinking about the other.

"You want to ride down with us?" I asked.

"You think I should?"

"Yes!" His reluctance frightened me. "Don't you want to be there with me?"

"I do. Actually. Only something like this is very private. For family."

"But Corey," I said nervously, "you're family."

He smiled. "I'm glad to hear you say that. It's just that I'm afraid of feeling out of place down there. At a time like this."

How could he treat it as something so trivial it called for decorum?"

"More important than that, Core...I don't want to run off and leave you behind. Right now, when so much is still up in the air."

346

"Meaning...?"

"Us!" I cried, shocked that he had to ask. "My betrayal of you, your anger with me. I can't go off and leave you alone with all that unfinished."

He remained uncertain. "But we've said everything that had to be said. I know I have."

Had we? Then why did it feel so incomplete?

"You were wrong and I forgive you. But none of that seems important now that this has happened."

Which was true. And yet.

The phone rang, Kearney this time, and I told him what I had to tell him. His righteous anger was back and he sounded so intent on using it against someone—Liza, Joan—that I told myself I should worry about him, not Corey, not myself. We had an enemy out there who made all my other fears seem only imaginary.

12

RAIN SLANTED BENEATH the street light, drummed on the hoods of parked cars and the lids of empty trash cans. The outer doors were propped open and an occasional breeze threw bits of rain across the tiny white hexagons of the front foyer floor.

They were an hour late.

The longer we waited, the more real the danger became. I was certain Kearney had to be somewhere out there, watching us, waiting. Corey and I stood with our backs pressed against the foyer wall so that we were visible only at a narrow angle from the one-way street outside. Kearney could drive past the building and it would give the game away if he saw the two of us on the porch with an overnight bag.

"Maybe one of us should go back upstairs and give them a call?" whispered Corey. The suspense of waiting caused even Corey to whisper.

"Let's give them five more minutes." I held his shoulder while I leaned out to look up and down the street again. All I saw was the black, wet pavement of the street and a single passerby, a man hurrying down the sidewalk with a newspaper over his head. The doorway across the street was empty except for a woman in slippers checking her mail.

"I think he'll be more subtle about it," said Corey. "If he tries anything."

"Maybe I should go out and check the building next door again. He might be waiting there."

The thought of Kearney waiting in ambush had begun as only a faint possibility, but the longer we waited, the more likely it seemed. He knew where we lived; he should know I'd probably go to Virginia with Liza. I was glad to have Corey with me now; he was larger than Kearney.

There was a trombone-moan of truck brakes from Amsterdam Avenue. Then I heard a car coming up our street, hissing like a wave. From our corner I saw a huge car stop out front, a door open and the interior light up. Liza and Jake inside: Jake smiling over something, Liza grim as a statue.

We ran through the rain. Corey jumped in while I paused to look back at the alley and the building next door. Nobody ran out from the shadows. There was only the ringing of rain on hollow trash cans.

I jumped into the back beside Corey and pulled the door shut.

"Oh, your friend's coming too?" said Jake in the rear-view mirror.

"Hello, Core. Hi there, Brother." Liza had turned around in the front seat. She spoke softly and tried to smile, with a mouth too hard for smiling. She touched my arm with three fingers, to give or take sympathy from me, then turned and did something for Joan, who was in the canvas box beside her.

"Well, more the merrier," said Jake.

"Corey's family," I insisted. "And it might come in handy having him with us. When Kearney shows up." We were moving now and I remembered to check out the store window on the corner, then the doorway of the bank on the other side of Broadway. All spun past too quickly for me to see anything but a blur of fluorescent light and the stick figures like slashes across bright windows and wet pavement.

349

"Not questioning his right to be here," said Jake. "Just surprised anyone would want to involve themselves in this sympathy mission when they could just as easily stand clear of it."

"Why're you so late? You had us worried."

Liza groaned and shook her head.

"Oh, had to drop by the theater and have a few words with the director, who's acting as my understudy. He's none too happy about my not being there tonight. But I told him, family comes first. Took a little longer than I expected, but not to worry. I'll get us down there in plenty of time. And we don't want to get there too early and wake them out of their slumbers."

"I don't think they're going to be sleeping," said Liza testily.

"Well, Kitten, even those in mourning need their sleep."

We barreled down Broadway, surrounded by cars and taxis streaked by the lights that raced overhead. I looked into the cab beside us and saw only a happily chatting party of four, the crushed head of a fox fur pressed against the window. Behind me I could see only masses of anonymous headlights that pursued us through the spray.

"No, Corey's more than welcome," said Jake. "But I don't think we're going to run into our old friend, Bob. No point in your looking around in case we're being tailed, lad. You've been watching too many movies. Uh, uh, Bob's fast asleep at some hotel right now, resting up for the big reconciliation. I'm sure of that."

I didn't like being mocked. "Yeah? You've been sure about other things too. Like Kearney having only three days leave. His three days were up this morning, Jake, and he's still here."

"Yes, well. I've been wondering about that myself," he blithely admitted. "Maybe he does have some sort of extended leave. Although I can't help wondering if maybe the good captain's gone AWOL."

Liza snorted. "No way. Like I said, you don't know

Bob. He loves the army more than he ever loved me. He wouldn't desert." But it didn't seem to matter to her one way or the other.

"Not desertion exactly. Just taking his leave without clearing it through the proper channels. Although it does have a nice, poetic ring, doesn't it? Desertion of a wife followed by desertion of the husband. One good desertion deserves another. All *just deserts*. Ho ho."

We stopped listening to him and I turned around to wipe off the rear window that was fogging up with all this talk. All I could see were disembodied headlights and the silhouettes of drivers, any one of which could be Kearney.

"But you talked to him?" asked Corey.

"Yeah, I talked to him," said Liza indifferently.

"And? What was it like for you? Talking to him again?"

"He can't mean flip to me now." She didn't turn around to face us. "Oh, it burned me when he talked like this was all Joel's doing, like he'd been keeping it a secret from me that Bob was even over here. Burned me even more when I had to pretend to him that something could be worked out. So he'd think I was going to meet him tomorrow."

"Do you think he believed you?"

"I don't know. Can't care, really. Told him I couldn't leave until tomorrow because I had to find a sitter. I came right out and said I was hiding Joan from him as insurance. So he wouldn't pull anything. And he *agreed*. I don't know if that should make me doubly suspicious or believe that he's being sincere."

"I think he might've been sincere," Corey suggested.

"Not that that changes anything," said Liza. "It doesn't."

Corey could still put in a good word for Kearney, and it annoyed me. He was asking Liza all the questions I should've been asking her, but couldn't because I was watching for the enemy that Corey so dutifully understood. His whole dutiful involvement irritated me, as if Corey were a stranger who had usurped a role that should've been mine. He wasn't a stranger, but all that seemed to tie him with us was his sense of duty.

"If Bob *is* AWOL," said Jake, "you kids might try ringing up the military police when you get back to town. They'll get him out of your hair. Unless, of course, it is an extended leave. But that's something you'll never find out without trying."

We followed the column of cars into the smoke-stained whiteness of the Lincoln Tunnel. It was bright enough for me to clearly see the dozen cars that descended behind us. Kearney's car wasn't with them. He knew where we were going; he wouldn't have to follow us. But when we burst into the rain again and flew up the ramp that swung beside the Hudson, I looked at the bleary constellation of lights across the river with a great sense of relief, as if we'd successfully escaped something. There was no longer the confusing weight of buildings and lights overhead. That was all in the distance now, beneath a low ceiling of clouds that turned the city's smudged aura back upon itself, like colored gas. A slight breeze could've dispersed it all: city, Kearney, confusion and everything that had happened to me there.

Everything ran in one direction now: south toward home. New Jersey thinned itself out into a long highway, streams of tailights that bleared with each slap of the windshield wipers, the bright billboards that floated by on high stilts out in the darkness. And here we were, the five of us sealed safely inside this car.

I leaned forward to look down at Joan. She slept soundly in the soft green glow of the speedometer. "Look at her," I whispered. "She has no idea of where we're going. The sleep of innocence."

"Uh uh," said Jake. "The sleep of Valium. We ground up a smidgin of one of mine and put it in her apple juice."

"Do you think that's safe?"

"She'll be fine," said Liza sharply. "I have too much on my mind to have to deal with Piglet all the way down."

"I guess. Yes, is a long drive." I looked at her sitting so stonily. I could be concerned about her now, curious about what she was feeling, fearing. I wanted to talk to her so I could unlock some of the emotions I knew I should be feeling right now. "You worried about not getting there in time?"

"No. Just . . . thinking." And she shifted her shoulders as if a change of posture could make her more alone.

I sank back into the back seat, telling myself that of course Liza would want to be alone with her thoughts, and that it was childish for me to feel excluded. I tried thinking about Gram, but all I could picture was her auburn wig.

A truck thundered beside us, then pulled past, a cloud of water spinning behind it.

Corey said, "Your grandmother's how old?"

I couldn't remember, but before I could even give my guess, Liza said:

"Sixty-eight."

"Really? Sixty-eight? That's not really that old."

"She married young," said Liza. "Was nineteen. The first marriage. Twenty when she had Mom." Liza turned so she could face us, her arm on the back of the seat. "Yes. Even younger than me when I got married. She always said it was a mistake marrying young."

"Married the baggage handler at a Greyhound bus station," I said, knowing I'd already told Corey that a hundred times but was determined to make myself part of this conversation.

Liza rested her chin on her arm. Her profile looked like a broken plate in the glare of the headlights behind us, and her lowered eyes showed no rapport with Corey. She was only talking to herself. "I think it hurt her feelings that I didn't learn by her example. But she didn't learn herself. Divorced Sullivan after three years, then five

353

years later married a man named Bolt. Who was with the government or something. Maybe she did learn, because that marriage lasted only a year."

"A fine old family tradition," said Jake.

She ignored him. "Our grandmother didn't have an easy life. But she had courage. She had to have courage, because she was ahead of her time. All this was back in the thirties and forties, and women just didn't do that sort of thing back then."

"Sure they did," said Jake. "Just not as frequently."

Liza narrowed her eyes at him. "You don't know what you're talking about!" she snapped. "This doesn't concern you anyway."

Jake adjusted his hold on the steering wheel. "Sorry," he said. "Didn't mean to touch such a . . . But I respect Mother Bolt. Always have. Just expressing a different perspective, that's all."

He too needed to be part of the conversation. We were involved in something that should've drawn us together, and yet we were each alone.

"Actually," said Corey, "there was divorce, but only for the rich. Women with money were the only ones who could even think of living without a husband. That's why the divorce rate was so low. Statistically."

Corey's pedantry irritated me as much as Jake's flippancy irritated Liza.

"Well, Gram wasn't rich," said Liza. "Far from it. And when she divorced those men, she had nothing to fall back on but herself. She had to work as a bookkeeper, and this was at a time when working women were looked down upon."

"They weren't exactly—" but Jake bit his tongue and didn't finish.

"A woman ahead of her time. I like to think of Gram as a pioneer. I do. And I want to think I've got a lot of Gram in me. I sometimes worry that I don't have the right to say that. But I hope it's true."

354

Liza was taking full possession of our grandmother, making her over into an icon that could mean something only for her. She left no room for me to feel anything. I wanted to remind her and myself that Gram was human.

"But she could be selfish," I said. "Not exactly selfish, but cool. Aloof. In a gentle way. She had the kindest way of being aloof."

"No! How can you say... okay, when she tuned you out, she literally tuned you out," Liza admitted. "Her hearing aid. But that wasn't selfishness. Or if it was self-ishness, it was a self-preservation kind of selfishness."

"Liza, I wasn't condemning her. It's just what I re-member about her."

"And who wouldn't be a little selfish after all she's been through? She had a very rough life. Worked her whole time, keeping track of other people's money, when what she really wanted to do was paint. She was a wonderful painter; I'm nowhere near her league. But when she re-tired and finally had time to paint? She got that arthritis and couldn't even hold a brush. She couldn't do anything but... read whodunits!"

"One right after another." I finally had a picture of her. "Like cigarettes," I said fondly.

The image saddened Liza. "Ugh. And when she read the ones she had, she'd go right back and read them all over again. Because she never remembered how they turned out."

"But she was content," I argued. "She was happy with what she had." I remembered resenting her contentment my first winter on the farm.

"No. She wasn't truly content. Not with how little she had to show for her life. She couldn't have been." Liza became very quiet.

I couldn't understand why she couldn't grant Gram this happiness, small as it was. Because the memory of my envy was making Gram real to me, making her into someone who had a life independent of anything we might think or need from her, someone whose death could mean something. She loved us, but carefully, from a distance, where we couldn't break into her contentment. I suddenly admired her enlightened solitude. I wanted to feel grief knowing we would lose it.

Then Corey's voice broke into my thoughts. "She had more to show for her life than many people do."

Grief was blocked by annoyance. With Corey for commenting on something that didn't concern him. The annoyance surprised me, because he hadn't really said anything. All he'd done was remind me he was here.

"We're born, we have children, we die," Jake said cheerfully. "What else is there?"

Liza sharply turned around and faced the highway again, sorry she'd talked about something that couldn't mean to us what it meant to her.

Jake's remarks meant nothing to me; they were only Jake. But Corey, sitting so dutifully beside me, had a presence that suffocated everything I was trying to feel. I breathed deeply, trying to pull myself free.

Corey thought I was breathing grief: he piously put his hand on my knee.

I let it lie there, not touching it with my own hand, not even turning to look at him. Until Corey slowly withdrew the hand.

Because I was admitting what I'd refused to admit since this afternoon: I was angry with Corey. For his failure to be angry with me.

We were involved in something that should've engaged me completely. But in the silence that followed the failed conversation, all I could think about was Corey's failure to be upset by what I had done. I thought about how much fear and worry I'd spent over something that meant so little to him.

He didn't take me seriously enough to be threatened by what I'd done.

He didn't love me enough to feel hurt by it.

I knew how absurd it was to be angry with him, especially now. Five hours ago all I had wanted from him was forgiveness. But his forgiveness felt so thin to me now, so meaningless.

He looked out his window, benevolently worrying about something. Why did he have to be here? Because I had asked him, because I had stupidly thought I'd feel better having him with me. His presence only got in the way and gave me strange ideas.

Jake drove sulkily. He seemed to think our silence was directed at him, as if his idle comments had shut everyone up. He nervously cleared his throat, then announced, "Here I am. Taking my family to be with their grandmother. I'm not such a bad parent after all."

"Dad," I said, leaning over the back of his seat. "Want me to drive for a while?"

"Uh, no. I'm fine," he said, surprised. "I wasn't complaining."

"I know. But when you want a change, give me the word. I'm getting buggy back here, just being a passenger."

We didn't change until Delaware. We were at a service station, in the harsh light beneath a roof that hovered like wings over the gas pumps. The rain had stopped. There was a haunting quiet: the drip of water from the trees, the purr of the pump, the whine and stutter of a truck on the interstate a half mile away. The cool air smelled muddy and green.

Jake did a few warm-up exercises beside the car, then walked over to me and said, "Think I'll take you up on your offer, lad. I must be getting old. I'm bushed. A little nap and I'll have my wits about me when we confront your mother."

"Here. Joan and I will join you," said Liza, hoisting the canvas box over the seat. "I can't sleep with all that road coming at me."

Corey returned from the soda machine and saw Liza taking his place. "Liza? That's okay, I don't mind sitting in the back."

"Joel's driving now. You ride shotgun and still get to sit with your buddy."

But Corey had already seen me get behind the wheel. "Never mind," he muttered, lowered his head and climbed into the front. "Uh, anyone want soda?"

It was good to be driving, to feel in control of something. I hadn't been at the wheel of anything for eight months. Even with its power steering, the car felt wonderfully huge as I took it back out to the interstate.

Behind me, there was a rattle of something like candy. Jake said, "Valium, anyone?"

"No thank you," said Corey.

"Sure," said Liza.

"Corey? You sure you won't partake? You seem a tad keyed up."

"No. I'm fine, thank you."

Jake and Liza quietly discussed their experiences with Valium until Jake began to snore softly. A minute later I looked in the mirror and saw Liza sleeping with her head on Jake's shoulder.

Even for Liza, the trip was too long to keep its urgency. We'd been on the road for almost four hours now and no longer seemed to be racing towards something. We seemed to float, suspended somewhere in the night between New York and Virginia. The Cadillac sat so high on the road that there was no sense of speed. The interstate took away the illusion that I was in command of anything. There was nothing for me to do but keep the car on the road; the highway did the rest. I found myself sinking back into anger, only anger had burned itself out and now was an irritable exhaustion, a nervous unhappiness.

"Watch it. Speed limits are now fifty-five, remember."

"I know what I'm doing," I snapped at Corey.

He sniffed, then his hand appeared at the dashboard, turned the radio on and promptly turned it off again.

"Worried about your grandmother?" he said.

"Of course."

"And that's all?" he whispered.

"Isn't that enough?" I whispered back.

He glanced into the back seat, then scooted down until his knees were pressed against the dash and the back of his seat shielded him like a wall. "There's not anything else eating you?"

"Something," I admitted. "But I'm not ready to talk about it."

A little air hissed through his nose. He turned the radio back on. It sputtered and whined while he changed stations, until it landed on the sound of a man crying into a telephone.

"You sit there in judgment, telling people who're unemployed that it's all their own fault when if your Daddy didn't own the station, *you* wouldn't have a job! Goodbye!"

"Okay. Why're you pissed at me?" whispered Corey beneath the voices. "What have I done?"

"Nothing." I intended it as a denial, then used it as an accusation. "Absolutely nothing. That's why I'm pissed at you."

"Something I didn't say? Something I didn't do?"

"If you don't know already, what's the point in my telling you?"

"Come on, Joel. Stop being evasive about it. You don't want me here and it's driving me crazy dammit." He folded his arms around his chest as if he were freezing. "You wish I weren't here, don't you?"

"You at least picked up on that," I muttered.

"Okay. You want to let me out? Drop me off and I'll hitch back."

"Don't make yourself into a martyr."

"I'm not playing martyr! I really want to get out of this

car and hitch. Because anything is preferable to your cold shoulder and whatever it is that's eating you. You wanted me along, remember. I didn't ask to come."

"I was stupid."

"Okay. If you won't let me out, you can at least tell me what it is that's eating you."

But I didn't want to go into it with so many people behind me, even if they were drugged and asleep. "Corey. I'm sorry I'm being so difficult. But you'll just have to bear with me. It'll pass."

"What will?"

"My disappointment with you."

"But what did I do?" he pleaded.

"I know I have no right to be disappointed, that it's all me. But this isn't the time or place to go into it."

There was a spot of music on the radio and Corey waited for it to pass and the cover of other voices to return.

"It's what was said this afternoon, wasn't it?"

I let him know by my silence that he wasn't so blind after all.

He softly growled to himself, then said, "I don't think I was being unfair by being angry with you."

"Oh no. You were the epitome of fairness. You were nothing but fairness."

"I was trying not to be angry," he said, thinking that my sarcasm meant that he was.

"Come off it. You didn't feel the slightest bit of anger. It didn't faze you in the least."

"Good God, is that what's eating you?" But before he could let his surprise turn into anger, he suppressed it. "Oh Shirts," he moaned.

The nickname I had once liked because it was Corey's was now painfully similar to Shirtsy, the name used by those who didn't take me seriously.

"You think it didn't faze me? You hurt and confused me. What else can I say? Come on, I thought we'd been through this already."

"See? You've already tied it all up and tossed it aside. It means that little to you."

"I haven't tossed it aside. It's just that I can't bring myself to dwell on it, especially not now."

"If it meant something to you, you'd be thinking about it, too. Even now."

"Okay," he admitted. "Your being annoyed with me has been making me think about it."

"And?"

"And I still can't hate you for doing what you did. I can be angry with you for being angry with me right now. But the other thing is . . . small potatoes. You were curious and you had time on your hands. You did what you did a few times. So what?"

"I didn't bother telling you until I absolutely had to."

"No. You didn't. And that still hurts. But even *that* I can understand. You wanted to protect me, you were afraid I wouldn't understand. But I can understand, and even though I can be hurt that you kept it from me, I can also be grateful that this wasn't something you did to rub in my face. I know you meant no harm."

He only made it worse, denying me even the moral will that was necessary to harm him.

"If you had done it to me," I said, "I'd want to kill you right now."

"Yes?" The idea surprised him and he thought about it for moment. "Yes. In fact, I'd expect you to feel like that."

"Because I love you. Because I'd feel threatened by it. Because you're the most important thing in my life, Corey."

"No, I don't feel threatened," Corey whispered, suddenly sounding very defensive and timid. "But that doesn't mean I don't love you."

There. He said it himself, and so guiltily I felt justified in thinking it.

"And if I can't get worked up about it, it's not because I'm indifferent. You know how my mind works. I get rational to protect myself from getting upset. It's my way of keeping a grip on myself."

That wasn't true. I had seen him lose his temper over this or that social iniquity with a passion he hadn't come close to showing with me.

"I know it can seem cold at times. But I'm not cold. I do care. I am hurt."

"But no so hurt that you've had to give up this rationality you're so proud of."

"I'm sorry if it seems like a poverty of emotions for me to be so rational right now, but I would've thought you knew and trusted me enough to understand. . . . " His whisper disappeared into the tumble of doubt it had come from. Then, "Why is it that *my* love's on trial right now?"

The answer was so obvious I said nothing.

"You were the one who was in the wrong. I've been faithful to you. Why am I talking like I'm the one who's . . . " But he was more amused than angered, until a new idea came to him. "Is that why you were doing what you did? As a way of testing me?"

He was imputing his own rationality to me and I rejected it. "No. There was nothing devious about it. I did it out of selfishness and stupidity."

"And that's how I've treated it. As a product of selfishness and stupidity. What makes you want to turn my understanding of you against me?"

"Because what I did was so wrong it would've enraged you if you cared about me."

"I do care and . . . It's ridiculous for me to apologize to you for not being enraged. What do you want from me? What? Would it really make you feel better if I went berserk about it, like your friend Bob back there?"

I didn't envy my sister, but Corey was right: Liza was definitely loved.

"That's not my style. I'll lecture you and tell you you're wrong. But I can't stay angry with you or want to punish you. Why are you punishing me?"

"Shrimp's done something wrong?"

The new voice only whispered, but was so close to my ear and unexpected it was like a shout.

Liza had thrust her face over the top of the seat.

Corey looked up at her, but remained slouched down.

"No. Nothing. Just a little domestic problem, that's all."

"Sorry I'm being nosy, but Joel's been seeing somebody on the side?" She was only half-awake and uncertain that she'd heard correctly.

"No. No, not really," Corey hurriedly chattered. "Couple of fibs, that's all, nothing worse than that. Long night, Liza, you should get some sleep."

I concentrated on driving and waited for Liza to sink back into her corner. But there was a strong temptation to bring in someone else, if only to reassure myself that what I was feeling was not as ridiculous as Corey made it. "Not fibs," I said. "Lies. About all the people I've been seeing on the side."

"*Really?*" she asked me. "Really?" she said to Corey. "Oh Joel," she groaned.

"A few one-night stands," said Corey. "Nothing serious."

"But I'd been hiding it from Corey. Until this afternoon."

"Jesus, Joel, you've been . . . oh, Corey, I'm sorry I . . . I never dreamed anything like this was going on. I thought the two of you were the one solid couple I knew. Why, Joel? I thought you loved Corey. No, not thought, knew. The whole time I lived with you."

"He was curious. And horny. This sort of thing happens all the time among homosexuals. Doesn't mean they don't love each other."

"Ever since Christmas, Liza. I've been deliberately going to bars and going home with total strangers. Without telling Corey. He never suspected a thing, until I confronted him with it this afternoon."

"You creep, Joel! How could you do a such a thing?"

I smiled to myself; she knew the right response for my behavior.

"I don't know what kind of devotedness gay men expect from each other, but for you to do something like that to someone like Corey! Don't you love him anymore?"

"Oh, he still loves me," said Corey. "Not even Joel has doubted that." Corey accepted Liza's intervention thinking he could use her to prove his point.

"Oh Corey," she said worriedly. "You know what a ditz my brother can be. He didn't mean any harm by it, I'm sure. You poor guy. How did you find out?"

"Joel told me himself."

"Really? That's good, isn't it? Doesn't it mean that there's hope, because he could confess it to you himself? When did he tell you?"

"This afternoon."

"Lord. Then it's still very raw for you, isn't it? But . . . *this afternoon?* This afternoon, Joel?" Her tender concern instantly broke. "Why the hell this afternoon? Don't we have enough to worry about without you?"

"I had to."

"Had to? Why? Don't get me wrong, Corey. I'm not saying he shouldn't have told you. But couldn't it have waited? If it's been going on since Christmas, why in blazes did you have to pick *today* to be virtuous?"

I wouldn't tell her; I had to keep Kearney out of it and leave myself in the worst light possible.

"But you couldn't wait, could you? With everyone else up to their necks in grief, you had to grab a little attention for yourself."

That angered me, but all I said was, "Lower your voice. There's people sleeping."

She snorted at me, but softened her voice to say, "You're making it awfully hard for me to take your side, Joel."

"I'm not asking you to take my side."

"He's right, though," said Corey. "He had no choice in the matter. Your husband found out."

"Bob? What can Bob have to do with my brother's...?"

"He wanted to blackmail him with it. So rather than tell Bob where you and Joan were, Joel had to tell me what he'd been doing. Which is why he did it this afternoon."

"See? I did it only because I had to. I might've *never* told Corey if it hadn't been for that."

But it was too late. There was no way that Liza could show Corey the indignation and disgust my behavior deserved once she heard how she was involved.

"Oh Joel," she sighed. "What a jerky brother you are. You shouldn't have put yourself in that position in the first place, but...thanks for not telling him. I'm sorry. Lord but that Bob can be a bastard!"

"He was only doing what anybody in his position would do," I said in a halfhearted attempt to keep Kearney's badness from upstaging mine.

"That stinking son of a bitch. I don't know what to say, Joel, except..." She put her hand on my shoulder and gave me a loving, chiding squeeze. "See, Corey? He's not such a bad guy after all. Not always the brightest, but in the long run, he's someone worth keeping. Don't you think? I know it's going to be difficult for you, but you know he still loves you. You can forgive him, can't you?"

"I can and I do. I forgave him this afternoon."

"You hear that, Shrimp? He does forgive you." But Liza sensed something was wrong here as she said it; she knew her few words hadn't brought about this reconciliation. "What's the matter, Joel? You don't believe him? Are you being sincere, Corey? You really do forgive him?"

"I do and Joel believes me. That's not the problem."

"Then...? I don't get it. What were you two arguing about?"

"Joel thinks that my forgiving him is proof that I don't love him."

"What?"

"That's not it at all," I said angrily. "If he had had any trouble forgiving me, it would've had some weight to it. It would've meant something to me. But it was so quick and automatic, it was like I didn't mean a thing to him. Like he didn't take me seriously enough to be upset by what I'd done. He forgave me without batting an eye."

"I batted an eye," said Corey.

"Yes, you brooded for a few minutes. Big deal. It didn't hurt you enough for you get angry with me."

"Are you two pulling my leg?"

"No! I'm dead serious. He couldn't even take it seriously enough to lose his temper with me."

And my own sister, damn her, began to laugh.

"It's not funny."

"I'm sorry, but it is, Joel. You must be out of your tree. Oh Joel. You do something wrong and it upsets you when you're forgiven? You goofball! Don't you know how lucky you are?"

"You'd feel the same way if you were in my shoes."

"Lord, Joel. I'd give anything to be in your shoes. To live with someone who could keep a cool head and forgive me when I stepped out of line? I've never done anything even close to your running around behind Corey's back. But if you'd been through what I'd been through—tempers exploding over nothing, apologies so passionate they were oppressive—you'd realize you were living with a saint."

I should've known that, fleeing from Kearney, Liza was the last person on earth to understand what I wanted.

"You must be a bit bonkers yourself," she told Corey, "to be able to forgive him like that. But, knowing my brother, you must've had lots of practice forgiving him. Don't sulk, Shrimp. I'm only teasing. I'm sure there've been occasions when you've had to forgive Corey."

"What I think has happened," said Corey, "is that Joel here was so prepared for me to be angry with him, counting on anger of one kind or another, that when it

366

didn't happen, he's had to fill up the empty space with anger of his own."

"Or maybe it's because my life's such a mess, Joel feels left out and wants his life to be as much an emotional stink as mine is."

"Bullshit!" I snapped. "Both of you. Don't tell me what I'm feeling, because I know what I'm feeling is justified. I've fucked and been fucked by total strangers, and if it doesn't mean shit to you, it certainly does to me."

There was a moment of silence, and then Liza said, "How wrong is it for gay men, what Shrimp's been doing?"

"Not as wrong as he seems to think it is. There are open relationships and there are closed relationships. I'd always thought ours was a closed one. But I can live with it being open. It upset me only to learn that it'd been open all this time without my knowing it."

"Open, hell. I was in the wrong. It's a closed relationship or it's nothing."

"You're the one who opened it," said Corey. "You're free to close it again."

"Open and closed. Opened and shut," mumbled a groggy voice from Jake's corner. "What're you kids talking about up there?"

Liza groaned. "Nothing, Daddy. Go back to sleep."

"Was asleep. Was woken up by sibilants. The siblings' sibilants. Like snakes." He seemed to be talking in his sleep and I thought we were safe until he said, "Am I misconstruing, or has my son been sleeping around?"

"You were dreaming," said Liza. "Go back to sleep."

"Yes'm. Outside my domain anyway. Never could understand homosexuality. One of the things I like about men is that you don't have to sleep with them."

"Shush, Daddy. Sleep!" But he was only comical to her now; Liza covered her mouth and giggled through her nose.

"Okay, I'm sleeping, I'm sleeping. Don't mind me. Only the father."

367

Nobody said a word while we waited for his snoring to resume. And in the silence that followed the comedy, it was difficult for anyone to remember what they'd been saying. The road droned on; flights of green traffic signs flashed overhead.

"I think I'll bug out, too," said Liza in the tiniest whisper. "Nothing I can tell you that you don't already know, Joel. I can't tell you what to feel, but I really do think you're being silly. You'll think so, too. Just give it time. Drive safe." She lightly kissed me behind the ear. "Patience, Corey. But you don't need me to tell you that. See you." And I heard the squeaky pip of the kiss she gave him.

And suddenly we were alone again, as if all that talk had been a dream.

"Been repeated many times before," said the toneless man on the radio, "but it bears repeating: When the going gets tough, the tough get going."

Miles of highway were pulled beneath the car without getting us anywhere, as if the car were pulling at an elastic ribbon that stretched as you pulled it and the highway in the distance unwound itself only in sleepy fits and starts.

For ten miles, twenty miles, the dream of being laughed at hung in my head as if it'd just happened and I could still answer it. They had treated me like a child. But after Liza's laughter and Jake's interruption, I couldn't quite reconstruct my anger with Corey.

"What're you thinking now?" he whispered.

"Nothing."

But Corey didn't sound as confident and rational as he had when Liza was with him.

Jake began his tenor snore in the back; Liza's breath became regular and whistling.

"If it makes you feel any better, I can tell you I'm angry with you right now."

"No. You're angry with me only for being angry with you. That's not good enough."

"Take it how you like. That's how I feel." And he

368

turned away from me, turned his face toward the door and window.

I tried to be angry with him for being angry with me and keep the vicious circle going. But it didn't work. Anger remained, but I couldn't direct it at Corey.

Liza's remarks had destroyed my right to be angry with Corey, but they had only removed the outlet for my anger, not its source. As if anger itself had been an outlet for something else.

A free floating unhappiness with nothing to explain it.

I tried to be angry with myself for what I had done to Corey, tried to do for myself what I had expected him to do for me, but that wasn't it, either, because even that had been washed away by their cavalier treatment of it and my crimes were exactly what they said they were: discourtesies, errors of judgment, sexual nothings. The cause was gone, but not the effect. Anger remained. Without a target or an explanation, it seemed less like a momentary emotion and more like a sudden understanding of something.

I hated myself.

Not for anything I'd done, but for who I was.

Petty, selfish, childish, stupid... But none of the names seemed to help me contain the hatred I was feeling for myself. Hatred spread into every part of my life, until there seemed to be nothing worth saving.

Corey's silence pressed against me like hatred. I could resist it only by hating him back, but even that turned against me, because I hated myself for hating Corey. If only there was just cause to be angry with him about something, then the circle would be broken. But Liza was right: Corey was too good for me, and I hated myself for hating him even as I hated him for making me hate myself.

I kept altering the sequence of my emotions, reversing the cause and effect, without ever changing the results, as if what I was feeling were only an evasive dance around a single, hard fact.

I did not love Corey.

Which explained why I had done what I'd done, how I had done it so easily. Acknowledging them as sexual nothings only made it worse, because those nothings had thrown everything into question. As if there had been so little there to begin with that the slightest breath could disperse it. Who hated whom for whose anger or failure to show anger, who forgave, who forgot, who recognized the absence of love in the other before he recognized it in himself—none of it mattered once I understood that Corey and I did not love each other.

I glanced over at him, to see what I might feel for him.

He was slouched against the door, hands pressed between his thighs, chin tucked into his shoulder.

I glanced again, just as another set of signs and lights swept over his head.

In the brief flare of light, I saw his slack mouth and closed eyes: He was sleeping!

I angrily turned away. Even now he could sleep; he didn't love me, either. He might claim he loved me, but love was only a routine for him, like putting on a tie when he went to work, a routine you put aside when you want to sleep.

But it wasn't an image of him sleeping that I saw when I stared out at the highway again. I remembered him in Switzerland, when I had looked and looked at Corey, wondering who he was that I could love him. My bewilderment had been an exciting wonderful mystery then.

I had been an idiot back then. I now saw the beautiful mystery as a cold fact: I did not know the person I loved.

I didn't know because it didn't matter. Because I didn't love him. I hadn't then and I didn't now, and what I thought had been love was nothing but a trite convention between two people who had lived too long together.

I seemed to have been in love with him once. When? All I could remember was my joy the night I had recognized love and poured coffee on my head. For four years I'd only been living off the emotional capital of that moment. And even that, the more I thought about it, did not really feel like love. Perhaps it was only my homosexuality I had recognized that night. I'd mistaken a love for men as a love for Corey Cobbett, and had lived inside that mistake for the past four years, as if asleep. I had only been dreaming I was awake. I was finally waking up and I blamed Corey for all the things that had been done to me in my sleep.

A city and a harbor appeared in his window: lights on black water and a white burning inside an iron shed. Wilmington? No, it was already Baltimore, because we descended into another tunnel. It was bright enough down there for me to look in the mirror and see that I was alone. Everyone else was sleeping. Only I was awake and they were in my hands. I could deliberately ease the car into the other lane and kill us all. But it was only Corey and myself I wanted to kill. My obligation to protect the others was the only thing left that I could like about myself.

The tunnel's stale white light fluttered on a face that was as shapeless as a ball of clay. His shoulder pressed his glasses into his face. He did not seem worth pain, worth hatred. We had nothing in common, that was all; we'd never had anything in common, not even the shared interests two friends might have. With the people behind me it was different. I shared no interests with them either, only accidents of birth and family, accidents that made any pain they caused me more bearable, because the accidents weren't my fault. But Corey was my own mistake. I had chosen him on my own. There was no accidental circumstance to bind us together. There was not even a legal tangle of marriage to hold me to my mistake. No divorce was necessary for us, only a simple good-bye. You wake up the next morning, take a good look at the person you went home with and you simply say good-bye.

It was after four when I took us across the Potomac. The sky over the river was surprisingly light. The low,

371

flat water was grey and wide open, the woods on the shore as black as ink. Washington was only a thickening of the horizon at the far end of the river, a dark blur sprinkled with lights. The bridge carried us over to the other side, where it was night again. It was Virginia.

There was no sensation of coming home. Only in New York had I been treated as a Southerner, and I'd never thought of myself as a Virginian. And yet, I had passed through here, again and again. To the south was Charles City, Williamsburg, Camp Wolf. Somewhere off to my right, west of Alexandria and the clusters of bedroom communities that ringed D.C., was the brick house where we had lived before the divorce. That house existed in another country now. The boy who lived there had nothing to do with me. He had promise and he knew it. He loved the world so much he couldn't wait to go into it. Being a child bored him.

And I had shown promise. Everyone said so. Mrs. Robertson in fourth grade had told my mother, "Joel has many abilities; he'll be able to do with his life whatever he wants." But what had I done with my life? Absolutely nothing. I had no education, no job, no love.

What had gone wrong? I'd loved the world so much. That's what it was like: an unrequited love for the world. Ambition, power, importance—I had dismissed those things as childish, but how else does one make contact with the world? My father had closed that door to me. And I had given up my gorgeous love of the world for the petty love of a single person.

But no, I couldn't blame Jake now. I was too old for that. If I'd tried to succeed, I still might've done it, if not by way of Harvard and Wall Street, then up the backstairs; motels or restaurants or whoever would have me. No matter what disadvantages I had started with, no matter how depressed the economy was, I still should've tried. But my nerve had failed me and I had settled for romantic love. Which had obviously not been enough, even when I'd believed in it, because I had had to supplement that love with music, novels and sex with other people. I had nobody to blame but myself. I could not even blame the proof of my stupidity who slept by the door. He was not the lover I needed anyway. I needed someone who would know what was best for me, who would keep me to my task. In that indifference which Corey disguised as tolerance, I had decompressed and lost all shape. I had become a lazy monster of appetite and self.

The sky grew more light. A landscape without color rose up on either side of the interstate. It was the hour of the night clerk, when every thought is so burnt and bitter you feel you're finally seeing your life as it is, without illusions. I thought of my grandmother. And, like before, I envied her and wished only that I too could grow old and get it over with. Twenty-three felt very old to me and it seemed only a matter of counting the days before I too could sit achingly in a chair, read without purpose and wait for it to be over.

But it was selfish to use my grandmother's death like that. I guiltily turned my thoughts back to her, wanting to grieve for her and not myself. And my failure to grieve only brought me to the hardest fact of all: Corey couldn't love me because I was not worth loving. I did not deserve to be loved by anyone.

I cracked open the vent to let in some air. I heard it pop, then whistle. The noise woke up Joan.

She woke up crying, but I couldn't do a thing for her. I looked for a place to turn off while I waited for one of the others to come out of their stupors and take care of her.

Finally, I heard Jake moan, "Uh, son? Baby's crying?"

"Hungry," Liza murmured. "Your turn to feed her, Bob."

"No Bob, here, Kitten. Only your old man."

"Huh? Oh? Where...? Oh." Liza woke with a start, caught her breath and sank back. "I dreamed I was in a glass box with Bob and... Whew. Come on, Piglet. We're safe. Don't fret."

The crying stopped when Liza lifted her.

A city skyline slid in front of us, a few tall shapes against a pink sky.

"Hm," said Jake. "Looks like Richmond. Must be almost there."

We drove past Richmond with sighs and groans while Jake and Liza stretched. Just below Richmond, we came down off the interstate to Route 1. The hum of the highway changed its pitch to something lower and less modern. The older road ran beneath the trees and followed the rise and curves of the knolls and ravines. The constant turning slowly shook Corey awake. I stole glances at him, watching his sagging face go from befuddlement to awareness to pain, as he remembered where and who we were. I watched only to see if he knew now what I knew.

But all he said was, "Where we going first? Straight to the hospital or to the house first?"

"Don't even know if she's in the hospital," said Jake. "She was still at home when we talked to your mother last."

"I hope we're not too late," whispered Liza. "Something tells me we are."

"No, Kitten, I don't think we have a thing to worry about. We've made good time. And death is one of those things you can never predict for certain. Might prove to have been a false alarm. In fact, if Mother Bolt were still at home yesterday, I think there's a very good chance it was a false alarm. No, wouldn't surprise me in the least if when we come rushing in, we find her sitting up in bed, engrossed in one of her whodunits."

The highway swung gently left and right and we flew beneath the trees with more speed and urgency. I became more nervous, more excited, more guilty. Jake's scenario was too convenient. I refused to believe I could be so guilty over a false alarm.

"Everything's green," Corey mumbled at his window. "Already spring down here."

Just the sound of his voice and his ability to notice something caused me to cringe.

But he was right. The trees that had still been bare in New York were in fresh, full foliage down here, as if the night had lasted for weeks and spring had come overnight. The highway swooped through clouds and curtains of chalky green leaves. The sun came out. Gold light raced and wheeled through a riot of soft greens spinning past us.

13

LESS THAN HALF of the field was plowed. The last swath of turned earth, black from last night's rain, crossed the field that was framed by the window, and abruptly stopped. There was an absence of something and I realized I was missing the croak of crows. The woods beyond the field were blurred with green, but no seeds had been planted and the crows had gone elsewhere.

I looked again at the badly made bed beneath the window. The living room was dominated by the bed. Without saying a word, without any kind of greeting, Catherine had led us here and sternly nodded at the room, as if we were children who'd done something to it that left her too angry for words. Her arms were folded, her sleeves rolled, her neck tightened against an outrage she refused to swallow. She alerted me to everything in front of us: the empty bed, the field outside, Gram's painting of her on the wall, even Gram's wig seated foolishly on a Styrofoam head on the bookcase. This was Gram's room now, to save her from the stairs. Under the bed was the aluminum bowl I had used a hundred times for cooking, but in the wrong room now, like the bed, with a twisted washrag tossed into the batter that filled the bowl.

Everything registered, mechanically, precisely. Even Max sitting in the armchair, muzzle now speckled with grey, but still looking like dachshunds always look, as if everything were fine. Only he was curled up on my grandmother's silk nightgown. And I finally acknowledged that I already knew what everything meant. The empty bed wasn't empty.

"Ohhhh?"

But it was Liza who moaned. She took hold of Catherine and buried her face in her mother's shoulder.

The empty wig, the bowl of vomit, the body beneath the sheet—the facts of death rushed into me, knocking away everything but the feeling that this was what had frightened me most, that I had thought about myself only to keep from facing this.

There was a sour stink in the room. The shiny bowl with its familiar dent sat in the shadow of the bed.

Her head held high, Catherine had folded her arms around Liza. Her hard face was not as hard as it seemed. The depths of her eyes kept changing as water passed over them, but not enough water for tears. She drew deep breaths, as if needing to breathe the odor of her daughter's hair, as if that smell could cancel out the other. But she kept her chin raised and her lips pinched and, when Liza drew back to look at her, Catherine did not seem to see her.

I couldn't look at the bed without thinking of the bowl. I wanted the bowl out of the room; I wanted death to be as clean and abstract as it would've been in a hospital. It was as though I did not want to know that my grandmother had once been alive enough to puke. I held my breath and stepped towards the bed, to remove the bowl.

But when I reached the bed, I'd forgotten the bowl. The body was so short and flush with the mattress that the sheet covered it as if there were nothing there. But a twirled lock of hair, like a frayed white ribbon, poked out between the sheet and pillow. I drew the sheet back.

Lightly closed eyes, parted lips and all the cliches about how the dead look like they're only sleeping. But she didn't look anything like she did when she was asleep. Her face was unnaturally white, as though she'd been dusted with flour. Without their color, her rich wrinkles seemed to have been ironed back into her face. She was naked under the sheet and the skin that was stretched over her collarbone looked like silk splotched with flour. Only her hair had ever been alive. The few curled wisps no longer hidden by her wig lay around the spare bristles on her scalp, reminding me one last time of an elderly states-man, a diplomat from another century. I thought of all the games of chess I had failed to play with her.

A set of leathery fingers stroked the high white fore-head, tugged the sheet out of my hand and drew it back over my grandmother's face.

"Isn't dressed," Catherine whispered. "Was going to bathe her."

Liza's hand touched the sheet, then drew back when she felt someone beneath it.

"When?" asked Jake from the far end of the room.

He and Corey kept their distance, Jake with his hands in his pockets, Corey holding Joan and looking only at Joan, ashamed that he was here.

"4:23. By the doctor's watch." Catherine's voice caught in her throat and she angrily swallowed before she re-peated more firmly, "4:23. Was 4:23 when Mom died."

"There was a doctor present? Good. Then you weren't alone when it happened," Jake said solicitously.

Catherine nodded and looked away. "No. Wasn't alone. Doctor was here. Nothing he could do but fill out the death certificate. Not that I blame him for anything. Nothing he could do. No, there wasn't."

She hadn't spoken to anyone in two hours and even now, she couldn't talk to us, only to herself, straightening her back as she spoke, facing the wig on the bookcase without seeming to recognize it.

"Turned out . . . she'd only been getting by on a wing and a prayer. And when one thing started to go, every-thing started to go. Click, click, click. Like somebody was turning off all the lights for her. Her mind, her lungs, her heart. Click, click, click. So there was nothing any doctor or hospital could do for her. Hospital was going to

admit her tomorrow if she didn't show any improvement
—meaning today, I guess? *Is* already today, isn't it? But
since it was going to happen, I'm glad it happened here.
Not in some cold, podunk hospital, but here, where I
could be with her. One last time together. I'm glad it
happened the way it did. I have nothing to blame myself
for, letting it happen the way it did. I really don't."

"We tried," Liza pleaded. "And we almost made it. I
wanted so badly to be here when it happened. And with
you, Mom."

"Not important. Wasn't anything to see, actually. She
slept right through it. She did. I heard her get sick—she
knew to use her dish—and I went down to the kitchen to
get her a glass of water so she could rinse her mouth out.
And when I got back, she'd already gone back to sleep. I
tried waking her up so she could rinse out her mouth..."
Catherine paused. Her voice became smaller, more distant. "She wouldn't wake up. That's all. Nothing I could
say to her could wake her up. And then Dr. Tarbell came
and... there wasn't even any point in calling an ambu-
lance. Nobody at the funeral home until nine. Dr. Tarbell
offered to stay with me until they came. But I said no. I
preferred to be alone with Mom. Told him I was fine.
And I am fine. I'll miss her. No doubt about that. But
she's happier now. Wherever she is, I'm sure she's happier."

Catherine blinked the brightness out her eyes and
smiled at us. A stiff, chilling smile.

"So I thank all of you for coming, but I'm fine now
and you can go about your business. I want to wash her
and dress her in something nice before the people from
the funeral home get here. So run along now, please. I
don't need you."

It was as though she didn't know who we were. All of
us just stood there, too confused to move.

"Can't I help you?" asked Liza. "I mean, I should,
shouldn't I? I want to."

"Only takes one person," said Catherine brusquely,

"and I don't see why you should—" She pinched her mouth shut, closed her eyes, then nodded. "Yes, I guess," she said resentfully. "If you feel that way, you should. You were her granddaughter."

"And me," I said. "Is there something I can do?"

"No!" she snapped. She tried to recover her temper while she angrily shook her head. "I'm sorry, but I'd rather be alone with this and I don't need any... Just take your friends and go! Please. I don't need all these people seeing me like this."

As if we were nobody, as if we were strangers.

"Yes. We will get out of your way," said Jake. "I understand. But before we go, you wouldn't first like to take a look at your granddaughter?"

"What?" And she saw Jake. She stared at Jake, then followed his nod to Corey and the baby. "Joan? That would be Joan," she muttered, not knowing what a baby could mean to her right now.

Corey lifted Joan so that Catherine could see her better. Joan watched everything with huge eyes.

"We wanted her great grandmother to see her," said Jake. "Your granddaughter. We lose one grandmother only to acquire another."

And his prattle caused her to turn away from Joan and glare at him. But it wasn't his clumsy attempt to console her that angered Catherine. It was the fact that he was Jake and she had finally recognized that he was with us.

He understood her stare. "Kids needed a ride," he explained. "And even if your mother and I never saw eye to eye, Catherine, I did have a fond respect for the old girl. I wanted to pay those last respects."

"Dammit to hell!" she shouted. "Dammit and I can't give a damn if you're here or not, Jacob Scherzenlieb! Not now! Just go, will you? Go! All of you. If there's anything to discuss, we'll discuss it later. Go to the kitchen, shut the door and leave me in peace with my dead! Please. Stayed out of my hair for this long. Don't see why in blazes you had to barge into my life now."

"I understand how you feel," said Jake. "And I'm sorry. Come on, lad. Corey. We should do what she says."

"Not you, Liza," said Catherine. "You stay. Mom would want you to stay. There's a bucket and sponge behind the chair."

It hurt me to be classed with the others, but I followed the men when they trooped guiltily out of the room. Upset by the shouting and being taken away from her mother, Joan began to cry. I tried to make myself feel better by taking her from Corey. Corey closed the door behind us as Liza solemnly rolled up her sleeves.

"Don't be put out, lad. It's traditional that the women lay out the body. At least in cultures where they still do that sort of thing. And if you feel rejected, just imagine how I must feel. Well, can't say I'm surprised. I knew what I was walking into."

I ignored my father and concentrated on giving Joan breakfast so she'd stop crying.

"Here. I'll hold her," said Corey.

"Thank you."

She became happily squirmy as soon as I started spooning pudding into her mouth. Was she the most selfish of us, or simply the most honest? I could think of nothing but the corpse in the next room.

"Liza was romanticizing on her way down," Jake told Corey. "Understandably. But Mrs. Bolt *was* an interesting lady. Not as clever as she thought she was, but then who of us is? Understood me far better than her daughter ever did. But then Mother Bolt knew the advantages of looking at the world with low expectations. Short of homicide, nothing I did would've shocked her. Well, I'm going to miss knowing that, somewhere on this planet, Mother Bolt is defending me, in her what-do-you-expect sort of way."

Corey only nodded. He'd been watching my hands while I fed Joan and now looked up at my face to test his sympathy upon me. My refusal to look back at him only made him sigh and hold Joan more snugly in his lap.

The door opened and Liza came in, carrying the aluminum bowl in her hand and Max under her arm. She spilled the dog onto the floor, emptied the bowl into the sink and let the spigot run.

"How's it coming, Kitten?"

She didn't answer. She had her mother's stern sense of purpose now, her angered look of solitude. She returned to the living room and shut the door.

"Give them a couple of hours together," said Jake as he looked at his watch, "and maybe have some breakfast. Then we should be heading out."

"So soon?" said Corey.

"We have to get Liza away from here before this afternoon, when you-know-who shows up. And I have a show to do tonight. No point in sticking around anyway. Funeral be something of an anti-climax after this."

"Yes. I guess you're right," said Corey. "I have to go to work tomorrow."

"I think I might stay," I said. "For a day or so."

"Doesn't look to me like your mother needs you, lad."

"I know. But there's a lot of things down here that have to be done. Mom's way behind on her spring planting. Because of Gram, I guess. Might be good for me to stay down here a few days and help her catch up."

"You can offer," said Jake. "But don't be surprised if she nixes it."

"You don't want to...?" Corey looked at me worriedly.

I wanted to stay behind to make myself a useful part of my mother's grief, just as Liza was now. "Want to what?" I said.

"Want to... what about your unemployment? Won't they cut it off if you don't show up?" He was afraid to mention the other thing.

"Too late," I said. "I didn't go Friday and this is Sunday. They've already cut me off. Only had a few more weeks of benefits anyway. So, there's nothing up there I have to get back to."

382

"No?" He lowered his eyes again. "No, I guess not."

"Stay down here a few days, a week maybe, maybe two weeks, then take the bus back. Yes, that's what I think I'll do."

"Two weeks?"

"Or however long it takes. You'll see me when you see me."

"Yes? You want to stay here that . . .? Uh, you want me to mail you some of your clothes when I get back?"

"Maybe. All I brought with me was a change of under-wear."

Were we talking about the same thing? We were being so cool and practical about it, but both of us seemed to sense that I might be saying good-bye for good. The death in the next room prevented either of us from press-ing the matter.

There was a crackle of gravel in the driveway.

Jake stood up. "The iceman cometh," he said and moved toward the window. "Wonder if they still use pine boxes in this part of the country?"

"Gram believed in cremation," I said, repeating what Catherine had repeated to me a dozen times when death was only hypothetical. When I said it now I was horri-fied; that white but familiar face and the skull beneath it, burning.

"Jiminy Christmas," Jake grumbled at the window. "Looks like Liza's Bob."

I threw down the spoon and snatched Joan from Corey's lap. I was on my feet, ready to run with her, but where? I was surrounded by closed doors. "You stupid ass!" I shouted at Jake. "I knew he was going to follow us! You wouldn't listen to me! I knew this would hap-pen!"

Jake stepped quickly to the back door. "I'll talk to him outside. Tell him what's happened and explain why he can't come in. Calm down, I'll take care of this."

But as soon as he opened the door, he was hurled back into the kitchen.

Corey jumped up to stand between me and the door.

I backed against the door to the living room, turned sideways and hunched over Joan to hide her. She was kicking and screaming.

Kearney stood in the back door. He lowered the hands that had pushed Jake, set the hands on his hips. He stood there, tapping one black shoe against the floor while he coldly looked at each of us.

"Mom!" I hollered through the closed door. "Kearney's here! I think he's looking for Liza!" I thought they could lock the door, or maybe Liza could escape out the front.

Max was barking, shrill yips directed at nobody in particular.

Joan howled and tried to wiggle out of my arms.

And Kearney saw his daughter. His lips parted. His eyes grew wide, then pained. His whole face fell on the sight of Joan.

"I'm sorry, son, but you shouldn't be here right now." Jake had recovered from his shove and laid a friendly hand on Kearney's arm. "Let's step outside and talk. We've got a dead grandmother in the next room."

Kearney brushed the hand away without taking his eyes off his daughter. "I'm not going anywhere." He nodded at Joan. "Not without my little girl. Or my wife."

"Liza's not here," I shouted over Joan's crying.

"She's in the next room," said Kearney.

"She's with her grandmother," said Jake. "Her grandmother passed away only a few hours ago, Bob. You can't go in there."

Kearney was frowning at me. "You're making my daughter cry. Let her down. She wants to come to her father."

"No she doesn't! She's crying because you're here. You're upsetting her."

Kearney stepped towards me.

Corey blocked his way.

Kearney's calm was like a trance. I waited for the split

second when the trance would break and he'd knock Corey to the floor. But he only tried to step his way around Corey.

Corey stepped with him, dragging the chair he was prepared to lift and swing at him.

Kearney stopped. "Only wasting your time," he assured us. "You're only postponing the inevitable. She's my daughter. I don't have to fight you for her."

"Okay, Bob," said Jake, trying for authority. "You're trespassing. If you don't step outside, we'll have to call the police."

"Go ahead. It'll save me from calling them."

That bluff again, I told myself, but he was so arrogantly confident I became panicked that he really did have something he could use against Liza.

Joan cried and Kearney bit his lip.

I moved away from the door toward the window so that the table would be between me and Kearney. If he got past Corey, he would have to chase me around the table to get his daughter. And there was Catherine's shotgun in the closet. If only I could get to that.

"The police're going to get my family back for me. One way or another." Kearney watched me and Joan.

"That's not the way it works, son. Law tends to side with the mother. I know. I've been down that road myself."

"You haven't been down that road," sneered Kearney. He glanced at Corey, at me. "You washed your hands of your family without so much as a . . . whimper!" He lunged at the table as he shouted the word.

Corey leaped back to cover me.

And Kearney spun around to lunge through the opening left by Corey. He lunged at the door and, before Corey could grab him from behind, threw the door open.

"I love you, Liza! You screwed me but I still love you dammit!"

He stopped.

Corey froze, without laying a hand on Kearney.

385

I came around the table to go for the closet, but stopped when I looked through the door.

The sheet lay on the floor. On the bed, fish-belly white, was a naked woman.

Worse than naked, because a pair of frilled drawers had been pulled on her, old woman's drawers that came all the way up to her ribs. There was a tan stocking on one blunt leg. Liza was stopped in the act of unrolling another stocking up the other leg. She paused, with the rolled silk around the ankle. She didn't look up. Then she continued, until the stocking like a shadow was tugged snugly over the thigh.

Corey turned away from it. "Dammit, Bob? Show some respect for the dead."

Catherine knelt over the breasts and face, her back to us. She glanced at us over her shoulder, then went on with what she was doing. Both of them went on, as if none of us were there.

"Liza. I'm sorry about your... Can't you let your mother take care of that? Do you have to be handling... Come on outside and talk to me. Please? You can talk to me, can't you?"

Jake stepped into the doorway and blocked my view. I set Joan on the floor, thrust a toy at her and hurried over to the door.

Kearney stood well inside the room now, but kept his distance from the bed. "Come on. I need to talk to you."

Liza knelt behind the bed and body.

"Please! Can't you even speak to me?"

"I have nothing to say to you."

"Nothing to say?" he muttered. "You walk out on me and you have nothing to say about it? I love you, girl! You're my life, dammit. You and my daughter are my whole frigging life! We're not some nothing thing you can throw away... without talking about it!"

"Lift her waist," Catherine told Liza. "So I can get this around her."

Liza did and angrily cut her eyes at Kearney. But when

the body was lowered again, she busied herself with the snaps that connected the stockings to the girdle.

"Can't you forgive me enough to even talk to me? I don't know what it is I've done, but if you'd only... Look! I can forgive *you*. You left without a word; you hid from me when you knew I'd come all the way from Germany; you lied to me. I wasn't born yesterday, Liza. I knew you were feeding me a line when you said you'd ride down with me today. I knew you were lying through your teeth, girl. Knew I was going to find you down here. Knew it all along, but it never took away from the fact that I love you. You tried my patience, you tried my love. But my love's survived, babe. Through all that. Because it's real. It's all that's real. I don't know what they've talked you into believing, but my love for you is real. Haven't I proved that by—"

"Nobody's talked me into anything!" Liza snarled. "Woke up. On my own. Yes, you love me. Big deal. I don't want to be your life, Bob. Enough trouble with it being my life."

"And you will be your life," Kearney insisted. "I'll give you your life back to you."

"You can do that by giving me a divorce." She went back to work, ashamed that she'd said so much.

"No. Not a divorce. We don't need a divorce. Okay, I know your life isn't mine to give. I shouldn't have said it that way. But I can change the way I am. I've changed before, I can do it again. For your sake, Liza. For the sake of our daughter."

"You'll have to sit her up so I can pull her dress on over her head," said Catherine.

Liza moved to the head of the bed and eased the shoulders up so she could get an arm under them.

"There's a lot of me in our child, Liza. But you love *her*. So you must love me some if you can still love her. She can't help but make you think of me."

With Liza's weight behind her, Gram suddenly sat up. A head fell forward. A green print dress was thrown over the head. Catherine hurriedly pulled the limp arms through the sleeves. The collar parted; the white face reappeared.

"You do!" Kearney cried desperately. "You do still love me! That's why you're afraid to even talk to me, Liza. You still love me and you're afraid to even admit it."

They laid the body down and smoothed the dress around her.

Kearney feverishly looked around the room. For his audience? For a weapon? "But I can make you see that love. I can make that love hit home, Liza. Hit home so it hurts. You want to see how badly love can hurt you?" He grabbed the phone and started to dial.

Who? The police? But what could the police do to Liza?

"This is going to hurt me more than it hurts you. But I'm doing it out of love."

Liza was on her knees, staring at Kearney.

"Watch this. All of you. I want you to see what real love can do." He gripped the receiver like a knife. "Hello? Hampton, the number for Fort Eustis, please. Military police, if there's a listing."

I rushed across the room to yank the phone cord out of its jack.

Kearney blocked me with his elbow. "There is? Can you connect me? This is an emergency."

I ducked under the elbow to get to the cord. Kearney's knee slammed my chin and knocked me backward.

"Let him call!" said Liza. "His M.P.'s can't get me back for him!"

"You try it fucker. Try it again. See if I don't knock you on your ass."

He was ready for me now, his free hand balled into a fist while his other hand held the receiver to his ear. He took a swing at me with his foot, but wasn't treating me as a serious threat. The shotgun was still in the kitchen closet.

"Don't think that because you're a captain you can

have me arrested. This is the real world, Bob. You're not on base. You're captain of *nothing* here."

"Hello? Military police, Eustis? This is Captain Robert Kearney, 28th Infantry, Mainz. I'm calling in regards to a case of desertion."

"He's bullshitting!" Liza insisted. "They can't do a thing to me!"

He stood at attention, but his eyes were soft and full. He gazed at Liza. "Stationed in Mainz, yes. Kearney. K-e-a-r-n-e-y. Correct. Yes, I would like to be connected with the duty officer. Okay, I'll hold. I'm not going anywhere." He lowered the mouthpiece so that it was at his throat. "There," he said. "You see how much I love you?"

"I don't see how calling the army, who can't do a damn thing . . .!"

"Dammit girl! I've gone AWOL for you! Absent without leave. For you," he said proudly. "Because of my love for you. The fuckers wouldn't give me a leave. They wouldn't even let me borrow any leavetime, but did that stop me? Hell no. Because I love you and Joan so much it hurts."

He seemed so confident, so pleased over his sacrifice. The rest of us could only stare at him in bewilderment.

"And now you'll turn yourself in?" said Jake. "Pardon me for saying this, son, but I don't see how you stand to gain a damn thing from what you're doing."

"I stand to gain everything," he told Liza. "My wife. My child. Because it's not too late, Liza. I could hang up this phone and everything would be the way it was. Back in Mainz, they still don't know that I'm gone. The C.O.'s a shit, but a couple of my buddies are covering for me. Only if they catch me over here will they know that I'm gone. That I'm AWOL. Which means prison for an officer. You want them to catch me, Liza?"

She closed her eyes.

"See? You do still love me. You do. Okay then. Come home with me, Liza," he said tenderly. "We can catch a flight in Washington, be back in Germany in a few hours, and they'll never know what I did. I love you, babe. I'll change. I'll make things right again."

We watched Liza. Corey was beside Jake in the kitchen door. Only Catherine looked at Kearney—blindly, bitterly.

"You really like blackmail, don't you?" I said.

"Not blackmail," said Kearney. "Just the way things are. Because, army or no army, Liza, I'm not going back without you and Joan. Only other way I'll go back is in handcuffs. It's not meant as a threat. It's just the way things are. How about it, Liza? Yes? I know you. You do love me enough not to want to see me destroyed because of this."

Liza drew a sharp breath, opened her eyes and straightened her grandmother's collar.

"You do, don't you? Don't you? Answer me! You *want* to see me go to prison?"

Without raising her eyes, Liza quietly said, "Joan and I are staying. What you do, Bob, is no concern of mine."

His face turned pale. He turned his free ear at her.

"If what you say is true, son, then my advice to you is that you hang up that phone, forget your family and catch the next flight back to Germany, pronto."

"Liza? Do you realize what you're saying? You do," Kearney muttered to himself. "And yet, you can just sit by and let it happen. Without feeling the slightest . . ."

He studied her for the longest time, his jaw moving, the teeth on one side of his mouth lightly grinding together. He watched her for a signal, a hint, something to show that she cared enough to feel hurt for him.

And she only smoothed the ribbons of hair on our grandmother's head.

And I suddenly felt sorry for Kearney.

There was a buzzing in his ear. I could hear it from where I stood, but he remained fixed on Liza. Finally, he swung the mouthpiece up. "Hello? Yes, still someone here. Lieutenant McKenna? Captain Kearney here." He

390

threw his shoulders back and coolly said, "I'm absent without leave from the 28th Division in Mainz. I've contacted you to turn myself in."

Liza's hand stopped. Her fingers covered her grandmother's head and she refused to look at Kearney.

"I'm in a house on Route 423 east of Charles City. I request that you send your people here immediately and place me under arrest."

I was stunned by what he was doing. Jake and Corey looked stunned, too, baffled by it, even awed. It was such a stupid but beautiful gesture: to destroy yourself for love. Catherine stood up and watched contemptuously. Liza remained as still as a stone.

"Pardon?" Kearney's look of purpose wavered. *"No. No, I'm sorry but I won't 'just drive over and turn myself in.' You'll have to come and get me."* He swallowed, afraid this detail spoiled the effect. "It's imperative you come out here and arrest me, Lieutenant. I don't care how it affects my case. Okay. You do that. Talk to your superior and see if he doesn't tell you what your duty is. Yes. Of course I'll hold."

"Hear that?" he told Liza. "I'll make you a witness to what you've done. This isn't any lousy bluff. You're going to see me arrested."

She drew a long breath and said nothing.

"What? Still don't believe me? You think I'm talking to air? Here, Liza. You talk to this asshole. Tell him how to get out here. Finish what you've started. Here, I'm giving you the knife."

Nothing.

"You don't have the guts, do you? Can't do it to my face, can you? What about you, Shirtsy? You been fucking me for days now. Here. One last fuck. I'll roll right over and let you fuck me for good. No? What's the matter? Too direct for you? Too direct for any of you, isn't it?" he cried. "Cold bastards and bitches, all of you. Cold fucks. Just stand there gawking like cattle, not feeling a damn... What? Yes!" he shouted into the phone. "Good then! Damn straight it's your duty. *Okay.* Route 1 to Charles City Courthouse! Turn right at the Baptist Church! Left on Route 423! Past a bunch of shacks! Rundown farmhouse on the left, Scherzenlieb on the mailbox. Scherzen-fucking-lieb, dammit! No! I'm fine! No, I'm not crazy! An hour? Okay. I'll be here!"

He slammed down the phone. He breathed heavily and looked hard at Liza.

Her head was bowed over her grandmother's face.

"You've done it now," Kearney whispered. "Yes, you actually did it, Liza. They're coming. I was wrong. You *could* do it. You actually did it," he repeated, trying to make himself believe that what had happened had actually happened. "Well," he sighed. "Yes, well. I only hope you can live with yourself. For what you've just done to your daughter's father."

"You dumbass!" cried Liza. "You stupid, arrogant bastard." She jumped to her feet, face twisted in rage. "Arrogant! *Yes.* You're not going to make me feel guilty. You did it yourself, you bastard." She went at him; she stood directly in front of him. "Asshole!" she hissed. "Don't think you're going to make me feel guilty, because I'm not going to feel a damn thing. Nothing, hear!"

He cautiously raised both hands to touch her shoulders.

"No!" She slapped the hands aside. "Think I feel sorry for you? Sorry enough to hug you good-bye? No way. I don't want you *near* me."

Kearney looked to us, before he remembered who we were.

"No. I do feel something. I feel grateful to you, Bob. Yes, grateful. Because your little *show* here—your *tantrum*... With one stroke, Bob, one quick stroke, you get yourself taken out of my life. *And,* make me see again that your love—this love you're so damned proud of—is nothing but horseshit!"

His mouth and eyes hardened, as if he were going to hit her. But then, just as abruptly, all the fight went out of his face.

392

"Manipulative, selfish, horseshit. Tricks, Bob. Plays for my sympathy. But I'm safe now. Because I've got no sympathy left. All my sympathy is with *her!*" She thrust one arm at the bed behind her. "A woman... a woman who loved me with no strings attached. But who I let pass away—pass out of my life!—without so much as a good-bye, because I was too snarled up in your horseshit. Either fighting it off or, before that, telling myself that it was what I should want from life." The tears spilled over the angry folds and lines in her face. "But I say, fuck you. And I say, thank you. Yes, thank you, Bob. Because you trying to manipulate my feelings, even now, when the only thing I can think of is *her* makes me see what a self-centered, arrogant thing your love has always been. I'm so grateful, I'm so grateful, Bob, I should shake your hand. Yes, Bob. Allow me to shake your hand," she sobbed; she gave up her anger to be sarcastic but without her anger, she broke into sobs.

Kearney watched as she took his limp hand and mechanically pumped it.

"Thank you, Bob. Asshole!" She threw the hand down and walked toward the window, her palms angrily wiping her face and hair.

And Kearney just stood there, following her with his eyes.

Catherine addressed him. "Does this mean we're stuck with you until the police come?"

"What? Uh, yes. Does." He looked at her in bewilderment. We had denied him everything, even his right to suffer.

"Not too late," said Jake. "You could still take off before the M.P.'s get here."

Kearney numbly shook his head.

"If it's face you're worried about saving, son, I think you're making a big mistake. Sincerely doubt that anyone here who matters could think any less of you if you headed for the hills. Hurts to lose a wife, Bob, but there is your own ass to think of."

"Uh uh. Meant what I said. Wasn't trying to manipulate anyone," he said softly. "Wasn't. I *want* them to put my ass in jail. Nothing else left to do with it. Nothing. Right?" He looked across the room at Liza's back, then closed his eyes. "Would like to say good-bye to my daughter, though. Will you grant me that much, Liza? Will you at least let me share my ... horseshit with my daughter for a few minutes?"

Liza stiffened at the window and said nothing.

Catherine shot an impatient look at her, then turned to Kearney. "Yes! Say good-bye to her. If she means so much to you, you *should* spend your time with her before the cops get here."

"Thank you," Kearney mumbled and continued to stare at Liza's back.

"But in the kitchen!" Catherine pleaded. "Please. All of you. In the kitchen and give me some peace. This damn circus has gone on long enough."

"I'm sorry about your mother, Cather—" but Kearney didn't really want to say that. He went into the kitchen, escorted by me and Corey.

"One person's tragedy is another person's circus," chided Jake. He smiled sheepishly at his ex-wife and followed us out of the room, closing the door behind him.

Joan sat on the floor, studying Max. Max kept sniffing her, but jumped back whenever she touched him. They were warily fascinated with each other. Kearney sat down, pushed Max away and lifted Joan into his lap. She began to cry.

I stood at the back door, in case Kearney tried to run out with Joan, but it no longer seemed likely. I was surprised by how totally defeated Kearney looked, this man who'd been so full of threats all week. But he was all played out.

Not even his daughter's rejection could faze him now. He jiggled her for a moment, then swooped her over his head a few times until the swoops stopped her crying. But even then she wanted down, to be with Max, who'd perched his paws on Kearney's knee to get a better sniff of this new animal.

"Okey-dokey, monkey," Kearney sighed, carefully set her down on the floor and pushed the dog towards her. He sadly watched the two be oblivious to everything else but themselves.

"Kids," said Jake. "They're in a world of their own."

"I was so sure she loved me."

"Joan?" said Jake. "Oh. You mean Liza."

"I was sure I could count on her love. When I showed her what I was willing to risk for that love, she'd come to her senses. But nothing. My sacrifice gets thrown right back in my face. All these years, through all our squabbles, I was so sure she loved me. But to find I'm... *nothing* to her. Like I'd been fooling myself all these years."

I was sorry for him. He had done it to himself; I remembered who he was, but nevertheless, I was sorry for him. I was surprised by the intensity of my pity. But Robert Kearney, who had seemed so distant and solid when he was a threatening enemy, had become a blur in defeat. Feeling sorry for him was as natural as feeling sorry for myself.

Corey leaned against the sink and looked down at his feet.

"Well," said Jake. "You probably don't need to hear this right now. But I suspect Liza still loves you some. In spite of herself. You overestimated the power of love, that's all. There's some wounds it can't heal. But you're young, son. You're still a romantic. You'll do better next time. Learn by your errors."

"Next time?" Kearney shook his head. "Won't be time for a next time. Not after I get out of the brig."

"I sincerely doubt they're going to put you in the room with striped sunshine, Bob. You've been AWOL, what? Five days? Clean record, I presume. No, I suspect they'll just give you an Article 15 and a discharge. Which means the end of your career in the army, of course, but you'll still have the rest of your life ahead of you."

It was good to know that Kearney hadn't completely destroyed himself, but there was something cruel in the way Jake took Kearney's tragedy away from him.

"Nothing else I want from life. There was my family, and the army. That was it. Nothing else."

"You'll find something. Another woman. Another occupation. Ever given any thought to the theater?"

Kearney looked at him as if Jake had mocked him.

"Just a suggestion. You have the face for it. And you certainly have a flair for the dramatic. I was thinking it while I watched you in the other room just now."

"I wasn't play-acting!" said Kearney indignantly. "That was real! I laid my life on the line for the sake of my family!"

"I know. Not disparaging your sincerity, Bob. And I know what you're suffering right now. But I couldn't help noticing the theatrical aspect. Especially when you were on the phone with McKenna. It was McKenna, wasn't it? Well, I found myself admiring your use of... deus ex McKenna."

Nobody reacted. Not even Corey and I, who understood the joke.

Jake apologetically smiled. "Sorry. I don't mean to be callous, punning at a time like this. But there are moments when one has to laugh to keep from crying." Jake thought for a moment and became serious. "You've still got your heart set on being here when they come for you?"

"Yes."

"If that's your decision, it's not my business to talk you out of it. If I don't seem to be taking this in the proper spirit, Bob, it's only because I think that what you're doing is a very foolish, pointless gesture. But who am I to tell you that? A selfish old man who never cared for anyone's ass but his own." He smiled at all of us, then announced he'd fix coffee for anyone who wanted it.

* * *

396

An hour later, we heard them pull into the driveway.

Joan was back in her father's lap. He kissed her good-bye before giving her to me. He stood up, straightened the line of his belt buckle and shirt and, one last time, faced the closed door to the living room.

But out in the driveway was a hearse. Two fat men stepped out of it, one bald and solemn, the other blond and sunny.

We all sat down again. Kearney didn't ask for Joan back. The undertakers entered through the front door and we could hear them in the living room.

"Mrs. Bolt. My heartfelt condolences. Dr. Tarbell called us first thing this morning and told us of the terrible event. We came as soon as we could. I am Dr. Billy Pusey and this is my son, Phillip."

"Hi," a boy said cheerfully.

"Ah. And this is the departed. Hmmm. I see you've gone to the trouble of dressing her. That wasn't really necessary. It's a delicate process, preparing the departed and we prefer... never mind. I understand. My, what a stately woman. I know you're going to miss her very much."

There was another crackle of gravel outside and I went back to the window. A dark green car with numbers stenciled on its door pulled up alongside the hearse. Two soldiers in khaki and braid got out, made faces at each other over the hearse and fell into step together as they went around to the front door.

"Around back!" we heard Catherine shout. "You can't come through here! Go around to the door on the side."

A moment later, shoes crunching gravel, their caps bobbed past the kitchen window. They knocked at the back door and I opened it with Joan still perched against my hip.

"Captain Kearney here? Which one of you is..."

They saw the man with the short haircut and patchy growth of beard. He stood facing them with his feet apart and his hands clasped at his back.

"Captain Robert Kearney? You're under arrest. Are you going to come along peaceably?"

"Yes, Corporal. I place myself in your custody." But he stood where he was, with his ear turned toward the closed door.

"I've made up my mind," Catherine was insisting. "No embalming. No waterproof casket. Nothing but cremation. There's no point in giving me time to think it over, Pusey, because that's what I want."

"Captain. We have a long drive to get back to Eustis. If you're not cooperative, we'll have to take you forcibly."

The corporal spoke and moved like an automaton, but the other man, who had freckles and a blond moustache, looked uncomfortable. "Pardon, but... did somebody die?"

"A grandmother," said Jake.

"Yeah? That's tough. I'm sorry, man. Had to go AWOL to be at your grandmother's side? Officers get the flak, too, huh?"

"Can it, Walker. Captain Kearney, I have orders to have you back by ten hundred sharp and if you aren't willing to—"

"Got a turd in your pocket, Corporal? I told you I was coming. Here." He held out the backs of his hands. "Put the handcuffs on me and let's go."

"Handcuffs? I don't think that will be necessary, Captain."

"I think it's necessary. Do it, soldier! Move!"

Shaking his head, the one with freckles pried a pair of handcuffs out from under his belt and gingerly snapped them on Kearney's wrists.

"You tell Liza what you saw," Kearney ordered. "Tell her I did exactly what I said I'd do, with no second thoughts. Okay, Corporal. Get your ass in gear. Haven't got all day."

We followed them out the back door and watched from the porch as the soldiers escorted Kearney down the driveway. The corporal gripped Kearney's arm; the soldier with freckles rested a hand on Kearney's back, as if to console him. All three automatically fell into step together.

Joan wiggled around in my arms and pointed. "Bye? Bye-bye? Bye!"

But Kearney didn't seem to hear her. He looked up at the living room window as he was marched past it, hands bound in front of him. From where we stood, I couldn't see anyone watching from the window.

The undertaker and his son came around from the front of the house, struggling with a stretcher that was covered with a sheet.

The M.P. with freckles saw the body, nudged Kearney and removed his cap.

Kearney was put into the car, our grandmother into the hearse.

The car backed out to the road and turned right. The hearse backed out more slowly, turned left and was gone. The open field on the other side of the road was covered with tiny sprouts like light green down.

We went back inside again.

The door to the living room opened, and was left open. Catherine passed through, carrying an armload of blankets that she absent-mindedly sniffed one last time. I could see Liza alone in the living room, sitting sideways on the tweed chair, her eyes closed, the corner of her fist pressed against her mouth.

Catherine returned from the back room, rubbing her bare arms. "Morticians," she muttered. "Sell you the moon if they could." She took Joan from me and sweetly cooed at her, "You been fed, pumpkin? I bet in all this commotion, nobody remembered to feed you."

"Your son fed her," said Jake.

"Yes? Is that so, pumpkin? In that case, Gram better not feed you, too. We don't want you turning into a little butterball, do we?" She stroked her granddaughter's silky hair, set her down on the floor and looked around for something to do. With death removed from her house, she was suddenly antsy.

I waited for a collective sigh. I waited for us to become ourselves again. But who were we to each other? Nobody seemed to remember.

Jake's facetious remarks stayed with me: It *was* like a play, and the play was over. The bodies had been carried off-stage, the curtain had fallen, everything had been resolved. I felt so blank, so emotionally drained, it was as if everything had really been resolved. Only slowly did I remember that I had been only a part of the audience. And if the play had been about fears and needs that seemed to be mine, because those feelings had resolved themselves in the play did not mean they had resolved mine as well. In the calm that followed, my life came back to me, the prolonged mistake I had discovered on the journey down here.

Corey slouched in the corner, eyes glancing up from one person to another. He was unnecessary here, annoyingly so, the extra who had missed his cue and failed to go off-stage with the others. He was motionless except for that shift of eyes and an occasional squirm of hands in his empty pockets. His eyes touched me, then darted away. He sighed and shook his head at something.

"Think I'll go outside and have a look around," I said. "See what needs to be done."

"Oh I can tell you that without looking," said Catherine. "Everything."

"You don't want any breakfast, lad? Was going to fix omelets for those who want them."

"Not hungry," I told him.

"Well, try to stay within shouting distance. Probably be heading out right after breakfast. Uh, you won't mind if we stay long enough to have some breakfast, will you, Catherine?"

"Suit yourself," she said. "You drove all the way down here. I won't deny you a bite before you take off again."

They looked at each other curiously, then looked at Corey to see if he'd go with me. Because of something they wanted to say to each other, or because they had nothing to say to each other, they didn't want Corey here, either.

But Corey belligerently stayed where he was, not even taking his hands from his pockets. "You asked her yet?"

Jake had forgotten my decision, but Corey hadn't. And that it could still be on his mind, after all that had happened, made me think it was something he wanted too.

"No. You tell her. I have to get outside and start on something." I escaped out the door before the questions could be asked.

Blue sky. A half-circle of pale green woods. A crust of dirt that was broken apart by the steady churn of blades and mixed into the darker, damper ground beneath it. After so long, it was good to accomplish something you could see.

My ears were filled with the roar of the cultivator. The wet earth stuck to the blades and the machine lurched from side to side, shaking the handle so that it rubbed my hands raw. My hands had gone soft in the past year and the muscles in my arms jiggled like those of an old woman. But to have so much agitation outside of myself, and controlled by myself: I was filled with calm.

Work like this was such a solemn thing, it felt like mourning. It was an act of respect to my grandmother. She would understand.

At the end of a swath, I looked up and saw Catherine in her cage, slinging feed at her chickens. She knew work wasn't disrespectful to the dead. She shielded her eyes with one hand to look out and see what I'd done so far, then went back to her chickens. A shout or a raised hand wasn't needed by either of us to show we connected.

I steered the cultivator back and forth across the unfinished plot. Shirtsy comes home. And home didn't seem so bad. My mother didn't seem so crazy to me now. You go out into the world, bang your head against a few closed doors, and then, if you can learn from your pain, you go off by yourself and create a world of your own.

Catherine's world was a small but honest one, a safer world. The point was to keep your life uncomplicated by illusions. There would be pain enough anyway, when those who genuinely mattered to you died. Illusions end in theatrical noise. Real love ends only in death.

The blades were on the sides of the machine, so you missed the ground in the middle and had to make each trip across the plot overlap with the last. A brazen crow appeared, expecting grain but settling for the worms I unearthed. My shadow grew shorter. So much had happened today, it was difficult to believe it was still morning. I kept stealing looks toward the house, but all the vehicles were still there: the pickup truck, Jake's borrowed Cadillac, the rented car Kearney had left behind. I hoped they would leave without saying good-bye. I didn't want to talk to anyone, even if it was only to say good-bye.

Out across the field, a door opened and shut.

I didn't look up until I was pivoting the machine around and saw that Catherine was gone from her cage.

And then I saw Corey coming across the field. He was hunched over like a bird, looking where he stepped as he stumbled across the soft clods I'd plowed up. He kept wetting his mouth, as though he had a great deal to say.

I wanted him to understand already, and had thought he did understand. But here he was, ready to make a scene. I released both levers on the handle, disengaging the blades and wheels. If I wanted to avoid a scene, I should be civil to him. I even shut the motor off. A dog barked somewhere in the distance.

Corey raised his head and casually announced, "We're getting ready to leave."

"Could you tell my father good-bye? I'm at a place where I can't stop. He'll understand."

Corey frowned.

"Oh, and thank him for me. And have a safe trip back. I'll call you in a week or so and let you know what's what."

He dug the dirt with the heel of his shoe.

"Catherine didn't object to me staying, did she?"

"No. No, she didn't," he muttered. "Said she could use a hand through the spring. Liza's staying. Of course. She told Liza she could stay as long as she liked, but not to plan on tying herself to your mother's apron strings." He looked hard at me. "You plan on staying all spring?"

"Or as long as my mother needs me."

"And then what?"

"Go back to New York . . . probably."

Our eyes met. We stared at each other through Corey's glasses.

"What's the matter, Core?" My faked innocence sounded contemptuous, but I stuck with it. "Don't you want me to come back to New York?"

He closed his eyes. "Will you cut the crap, Joel?"

"What do you mean, Corey?"

"You know damn well what I mean!" But he regained his temper as quickly as he lost it. He nodded toward the house. "Come on. Your father's waiting for us. We should ride back with him."

"But I already told you. I'm staying. Nothing I have to do in New York. Plenty that has to be done down here."

Now I was the one who didn't want to be emotional. Kearney's defeat had been so confused and pathetic because it had been so emotional. I was determined to be calm, rational, civil. I didn't want us to look anything like them.

"Joel. Ride back with us. If you're so intent on helping your mother, you can come back down here next week. I'll even buy you the bus ticket to come back down here."

"But why? I can save you the money just by staying here."

"Joel. Look. I'm not so fond of you either at the moment. But if we separate now, with all this still fresh in our heads, it's going to be even more difficult for us to set things right with each other."

"Who said anything about us? Quit being so egotistical. All I'm talking about is staying behind and helping my mother. Is that such a threat to you?"

"That's not what you're talking about and you know it."

"Oh no? Then what am I talking about?"

He grimaced, annoyed that he had to say it himself. "You're thinking: what a convenience. You stay. I go. In a week or two, I ship you your things. The end. Without tears."

I was surprised to find him one step ahead of me. He said out loud what I hadn't been able to think about, only acknowledge as a vague possibility in the distance: We were saying good-bye for good. The suggestion pleased me, but what I said was, "You're being theatrical."

"Cut the crap, Joel. It's what you're thinking, too."

"Okay. It's a possibility that has crossed my mind. But if it happens, it happens."

"Look. It's something that appeals to me right now too. Because it's the easiest solution to all the grief you're putting us through. But it's an impulse I know well enough to fight it."

"Why? If it's there, why fight it?"

"Out of common sense. Out of..." His hand went up and repeatedly snatched at air. "...respect for our past together. For how long we've been together. Out of..."

"Love?" I said skeptically.

"Love?" He looked pained.

We'd heard the word too many times this morning. It carried no weight for either of us.

"Okay. It's true," he confessed. "It's difficult for me to feel much love for you right now. Your doubting my love has made *me* doubt it, made me take a long, hard look at something I'd always taken for granted and...I'm too confused now to be able to tell what's there. But I do know this. I have a duty towards us. Towards who we were and how long we've been together. And I don't want to see that thrown away over...over something that, in the final analysis, Joel, is nothing but chickenshit!"

"Well, if all it took was chickenshit, there must not have much there to begin with."

"I don't think that. Won't. I can't believe for a minute that we're just another one of those gay couples who bump together, admire their reflections in each other's eyes for a while, then break up the first time one of us blinks."

A rehearsed sentence: He'd been giving it long, hard thought.

"Oh. So that's what matters to you. Hurts your pride to think we might be just another case of homosexual... narcissism."

"No. Pride has nothing to do with it. I'm feeling a duty towards us, and the idea of us."

"Well, if all I am to you is a duty..."

"Yes. At the moment that *is* all you are to me," he said gravely. "But at least you're that much to me. Duty can give things continuity, Joel. Because right now I suspect —assume... I feel that right now you don't even feel *that* towards me, only anger."

"Yes. At the moment," I admitted. "But it's a more honest reaction than your duty."

But I was finding myself reluctant to continue along this line. Because of the emotion? Our voices had not grown loud enough to frighten away the crow who continued to hop around on his patch of ground, but we seemed to be performing what I had wanted to avoid: the final theatrical good-bye.

It was the finality that was making it theatrical. I retraced my steps. "But time will tell," I claimed. "This is only how I feel at the moment and... what happens, happens," wanting us to pretend that the door was still half open.

He inhaled a desperate chestful of air, then surrendered it in a long, weary sigh. "Okay, Shirts. If that's the way you think it is—"

"It is."

"Stay here for a week or so. Do what has to be done.

And then, who knows? Maybe all we need is a little vacation from each other." He could surrender only by taking up my claim that we'd left the door open, but he took it up without conviction.

"Maybe," I said. "Who knows."

We nodded at each other, tried smiling at each other, but our smiles felt like sneers. I turned away to dicker with the primer and cord again, showing I'd thought we'd said all that needed to be said.

But before I could start the engine, whose noise would force us to keep our good-byes simple and allow us to simply shake hands, Corey said, "I'll tell your father good-bye for you. And give him your thanks," then wheeled around and walked briskly toward the house.

Without saying good-bye to me.

If what we were saying was good-bye.

I angrily yanked the cord. The engine started and the crow leaped up with a panicky flapping of wings. When I could bring myself to look towards the house again, Corey was gone. But my way was better than Kearney's, I told myself. It was. My only regret was that that damn Cadillac was still parked beside the barn.

The cultivator waddled back and forth, weaving its pattern of turned earth. Its noise wasn't loud enough for me now, it went too slow for me. Maybe I could talk Catherine into leasing a tractor tomorrow and we could get something planted in this ground before it was too late. Each time I turned the machine around, looked up and saw the car still by the barn, I muttered, "Leave dammit! What're you waiting for!"

"What the hell do you think you're doing?"

The words were hollered through the howl of the engine and I looked around. Liza had come up behind me. Her eyes were still red, but she stood there with her hands clasped together and resting on top of her head.

I released the levers. The noise became thinner when it didn't have to strain against anything, but was still loud enough to force us to shout. "What do you think! I'm staying behind to help Mom."

"Bullshit!"

I had nothing more to say about it, not even to my sister. I swung the machine around, pressed hard on the levers and attacked the next strip of ground.

But Liza stayed beside me, walking on the stubbled, uneven earth I hadn't plowed yet. "You're making a big mistake!" she shouted.

"That's none of your business!" I shouted back. "You have enough to worry about right now! You don't have to worry about me!"

"I do have a lot to worry about! I'm sick over it! But I couldn't sit in there, Joel, and let you do something so stupid!"

"I'm only following your example!"

"Don't! I'm not proud of what happened in there! It's something I'm going to have to live with the rest of my life! Don't make it so I have to have you and Corey on my conscience, too!"

"It has nothing to do with you! It's between me and Corey!" I didn't really think I'd been following her example; I'd said it only because it was the easiest argument to shout at her.

"I got you into it! You can at least listen to me, can't you!"

I shook my head. Suddenly, she was no longer beside me. I was alone with my work again. But when I reached the end of my row and turned around, I found Liza still standing in the middle of the field, arms fretfully folded under her breasts, a distressed look in her face while she waited for me to return. I had to dismiss her anguish as something that had nothing to do with me. She was only using me as a way of getting away from her own anguish.

I braced myself for her next plea as I chewed my way towards her. I was almost level with her when she suddenly turned toward the house, as if she had heard something.

I heard it too: the honking of a horn.

I stopped and saw our father standing behind his car, waving and shouting at us.

Liza waved back at them, not "Good-bye," but "No!"

He was too far away for me to hear what he shouted through the engine before he disappeared into the car. The windows were up and all I could see inside the car was the knob of Corey's head. At this distance the shape of his head merged with Jake's and he seemed like only a thickening of the headrest.

"Dammit! They promised me they'd wait until I had a chance to talk with you!"

But the car swung around the yard, disappeared behind the house, then reappeared, racing down the drive, paused, turned on to the road and disappeared behind a screen of trees.

And that was that.

I was surprised by how easily it had been accomplished. I turned off the engine. I could deal with Liza's admonishments and accusations now that it was too late for her to accomplish anything with them.

But all she gave me was a sympathetic "Well. Welcome to the club." She rubbed her eyes with the heel of her hand and shook her head at me. "Make a deal with you, Shrimp. I won't cry on your shoulder if you don't cry on mine."

"No need for that. You're welcome to cry on my shoulder, but I have nothing to cry about. Corey and I are only taking a brief vacation from each other. That's all."

"Uh uh. You might be telling yourself that, but I know how your mind works. Out of sight, out of mind. It's going to be up to Corey to fix things. But your doing this to him has left him so pissed he's never going to want to see you again. Can't say I blame him."

I was glad to hear her make this mean what I wanted it to mean.

"But. What's done is done. For both of us. And here we are, right back where we started from. I don't know about you, but I only intend to hang around this dump long enough to find my feet again. I didn't screw over Bob just so I could crawl back into the nest again. I hope you had a better reason for screwing yourself than that."

I leaned impatiently against my machine.

"Okay. I'm not ready to talk about it, either. I only came out here because I thought I could...but what's done is done. We're going to have all the time in the world to dwell on it. See you later." She walked away wrapped in her own arms and with her shoulders bunched around her neck.

I started up the engine and threw my back into my work again. The earth was too wet to kick up any dust. There was a smell of clay, a sharp clean odor of gasoline and the sweet smell of hot oil, like burnt cocoa.

My crow returned, skipping over the raw ground with its head bent down. Then crow and field suddenly blurred, as if some sweat had spilled into my eyes. But it wasn't warm enough today for my face to perspire. I was crying.

I tried to think nothing of it. I hadn't slept in twenty-eight hours; my eyes were only watering from lack of sleep. Because I had nothing to cry about. No matter what Liza said, we *had* left the door open. If I changed my mind I could still go back to New York. I could still go back to Corey. And if this were what I wanted, I had nothing to cry about. Nothing was final but death. There was nothing for anyone to cry about but death.

There had been so much today that justified tears and I had no need to feel ashamed. Nevertheless I waited until I was all cried out and the two acres beside the house completely turned over before I went back inside to join the collection of solitudes that was my family.

14

One Year Later

*. . . So how do you live your life? How do you accommo-
date self and world?*

*We do not want to be alone but we can connect with others
only through self or the suppression of self. The community
of appetite or the community of duty.*

*Know thyself? A headache and one I could ignore before I
found myself stranded in a life I still don't understand.*

*We know the world—and ourselves—only by the use we
make of the world, a use best represented by work, or better,
ambition. I should look for myself there, only I have no ambition anymore. My good works were genuinely motivated
but they had no practical results and my concern for others
only distracted me from my own failings. My leftist politics
were only a guard against pity or outrage, and with the cause
for pity gone, my radicalism is only old clothes. (Not quite
true. But it does seem to be in suspension, hibernation. All I
need is a cause and . . .)*

*It is good to start all over. If only I didn't feel nostalgic for
the way things were. Reject anything and you find yourself
defining yourself by that act of negation. (There is love—negation or position? A negation when unrequited, a position
when requited. Who said that love is not so much a sentiment
as a situation? Which sounds like work: "Situation wanted."
Which makes it sound like servant's work, but often preferable to unemployment.)*

*Abstract pretentiousness that shows no evidence of the feel-
ings that caused me to sit down here in the first place. I cannot
confront myself directly. This journal functions best as a*

record of things done and not done (and there is no goodness in us). Reading the above I am surprised by how unhappy I sound.

March 14, Sunday

The myth of rural goodness: wishful thinking sown by the media. Even the farmers believe it. Agriculture is corporate business and the glow from farmhouses at night is the glow of color televisions. Foozball is the most important thing in most kid's lives. Even religion comes into the home via satellite. And yet people will have you believe they're just like the Waltons.

The cause for my indignation (unjust, because if people want to believe they're the Waltons, it's because they don't know who they are anymore) is that this rural romanticism has now infected me. I suffer an inordinate, fetish-like attachment for that farmers' market snapshot of me and Joel.

There we are with the vegetables last summer, shirtless and overalled, in front of the pickup truck in Williamsburg, two sunburned farmboys grinning for the sentimentalizing camera—Liza's camera. You look at such a picture and envy such a pair. You forget the annoyances you were feeling that day, the uncertainty about your future, the suspicion you were only delaying before you declared it was over. You read into it a shared happiness as simple and whole as a potato. How bucolic. We look like an advertisement for fresh gay produce. My wishful thinking can be as corny and sweet and false as everyone else's.

We wait for anchor cables and insulators before we resume work on Catherine's project, but the project waits anyway until we finish the planting.

The fine, blue mouse-scribble skipped a line, continued down the page and filled the next page, but I couldn't go on. I snapped the notebook shut and laid it on the desk where I had found it, where Corey had left it out.

I hadn't intended to read so much, hadn't even known it was a diary until I started reading. I'd idly opened it

411

while I changed my clothes, thinking it was only Corey's substitute teaching notes. I sat on the bed with my hands pressed between my knees, my Ramada necktie unknotted but still stuck in my collar, my thoughts fumbling with what I had found.

But I had promised to help outside as soon as I changed. I lowered my head to look out the window. I saw the farmhouse standing out there in clear afternoon light. Liza and Catherine walked by, carrying a long wooden ladder. It was still odd to see house and yard from this raised spot outside it, and to see it while sitting in a bedroom, as if our trailer were a compartment on a train and we had stopped just long enough for me to notice a house beside the tracks. I turned away and looked around the trailer, a small, square space doubled by the mirror bolted to the paneling above the desk. And taped to Corey's corner of the mirror was that licked-candy color snapshot of us. The two sunlit boys with timid smiles, the big one's arm across the smaller one's shoulder, had the enviable completeness of a couple glimpsed from a passing train.

Corey had not been in the car when Jake had driven off a year ago. Corey was still here.

I had wondered why Corey put that picture up when all he had to do when he wanted to see us was look in the mirror. And the picture always embarrassed me, because we looked so wholesome and insipid, because we looked fake. But now I knew why Corey needed it. It took away some of the uncertainty of where we were and what we were. I could understand his needing it. After reading his journal, I needed it too.

I couldn't move from the bed. There was guilt for reading something private, and the vertigo of seeing familiar things from a reverse angle. But what paralyzed me most was the shock of recognizing my confusion in Corey's.

We had placed ourselves in a life we still didn't understand.

I already knew that, whenever I stopped to think about it. But over the past winter I had come to believe that Corey knew something I didn't. Seeing his confusion written out brought back my fear that we were only fooling ourselves again. Our past year should have had more to show than this shared bafflement.

Jake had driven off without Corey. He had been in such a hurry to get back to New York that he forgot Corey was going with him. Or pretended to forget. But Jake left Corey here.

That didn't explain us, but my mind locked on it now, as if it were the only thing that justified why we were still together. I had walked back from the field, bitterly proud of my resolve to live a solitary life, a life where I would never again fool other people or myself. And then I had opened the door to the kitchen and the marshy shadows.

Corey sat at the table.

I stood petrified, frightened to find him still here. And frightened by the impulse in my arms and legs to fall on Corey, embrace him, as if someone in me were overjoyed that he wasn't gone. I closed my eyes and opened them again. Corey was still there.

He looked down and said, "I'm sorry. Your father drove off without me. I'll have to find another way back."

So it was only an accident, nothing more. My fear subsided and I walked over to him, touched his shoulder—almost pushed at his shoulder. Then I touched his chest, his neck, his hair.

He sat there blinking, never unfolding the hands in his lap.

And I had to admit what I was feeling. "Dammit, Cobbett. It was going to be so clean and simple. Okay. Yes. I love you. But you can't love me because I'm not worth loving!"

"No. But I do love you. Stupidly."

"Then you're an idiot."

"We're both idiots."

413

The same self-denigrations that had once been giddy with the surprise that requited love was possible. Only Corey and I believed every damning word.

I saw Liza watching from the doorway, then heard her quick retreat up the stairs. I asked Corey to come outside with me, where we could talk and think away from the house and everything that had happened there that morning. We walked to the woods and I saw Kearney's rented car sitting in our yard. Corey could always drive back to New York in that, but I didn't want to suggest it yet. The new, burnt-orange car continued to sit there like an example, a temptation, a threat, every morning for a week, until somebody came down from Richmond and took it back to the agency.

If only there had been a moment of joy from that time, a memory of joy like a bolt of lightning that had magnetized us forever, then I wouldn't feel so worried reading his dissatisfaction and uncertainty. But I'd been struck by lightning once before, when I poured hot coffee on my head, and that had gotten us nowhere. This time I wanted it to mean something different that we were still together. I wanted this trailer—smelling like a plastic jug and tumbled with our things—I wanted this space to mean something. Something like wisdom. There seemed to have been times this past year when it had meant that, but I couldn't remember any today. Even the patience I had learned, which sometimes felt like wisdom, today only felt like laziness or even cowardice. Without learning anything, we had merely let life close over us again.

What had we said in the woods a year ago? I remembered us saying everything that could be said, without arriving anywhere. I had guiltily accepted Corey's accusations—"What makes you so damn impulsive?" "My selfishness. And my stupidity."—until I could accept no more blame and started to pour it back—"You are such a cold fish!" "Anger frightens me, so I kill it, which is wrong, but I do."—blame flowing back and forth, the poles repeatedly reversing themselves while we tried to argue ourselves back into existence. But all we had created with our anger and explanations was a mood, something as sadly vague as the woods where we sat. The sky clouded over before sunset and all color faded from the trees, briars, sprouting stumps and bed of dead leaves. There was a grey smell of mold.

We tried touching each other, until we were lying on dank ground with our pants undone. It was nothing like sex. We only wanted to make each other come and see what was left. Afterwards, we sat up, leaned against a tree with corky bark and said nothing while we watched the woods sink backwards into darkness.

When we finally went back to the house, we held hands. We had to. The blackness under the trees was so complete it was dizzying. I couldn't see, couldn't even believe I stood up unless I held on to something. That Corey thought he was upright with his feet on the ground helped me believe that I was too. We felt our way together towards the lighted windows of the house.

That walk was something I often used to tell myself we weren't so dumb; we needed each other to get our bearings. But all it seemed to say to me now was: I needed to love and live with someone, why not Corey? We preferred each other to unemployment.

I picked up the notebook and opened it back to "stranded in a life I still don't understand." It was my why-not-Corey and his why-not-Joel that had stranded him here. Love is servant's work? Only when you attempt to build a life around it. Corey had no real purpose down here, except me, and love was no more Corey's vocation than it was mine. That was what he referred to with his jottings about position and ambition: his job in New York. Even now, one year later, he regretted leaving it?

He had called in sick every day for a week while he helped us out in the field so that everything could be done

415

and we could go back to New York together. Then one day he called New York and quit.

"You're not the only one who can be impulsive. I never liked that job."

"But Core? What're you going to do?"

"Don't know. Spend the summer here, I guess. See what happens."

It was so unlike Corey. It was unlike him to saddle Ed with the chore of shipping us our things. My selfishness was rubbing off on him? But he gave us more time to decide, a whole summer, and when we decided we could leave either together or separately.

We hadn't left, which seemed to mean we hadn't decided.

I found myself reading the next entry.

March 21, Sunday

Joel at work. In necktie and blazer he has the cockiness touched with belligerence associated with short people. When he walks, he charges, stepping so quickly he loses the slight side-to-side roll he has at home. He walks in the motel like someone in charge, only his boyish face betrays him. He compensates for youth by being formal, but still beams in surprise whenever anyone defers to him. Naked, his body is a short, freshly cut plank, but as muscular and hairy below the waist as any adult.

I can't continue this. The above was written only because of guilt over how infrequently I mention Joel in these pages, and because I suspect you've been reading this, Joel. Some things you said the other night about nostalgia for certainty.

But I hadn't read his journal until today! Those were thoughts arrived at on my own.

It doesn't upset me. Looking this over, I find nothing I haven't told you already, directly or indirectly. But the writing down of isolated thoughts presents a false impression. I become critical when I start using words, which is why my

brief portrait of you might sound unflattering, and why I'm
shy of using words with anyone close to me.

If you are not always here in these scribbles, Joel, it's
because you're too much part of my everyday life for me to
write you down. We are not one. I can never pretend we are.
When I mentioned your boyishness I didn't mean to imply
that that's all I love about you. It wasn't for a boyish face
that I quit my job a year ago, just as it wasn't for a hairy oaf
with glasses that you chewed up your life while you chewed
up his. But exactly what we are to each other still eludes me.
After five years. The romantic conventions don't quite fit us
(perhaps do not fit anyone). And yet, if we are sometimes not
emotionally enough for each other, a world unto ourselves, it
might be said we are never emotionally too much. Friends in
the role of lovers? Lovers who've tamed themselves by taking
on the role of friends? We are too different. I am so unsure of
self I long for selflessness, and so your love of self often looks
good to me, even with its moments of selfishness. We round
each other out, complete each other. Maybe we're one of those
homemade inventions that is never quite finished, but we are
the sole witnesses of our inventing. Like it or not, we have
made ourselves the chief witnesses of each other's life.

After all that, I realize there's a good possibility Joel won't
see this. His guilt takes hours, sometimes days to catch up
with him, but then he'll feel—

There was a banging at the window.

I hid the notebook between my legs.

But there was only a fist at the window and Liza's voice outside. "What the hell you doing in there? Get off your butt, we need your help!"

"Sorry. Out in a minute," I called back. I heard her walk away.

I resumed changing, but left the notebook open on the desk, so I could reread Corey's explanation of us while I changed. It sounded so nice, what he said. I was touched by his attempt to say something, but I didn't think he was right. I didn't always love myself. And we had been emotionally too much for each other, one time in particular. No, his reasons might sound better than mine, but he too felt the need to justify us, as if we bothered him, as if we were an unsolved problem. And his words couldn't solve us. Like it or not, we *had* made ourselves each other's witness, only we were such unreliable witnesses. But I had taken the afternoon off so we could finish our mother's project. That's what I should be thinking about now. I tried to place the notebook on the desk exactly as I had found it.

Everyone was gathered at the side of the house, all waiting for me.

"Uncle Joel!" cried Joan, sitting in the sandpile left over from our cement mixing.

"About time," grumbled Liza. "What were you reading in there anyway?"

"I wasn't reading. I just wanted to catch my breath."

"Bad morning at the Ramada?" asked Corey.

"The usual." Actually, it had been a bad morning, one of those days when being an assistant manager did not mean I had any authority, only that they could get more work out of me. But it was Corey I wondered at, seeing him standing there in a rust-stained sweatshirt and torn overalls—things were always snagging on Corey. He didn't look discontented. He seemed his usual calm, homey self. It was difficult to believe that this was the same person whose diary was so full of questions. He could be such an easygoing sphinx.

"All right!" said Catherine, rubbing her hands together. "How do we want to do this?"

The arm of a crane lay on its side, one end hinged to a block of concrete set in the ground, the other end propped on a sawhorse with the old windmill blades now bolted to it. This was the homemade invention that was never quite finished. Catherine wanted the farm to have its own electricity, without further need for a public source. We had tried a single airplane propeller perched

418

on the roof—it was up there now—and that gave us some electricity, but not enough. We had tried attaching these windmill blades directly to the roof, but the house couldn't bear the weight and we had to call a roofer to repair the damage we'd done. So now we were trying this, a tower beside the house that would be anchored to the ground with cables. It was ready to go. All that remained was to raise the unwieldy thing. I went to the end and tried lifting it from the sawhorse; it was as heavy as it looked.

"We tried it with all of us," said Corey. "But even with a fourth body we can get it up only so high. Then, you know, the fulcrum effect."

"Maybe a rope. And one of us on the roof?" I suggested.

"Maybe me," said Corey. "I'm the heaviest. I'll get the rope from the barn."

I went with him, wanting to be alone with him for a moment, hoping that would be enough to put my mind at ease. But I didn't want ease, I wanted honesty.

"Today's the day," said Corey eagerly as we entered the barn. "I think it's going to work this time."

"Corey? I was wrong to do it, but... You left your diary out and I've been reading it."

"You...?" He stopped looking for the rope to look at me. "Oh. Not a diary, really. Just thoughts. I sort of suspected you'd been reading it. I'd rather you didn't but..." He resumed looking for the rope, without seeing the coil on the workbench in front of him.

"But I haven't. Not until today. I shouldn't have and I apologize. It's an invasion of your privacy and I had no right to do it."

"It's not that. It's just...you *haven't* been reading it?" He frowned and looked pained. "I hope you weren't hurt, then, when I accused you of reading it." In his usual Cobbetty fashion, his chief concern was that he had caused *me* pain.

"No. How could I be hurt when you accused me of doing what I was doing? And I liked some of the stuff it made you say."

"Good. Good then." But he looked like he was trying to remember what he'd said; he'd written it weeks ago. "Still, I'd rather you didn't read it, Joel. I get pompous when I write. And critical. Was there anything in there I hadn't told you already? In one way or another?"

"No. Not really," I admitted. "Except... you seemed so unhappy in it."

"Unhappy?" The idea surprised him. "But I'm not unhappy."

"You are! You must be."

He laughed, finally saw the coil of rope and hoisted it over his shoulder. "I'm not unhappy. Really."

"You've stranded yourself in a life you still don't understand," I reminded him.

"But that doesn't mean I'm unhappy. Confused maybe. But not unhappy."

"Dissatisfied then. Or critical." Was he serious? Without his notebook in front of me, I wondered if I'd been reading it wrong.

"Oh, uneasy now and then. But only with my situation here."

Love is not so much a sentiment as a situation?

"Because I know it can't go on forever. I mean, look at me. I've got the farm and you and a real live baby underfoot. I substitute teach now and then, work with a Boy Scout troop. I've never had such a varied life. Really."

I wasn't his sole reason for being here. I was only one thing among many, which was a relief to hear. I was not yet good enough for him to build a life upon.

"And now we're building this *thing,* which excites me. It's an experience I never would've had if I weren't here. Why're you being so scrupulous? You sound like me on a bad day. Which is another reason why I rather you didn't read my journal. I usually write in it only on bad days." He rubbed my back and laughed.

I followed him out of the barn, wanting to believe him but wondering if his happiness were only today's mood and based on Catherine's project, nothing else.

Catherine saw us coming and hooted. "Corey. You look like a mountaineer in all that rope."

"Like a real man?" he joked.

Catherine looked embarrassed, then solemn. "Now don't say that. Nobody here thinks you're less of a man," she insisted. She still didn't know how to respond to that aspect of us. If only she approved of us fully, maybe then I could feel that Corey and I were justified. But one of the nicest things about Catherine was that she was too definitely Catherine in my eyes to have the authority of a mother.

"I wish someone here would treat me as less of a woman," Liza grumbled. Apparently she and Catherine had been having one of their arguments, Liza revolting against the role of daughter, Catherine pointing out that nobody was forcing her to stay. But Catherine liked having her here, and Liza liked being in this family that was too extended and motley to pinch like a real family. We'd heard only last month from Kearney's lawyer that Kearney was now a policeman in Houston. All news of him came through his lawyer, as if he were still ashamed that he'd been discharged from the army without spending any time in the brig.

"You do the knots," I told Corey and helped him loop the rope around the cross-brace beneath the blades and generator. We took the rest of the rope to the ladder that leaned against the house. He fastened the rope around his waist. I steadied the ladder for him.

"Ouch!" He stepped on my thumb and I remembered how clumsy he could be, especially when he was excited. "And be careful!" I shouted up to him. "Get a steady seat up there! If it starts to fall, let it! Don't let yourself be yanked down by it!"

"All righty," he sang back, scrambling up the tin roof on all fours.

I joined Catherine and Liza at their end. Catherine was very breathy and excited. Liza looked prepared for the worst. "Here goes nothing," she said and pulled on her work gloves. "I wonder what'll go wrong this time." She still thought we should be trying something with solar batteries.

I knelt down to fit my shoulder under the frame.

Catherine curled her hands under it, rocking from side to side like a weight lifter. "Ready? Okey-doke? *Lift!*"

We heaved our end off the sawhorse.

High above us, straddling the peak of the roof, Corey hauled the rope.

Liza grimaced at me and strained at the weight. We got it high enough for us to get under it. Then we worked our way down it, the few feet behind us increasing the weight, until it become immovable.

"Corey dammit! Pull harder!" Catherine shouted.

"Dammit I'm pulling!"

"More weight on his end," I grunted. "Let me just . . . Can you hold it without me?"

Catherine and Liza clenched their teeth and nodded.

I ran to the ladder and raced up it. The tin roof buckled and popped as I crawled over it. I joined Corey on the peak, sat facing him and grabbed hold of the rope. When I added my weight to his, we heard a groan of relief from below.

We sat with our knees poked into each other and pulled at the rope. Arms got tangled together. Fingers were pinched in each other's grip. But we worked out a rhythm, pulled hand over hand.

And the tower began to lift. Lifting, it lost more of its weight and gently came up, now level with the eaves, now floating above the roof, its blades hovering there like a great steel sunflower.

"No more!" called Catherine. "We have to anchor it now!"

Corey and I held the rope and supported the tower two mismatched pairs of arms wrenched taut by the weight. We heard the rattle and strum of cables as Catherine and Liza ran them out to the anchor blocks. But Catherine couldn't find her pliers and Liza had to shoo Joan back to her sandpile—what if the tower fell?—so Corey and I were left up there gripping the rope for an impossibly long time.

"Joel?"

"Yes?" He spoke so timidly I was afraid he had a terrible confession to make.

"My nose itches."

"Oh. Okay. What if I just—" I scratched it for him with my teeth.

"Ow!" One of my canines nicked him. "Ah. That's better. Thanks. I wish they'd hurry up. I want to see if the darn thing's going to work this time."

The wobbly blades that leaned back from us did not inspire confidence.

My knees and ankles pinching the roof, my arms going numb, the two of us knotted together; I began to laugh.

"What's so funny?"

"Us!" I said. "Inventors of ourselves? What you wrote in your journal? Oh, Corey. We're the Laurel and Hardy of inventors."

"You think so?" But Corey was grinning, too. "Well. This is another fine mess you've gotten us into."

And it was a fine mess, today at least. Okay, I wasn't any smarter than I'd been a year ago. I still lived in a dream of self, only to wake up periodically, wildly look around and grab for something that proved I could control my life. I'd learned only not to grab too quickly. But up here on the roof, there was no need to grab for anything. Or maybe it was only because, locked up here with Corey, I couldn't afford to worry about us. But enjoying our situation did not feel dishonest to me.

Down below, Catherine and Liza were bickering with each other over the correct way to tighten the cables. Liza often talked about moving to Richmond with Joan. If she did, Corey and I would probably leave, too; I couldn'

423

imagine us living alone with my mother. We were a household, a family, only by accident. There was no authority to follow or react against. Corey and I were only an accident, without Corey's journal or my feelings having enough authority to justify or condemn us. There was no telling what would become of us. But here on the roof, the two of us straining every muscle yet remaining perfectly still, grinning at each other to distract ourselves from the buzzing in our arms, the accident froze a few minutes and felt as permanent as knowledge.

Then Liza hollered, "Crap!" A rusty ring bolt had snapped off the tower and a cable dropped to the ground. We had to lower the damn thing and put a new bolt in. We weren't finished yet.